For Liz, forever.

ANGELS BLEED

MAX HARDY

Copyright © 2013 Max Hardy

ISBN-13: 978-1494298647

ISBN-10: 1494298643

The moral right of Max Hardy to be identified as the author of this work has been asserted in accordance with the Copyright, Designs and Patents Act, 1988.

All rights reserved. No part of this publication may be reproduced or transmitted in any form or by any means, electronic or mechanical, including photocopying, recording, or any information storage and retrieval system without permission in writing from the author or publisher.

Selected Lyrics from 'When Doves Cry' © Prince

By Max Hardy

Novels

Angels Bleed

Her Moons Denouement

The Murder Path

Poetry Collections

Soul Whispers

My Dark Disease

The Alchemy Of Swaying Hips

Angels Bleed

Pigments of pain

scream scarlet.

A swelling stain

in the relief

of his tapestry,

where angels bleed

in the ignominy

of his seed.

His omnipotence cedes

impotence, portents

inked in blotches

left diseased,

as angels bleed

their last refrain.

11:54 pm

The crystal chandelier shimmered an iridescent pink from the blood spatter that coloured it. Above it, the ornate white ceiling rose was equally covered with a dark red dotted trail. The trail spread out in two directions over the ceiling, one down a large bay window wall, where its path was lost temporarily in the deep burgundy of the closed suede curtains before it reappeared on the plush white carpet. In the opposite direction, the arterial arc added a macabre lustre to the fruits on Cezanne's 'Basket Of Apples' original painting, before heading off into the carpet back to its source, the congealing pool of blood circled in halo around the battered head of the naked dead body in the centre of the room.

DI Saul knelt on his haunches, gently rocking to and fro just at the side of the body, an arm resting on his knee, the hand holding his chin. His brow was furrowed, a slight frown disturbing designer stubble. He sniffed a few times and murmured an audible 'Mmmm.', before taking the pen that was in his hand and poking a blood free spot on the forearm of the corpse.

'What's wrong with this picture?' he asked, rhetorically.

PC Buglass, a young skinny lad, uniform looking oversized on his small frame, was standing directly behind Saul with an open pad in his hands taking down notes as directed.

'You mean apart from the obvious dead body, gallons of blood and that huge crate in the middle of a drawing room?' Buglass replied.

'Just thinking out loud Buglass. The blood looks fresh. It's starting to congeal slightly around the edges but is still fluid where it's pooled. Above the overpowering scent of those candles there is also a distinct odour of decomposition, which suggests to me that the body has been here for some time. It's fairly stiff as well. It feels like rigor has started to set in. Have we got an ETA for SOCO and the Duty Medical Officer?' Saul asked.

'Should be here any minute, they said about midnight.' Buglass replied, sniffing the air furtively.

Saul stood up and looked around the room once more. Apart from the arterial spatter circling out from the body in two directions, there were no other visible signs of blood on the walls or furnishings. There weren't any smear marks where the corpse had fallen and no sign of any disturbance or struggle at all. Even the white carpet was spotless save for the pool of blood around the body, not a single drop evident outside that area.

Each corner of the room contained wrought iron candelabras with six, recently lit foot tall candles flickering on each. In front of Saul was a wall with a large open fire, orange flames dancing on the burning logs in the grate. Insidious gargoyles chased playful, teasing cherubs around a gothic style black granite surround and mantle. Above this and looking slightly out of keeping with the rest of the room was a large plasma TV hung on the wall.

In an arc around the corpse and crate and facing the fire were three antique black leather Chesterfield sofas. Behind them was a Steinway grand piano and on the full length and height of the wall behind that, rosewood bookcases filled with old leather bound books. There was an occasional table to the side of the window. On top of it was a white Bakelite telephone and a TV remote control.

'Were you running this weekend?' asked Buglass, doodling on his notepad.

Saul was still surveying the room and took a few seconds to answer. 'Yes, down in Manchester for the half marathon. I was just on my way back when I got the call about this.' he walked over to the Cezanne as he was talking. 'It was a good race. I managed to knock six seconds off my Personal Best.'

'You must be nearing world class now with the amount of running you do. How much did you raise?'

'Hardly world class. Hopefully about three thousand this time: as long as you tight bastards put your hands in your pockets and cough up. It all helps.' He turned around to face the room, then back to the picture again.

'The interesting thing about this picture Buglass, is its disjointed perspectives. Cezanne painted it from two different viewpoints. If you look at the table, the left side is on a different plane to the right side. The tilt of the bottle and the incline of the basket are at different angles to the other items, so when you look at it closely, things don't seem quite right. I'm getting the exact same feeling about this scene.' he said, turning back to face Buglass. 'You have a large country house which to all intent and purpose is derelict apart from this one room: one room opulently decorated and full of very expensive and particular furnishings, a corpse and a crate. It feels like a Tracey Emin piece.'

'A what? ' asked Buglass quizzically.

Saul shot a fleeting derogatory glance across to Buglass before taking in the room again. 'She's an artist: allegedly. She is the woman who put her piss and cum stained bed sheets, condoms, dirty knickers and other paraphernalia from her bedroom onto a bed in the middle of an art gallery.'

Just then Saul's mobile rang. He took it out of the inside pocket in his tuxedo jacket, looked at the screen and sighed heavily, frustration evident in the way he stabbed the 'Decline' button. He put it back into his pocket.

From outside the open door of the room Saul heard a resonating guffaw. 'Oh Christ, please tell me Darrie isn't on call tonight.'

'Based on that laugh, I would say he definitely is!' Buglass answered, a look of disdain crossing his face.

A short, rotund character appeared in the doorway. Candle shadows danced over the food stained Onesie he was wearing beneath a creased and dirty Hacking jacket that was two sizes to small, accentuating the girth of a stomach that arrived before he did. The stylish garb was bottomed off by pink spotty Cath Kidston wellies. Candle light shone from the perspiration meandering down the brow of his bald head, which joined the droplets forming from the pores on his ruddy cheeks.

'Oh my word, what and absolutely sumptuous room. I wasn't expecting that. Saul!' Darrie exclaimed extrovertly. 'My good fellow, that Tuxedo looks dashing on you tonight. Have you dressed especially for this location, or have we dragged you from one of your high society occasions? Am I OK to come in and where can I walk?'

Behind Darrie a bespectacled head wearing a plastic PPE hat seemed to float from side to side, its body hidden behind his full figure. 'Hold up Darrie, you need your shoe covers on.' said the head, which belonged to Harris, the Scene of Crime Officer.

'Be a darling and slip them on for me would you Harris?' asked Darrie, lifting one of his feet backwards while holding onto the door frame coquettishly. The floating head rolled its eyes.

'Good evening gentlemen. You are fine to walk from the door up to here, in front of the body. This side of the room seems clear. Harris, can you start taking a few pictures of the body. Darrie, I want you to take a look at it straight away, there are a few things about the corpse that are troubling me at the minute. No, no social occasion tonight. I was supposed to be out with Sarah for our wedding anniversary.

'In a Tux, my, aren't you the gentleman. How are you Buglass, still enjoying life in the closet? I have the address of a lovely lithe Latino lothario if you are interested? Loves cock, especially cock in denial.' Darrie shared with a wicked glint in his eye as he walked across the room towards them.

'Piss off you sad queen.' Buglass retorted petulantly.

'Darrie, stop winding him up and let's focus on the body here, please.' Saul stated sternly.

Harris came into the room too, dressed in blue plastic PPE overalls. He set down his bag onto one of the Chesterfields, took out a camera and began taking photographs of the body and the immediate vicinity.

'Right Darrie, you'll need to squat down here to see and specifically smell what I need you to, as the vanilla scent from the candles is masking the odour unless you are up close.' advised Saul as he got down on his haunches again.

Darrie huffed, put one hand on Saul's shoulder and eased himself down onto his knees. 'You know, I really do wish more murderers would kill people on tables or benches. They just don't consider the stress it puts on the heart of a portly fellow such as myself, having to go down like this.'

He sniffed, the playful expression he had on his face, hoping someone would bite at his innuendo, instantly turning intent. 'That's decomposition. I wouldn't expect that so soon, not when you still have a pool of congealing blood.'

'I know. And look at this.' Saul responded, taking his pen and poking the arm again where he had previously. 'There is no give in the flesh at all. It feels like rigor has already set in.'

'That doesn't just look like rigor.' mused Darrie. 'Harris, I'm going to touch the skin on this one part of the arm, can you take a photo please. There's dark colouring on the top of the exposed arm which looks like Livor Mortis. It suggests to me that's where the blood has settled in the corpse. The problem is it's on the top of the arm, not the bottom. This body has been turned over a long while after death.' He put his hand on the forearm and sighed deeply. 'I can tell you now that the fresh pooling and blood spatter on these walls isn't from this body.'

'What do you mean?' asked Saul

'Well, if I'm not mistaken, and I rarely am, this fellow has been frozen and is currently in the process of thawing. Put your hand here and you will feel the cold coming from the skin, that's why there is no give.'

Saul did as requested, a look of incredulity crossing his features. He looked at Darrie. 'So, we've got a body here that's not recently deceased, setup in a scenario to make it look as though he's just been killed?'

Harris interjected. 'I would second that. If you look at the arterial arc on the walls, the pattern is far to uniform. It also starts on the floor from around where the throat is. The body looks to have fallen face down. That type of spatter wouldn't happen. If anything, you would expect to see spatter in a circle of descent on the floor where the body has fallen. You wouldn't expect to see a blood trail then hitting the ceiling above it.'

'That may not be all.' said Darrie. He took a tissue out of his jacket pocket. 'Harris, I'm just going to wipe a little of the blood off this fellows hairline, are you alright with that?'

'As long as it's a little, it's okay with me.' Harris answered quizzically, bending over the body with Saul and Darrie. Buglass also joined them, not wanting to be left out. Four shadows weaved a flickering dance on the walls, intertwining as they got closer to the body. Darrie rubbed away a patch of blood around an inch square from the hairline, revealing a row of neat stitching.

'Harris, can we turn this fellow over gently please, I have a feeling, either he has had a god awful facelift, or....'

Harris nodded and helped Darrie with the body, being careful not to disrupt the vicinity. It was fairly easy to do as the corpse was indeed still frozen. As they lifted, they noticed that the carpet below was still white, suggesting the body had been placed there and then the blood poured around it.

On its back, they could now see the almost blood free face of a youngish man. His eyes were closed. A dark shadow of eyeliner was visible on the bottom lid with mascara accentuating the lashes. The pallid cheeks looked to be made up with foundation, a slight blush of rouge giving them colour. It was apparent now that there was no cut to the throat which could have caused the spatter in the room. What was also evident, on the naked torso, were tramlines of stitching in a 'Y' shape, from each shoulder to the middle of the chest, then from the chest down to the stomach.

'Or he has had an autopsy.' Darrie began. 'Which suggests he has been dead for a very long time. Not only that, the make up on his face smacks of funeral parlour glam, suggesting he has already been buried: and given that he is here, presumably exhumed!'

12:20 am

The little finger of each hand was tapping out an indelible litany on the arms of the chair, syncopated with the slow turning of her wrists forcefully against the leather straps that bound them to it. The wrists oozed blood and puss from the lesions caused by the friction of the motion. On her exposed forearms, before another strap tying down the elbows, hundreds of scars, burns, cuts and gouges were visible: a battlefield of harm, a litany of war.

'Day 15 Rebecca, how are you feeling?' The nebulous voice echoed around the padded cell, the tinny tincture produced by the ceiling speaker it came out of not diminishing the deep resonance of the man speaking.

Above the elbows, yet more straps were wrapped tightly over her chest. Two more secured both her neck and her bald head to the back of the chair. Similar weals to those on her wrists were visible where she gently gyrated her head against the bindings. Her eyes were closed. The only thing she wore was a green hospital theatre gown which hung limply from her emaciated body.

A stuttering giggle escaped from her mouth. 'Feeling!' she slurred, partly due to the plastic contraption in her mouth that stopped it from fully biting closed and partly due to the gnawed and withered stump that used to be a tongue. It was too small now to reach the front teeth or top of the mouth to round her words.

'I try hard not to feel. The pain helps. It distracts my mind. There's not enough of it though, not nearly enough of it since you started to take me off my medication.' Her body tensed as she visibly pushed it wherever possible against her restraints, forcing the point home. 'No, not nearly enough!'

'I'm sorry about that, but we have to get you to a place where we can talk, off the medication. You and I both know what you would try and do if you weren't restrained.'

She began shaking furiously and screamed. 'Then why don't you let me! Why don't you fucking let me end this miserable desolation? I am beyond redemption, beyond saving, beyond repair!' She stopped shaking just as suddenly as she had started, slight sobs stuttering from her open mouth. 'What good does any of this do? It doesn't change a thing....'

Her fingers started their litany again, the wrists circling against the restraints. Her head was bald, pock marked with craters where large clumps of hair had been ripped out, taking the scalp with it. There were more cuts and burns visible here as well. Her legs were damaged in a similar fashion and also bound tight. Underneath the wooden chair, which was bolted to the floor, was a bucket from which the smell of stale urine and faeces emanated. A cannula was secured to her left arm, the drip tube going off to a stand that had three different solutions feeding into it: feeding her. There was nothing else in the cell, save for a camera on the ceiling.

'Your lips are whispering Rebecca. Your fingers are tapping. Is there music that helps distract you?' he asked.

Her eyes had been closed, but she opened them and stared directly at the camera, looking into it for a full minute before replying. 'Can you remember the first time that you kissed a girl?' she asked.

There was a few seconds delay before he answered, '1974. I was seven. It was a sunny summer's day in July, just before we were due to break up for the holidays. Our school was a mixed school but at breaks the girls and boys would play in separate playgrounds. The teachers would stop us from mingling with each other. However, if you went down to the railings at the bottom of the yard, they couldn't see you. I had fancied Carolyn for what seemed like aeons but was probably only since Maths that morning. Both sets of our friends had been daring us all morning to have a snog and at lunchtime we sneaked to the bottom of the fence and did it. We kissed through the fence. I even slipped her a bit of tongue. I'd like to say it was romantic and special, but seven year olds really haven't got a clue. To prove how much we didn't have a clue, I remember coming back to my mates who were waiting in the dinner queue, all pumped up with adrenaline, all excited from carrying out the clandestine deed. I think my exact words to them were 'I didn't just kiss her; I fucked her as well!' My seven year old peers had told me that's what putting your tongue into a girl's mouth was. How about you?'

She was still staring at the camera, wrists, head and ankles all straining against the restraints, inflicting the maximum possible pain.

'Aren't boys monsters. Taking something so pure, so innocent and wrapping sex around it.'

'I don't think that's just boys, I think it's what you hear, what you learn about relationships as you grow up. People tell you things and as a child you don't have the mechanisms in place to challenge if what you are being told is the truth or not. I think it was my seven year old girlfriends who told me about fucking. I would imagine you believed you could get pregnant from a toilet seat well into your teens. Tell me about your first kiss.' he asked again.

'When Doves Cry. The song is When Doves Cry.' she whispered, looking intently into the camera. 'Dig if you will a picture, of you and I engaged in a kiss.' Her body started to shake ever so slightly, eyes dilating as she appeared to be losing control, but then the quivering subsided and she returned to the rhythmic infliction of pain.

'The first time I kissed a girl was in 1984. I had no plans to kiss her. She was called Hannah Matthews and we had been good friends since primary school. I liked her a lot but the thought of kissing a girl had never even crossed my mind. We both loved Prince and it was the year Purple Rain was out at the pictures. Our other friends weren't really that into him, but we were purple through and through. It's funny what you remember.' She paused, drifting off into her memory for a few seconds before continuing. 'We went to the Regal Picture Hall in Blyth on the first night it was out. It was a fleapit and we were the only ones in there, so we sat right at the back in worn and ripped red faux suede seats. There were bits of popcorn all over the floor and your feet stuck to the syrup of spilt drinks. That didn't matter though. It would be a massive understatement to say we were excited. We talked about nothing else for weeks leading up to it and all through the trailers and adverts we were giggling and screeching out the songs at the top of our voices. There was no one else in there, so the ushers didn't care. We were spring loaded with pent up excitement, ready and impatient for the start, and in all innocence we were holding hands, trying to keep each other calm enough to be able to enjoy the movie. That's fourteen year old girls and hormones for you. The movie started and for whatever reason our hands just stayed entwined.'

She paused and the rhythmic circling against the restraints ceased. Her sunken, bloodshot eyes, the irises a faded green, looked down from the camera and what might have been warmth tried to break out in the contours and curves of her gaunt, haunted face as she retreated into the memory.

'The raking guitar of the first bars of 'When Doves Cry' screamed out. We were so engrossed in the movie I don't think either of us realised that the handholding had turned into stroking, the delicate tips of Hannah's fingers gently meandering up and down the inside of my arm. It was the static tingling born in the depths of my stomach that made me look, the growing glow of joy that began to consume every bit of me, made my skin shine and spark with the essence of her touch. The lyrics started, 'Dig if you will a picture, of you and I engaged in a kiss' and we looked at each other. We looked beyond the touch, beyond the skin, deep into the feelings that were curving her beautiful smile to radiance, deep into the emotions that were cascading from her eyes, from my every pore. It was undeniable, unequivocal. In that moment we were being consumed by love. We both leaned towards each other at exactly the same time and, eyes wide open, our lips tenderly touched. Within my veins, her essence beat, my heart palpitating with the absolute clarity of being loved, of being in love. It is the only time in my life that I have been absolutely sure of every single feeling, emotion and thought that passed through my soul. Our lips parted, and for the remainder of the song we just watched the enormity of that moment paint itself onto our faces.'

She fell silent again, her body still in the confines of her restraints, in the confines of the chair, in the confines of the cell, spirit free in her minds tapestry.

'Your son. Tell me about the first time you kissed your son.' crackled his voice over the speaker, breaking the moment.

Suddenly her body tensed and she glared up at the camera, the placation gone in an instant. The circling of her limbs against the straps intensified and the obvious veins on her bald head began to throb with the exertion of her movements. She started to shake within her confines and spittle dribbled from the sides of her wedged open mouth.

'He was sweet.' she whispered, her breathing frantic, the words full of venom.

'Sweet?' he asked.

'His tasted so, so sweet.' Her words were sneered now, sibilant, yet low and full of menace. 'As I sat astride, taking every inch of him inside me, laughing manically as I tore his chest open with my bare hands, ripped his still pumping heart from its home and ate it as he died in front of my eyes, yes: he was sweet!'

12:45 am

Saul walked out of the Drawing Room into the dark, stuffy corridor, the inane banter and joviality between Darrie and Buglass receding as he retreated to a safe enough distance not to be overheard. The flickering candlelight from the partly open door caressed the darkness in the corridor into penetrable shadows, which congregated around his person, consuming his abrupt features as he leant against the dusty wall. He took out his mobile, its screen chasing the shadows from his face as he dialled a number.

'Hey Jess, I didn't wake you did I?' he asked gently, his features noticeably softening as the call was answered almost immediately.

'No, just had a long luscious bath. I'm trying hard to relax! I didn't expect to hear from you this early, have you told her already?' asked the low sultry voice at the other end of the phone.

'Not yet, I got a shout about ten minutes from home, possible murder so I've been at the Crime Scene for the past hour. I think she's pissed off with me. I've had a dozen missed calls and about the same number of texts containing an escalating number of expletives.'

'Oh John, that's bad. Didn't you call her and let her know?' she asked reproachfully.

'Yes, it went to voicemail, and I sent her a text. I'm not that callous. I am putting off speaking to her now.' He said, sighing heavily. 'I know I have to and more importantly, I really, really want to, but....'

She gently interrupted 'I know how hard this is for you and I'm truly aware of everything that you will be sacrificing for me. If you aren't one hundred percent sure, you do know I will understand that too, don't you?'

His face broke into an obvious smile, casting circling shadows to flight as his eyes brightened. 'I do, and I know you will be there for me and Jacob. I guess I just have to man up. This crime scene is looking a lot like someone playing silly buggers rather than a real murder, so I'll be home in the next hour or so. I'll give you a call after that. I had such a wonderful weekend and I cannot wait to be with you all the time. Love you baby.'

'Et tu, my darling, Et tu,' she finished.

He hung up, the smile immediately disappearing from his face. Still looking at his phone, he opened the last text message received, from Sarah and replied 'Sorry, this should be wrapped up soon, see you in about an hour J x'. He lifted the phone pensively to his lips once he sent it and stared into flickering shadows for a few moments in silence.

As he leaned away from the wall, he heard a ripping sound as his jacket arm caught on a loose nail. He looked down to see a tear in the sleeve, which was also covered in dust. 'Shit, there goes the deposit.' he moaned as he walked back towards the Drawing Room, the banality of the conversations going on in there invading his ears once more.

'Right.' stated Saul, walking back into the room. 'We've all got homes to go to tonight, so unless you can show me some compelling evidence that we have a fresh, bona fide murder to investigate, I suggest we wrap for this evening and let the day shift pick this one up. Darrie, have you seen anything more to suggest that this guy wasn't already dead?'

'Oh, I do like it when you are this forceful and direct, speaks to my submissive tendencies...' Darrie started.

'For fuck's sake will you give it a rest! It's getting very late and I am really not in the mood.' cut in Saul. 'Is there anything else?' he finished abruptly, staring at Darrie in frustration.

Darrie postured and pulled a handbag face, but then answered calmly. 'No, everything suggests that the cadaver has been dead for quite a while and placed here recently. It was definitely frozen after exhumation. The only thing, as we saw, was the slight scratch on the head which could be as the result of a knock and the stitching around the chest area which may or may not be to do with the autopsy. I will know more once he's back on the slab, but there is nothing that stands out for an urgent chase up. What's more urgent, in my humble opinion, is that you find a sense of humour in that uptight arsehole you've got!' he finished with a challenging smirk back at Saul.

Saul just sighed. 'Harris, have you seen anything else significant at this stage?'

'The significant things really are what's absent to be honest. There are no finger prints on any of the surfaces, not one, anywhere: not even on the crate. Lord knows how anyone got that in here without leaving some kind of print. Even the candles and the fire which have only recently been lit have none. That suggests the room was cleaned thoroughly after the body was staged. I can confirm that the blood around the room is not human. It is some kind of animal and tests in the lab will tell us what. The only thing I have found that may be of any significance so far is what looks like a hair and some dried blood on the corner of the fireplace. It has been there a while and is human so we can do a trace on that. I've taken swabs and samples from the body too. I still have quite a bit of processing to do, but you can leave me doing that if Buglass is okay to hang around for an hour. I want to check out the main corridor and the entrances as well. After that I'll get back to the lab to run DNA tests and try and work out who this guy is.'

'Buglass, are you OK with that?' asked Saul.

'Yes that's fine with me. I'm on shift until six anyway and will probably need to stay here until the day shift arrive. I'll do another recce around the rest of the building, although there was nothing obvious first time.'

Just as Buglass finished his sentence, the Bakelite phone on the table started to ring, an old fashioned brring, brring. Buglass, who was closest to it, looked down at the phone, then up to Saul with a quizzical expression. 'Should I get that?' he asked.

'Yes, get it!' said Saul, obvious annoyance in his tone.

Buglass picked the ringing phone up and said 'Hello.' into the handset. He looked up at Saul again, surprised, holding the phone away from his ear. 'It's someone asking for you?' he said, proffering the phone over to Saul.

'For me?' Saul asked, perplexed as he walked towards Buglass. He took the phone from him and said 'Who is this?' into the receiver.

'Do I have your attention, Mr Saul.' asked a male voice, clipped and precise in intonation into Saul's ear.

'Pardon, who is this?' Saul reiterated. Harris and Darrie came closer to the phone too, picking up on the confusion in Saul's tone.

'Who I am is irrelevant. Why you are here is not irrelevant. Why the body is here is not irrelevant. Why the container is here is not irrelevant. So, I ask you again, do I have your attention Mr Saul?' the voice reiterated, calm and measured.

'You have my attention, what can I help you with?' asked Saul while acting out a writing mime in the direction of Buglass and then mouthing 'Take notes!' to him silently once he finished the sentence.

'I was really hoping you could help me Mr Saul. You see, I am in a bit of a predicament. I have certain information which relates to the murder of the gentleman lying on the floor in front of you, but have reason to believe that you will not act on that information willingly.'

Saul's eyes were darting between the men in the room in front of him, a dozen questions visible in them all at once. He plumped for 'Why don't you think we would act on the information willingly. If this is a murder, any information you may have that could assist our enquiries would be invaluable.'

'Oh it is most definitely a murder, it is just that someone has already been convicted and incarcerated for the crime. Unfortunately, it is the wrong person and a gross miscarriage of justice has taken place.'

Saul paused for a moment and put his hand over the receiver. 'Buglass, are you getting this?' he said quickly. Buglass nodded. 'Darrie, can you quickly ring HQ, give them this address and see if they can get a trace on the call?' Darrie nodded and backed off out of the room.

'So, just to be clear in my mind. Did you set this scene up to attract our attention so that we would listen to the information you have?'

'Just to be clear Mr Saul; I wanted to attract *your* attention, but yes, I set this up. I have it on good authority that you are an excellent detective, fastidious in the detail with an unwavering moral compass. I believe that while the information I have is important, if I were to simply visit the station and offer it openly, it would just be disregarded. To be honest, I do not have sufficient evidence to back up what I know. Now you, on the other hand, given the right encouragement, have the skills to be able to gather that evidence.'

'Sir, I would like to inform you at this point that your actions in setting this scenario up could in themselves be considered a criminal act and may lead to prosecution, you are aware of that?'

A humorous, resonating laugh broke out of the phone, startling Saul to move the phone from his ear. Buglass and Harris heard it too, their expressions becoming even more bemused.

'My dear, dear Mr Saul, please be assured that I fully understand the implications of my actions. Thank you for your candour in pointing them out. Equally, I am also aware that you have sent one of your colleagues off to try and get a trace on this line, that rotund bumbling character with the sewer mind, Darrie I think you called him. Could you do me a favour please and switch the TV on? The remote control is next to the telephone. You only need to press the red on/off button at the top.'

Saul bent down and picked up the remote and did as requested. After a second, the blank screen burst into life and he found that he was looking at himself looking at the TV. Half the screen was taken up showing the room they were in. He turned and looked toward the bookcase, and his image on the screen did the same. The other half of the screen showed what appeared to be a blanket with an arm slightly visible. The aspect looked confined and the lighting was fairly low. Overlaid in the top corner of this part of the screen was a heart rate monitor, with a solitary rhythmic beep coming from the speakers of the TV.

'On the left screen, Mr Saul, is a real time video stream of this room. I have been watching you since you arrived and know that you have already gathered a great deal of evidence that will be crucial in identifying our poor friend's real killer. So yes, I know that Mr Darrie is currently calling Headquarters to ask them to put a trace on this line. It will do no good, but let him try.'

Saul had an agitated expression on his face as he looked between the TV, the bookcase, the body and the nonplussed expressions of his colleagues.

'Sir, I don't quite understand the necessity for these theatrics. Surely if you just give me the information you have we can see how it pertains to the murder. I'm not at all sure what you gain from this.' Saul finished, casting an expressive arm in an arc taking in the room and looking directly into where he though the camera was.

'Mr Saul, let me cut to the quick and get you focused on what you need to do. You are the detective. In this room, there are enough clues to allow you to progress your investigation. You have a body. You have a crime scene, and within a few hours you will have the identity of that body and who was convicted of killing him. From there, you will have all of the transcripts from the investigations and the subsequent trial. I am giving you most of this on a plate. My challenge to you is that I want you to bring the real murderer back to this room by midnight tonight.'

Saul looked from the TV back to the camera. He held his arms out in exasperation before he put the phone back to his ear. 'Well, I am sure that we can start to look at the evidence we find in this room, but I think you are being unrealistic in your expectations of getting any conclusions in a day. There are processes to go through if new evidence is brought to light for previous convictions.'

'I am well aware of that. That is why I mentioned earlier that you may need a little encouragement. Please take note of the image on the right side of the TV. That is a real time video feed as well. A real time video feed of a real person. A real person currently ensconced in that container you see in front of you. Don't worry, they are perfectly safe: for now. They are sedated and blissfully unaware of the predicament they are in. However, if you do not bring the real murderer into this room before midnight tonight, that will be a different matter entirely.'

Saul's face fell, 'Look, I'm sure if we talk through this, understand what information you have and see what we can...' Saul was interrupted.

'Mr Saul. I understand how the system works. You also need to be aware that the container in front of you is lined with Semtex. Do not attempt to open it, or it will explode. Do not try and disrupt the video stream coming from it or it will explode. Do not try to tamper with the casing in any way, shape or form or it will explode. Do I make myself clear?'

'Crystal.' rumbled Saul staring in anger at the bookcase.

'Just so we are crystal, Mr Saul and you fully understand what I *need* from *you*.' the voice continued, 'If you do not bring the person responsible for his murder into this room before midnight tonight, the container will explode. Now Mr Saul, I ask you again, do I have your attention?'

1:30 am

The slightly wavering barrel of a gun appeared through the frame of an open door, pointing towards Saul's head. As it moved forward, slim, elegant fingers with immaculately manicured and painted nails came into view wrapped around the handle. The index finger was wavering over the trigger, its false nail missing, underneath, the real one bitten back to the skin which was red raw and angry. Not quite as angry as she was.

'Bastard!' she slurred and pulled the trigger.

A jet of water shot out of the plastic gun in a spectacular arc, splatting straight into a photograph of Saul and Sarah on the far wall of their minimalist living room. Sarah shuffled through the door into the room, waving the water pistol in front of her.

'Gotcha you knob jockey!' she exclaimed while raising the half empty bottle of wine she had in the other hand to her lips, guzzling down the contents voraciously.

There was a point, earlier in the evening, when she had looked stunning: dressed elegantly, her hair and make-up professionally done, having spent two hours in a beauty salon getting ready for their anniversary dinner. Now, that perfect porcelain façade which accentuated her elfin features was gone, replaced by a tirade of tears and smears. Bright rouge lipstick now adorned her chin and cheeks, mascara flowing in torrents with earlier tears, carving black shadows into her beauty. Hazel shoulder length hair had been straight and pristine. Now it was tousled and tangled, the ends caked with running make-up. She still wore the fitted scarlet YSL dress, cut low at the front, accentuating the gentle swell of her cleavage, highlighting the slender curves of her hips, her long legs still wearing black stockings. Sparkling Jimmy Choo high heels had been kicked off long ago and replaced with a pair of tatty Uggs. Over her dress, she was wearing a thick cotton dressing gown which was stained with, and stank heavily of a child's milky vomit, slightly overpowering the subtle odour of the Chanel perfume she was wearing.

Gently swaying, mumbling curses under her breath, she stared at the photo of the two of them, their heads inclined in and cheeks brushing. They were smiling from their eyes, a tacit intimacy evident in the glow from them, not just from the jet of water that she had sprayed. There was a time when they had been happy. Her gaze moved right, to a large canvas portrait over the wall mounted fire.

A fleeting smile wiled its way onto her lips, stopping the grumbles for a moment as she took in the image. The canvas was a pencil sketch drawing of her. She was draped seductively over a table on her back, long tousled tresses of hair cascading over the edge as her head tipped backwards looking out of the picture. Her beckoning eyes were suggestively following those of whoever was taking in the image. She was naked, the sensual placement of an arm here, the bend of a leg there discreetly covering her modesty. She adored the sketch both for what it was and for the moment it captured: the moment she met John, the moment he exposed her soul bare.

That moment was the 3:00pm on Thursday the 2nd May 1996. She was in the last week of the last year on her Performing Arts degree at Newcastle University and was putting together her final portfolio of photographs and images. She needed something alluring to complete the collection so had agreed to be a nude model for the Art class. There had been a fleeting moment of concern about the idea of 30 plus testosterone loaded Art student's perving over her. Very fleeting, before her naturally extroverted tendencies kicked in and reminded her if she ever wanted to be an actress, this was the type of thing that you needed to be comfortable with: or at least act like you were comfortable with it.

She was attracted to John immediately. Yes, he was handsome, with an angular profile which could be soft or sharp depending on his mood. He was tall, well over 6ft with a toned physique honed by hours spent playing football and at the gym. But it was his eyes that drew her to him. Most of the other students were looking her up and down, lust in their actions as they were sketching. John hardly ever veered away from her face and there was an obvious intensity in his gaze as he looked deep into *her* eyes. Rooms in the recesses of her memories opened, proffering up personal thoughts and feelings willingly through the dilating pools of the facade she was trying to portray, straight into the resonating emerald of his irises and out of his dextrous fingers onto the canvas.

During the sitting she had been on a chair, legs crossed to cover her lady garden, breasts exposed. Most of the sketches took the pose verbatim, with varying degrees of caricature and accentuation of her assets. John's didn't. The physical nudity of his sketch was discreet, the pose totally different, with attention drawn away from the luscious form of her body to her face. A face which conveyed the naked truth of her innocence, insecurities, beauty, temper, avarice and wanton soul breathing from every stroke of his pencil on the canvas.

'Why aren't you like that now, why can't you see inside me, why can't you read me anymore?' she blubbered out as she raised the gun again and shot a jet of water at the sketch. The droplets started to trickle down, smudging the pencil in trails that mirrored the current state of her mind and body, blurring the clarity of what had made their relationship so special.

On the coffee table in the middle of the lounge stood an empty wine glass lipstick kissed, an already empty bottle next to it, sitting on top of a weighty tome on Renaissance Art along with her mobile phone and a brown envelope with the ear of a photograph sticking out. She shuffled into the room and put the current bottle down on the table, picked up the phone and dialled a number at the top of the recent call list. It went to voicemail, and she collapsed back into the brilliant white leather sofa behind her in disappointment.

'Hi Rob, just me again.' she stuttered with a determined expression on her drawn features. 'Guess you are probably out on a call or in bed: probably with your girlfriend! Ha, Ha, HA!' she burst out laughing and then shushed herself.

'Sorry didn't mean that. You might have got my other messages about being sorry for making a pass at you earlier. Well, I'm not!' she proclaimed while raising the water pistol and taking another pot shot at a different picture of Saul on the wall.

'Cunt.' she announced.

'No, not you!' she apologised quickly into the phone 'My git of a husband. He has no idea, no bloody idea what I go through every day trying to keep some normality and perspective in this bubble world with Jacob. You seem to understand, you seem to have a lot of empathy for our situation, a lot of feelings for me...and you are hot, god you are hot!'

She flushed, a look of pained embarrassment replacing her determination. She started to nibble on the nail less index finger as she carried on. 'Shit, did I just say that! Sorry, Jesus I'm so, so sorry! Oh fuck!' she finished and hung up, dropping the phone on the sofa.

'Silly bitch.' she whispered, chastising under her breath while leaning forward, grabbing the wine and taking another huge swig of the contents.

Rob was Jacob's consultant paediatrician. He had been working with Sarah full time for three months now, carrying out research along with other specialists into the neurological disease Jacob had suffered since birth, four short years ago. Although suffered was probably too strong a word given that he seemed to be in a permanently comatose state, oblivious of the world, not even seeing it unless you physically opened his eyelids. The only general reaction his body gave to any kind of stimulus was his eyes dilating under light. They had a daily cleaning and massage regime to keep his body supple and exercised, and the water pistol was a tool they used to see if the gentle sprays would shock his muscles into action. It had never worked, but they kept trying. His body would spasm involuntarily into fits, at least a dozen times a day. He had a mouth guard in place to hold the tongue down so he wouldn't choke, but the spasms would invariably induce vomiting. Feeding was done via a tube that was fitted directly into his stomach. Full time supervision was a necessity, but most of the time this was generally at the end of a baby monitor now. He wore a motion activated alarm on his wrist which looked like a watch, a picture of Pinocchio on the face.

The only occasion he had ever looked like he had a body movement under his own volition was when he was three. Sarah still tried to do all the usual things you would do with a young child as routine, right down to reading him a bedtime story, closing the blackout blinds and kissing his delicate forehead goodnight. On this occasion, she was reading him Pinocchio and had just reached the part in the story where Pinocchio was being tempted by the 'lame fox and the blind cat', to plant his coins under the magic tree. A huge grin surfaced on Jacob's face right at that point and the slightest of noises which she convinced herself was a laugh came out between his lips. The utter exhilaration that overtook her in that moment at the idea of her son coming to life, her son becoming a real boy was equally matched by the devastating anguish that consumed her when, after days of testing, the doctors concluded that he had just had his first wind smile. From that day, they named his condition Pinocchio Paralysis.

Once a month Jacob would go to a private paediatric unit in Newcastle to give Sarah some respite from the demands of his disease. Rob had taken him there yesterday afternoon so that she could get ready for her anniversary evening with John. It was as he leant in to peck her cheek in a friendly goodbye that she had turned her head and kissed him fully on the lips. At first he responded but then after a second pulled away, very apologetic, fumbling back from her, being very clear that while he liked her, he couldn't get involved in that way. Her face flushed red with the embarrassment of the moment as it swirled through her drunken fume.

'Twat Face!' she shouted, another stream of water flying from the pistol, smacking into a photo of John with Jacob in his arms on the day he was born. She clumsily managed to stand up, glugged the last of the wine, dropped the bottle on the floor, picked up her phone and rang John. Her fury was evident as it went to voicemail and she scowled into the handset.

'You are a piece of work John, you really are!'

Shuffling toward the photo, she fired again.

'You have been gone all bloody weekend. I know. I know, you are the big I am. Look at me! Away supporting my son, raising money to pay for research into his illness!'

Closer still she moved, to within a few feet, where another shot was dispatched.

'You are a cock. A bona fide one hundred percent knob. You can't even make time for our wedding anniversary. Our fucking wedding anniversary John! What is it? Why not! Are you scared? Or just bloody bored!'

She was right up to the photo now, the muzzle of the pistol in John's face, where she forced it hard into the glass with an obvious vitriol.

'Or are you just avoiding me, so we don't have to continue the conversation you started the other day. And where did that come from, how the hell did that curve ball pop into your head? What warped world does your mind live in that thinks its okay to consider killing our son!'

2:15 am

After more than an hour in silence, the insidious glare on her face abated, the prolonged straining of every sinew against the restraints dissipating in a second as Rebecca figuratively slumped back into the chair. A huge sigh escaped through caged lips as she spoke. 'That wasn't the first time I kissed him. It was the last.'

She fell silent again.

'Well done Rebecca, it may have taken a while, but that's the first time in two weeks you have been able to answer that question and remain rational.'

She burst out laughing, a further release of pent up tension apparent. 'Doc, for the things I can explain, my mind has always been rational. It's the things I can't explain that test my lucidity. I don't think it's insane to want to kill myself for the things that I have done. I am sure if you went out and canvassed opinion, asking people if a multiple murderer should be allowed to commit suicide, they would consider it reasonable. They would probably offer to help!'

'Multiple?' he questioned.

Silence again, then after a moment, in which she resumed the slow grinding of her wrists against restraints, Rebecca continued.

'The first time I kissed my son. Hannah was in labour, more than eight centimetres dilated with contractions coming every two minutes, well into the second stage. We had wanted a home birth, fully natural, just the two of us. The pain was getting too much for Hannah though and

I thought that the baby was breach, so I decided to take her into hospital, which was only a ten minute ride away.'

'She was lying on the back seat of the car, panting through the contractions and swearing profusely at me for letting her do the hard bit. It's the only time in our relationship that I ever felt like the man. It was only for the briefest of moments though, as through her controlled breathing rose the most gut wrenching scream. I was trying to concentrate on the road, with my left hand swapping between changing gears and seeking out to hold hers with what little comfort I could offer in the circumstances. The scream reached a crescendo and she started to shout 'He's coming, he's coming, he's coming!' at the top of her voice.'

"Cross your legs you silly bitch, he's nowhere near yet.' I sympathetically said, my attempt to keep the mood light while trying to quickly turn around and see how far on Hannah really was. She was fully dilated now, and I could just make out a little vernix as I glimpsed the baby's scalp. That told me he wasn't breach but that he was fully engaged and on his way.'

'As I turned back to look at the road I just caught out of the side of my right eye a lorry heading straight for the car, the rising drone of its blaring horn drowning out Hannah's groans. Ironically, the words 'We Deliver Your Promises' flashed past my startled eyes as I realised I had just gone through a 'Give Way' sign at a crossroads, straight into the path of the lorry. I put my foot on the accelerator, not panicking but realising I had a better chance of driving past it now. I was too late.'

'Huge plumes of acrid black smoke began to rise from the braking delivery lorry as its front end slammed into the rear wing on the driver's side of the car. It was sent spinning with a wrenching screech of metal on metal. I tried hard to steer into the skid as the impact buffeted me in my seat, braking now as well. Panic overtook me as I heard Hannah screaming my name, felt her arms slap into my side, as without a seatbelt on, she was ungraciously thrown around the back seat.'

'In that panic, I still managed to count four complete spins of the car, right across the crossroads, as my gaze agonisingly darted from the windscreen, to the side windows, then behind me, trying to see what we were going to hit next.'

'What we hit next was the trunk of an old and wizened oak tree that stood in an open playing field at the far side of the crossroads. The rear of the passenger side slammed into it, glass shattering as the back door was crushed on impact, stopping the car dead. I could see Hannah being hurled back as the glass flew in, her head banging into the bark of the tree. She screamed. My god did she scream, not just with the impact of the crash but as the next contraction overwhelmed her. There was very little damage to the driver's area and apart from a few scratches from flying glass I was relatively unscathed. I tried to jump over to help her but my seatbelt was locked tight. I quickly fumbled and released it and started to scramble into the back seat just as Hannah's contraction reached its crescendo, just as a fountain of blood spurted from an open wound visible on her neck where the glass had severed an artery.'

'She was jabbering, shaking in shock, in agony, in the last stages of bloody labour, with cuts all over her head and blood seeping down her face, mingling with tears and sweat. She was awake though and in her next breath she screamed at me 'The baby Becca, the baby!', a look of terrified concern consuming her.'

'I didn't know what to do first, find something to stop the oozing from her neck, which had eased off as the contraction passed, or to check between her still open thighs. I froze in absolute shock and did nothing until she slapped me a split second later and said in a calm yet purposeful tone 'Becca, please check our baby. I'm okay, I will be okay and you need to see if he looks alright, please?''

'That's my Hannah, in a nutshell: absolute clarity in her purpose, absolute courage in her convictions. I finished scrambling over into the back seat, gently positioning myself as best I could between her thighs. She was fully dilated now with the baby's head crowning. I couldn't see any abrasions on his visible skull, or any injuries to her vaginal area. 'He looks okay.' I said, obvious relief in my voice, which echoed in her otherwise pained face. 'But I don't think we will be making it to hospital for delivery!''

'It was then I heard a voice from outside. It was the lorry driver in his bland brown delivery livery. He was frantic and blubbering. I let him know that we were both alive but did need an ambulance urgently. I later found out he was called Colin. He ran back to his cab to call it in on his C.B. radio. God, what did we do before mobile phones? Hannah was panting again, the next contraction starting. With her left hand, she had the collar of her blouse pushed into the wound on her neck, slowing the flow of blood from it. With her right, she held mine tightly, anxiously. 'Becca baby, when has anything in our life ever been normal.' Hannah said, raising our entwined hands to her lips and kissing my fingers gently. 'It's always been you and me against the world. It looks like we will be bringing our son into it the same way, just as we wanted.' With that, I could see the tension of the next contraction begin to contort her features, I could hear the low guttural growl start deep in her lungs and I could feel the pain as she crushed the bones in my hand.'

'She pushed. She pushed hard, banshee wails assailing the confined space in the car. As she pushed, blood started to pour profusely from the neck wound, even through the pressure she was applying to keep it in check. 'Stop pushing Hannah, stop pushing!' I shouted, hollow consuming my stomach at the sudden realisation of what was happening to her. 'Hannah listen to me. I know this will be hard, but you have to stop pushing until we can get that wound sorted or you will lose too much blood.' The contraction started to subside but the next one was only a minute away.'

"Becca, I have to push.' she told me, a look of inevitable realisation visible in her eyes. 'He won't be able to breathe for long in the canal, you know that. We have to get him out while I have the energy. The more blood I lose the less chance we have of that happening.' She was right. I knew she was right. Colin appeared back at the car, letting us know the ambulance was on its way and asking what he could do to help. I directed him to Hannah and he took off his brown jacket, scrunched it up and pushed it hard into her neck, taking over that duty. He was wearing a 'Fields Of The Nephilim' tour t-shirt underneath. I remember the image vividly, an angel sitting cross legged, naked on the ground, her wings battered, feathers broken and falling out.'

'I was sobbing uncontrollably now, my chest wracked with taut pain as my own breathing became laboured under the intensity of the emotions. My words came out, but they were broken and high pitched as I groaned. 'No Hannah, I can't let you, I can't.....' She interrupted me, grabbing both my hands with hers and staring straight into my eyes with a fiery, defiant determination. 'It's my choice; it's what I have to dooooo....' The sentence ended in a scream as the next contraction kicked in. I could see every vein and sinew pumping in her face, forehead and neck with the ferocity she was forcing into the push, blood streaming from her wound through the makeshift bandage. I looked down and saw the whole of his head crowned as the wave abated.'

'In between the tears I let out a squeak of delight at the thought that he was almost out, the thought that one more big effort would see him born and that Hannah just might not bleed to death. 'He's almost there, one more huge push and he will be out. You are doing so well, so, so well.' I said on autopilot. Hannah, lying there in the most exposed way, life force ebbing from her, exertion evident in every fibre of her being, fatigue apparent in the wry smile that formed on her lips, said to me as only she could, 'Becca, I know you are a midwife, but that has to be the most condescending line you could say to any pregnant mother under normal circumstances, let alone these!''

'Her face suddenly turned hard again. 'It's coming. He's coming!' she said as the next contraction began to bubble. 'Get your hands on your knees and be ready to let rip.' I instructed, positioning myself to deliver our son.'

''Dig if you will a picture...' she started to randomly shout between panting as the tidal force of this last, all-consuming contraction overwhelmed her. His head edged her cervix further apart, the top of an ear popping into view.'

''Of you and I engaged in a kiss....' she continued. Colin was pressing as hard as he could on her wound, but it wasn't stopping the flow of blood at all. 'Nearly there Hannah, keep this push up and he will be out!' I screamed over her tirade.'

''Can you my darling, can you picture this....' she finished, with a monumental wail, hands pulling her knees up with the effort, head forced forward looking down towards the delivery as, with a final gasp, she forced our son out.'

'His head was free, and his bloody blue body slithered out into my shaking hands. Seeing I had nothing to wrap him in, Colin took off his t-shirt and passed it over to me. I wrapped the baby up, wiping the vernix, blood and slime from his head and face, quickly checking his throat.'

'In a second he began to wail: full, raucous screams as I lifted him up onto Hannah's chest. With an effort she was still holding her head up, tears biting clear streams through her blood stained face as she said 'He's okay. He's okay.', while leaning over to kiss his head, cuddling him into her chest.'

Angels Bleed   Max Hardy

'I did the same, the first time I kissed my son, before reaching up and kissing Hannah full on the lips. The last time I kissed her. We pulled apart and she looked at me, the sheen covering her eyes not just due to the tears. She put one hand behind my head, pulled me in close to her face and whispered with her last breath 'Look after him. Now I know what it *really* sounds like, When Doves Cry.''

'That was the first time I killed someone.'

3:30 am

Brilliant white light exploded from two tall arc lamps bursting into life, the monotone chatter of the diesel generators powering them pre-empting the illumination of Featherstone Hall. Darkness was dispelled to reveal a bustle of uniformed Police Officers on various duties. Some were staking out lines from the edge of the Hall and erecting 'Police – Do Not Enter' tape. Some were chatting to their SOCO colleagues who were carrying items to the property. Some were transporting boxes from several vehicles to the large Major Incident Unit parked up on a grassy field about a hundred metres to the front of the building, the arc lamps flanking either end of it.

The Hall itself was built in 1801 in a castellated Tudor style. A rotund tower on the left rose beyond the height of the main building by about twenty feet and was topped with ramparts. Fake arrow slits were visible down the side along with many small shuttered windows. The central body of the Hall was over three storeys, the entrance flanked by two pillars that framed a large oak door which was distressed and rotting with age. A balcony jutted out from the central structure above the oak door, supported on the pillars, the large windows leading out onto it also shuttered, along with every window in the property.

A gravel driveway, overrun with weeds and blurring with unkempt lawns at its edges meandered through woods from the left of the property to a large open expanse at the front of the house. In the centre of this was a dilapidated fountain, an early Greek statue of Eros that was meant to be standing proud on a plinth in the middle missing its wings, arms and head, the remainder of it lichen stained.

A Range Rover rolled sedately down the drive, circling the fountain, the driver taking in the scene and the Hall before he drove up to the side of the Major Incident Unit. The car door opened, tan brogues coming into view, followed by the Moleskin suited DCI Jeremiah Strange as he stepped out of the vehicle. He was a tall, very slight man, his dark leathery skin especially noticeable in the sunken cheeks and around gaunt, haunted eyes. He still sported an Afro on his head, only with age it was now a shock of grey. Vapour wraiths escaped his mouth in the early morning chill as he blew through his hands.

PC Buglass was waiting for him outside the entrance of the Unit with a steaming cup of black coffee. 'Chief, here's a wake me up for you.' Buglass said, proffering the drink.

'Thank you son.' Strange answered, with a slight Jamaican twang evident in his gentle timbre. He took a huge gulp of the coffee and asked 'Who's managed to get their behinds out of bed so far?'

'Saul is still here, he's inside with Munro and Saxon. No other Detectives yet. Harris and Darrie have headed back to HQ with the body and the initial forensic evidence. They should be there by now. There are three more SOCO's on site and they are checking over the rest of the house. We've got half a dozen PC's just securing the perimeter and Tech are outback setting up comms and IT. There's an Army Bomb Squad Unit on their way from Otterburn, they shouldn't be long arriving. That's about it.' briefed Buglass.

'Not a bad turnout considering the time.' said Strange, pleasantly surprised as he climbed the steps into the MIU, coffee in hand. 'I guess you are designated scribe until admin turn up. Are you okay with that?'

Buglass shrugged. 'It beats real work.' he said, a cheeky look on his young, still spotty face.

The unit was decorated an industrial, lifeless grey. On the farthest, shorter wall was a bank of clean whiteboards. Along the entire length of the back wall of the unit ran a bench loaded with computers, monitors, telephones and a percolating coffee machine. Above these and secured to the wall was a horizontal bank of ten plasma screens. There were windows in the front wall of the unit that looked out over the Hall. In the middle of the room was a rectangular table around which were squeezed half a dozen chairs, three of them occupied by the DI's, who were all drinking coffee, Munro and Saxon listening intently to Saul.

'Morning chaps, thanks for coming out so quickly this morning, not the best start for a Monday, I know.' He placed a hand on Saul's shoulder as he passed, squeezing it gently. 'And John, thanks for leading on this so far. Like the tux by the way. Hopefully the coffee will kick in quickly and our brains just might start working.' he continued light heartedly as he made his way to the whiteboards. Buglass followed him in and sat down next to Saul.

'Right guys, the chain of command for the incident is as follows at the moment. I am Bronze Control; Super is Silver/Gold and will be in the loop once the Video Conferencing is up to HQ. Saul, as the first on the scene with the most information on this, are you okay to be lead Detective?' asked Strange. Saul nodded while drinking his coffee. 'Saxon, Munro you are supporting and at the moment Buglass is scribe. We will have more support turning up soon but given the time pressures we appear to be under, I would suggest we get started. Is everyone okay with that?'

Everyone nodded in acknowledgement, and they started, Buglass relaying details of the initial 999 call that had sparked the incident, which had come through at 11:00am the previous night. As he spoke, DCI Strange began to jot down salient points in a timeline on one whiteboard, while mapping out relationships with questions underneath on the next. Buglass finished his notes and then Saul brought them up to speed with the events since he arrived at the house.

'So, the upshot is, we have an ultimatum from an unknown caller to deliver the unknown real killer of their unknown victim, to the drawing room of this house by midnight or our unknown live captive will be blown up. That is a frightening number of unknowns to discover in 24 hours.' finished Saul, shaking his head.

'It is, but as our 'Unknown Caller' points out, we have a lot of evidence already and will have more as soon as we identify the body. So let's do what we always do. Get all the things we know on the table and the right resource focused on investigating the things we think, based on our collective experience, will get us a result. I can't promise this will be easy. We have a person's life at stake here but what we can't do is panic, or procrastinate, or lose our focus, and it's my job to make sure that we don't. So sup up your coffee and let's get focused.'

'Right, as I see it, there's three primary lines of enquiry we need to start down. Firstly, who is the dead person, who has been convicted of killing them and why is our 'Unknown Caller' so convinced they didn't do it? The 'who' bit will hopefully be incoming soon, and from there we need to try and figure out the 'why'. I see this as the main area of the investigation and John, I would like you to pick that up.' Strange started.

'Secondly, who the hell is the guy who set this elaborate honey pot up? Does he own this Hall, is it as simple as that? I doubt it, so if he doesn't, then who does? It's empty apart from that one room, so we need door to door co-ordinated with the surrounding farms and neighbours, see if they have seen any activity here recently. We need to be checking the data from the phone lines into the house, calls received over and above the one we managed to record the end of. We also need to be analysing that call to see if it's the same person as the 999 caller and if we can get any audio forensic from either of them.

Get the Tech Forensics checking out the AV setup and connectivity into that room as well. Finding out where those feeds are coming from should help us find this guy. Leigh, could you pick that up please?' he asked DI Saxon.

'On it Chief!' she said, obvious enthusiasm in her animated response.

'Thirdly, we have an unidentified person whose life is at risk in all of this. Have we had any missing person's calls in the last 24 hours from around this area? We might need to look back further than that. See if the Tech Forensics can glean any more from the feed into that crate. Any distinguishing features on the little we can see of the person that might help identify them. Mick, just you left, are you okay with that?' Strange finished.

'It's going to be like finding piss in the ocean, but yes, I'm on it.' DI Munro moaned, a surly look on his haggard face.

'Start with finding piss in the puddle, then the pond, then the lake before you start on the ocean. You know it's more likely to be a local, so let's maintain that focus.' Strange firmly directed.

'Right, do we all know what we are doing?' asked Strange. Nods of affirmation were forthcoming. 'Leigh, Mick, you can crack on. Buglass could you give Leigh a hand organising the door to door? John, you wait until we hear from HQ. We will catch up at 06:30 hours either here or on the conference bridge. We have 21 hours to find a killer, or to stop a killer. So let's get going.'

Saxon was straight up, barking instructions to Buglass immediately as they left. Munro slouched out of his seat lethargically, taking time to finish off his coffee before buttoning up his overcoat and leaving. Strange sat down next to Saul at the table.

'How are you doing John? I know you've been up a while but you are looking troubled. Personal or Professional?' asked Strange empathetically.

Saul had a nonplussed expression on his face for a second before he answered, a little tersely. 'Professional of course.'

Strange stared Saul out for a few seconds, a wry smile spreading over his face, shaking his head slightly as he said. 'Okay, if you don't want to discuss what you are doing here dressed up to the nines, on your wedding anniversary, when you should be with your wife, that is entirely your own business. If you don't want to tell me why you asked to be on call tonight, I'm not going to push it. I am here to listen when you are ready to talk. So, professionally, what's up?'

'He wanted to attract *my* attention. He was very particular about wanting *me* to investigate this. I'm wracking my brains to think if I recognise the voice or if there's anyone I've dealt with in the recent past who would have hatched this. I can't think of anyone at the moment and that troubles me.' Saul paused and let out an ironic laugh, then continued, 'This is professional but someone is trying to make it personal and I don't understand why. How the hell would he know it would be me turning up to investigate tonight? How does he know what I am like as a Detective and why has that got any relevance?'

'Keep thinking those things, as we get more facts on the table, run those questions past each and every bit of information we gather. He has the advantage, for now, but he is right on one thing, you are an excellent detective. Recognise your blindside John and make sure he's not trying to exploit it. Professional and Personal can never, ever be kept totally separate. No matter how hard you try, they bleed into one another. Just think on that.' advised Strange.

Just then, a low thrum burst from the bank of plasma's behind them a second before two of them powered on, one displaying the ruddy hue of Darrie stood behind the shimmering silver of an autopsy bench, his green gloved hands delving into the open chested cadaver of their John Doe. The second screen showed an empty office with a small sign saying Path Lab on the wall behind a desk.

'Georgie, how's it hanging my friend? Have you got any news for us yet?' asked Strange, turning in his seat to face the screens.

'Jerry! To the left you cheeky sod, always to the left. It's not often you are out of your boudoir and away from your harem of honeys this early in the day.' Darrie retorted jovially.

'They be waiting for me, gives me a break to recover, my body's not as young as my mind thinks it is. Do we know who he is yet?' Strange responded, entertaining the banter.

'I think Harris should be along any minute with some news, he's just running the DNA now. What I can tell you is that our JD had his heart ripped out. If you look along the line of the Y incision, you can see the uniformity of the cut.' he started, taking his hands out of the chest and pointing to the edge of the skin, moving up from the stomach. 'But when you get to this area of the chest, quite literally the skin has been ripped open. You can see the tear. The ribs around the cavity have been snapped outwards, lung pushed to one side, and all that's left of where the heart should be are the remaining ends of riven arteries. It's some ferocious effort that's been exerted to do this. Ripping skin is not an easy thing to do.'

Harris sidled into view on the second screen, consciously positioning himself in front of the camera at his end. 'Can you see me?' He asked, squinting into his monitor.

'Yes, we can Ian. What's the news? Have you got a match yet?' asked Strange.

'We have, and you aren't going to like it. Our JD is one Michael Colin Angus. Born 14th September 1989. Died, or should I say murdered on the 1st January 2012 at the age of twenty two by his mother's hand in her flat on the Crombie Estate, Edinburgh.' divulged Harris.

'His mother's hand?' asked Darrie quizzically. 'Are you sure? I can't imagine a woman causing the damage I can see?'

'Definitely. Rebecca Angus confessed to his murder under caution on the 2nd January 2012. She called the police to her flat on the 1st saying she had killed her son. They arrived, found her naked and covered in blood, gibbering and incoherent. He was on her bed with his chest ripped open. Forensic examination found that sexual intercourse had taken place between the two of them. She had bits of his heart in her teeth and chunks of it in her stomach. She was formally charged with his murder on the 3rd January.' Harris continued.

'Jesus H, that is sick.' pitched in Saul, his words conveying the feelings evident in everyone's expressions as Harris continued to relay the facts of the case to them.

'More than you know. He was wearing a black full body rubber suit with holes exposing the genitals and anus. A gimp mask, mouth bit and reins were by the bed along with numerous used sex toys.'

'That in itself is not sick.' piped in Darrie. 'Just playful.'

'Darrie, not appropriate at this point.' rebuked Strange. 'Let's focus. Carry on Harris.'

'Rebecca Angus was deemed unfit to plead due to mental illness but was convicted of his murder by a trial of facts on the 1st April 2012 as a result of the overwhelming forensic evidence. She was committed to a mental institution indefinitely. Open and shut case.' finished Harris.

'Shit.' sighed Saul, scratching his hands through his hair. 'How the hell does that tie up with our man making out a gross miscarriage of justice has taken place?'

'I said you wouldn't like it.' added Harris. 'The thing that's going to flip your lid even more is where she is incarcerated.'

'Why?' shot back Saul, staring at the screen.

'She's in the Fielding Institute, in Morpeth, under the authority of Dr Ennis. The same Dr Ennis that you collared for two deaths caused during Face Down restraint incidents. The same Dr Ennis that was acquitted last month.'

Strange took a deep breath and looked over to Saul, who was staring incredulously at Harris. 'Professional and Personal John, there's your starting point.'

4:15 am

A quizzical expression found its way onto Rebecca's restrained face as she saw a handle in one of the cells padded sections in front of her turn and a door open up in the wall. Through it walked a tall, broad man, hunched in the shoulders and limping lightly on his left leg as he entered the cell. He wore beige polyester slacks, a tan gingham shirt under an angora cardigan that was stretched in the pocket and sandals over white socks. He looked old, furrows sculpted into a brow tickled by the odd grey hair combed over his bald scalp.

Behind him, he pulled a metal chair which emitted a bone tingling screech as it was dragged over the tiled corridor, the sound stopping on the padded cell floor.

'You look a lot older than I thought you would be.' said Rebecca, her eyes not leaving him as he positioned the seat directly in front of her.

'I get that a lot. It's the soft Irish lilt in my accent, so they tell me.' he answered as he turned to her and began to loosen the mouth guard she was wearing. 'If we are going to have a proper conversation, let's get this thing out. Do you promise me that you won't try and bite your tongue?'

'I promise I will try hard not to, but I can't promise I won't. It depends on what questions you ask me. I thought you were about forty six. You first kissed a girl in 1974 when you were seven? Was that a lie?' she finished, wiggling her jaw as the guard was removed.

'I can see being insane hasn't impacted your cognitive abilities.' he smiled wryly as he sat down in the chair in front of her. He reached out and took her bound hand, shaking it.

'Hello Rebecca, it's nice to meet you face to face, it's nice to talk to you without your mind being in a drugged fug. Yes, it was a lie. I'm Dr Hanlon and I am here to help.'

Rebecca's eyes looked down to his hand which was holding hers, then shot a startled glare back at him. 'Are you sure? You haven't just come in for your *Kit-Kat*, have you?' harsh invective emphasised in every word.

'Kit-Kat? I don't know what you mean. I'm sorry, I should have asked if I could shake your hand.' he replied, removing his hand from hers, appreciating the distress that the contact had instilled.

As much as it could, her head tilted to one side, eyes darting over his face, trying to glean any sign that he might be lying again. 'You don't know what I mean, do you. It's what the staff call me, well, most of the staff. It's also what they do when they *'Have a break'*: come into my cell, slip two fingers into my cunt and frig me until I come. They think I don't remember. I mean, why would I, being dosed up on Diazipam and Haloperidol. I remember *every, single, time*.' She finished the last three words slowly, her stubby tongue trying to lick her lips lewdly. It looked grotesque.

Dr Hanlon leant forward in his seat, white knuckles evident as he clasped his hands together tightly. Shaking his head, eyes alive with anger he said, 'Rebecca, I am genuinely sorry for every single violation that has been exacted upon you under your care. Please believe me, I am here to help. I am here to understand the care, or lack of care that you have been given. I am here to understand your version of events and get to the truth of why you are here. I am here to let you know that I do not think you are insane. I think you have had a tremendous amount of trauma to cope with and that has caused you to behave extraordinarily. I believe I can help you believe again.'

He held her gaze intently in silence, then looked over her body at the lesions, bruises and burns. 'Were any of these wounds inflicted by the staff?'

Her wrists were turning again, and she was biting the corner of her bottom lip so much a drop of blood oozed out of the broken skin. She saw him look at it and frown, immediately stopping the action.

'No, not directly.' she started, calmness descending over her again. 'They are all my doing, either self-inflicted or from when they stopped me trying to kill myself. I believe I deserve every single one of them. It was only sex with the staff. They see me as a sexual deviant. I think I am complicit in that. I did nothing to discourage them, in fact, probably the opposite. It wasn't about pleasure though. It was about suffering, about pain, about living the hell I truly believe I deserve.'

'That doesn't excuse their actions Rebecca. You are not well and they have a duty of care to you, a legal obligation to look after your wellbeing. I won't let that lie. Why do you believe you deserve this hell?'

She burst out laughing, her chest wracking with the force of the guffaws, loud chortles able to escape her freed mouth now. 'Oh Doc, you are such a comedian, you remind me of Dave Allen with that accent. I think I like you, but you just might be deluding yourself if you think you can ever lead me to a path of redemption. Didn't you listen to how I killed Hannah? How I murdered Michael?'

'I did listen. What I need you to try and help me with now is to understand what happened, if you can. When you murdered your son...' he began before being interrupted.

'Michael.' she stated firmly, tension in her tone which quickly relaxed as she continued. 'Can you call him Michael please?'

'If that's what you want, I can. It may make it harder for you to talk about?' he suggested.

'Harder, it should be horrendous: it should be a living hell. They aren't once removed for me. They aren't a faceless fantasy that I have brought to life in their killing. They were the essence of me, my pulse, my breath, my being. 'Sorry Hannah', 'Sorry Michael' will be my litany until the last breath of life passes these lips. It's what I want.' A tear started to trickle from the corner of her eye as she finished. Her gaze didn't leave Dr Hanlon's questioning, concerned stare.

'Alright.' he said, nodding gently in appreciation. 'So, when you murdered *Michael*, you said that you were sat astride *Michael*, *Michael* was inside you, you ripped *Michael's* heart out and ate it laughing as *Michael* died. Is that what you remember?' he asked.

'It's what happened.' she retorted brusquely. 'You can't deny the facts.' she finished abruptly.

'No, I guess you can't.' he conceded, pausing for a moment in contemplation before a quizzical look came over his face and he continued. 'Which rib did you break first?'

'What?' she replied, stunned disbelief evident in her voice. 'What's that got to do with anything? Aren't you going to ask me why?' she added, frustration entering the tone, oozing into her actions as she flexed against her restraints.

'At this point Rebecca why isn't significant. How is. Which of Michael's ribs did you break first?' he repeated firmly, sitting calmly in his seat, holding her confused gaze without blinking.

She started shaking, tension escalating in the pulsing veins of her forehead, in the rouge that flowed up her face, in the blood that started to drip from the lip she was chewing.

'I...I....' she stuttered, 'The... the...' she continued, her eyes bulging now as she tried to hold his gaze.

'What T-shirt was Colin wearing in the car crash?' he said abruptly in a firm tone.

Within a split second, she answered, 'Fields of the Nephilim.' surprise overtaking her frustration.

'What line was Prince singing when you kissed Hannah for the first time.' he asked just as sharply.

'Dig if you will a picture.' Her animation was slowing now as she answered.

'What was the picture hall called where you went to see Purple Rain?' he fired firmly.

'The Regal.'

'It's funny what you remember, isn't it?' he finished, leaving the statement hanging in the air.

Rebecca stopped biting her lip, stopped shaking and stopped forcing her limbs against the restraints. She didn't stop staring at him intently and said in a tone wavering with bubbling emotion, 'I don't know which rib I broke first. I can't remember. I can't remember how we got to the flat. I can't remember why he was on my bed. I can't remember how I did that to him, I honestly can't.'

'That's fine. Let's start with what you do remember.' he said, the gentle lilt of his voice whispering encouragement.

Angels Bleed

Max Hardy

'Johnsons baby powder, rubber and copper. That was the mixture of smells that began to invade my senses as I was stuttering back into consciousness. I couldn't open my eyes initially. Jackhammers were pounding away at my temples and thoughts were nebulous things wafting into touching distance, then floating away the second I got anywhere close to making one coherent. I vaguely recalled lots of drink, lots of drugs, lots of dancing and lots of sex, but who with, where and how much all eluded me at that point.'

'I eventually managed to force one eyelid open and the vague blurriness ever so slowly began to focus. The side profile of a face started to coalesce into what looked like the serene, sleeping features of my son. At least that's what my mind saw. It also wondered what he was doing there, and I tried to speak his name but my mouth was far to parched to emit a noise, only a whispered breath escaping.'

'Some thoughts began to impress themselves upon me at that point as his image became clearer in front of me. Why is he looking so drawn and pallid? Has he been eating? Why does he smell of baby powder and rubber and what is that copper odour? He's got cuts to the corners of his mouth, what are they from? What are those red spots dotted over his face? I raised a thumb to my mouth and unsuccessfully tried to lick a bit of spittle onto it before reaching over to rub off the red spots. Mother's instinct? My hand and arm came into my line of vision as I did so, and it was red, it was all red. My sense of taste suddenly kicked in, enlightening my mind with the knowledge I had just licked blood off my thumb.'

'Every synapse fired, all at once, kicking a rush of adrenaline into my system. Both eyes shot open, and from a prone position I was on all fours next to Michael in a split second. I couldn't process all the information that was bombarding my brain in that moment. He was lying on his back, neck to toe in black rubber apart from two areas, one where his genitals were exposed, one where the latex was torn on his chest. Flaps of skin, bits of bone, trailing veins and rivers of blood all encircled a gaping cavity where I knew his lungs and heart should be. I screamed, or tried to scream. There was not a drop of moisture in my throat so all that came out was a hoarse moan. I shot one hand up to his neck, foolishly feeling for a pulse. With the other hand I scrambled round in the pools of blood that were forming from the rivers flowing from his chest to see if I could find his heart. How stupid is that? My mind thought that if I could find it, I would be able to push it back in, and he would be fine!'

"Michael!' I screamed, over and over, the constant use of my throat making it moist, making the sounds come, making the screams real and making everything real as the crescendo echoed around the bedroom. I couldn't find his heart, but that didn't dissuade my mind. I forced all of the loose bits of bone and skin back into the gaping cavity and started pumping it to try and resuscitate him. One, two, three pumps on the chest then one, two, three breaths into his mouth. 'Breathe, Michael, breathe!' I screamed in time with the beats.'

'I counted three thousand. Three thousand pumps. Three thousand breaths. It was about an hour before I gave up, before I tried one last time to breathe life into him, ending it with the gentlest of kisses on his lips. The last time I kissed my son.'

'I was in bits, tears streaming from my eyes, my whole body wracked with sobs as I stumbled from the bed in a daze, mumbling his name over and over again under my breath. I picked up the phone from the bedside table and dialled 999, turning back to look at the bed as it rang. It was only then I saw the bigger picture, saw the entire bed scarlet with his blood, even where I had been lying. I saw my own reflection then too, in the mirrored wardrobes opposite. I didn't recognise it as me. I saw a naked woman, hunched and quivering in shock, her whole body painted in shades of blood, the worst being caked around her mouth as she began to speak into the phone.'

''I've killed him. I've killed my son. He's dead. Oh my god I've killed him. What have I done....' I started to wail down the phone as I collapsed into the corner, sliding down the wall and curling up into a gibbering ball on the floor.'

'That's all I remember until the police arrived.' she finished, tears shining brightly on her cheeks, her body still, calm.

'So, you can't remember laughing manically? You can't remember ripping his heart out? You can't remember eating it?' asked Dr Hanlon.

'I can't remember doing any of those things. They are the things I can't explain, the things that test my lucidity.'

'What about sitting astride him. Can you remember that?' he asked.

She tensed again. 'Do you mean did I fuck him?'

'Rebecca, I am using your words, all I want to do is know what you know. I am not trying to get a rise out of this, please believe me.' he encouraged.

'Sorry Doc.' she answered, sincerity in her tone. 'My moral compass is totally demagnetised and spinning like a dervish. I do remember my son fucking me, vividly. It wasn't at my flat. It was after a party the night before, after we left there and went back to someone's house.'

'You went back to someone else's house? They were with you and Michael before he died? Did the police know this? Did they visit the house, question who you were with?' he asked.

Rebecca laughed through her still trickling tears. 'Doc, if only it was that simple. I don't have a clue where the house is that we ended up at. All I remember is the room that we had sex in, all three of us. It had a black fire place with gargoyles chasing cherubs around it. We fucked all over, on the Chesterfield sofa's, on top of the Steinway piano, on the plush carpets in front of a roaring fire, with huge candelabra's throwing flickering light onto passions shadows throughout. That's where I sat astride him.'

'So who was the other person? Surely they know where it is?' he pushed.

'You would think that, yes, she probably does. If you can find her, if she were ever real. I don't know where she came from. I met her in a particular kind of bar, and she introduced me to a world of pleasure I never knew existed. She became my dark disease, my fatal addiction. I never had a phone number, an address, any kind of contact information, just a name. I told the police everything I knew about her, which wasn't much and they checked at all the places we had met. Some people did recognise the description, but no one knew who she was, no one could recall the two of us being together and to be honest, that is the way those kind of places are. The police and Dr Ennis concluded that everything I told them about her and the house was all down to my psychosis, all just a figment of my imagination. I only knew her name: Madame Evangeline.'

5:30 am

The stuttering orange hue of streetlights illuminated the road out of Morpeth as Saul turned left into the entrance of St George's Park Estate, and started the meandering ascent up the side of the hill to the main hospital grounds which were housed on the plateau on top of it.

He dialled recall on the hands free phone as he took the bends slowly. The call went to voicemail. 'Just me again. Look, I can only apologise so many times, but I am truly sorry. I'll give you a call a little later, when the world wakes up a bit.' he finished, hanging up on the call to Sarah with a heavy sigh.

The beams from his headlights punctuated the darkness beyond the glow of the streetlights, highlighting tall metal fencing to the left and right on the winding road, 'Keep Out' signs fixed to them. Behind these, the lights exposed fleeting glimpses of boarded up houses. They were ancillary offices and accommodation of the old lunatic asylum that came into view on the right as his car rounded another bend. Security lights shone out from each side of the redbrick tower at the centre of the asylum, illuminating the derelict wings of the main building, the harsh glare against the darkness accentuating the detritus of dilapidation festooning the weed infested concrete pathways surrounding the boarded up structure.

He took a left into a driveway that passed the new Community Mental Health Centre, and ended at the security gates to the Fielding Institute, a large, modern structure totally enclosed within a ten metre high metal wall. He flashed his badge to the Security Guard. 'DI Saul to see Dr Ennis. I rang ahead, he is expecting me.'

The Guard checked his tablet. 'No problem Sir. Through the gate when it opens and please park in the visitor bay to the right then report to reception.'

A large red light began to pulsate on top of the tall steel gate as a loud beeping signalled its opening into a holding cage with a similar gate at the far end. He drove in and waited for the gate behind to shut and the one in front to open, which it did, in a similar manner. The car continued on and Saul pulled into the visitor bay.

He vacated the car and walked to short distance into the light, airy reception area, announcing his arrival to the polite, smiling young lady behind the smoked glass and aluminium reception desk. 'If you would like to take a seat Sir, I will let Dr Ennis know you are here.'

Saul returned her smile, thanked her and then walked the few paces to the waiting area with its metal legged black leather sofas, taking in the various pictures on the walls. His eyes were drawn immediately to an enormous canvas just behind the seats, fully five metres wide by about a metre deep. It depicted a Jesus like figure, long hair and beard, pious expression on his face, in hessian robes with palms held out displaying his stigmata. Two giant wings spread out either side of his body to fill the width of the picture.

'Impressive canvas, isn't it Saul.' came the impersonal greeting from a tall gentleman in a tweed three piece suit, striding down the corridor, thumbs tucked tightly into the pockets of his waistcoat as he arrived and positioned himself right beside Saul, shoulder to shoulder, taking in the picture. 'We found it in the old hospital, hidden under wood panelling removed from the main hall. Records suggest it was painted by an inmate, around 1899. Psychopath. Murdered three men. Partial to eating their genitals apparently. Also killed one of the guards, maimed and sexually molested two others before he was restrained, face down.' Dr Ennis finished, leaving the last statement hanging in the air as he turned his head to take in Saul's profile.

'Impressive brush work. His strokes have a feel of Munch, the face has a similar contortion to that in 'The Scream of Nature.' There are those that think Munch found his inspiration from a lunatic asylum near to the location depicted in the painting. His sister was in there at the time, apparently. Very apt. This guy might have been a psychopath, but he certainly studied the masters.' Saul said, before turning and offering a hand for Dr Ennis to shake, adding, 'Thank you for agreeing to see me at such short notice Doctor. I appreciate your time.' he finished, looking directly into his eyes, gaze unwavering.

Dr Ennis stared back for a moment, a simmering anger evident in his glare, hands still firmly forced into his waistcoat as he looked down to the proffered hand with obvious disdain. 'Yes, well.' he said, a tinge of red rising on his neckline above the brilliant white and perfectly starched shirt collar as he looked Saul up and down, snorting as he took in the tuxedo. 'Let's continue this in my office. Follow me.' he ordered while turning and striding off in the same direction from which he had come.

Saul sighed, shook his head and slowly followed him down the clean, white walled corridor and into his office. As he came through the door, the décor changed from crisp, clinical lines and materials, to paisley papered walls, mahogany furniture and classic paintings. Saul's attention was drawn to a painting on the wall behind Dr Ennis's desk and he continued to look at it while he was offered a seat and Dr Ennis took his.

'The Cezanne behind you, is that an original? I don't recall it being there the last time I was here?' asked Saul, motioning to the picture which depicted a table with apples spilt onto it from a fruit bowl, a pitcher beside it.

Dr Ennis looked up to the picture as he sat then turned to Saul with a perplexed look. 'I'm sure you haven't come here to ask me about art, have you?' he said, while resting his elbows on the table, steepling his arms and hands on the desk and resting his chin on the thumbs.

'Sorry, no, I haven't.'

'It was bequeathed to the Institute by one of our patrons. We received it amongst about a dozen other painting three months ago along with a large financial donation. We have all the paperwork if you need to see it.' he said.

'No, it's not why I am here. Just an interesting painting, that's all.'

'So, Saul, why are you here? Is it further allegations of brutality towards my patients?' Dr Ennis stated, crossing his arms and leaning forcefully forward in his seat, not able to stop himself bringing the subject back to his agenda.

Saul held his penetrating gaze and answered. 'Dr Ennis, I appreciate that you are unhappy with me and the investigation we undertook into those allegations, and if you want to vent your frustrations, then please feel free. What I can tell you is that we presented facts found in the investigation to the CPS, *they* took a decision to prosecute, and you and your staff have been acquitted. That is the process and the system that I respect and it has done its job. I am not here to harass, or hound, or claim any umbrage with regard to the outcome. I am here on a totally separate matter.' he concluded, holding Dr Ennis firmly in his eye line.

'Just as long as you accept that we were just doing our job. We deal with extremely psychotic individuals here, individuals that would kill someone in a split second with no reservation whatsoever. We need every tool available to us to manage them. I recognise face down restraint can be dangerous, but it is also effective: very, very effective.' Dr Ennis stated, anger still driving his tone.

'As I said Dr Ennis, I accept that due process was followed and an impartial jury accepted you were doing your job. I have nothing more to add to that. I do need to talk to you about Rebecca Angus though as a matter of urgency, so could we please move on to that?' asked Saul, his tone conciliatory, even if the statement wasn't forgiving.

Dr Ennis was still simmering with resentment, which was evident in how hard he was balling his fists, how his head was juddering and how his right eyelid was twitching under the strain of his own self-restraint. 'Alright Saul, let's leave it at that: for now. What do you need to know about Rebecca?'

'Thank you Dr Ennis. As I mentioned, we are investigating a potential murder at the moment and have reason to believe that Mrs Angus could help us with our enquiries. Do you feel she is in a position to be able to answer some questions?' Saul asked.

'Given what I know of her mental state, I doubt that very much. The other issue you have is that she is no longer a patient of the institute. She was moved to Broadmoor two weeks ago.' answered Ennis.

'Oh, right. Is that usual? Moving between hospitals I mean. I thought that there would need to be a court order to move care from the designated authority?' Saul questioned.

'It's not usual, no. In this situation however, her new consultant, Dr Hanlon and I thought it best for the treatment of her condition. And yes, it was approved by the court.' he finished tersely.

'Sorry, I don't mean to sound accusatory, I'm just surprised our systems haven't been updated with that information. Would you be able to get in touch with Dr Hanlon and see if it would be possible to interview her?'

'I can try.' Dr Ennis began, picking up his desk phone and ringing his receptionist. 'I'm not sure he will be in the office this early, depends what shift he is on. Celia, could you give Broadmoor a call and see if Dr Hanlon would be free to have a quick chat about Rebecca Angus please.' he asked as the call was answered. 'Thanks, just buzz through if you can get him.'

He hung up the call and continued. 'I still don't think you will be able to talk to her. For six months before she left us she was continually sedated to protect her and my staff. I very much doubt that has changed dramatically in two weeks.'

'Perhaps you can help while we are waiting. We know that Mrs Angus was committed to you for the murder of her son. In your time providing care to her, did she ever mention anyone else involved in his murder?'

'You do know why she was in here with us, don't you?' Dr Ennis asked, surprised.

'Unfortunately we don't have too much information at the moment. We only found out about a possible link to our investigation a short while ago and haven't got all the paperwork through from her original conviction. If you could let me know, that would help.' Saul answered.

'Rebecca was diagnosed with psychotic Dissociative Identity Disorder. She has multiple personalities. Two to be precise. One, the guilt ridden and suicidal celibate lesbian that worshipped her son, who we know as Rebecca. The other, a sultry, vivacious psychotic dominatrix who will eat you alive, literally, who she refers to as Madame Evangeline. We have spent the past year trying to bring out the Madame Evangeline personality, without any success. It's one of the reasons we moved her to Dr Hanlon's care, he has some innovative ways of treating DID.'

'If you haven't been able to bring that personality out, how do you know she has a multiple personality?' Saul questioned, slightly bemused.

'That comes back to your question about was anyone else involved in her son's murder. When you do eventually see the investigation transcripts you will see Rebecca continually referring to Madame Evangeline. How she met her, their relationship, her involvement in Michael's death. You will also see reports of prolonged periods of time where Rebecca can't account for her whereabouts or actions. The police could not find any evidence from any of the sex clubs she frequented of a Madame Evangeline. They remember Rebecca, but always being there alone. From a psychological perspective, the blank periods in her recollection and detailed observations about Madame Evangeline are classic symptoms of DID. We believe that the last act Madame Evangeline carried out, the brutal murder of Michael Angus, was so traumatic to Rebecca's personality that she has figuratively locked the room and thrown away the key that would allow us access to her. We have to try and find that key. It is the only way we will really understand why Madame Evangeline committed this murder.'

Dr Ennis stood up then and walked to a set of filing cabinets behind Saul. 'It might help you to understand more if you see what Rebecca looks, or looked like, and how she sees Madame Evangeline.' he continued, taking a file out of the cabinet and bringing it back to the desk. He took out two photographs and one drawing, placing them on the desk facing Saul.

'This first photograph is Rebecca before she murdered her son. Don't know when it is, it's just what she used to look like. You can see she is tall, very slim, yet curvaceous with a natural beauty about her. She has long flowing brown hair and bright green eyes, much like yourself. The second is a police artist sketch of what Rebecca thinks Madame Evangeline looks like. Notice she is tall, slim, curvaceous with a natural beauty, bright green eyes, but red hair. The second photograph is Rebecca just before she left. She pulled all her hair out, inflicted those cuts and bruises in many, many suicide attempts. She has no tongue to speak of now, pardon the pun.'

Saul paused for a moment, taking in the images, obviously upset by the last picture. 'So, there was no evidence at all to suggest that Madame Evangeline was real?' he said, rhetorically.

'None. In fact, while most of her recollections of Madame Evangeline have at least a basis in fact, her story about the night Michael died seems to be almost totally fictitious. We feel that is also part of the trauma during her last hours before killing him.'

Saul was about to speak just as the phone rang. Dr Ennis picked it up. 'Hello. Ah Celia. You have him, great. Can you put him through please?' he said, putting his hand over the receiver and addressing Saul. 'Dr Hanlon is in.'

'Hi Ben, its Gordon, Gordon Ennis. Sorry it's so early. Wanted to have a quick chat about Rebecca Angus if you have five minutes.' he began, listening for a second. 'Oh, sorry, bloody receptionists!' he exclaimed, skin suddenly reddening under his collar again. 'I was after Benjamin Hanlon, he's looking after a patient we transferred down there two weeks ago. Is he in do you know?' he asked, vehemently jotting down Celia's name on a pad in front of him, underlining and overwriting it harshly, over and over as he continued on the phone.

'No, he's an Irish fellow, in his sixties. Enjoys his single malts.' he paused as the person on the other end talked, face reddening continually, and the ferocity with which he was overwriting on the pad breaking through pages. 'Of course there is someone with that description working there. Is this some sort of joke! I have been dealing with Benjamin Hanlon for three months now. He is an Irish gentlemen. Three weeks ago a court order was issued in his name to transfer Rebecca Angus into his care. Two weeks ago we transferred her.' he shouted, standing up as he did so, listening to the reply.

'You can assure me as much as you want, Sir. I know there is another Dr Hanlon. I have e-mails, I have correspondence and I have been ringing him at your bloody hospital. Now I don't know what game you are trying to play, but....' he paused. 'Hello, hello. He hung up, the bastard hung up.' he stabbed zero on the phone. 'Celia, get me Broadmoor again, and make sure it's the right fucking Dr Hanlon this time.' he finished.

The colour started to drain from his angry features, his expression one of astonishment as he looked at Saul. 'That was Dr Hanlon. Not the Dr Hanlon I have been dealing with. But the only Dr Hanlon at Broadmoor. He is adamant about that. He is also adamant that there isn't a Rebecca Angus under their care. They have no record of her at all.'

6:02 am

Dr Hanlon came back into the cell, an empty bucket in one hand, a cup of steaming tea in the other.

'You've been gone a while, I thought you just went for a pee?' Rebecca asked rather curtly.

Dr Hanlon smiled at her as he positioned the clean bucket back under the seat from where he had removed it earlier. 'Rebecca my dear girl, you aren't the only patient I have to look after. Would that you were, life would be so much simpler. Now, I am going to take your head restraints off so that you can have a decent cup of tea without drinking through a straw. I am trusting you, so don't let me down.'

He expertly loosened the buckles on the straps with one hand. Rebecca let her head sag forward and then circled it around her neck, revelling in the release, her eyes rolling with the simple pleasure of the movement. 'That feels good.' she said as Dr Hanlon raised the cup to her lips and she took a few sips. 'That feels even better. I haven't had a cup of tea for...god I can't even remember how long. I can remember plenty of times tea being drank around me, when they were on their breaks.'

Dr Hanlon let her have a few more sips, then sat back down in his seat with a gentle groan as his knee bones cracked while bending. 'Tell me, was Dr Ennis ever involved in these break time sessions?'

'Oh yes, he was always involved. Perhaps not in the way you are thinking though. It was only ever six of the orderlies and eight of the guards that played with me. The women were the worst. By that I mean they were the more aggressive. The men were just trying to get me off, or get themselves off. I seemed to be some kind of challenge to the women, an affront to their femininity, an aberration they had to punish. Either that or they just got off on the violence of the action rather than the sex. No, Dr Ennis never touched me. He only ever watched. I would see him, his features framed in the oblong observation orifice of the door to my cell. I knew that look on his face. I had lived his voyeuristic eyes devouring every last morsel of the depravity that was being exacted in front of him. The frenetic vacillation of his face told me he was masturbating.' she said, calmly.

He leaned over, offering the tea again, shaking his head disconsolately. 'How can you be so calm about that Rebecca? It is abuse, plain and simple abuse. Regardless of the fact he never touched you, he was aware and involved in the act.'

'Perhaps. Don't confuse the legality with the morality of the act. They are very different. What you would consider to be morally reprehensible is not necessarily illegal.'

'I am very clear on the legality of what you are telling me, Rebecca. It's encouraging to see you raising the philosophical question. In this instance it is illegal. As much as you feel complicit in not discouraging them, as much as you have an empathy with Dr Ennis's voyeurism, as much as your sexual preferences may not be morally acceptable to some, you were allowed to be systematically sexually abused by fourteen people by a man who was charged by the state to look after your welfare, to protect and nurse your fragile mind. A mind I may add, that is showing me an exceptional level of self-awareness.' He gave her another sip of the tea. 'Tell me about Madame Evangeline?' he asked.

She smiled a crooked smile, a wicked glint in her piercing eyes. 'Well, now you *are* talking morally questionable. Hannah was the only lover I ever had. When I killed her, I promised myself that I would devote my life to bringing Michael up. And I did. Until he left home and went to University, I never had another lover, I never had a single sexual encounter and never even masturbated, not once in all that time. My focus was Michael, my life was Michael. When he left I felt utterly lost. Oh, I talked to him most days and he came home at least twice a month, mainly for me to do his washing. But he had his own life, his own interests and his own friends and didn't need his mollycoddling mum any more. I was alone. I was lonely. I didn't have a Scooby about relationships. There had only ever been Hannah. How sad is that. In my forties and not a clue how to date.'

'One of the girls from work was getting married and she invited me out on her hen night. I know she was expecting me to say no. I had every time anyone else asked me. This time I said yes. I had to get out there somehow and at least try to find some friendship, even if it was just with my work colleagues.'

'I fussed for weeks building myself up for that night. I bought and changed twenty six dresses before settling on the one I wore, a simple black A-Line, very short on the leg, but elegant. I had my hair straightened and my nails done. You might not believe it now but I used to be pretty. There were thirteen of us including the Hen and we initially went for a meal on the deck of the Cruz Bar, a boat on the river right in the centre of Leith, next to the Customs House. It was a great venue, good food, lots of smutty girlie talk and an ideal opportunity to people watch Leith life. I was nervous and very reticent in the early conversations, but after a few Jager Bombs, I loosened up a little, watching and talking to the girls more than people watching.'

'It was around ten when Sammie, the Maid Of Honour, announced that we were ready to head off to the next venue. She wouldn't tell us where that was. We all had to put on blindfolds. A slight chill of excitement, of anticipation ran down my spine as I put mine on. She then led us in a slightly drunken conga out down Bernard Street. We sang all the way, passing numerous pubs and clubs, being cheered on by the night time revellers, some of whom copped a sneaky feel or fondle, which was tantalising. After about ten minutes we arrived at our destination and Sammie led us, still blindfolded, into the venue. The crisp evening air outside immediately changed to a warm, close atmosphere, sudden aromas of musk and pot invading my senses, the gentle, disjointed confusion of light Jazz entering my ears.'

"Right Girls.' Sammie said, 'After three, take your blindfolds off: One, two, three!' she announced. We took them off and girlie shrieks, some of excitement and some of shock rang out above the ambient jazz, as we took in the room. It was dimly lit, with small booths around the walls, cigarette and pot fumes adding to the haze. We were in one of the booths, looking out into the room where there were tables in front of a stage. On the stage were two very voluptuous blondes, totally naked, pole dancing for the women seated at the tables. In the booths that were occupied, we could see lap dances going on with the women sitting in them. In one corner, a quartet of beautiful women, dressed in spats, white cuffs and collars, hair sleeked back, moustaches drawn on their lips, but naked otherwise were the source of the music.'

"Welcome to Labia's ladies, Leith's only lesbian lap dancing establishment. My name is Destiny and I am your hostess for the evening. Our desire is to see your desire fulfilled. What can I get you to drink before the entertainment starts?' asked Destiny, a very tall, very buxom brunette in a long white evening dress, split from the waist down on either side, her slim, tanned legs visible. She was stunning and I have to admit, my heart began to palpitate at the sight of her and of the other beautiful women in the room. Feelings, emotions that had been dormant for such a long time, since before Hannah died, started to nip at me, reminding me that as much as my mind had put me on the shelf, my libido hadn't!'

'It was strange watching the reactions of the girls as our 'entertainment' started. As far as I knew they were all heterosexual and they all knew I was gay. No one walked out in disgust, and everyone took it in the manner it was meant, a Hen Party Experience, but I could tell in the expressions of one or two that this was a bit more than fun. I could see the sexual chemistry simmering in their eyes, could empathise because I was feeling it too. Destiny was our 'entertainment' and for the next hour she danced for us, slowly and seductively stripping as she did, ensuring that she spent more time with the Hen, but paying attention to everyone. She was never overbearing, and would always ask, 'Would you like to....' before the girls interacted with her. A few needed encouragement, but with the drink and the pot that started to be freely smoked, eventually everyone at some point had Destiny in their hands, stroking her thighs, squeezing her tight buttocks, gently caressing her breasts, some even tweaking her nipples. It was honestly a giggle and I don't mind admitting to being seriously aroused.'

'Was that a pun in there Rebecca?' asked Dr Hanlon.

Rebecca laughed, 'Oh Doc, I am glad it's not mine. It's what Destiny would say throughout the evening as one or another of us was touching her. My eyes were wandering the room, people watching during Destiny's dances, and I couldn't help noticing that some of the 'entertainment' would take individual ladies away to a side entrance. Occasionally the odd single woman would go through the entrance too. Intrigued, I went to see what was going on under the premise of going for a wee. As I approached the entrance, which was draped in a black curtain with diamante sparkling from it in the dim light, another stunning hostess on the door smiled at me and asked, 'Would Madame like to watch? We have some free spaces.' Not really knowing what she meant, I nodded, and she directed me to bay number six, which was highlighted by a subdued light in the gloomy corridor beyond the entrance, as were a row of numbers, up to twenty. I thanked her and made my way down towards number six. The Jazz began to fade as I walked down the corridor, to be replaced by subdued moans and groans. I reached number six and went through another black diamante curtain, behind which was a small purple velour chaise lounge, edged with brass buttons, facing a black wall with a window in it which was eye height to the sofa. It was even gloomier in the confined space and it took a second or two for my eyes to become accustomed to the dark and make out what was through the window as I sat down.'

'There was a small room, the flicker of candles chasing shadow ghosts up the deep red walls. The whole floor space was taken up by a large bed which was festooned with pillows, cushions and throws. In amongst them I could see the gently writhing limbs of two women, totally naked, making love. One was on her back, her legs spread wide while the second was between her thighs, head right up to her shaven mound, tongue quickly flicking over her clitoris which was exposed and hard. She stopped for a second and both of them looked toward me and smiled, mouthing the word 'Enjoy' simultaneously before the second woman went back down on her lover. Every single part of me was alight at this point, my body tingling with the eroticism I felt watching two beautiful women in front of me pleasuring each other. I started to touch myself as I devoured their lovemaking, stroking fingers over my breasts through my dress, snaking striations down my stomach, to my own point of pleasure, which was aching with the desire to be touched, to be stroked, to be caressed. I did just that as I watched them, sliding a finger inside my panties, down over my mound to my slightly parted lips which were moist with my excitement. I slid the end of my finger inside, taking a little of the juice, taking it back towards my clitoris which I gently started to massage while being a voyeur, pleasuring myself while watching those two beautiful women pleasure themselves.'

She had a wistful look in her eyes for a second as she went quiet, before looking at Dr Hanlon again. 'Morally, some may find that unacceptable, but to me, then, it was exquisite, enticing, exciting. It was the start of a journey. A journey that led me to damnation.'

6:34 am

There was heavy, laboured panting in the almost consuming darkness. Moans and groans could be heard. A single piercing narrow beam moved quickly from left to right as the source of the panting and of the beam seemed to be dragging themselves tortuously, their body gyrating and contorting in time with the groans.

'Shit.' exclaimed Corporal Garry, the person holding the pen torch, as it settled on the eye of a webcam which was taped to the underside of a floor beam. He was underneath the floorboards of the drawing room in Featherstone Hall. He was on his back in the foot high void, snaking his body to move him further into the claustrophobic space. So far he had seen three webcams, six pressure sensors and a dozen motion detectors around the floor space where the crate was positioned in the room above.

'It doesn't look like we are going to get into this bloody thing from underneath.' he relayed into his mike, 'I'm coming out now.' he finished as he started to shuffle backwards, towards a hole in the floor which he then climbed out of and emerged into the main corridor of the house.

In the corridor, two of his colleagues had a small scanner on wheels facing the door of the drawing room. 'How's the scanning going?' he asked.

'No joy with X-Ray, the bitch is lead lined. IR is showing motion sensors all around it. Nothing coming up on UV. RF, fuck RF is going wild. There's a ton of transmissions coming from that thing. All seem to be from a spot in the top right corner. I can't see any hardwiring into it at all. Oh yeah, and I can confirm there's enough Semtex on the outside of that thing to blow this house to kingdom friggin' come.'

'Shit.' Garry said, again. 'I better go and give the Suits the good news. Thanks guys.' he finished as he walked off down the corridor to the main entrance. He was a short, slim yet muscle bound soldier, his army fatigues filthy from crawling under the floor, his ginger hair full of dirt and cobwebs, which glistened in the arc lights as he came out of the Hall. He jogged across the drive to the MIU and bounded up the stairs into the meeting, which was in full flow.

All available seats were filled in front of the white boards and half a dozen technicians and technical forensic staff were sitting at the computer screens on the back wall. All of the plasma Video Conferencing screens were on, showing the Path Lab, the Mortuary, a meeting room at HQ and the Chief Superintendent.

DCI Strange now had his jacket off, rainbow suspenders holding up his trousers and sleeve garters gathering his shirt arms up around the elbow. Those arms were leaning on the table, listening intently as DI Munro finished relaying back findings from his initial investigations.

'Okay then, we have ten missing persons to chase up. In the next two hours we need to have talked with every one of their families in detail to rule them in or out. Mick, have you got enough support to get that done?'

'We've got Henshaw, Simons and Gilbert on the case from HQ. I'll shout if we need any more resource.' Munro answered.

'Great. Now Leigh, where are we with finding out who this guy is?' asked Strange.

'So, none of the surrounding neighbours have seen any activity at the Hall for over two years, when it was boarded up. Jimmy Greeson, from the adjoining farm, told us it used to be owned by a 'Lord

Featherstone' up until he died. It had been in the Featherstone Family since 1800 or so, but the current Lord was the last in the family line. A bit of a recluse by all accounts. It was sold to developers on his death. They had grand plans to turn it into a luxury hotel. No one locally met these developers. Initial searches on the online Land Registry Service state an offshore holding company called 'Axiom' acquired the property in 2011. There is no one in the Land Registry Offices or Companies House yet to get any further information. Registered address for 'Axiom' is a PO Box in the Cayman Islands.'

Strange jotted down pertinent points on the board and then asked, 'Have you tried any escalation routes with those organisations?'

'Already on it, voicemails left with everyone we know and the organisations out of hours numbers but no answer back yet. Worst case scenario is the offices open at eight, but I would hope to get traction before then. DC Anderson is searching the net at the moment to see if we can find out anything else about Axiom.' filled in Saxon, efficiently, motioning to DC Anderson, a middle aged, stern faced woman, sitting at one of the computers.

'A waiting game there then. Phyllis,' Strange said, addressing DC Anderson, 'can you own that now and let us know what you find?' he asked, to which she nodded acknowledgement. 'Great. So Leigh, what about the calls and the phone lines?'

'Well, the phone line is also registered to 'Axiom'. No individual's names. Bills are paid via direct debit from an offshore account in the Cayman Islands. No further info at the moment. Mr Reynolds has been looking at the calls. Do you have any news?' she asked a very young looking, scrawny individual sitting at a bank of three monitors beside DC Anderson.

He turned his evidently twitching head to the watching audience, his pallid features flushing red as he addressed them. 'I c...can c...confirm,' he began, stuttering slightly, 'That the voice on the 999 c...call and the voice on the later c...call are the same person.' he said, pointing to one of the monitors on which overlapping voice waves were in synch. 'There are no other records of c...calls to or from the phone in the past two years. I am starting to c...check background noise to see if that can give us any c...clues on where he c...called from. Both c...calls were made from the same mobile phone. It's a pay as you go, so we have no way of telling who owns it. We are waiting on info back from the provider on the location of the c...cell the c...calls were made from. I will have that in the next half hour.' he paused, taking a deep breath.

'Good.' Strange said, in the gap. 'Well done, feedback that info as soon as you get it. Have you managed to check the feeds into or out of the room?'

'Not yet, I was waiting on the Bomb Squad c...checking it out first.' Reynolds finished, relief evident in his tone.

'Gaz,' Strange started, addressing Corporal Garry, 'what can you tell us about the crate and are we clear to start checking the room further?'

'There's two boxes, the wooden crate you can see, then inside that, a lead lined box. Between them is a layer of Semtex. At this point we don't know how it is armed or what the trigger mechanism is, but it looks to be inside the lead lined box. My guess at the moment would be the trigger is wireless given the amount of RF activity that's coming from the thing. I would suggest the AV is also being fed wirelessly as we can't see any cables going into or coming out of the box. We've checked under the floor to see if we can get into the crate from underneath without being seen. No Go. There's webcams and motion sensors down there. It's alright for you to start doing non-intrusive wireless scans but don't do anything invasive unless you talk to us first. As soon as we have finished our checks, I'll get one of the guys to sit with Mr Reynolds to see what activity is going on.' briefed Garry.

Just as he finished, the conference phone on the desk beeped, announcing that 'DI Saul' had joined the call.

'John, good of you to join us.' started Strange. 'Thanks Gaz, I know I don't need to tell you this, but the quicker we can work out where those feeds are going to...' he left the sentence dangling.

'I know.' Said Garry, holding up a hand. 'And as soon as we are sure the whole thing won't blow us all to hell, I will gladly let you in there.'

'Thanks.' Strange nodded appreciatively, then spoke into the conference line. 'John, how did things go with Rebecca, did you have a chance to talk to her? Do we have any leads?'

'I think what we have Sir, are more questions than leads. Rebecca has potentially been kidnapped. Either that or has been broken out.' he started, relaying the pertinent parts of the conversation with Dr Ennis. 'I've e-mailed over CCTV footage of the Dr Hanlon that took Rebecca. It was taken by the Institutes system when she was transferred into his care. It is very clear. We also have footage of the van that moved her and also of a guard who assisted. My gut is telling me that this is the same guy who set this thing up. Who else would have anything to gain from kidnapping her?'

'Possibly, but do we have any facts at this point to back that up. Didn't Dr Ennis say he had an Irish accent? Our guy doesn't. Have you run a PNC check on the van? What about facial recognition on the Dr and the guard?' asked Strange.

'Looks like the van had false plates. PNC has them registered to a 1999 Ford Fiesta, uniform are on their way to the keeper now just to make sure. No facial recognition yet, I've only just got the images.'

'We will pick that up John. What about the Dr Hanlon at Broadmoor. Are we sure he isn't involved in this in some way?'

'We can't rule him out yet and I have the guys at HQ checking out phone and e-mail records that Dr Ennis claim were to him. We do have a picture of him. He looks nothing like the Dr Hanlon we have on CCTV. At the time Rebecca was being moved he was on holiday in Cyprus with his family. HQ are co-ordinating a local Detective to interview him and to corroborate his story.'

Strange leaned against the table again, rocking gently back and forward, a pensive look on his face for a second before he spoke again. 'Do you have any evidence at this point to suggest that Dr Ennis is involved with this?'

There was a pause before Saul answered. 'No, no evidence. He has been open in providing the court documents, the CCTV information and the e-mail and phone records of his dealings with the Dr Hanlon he knew. He seemed genuinely shocked when he found out about the real Dr Hanlon. I watched him closely. While my gut tells me he is a bastard, at this point, there is nothing to suggest he is involved.'

'OK, thanks John.' Strange said, still mulling this new turn of events over in his mind. He turned back to the board and wrote the name 'Dr Hanlon' to the side of 'Unknown Caller', with an arrow pointing to it and a question mark above. He then drew a line down to a box with the name 'Rebecca Angus' in it and looked intently at that name. 'Did Dr Ennis say if Rebecca had mentioned anyone else being involved in her son's murder?' he asked, still facing the board, his features still ruminating on the information in front of him.

'He did. Rebecca talked about someone called Madame Evangeline. However, Ennis believes that this 'person' is a multiple personality inside Rebecca herself. Apparently there was no evidence at all to suggest that she was real. We need the detailed case files to confirm this.' answered Saul.

'We do need those files. John, a DI Bentley is on his way down from Edinburgh with the files at the minute. PC Buglass is rendezvousing with him to get them. It might be worth you going instead to pick his brains about the case, as we don't have Rebecca. Can you do that? He's only free for about an hour?' Strange asked, slightly distracted, still looking at the board, moving the marker between various bits of information, his mind still digesting everything in front of him.

'Yes, no problem. I'll give Buglass a call.' answered Saul.

Strange put the marker pen below Rebecca's name and slowly started to draw a line down, towards a box with the words 'Person in the crate' inside of it. 'The one thing we do have to consider, if our caller and the fake Dr Hanlon are indeed one in the same, and if she has been kidnapped rather than broken out.' Strange said, putting a question mark above the line he had just drawn before turning back to the room. 'Is that the person in the crate could be Rebecca Angus.'

7:07 am

Rebecca's head turned towards the high pitched squeaking that came from down the corridor beyond the open door to the cell. It grew louder and louder until a rusting old trolley, its wheels barely moving freely, came into view, quickly followed by Dr Hanlon pushing it into the cell.

'Do you know what it's like,' he said, puffing slightly as he rolled the trolley up to the side of Rebecca, 'to find anything decent to transport things on when the kitchen is shut. Bloody Impossible!' he finished, flopping into his seat.

'Now, what I have here is breakfast: Full English. You have a choice. I can either feed you, or loosen your arms so you can feed yourself.' he finished, looking questioningly at Rebecca.

She sniffed in the amazing aromas of the sausages, bacon, eggs and mushrooms, closing her eyes and savouring the smells. 'Do you know how long it is since I have smelt anything as delicious as that, let alone eaten anything that hasn't been liquidised or through a tube.'

She opened her eyes and looked back at Dr Hanlon, a slight smile on her lips. 'Do you think you can trust *me* yet? I think that when you pop off and leave me, you are going back to your little room, with its little monitors, and you are checking to see if I injure myself when I am alone.' she offered, the smile still there, her eyes wide and challenging.

Dr Hanlon's eyebrows raised, and he nodded gently. 'There's no pulling the wool over your eyes, is there.' They sat staring at one another for a few seconds, neither one wavering, before Dr Hanlon continued. 'I think I can trust you. There's only one way to find out.' he said, standing up and loosening the straps on her arms and wrists.

Rebecca stretched them out as he did, rubbing her hands together, letting the fingers play over the lesions on her wrists, pressurising them as she looked at Dr Hanlon. 'I am curious.' she said, running fingers up and down her arms, revelling in the movement that she now had, returning to her wrists again and again, and digging what finger nails she had into the open wounds.

'Curious about what?' Dr Hanlon asked.

'About why you are helping me? About who you are? About where we are?' she said, looking down towards the old trolley, then around the stained and ripped padding on the cell walls around her. 'This place is old, nothing like the facilities I've come across either as a patient, or when I was a professional working in healthcare. Where are the orderlies? Where are the guards? That door has been open for the past half an hour and I haven't seen or heard a single person walking up and down the corridor. Look at the floor out there, the parquet is lifting, the tiles are broken' she said, her gaze returning to look at him quizzically after sweeping the room. 'Can I have that breakfast now? I'm starving.'

'That's a lot of questions. A lot of curiosity.' he reflected, lifting a plate from the trolley and putting it onto her lap. He picked up a knife and fork -a metal knife and fork- and paused, looking at her intently, before handing them over.

She took them, holding the fork up to her eye line. She then brought it forward, pushing the end of the prongs into her soft, scarred lips, continually looking at Dr Hanlon as she did, deliberately defiant. She moved the prongs onto her cheek, digging them in, the cold metal leaving four red imprints in the hollow where she applied the pressure.

'I think,' she began, the fork snaking up her face towards her eyeball.

'At the moment,' she continued, the prongs now less than a millimetre away from her contracting iris, her hand as steady as the gaze which hadn't blinked at all while staring at Dr Hanlon.

'The urge to eat this breakfast is probably just beating the urge to kill myself.' With that, she dropped the fork to the plate and with the knife, cut off a piece of bacon and devoured it with obvious relish, saliva dribbling from the corner of her mouth as she continued to speak while chewing.

'So, who are you?' she asked mid chomp.

He sat down in his chair and crossed his legs, enjoying the vigour with which she devoured the meal. 'Who I am isn't important. But if it helps, I'm Ben Hanlon. I am a psychiatrist and I am here to care for you. Why you are here is important. Do you know why you were committed?'

She stopped chewing and laughed on a full mouth of food, little bits of bacon popping out of her lips. 'I think that is pretty damn obvious isn't it. Raving psychopath, rips the heart out of her son and eats it.'

'You might think it's obvious, but it's not. You have no recollection at all, either consciously, or subconsciously of carrying out that act. Dr Ennis believes you suffer from a condition known as Dissociative Identity Disorder, that's why you were certified. Do you know what that is?'

'Multiple personalities.' she shot back, straight away, devouring the last of her sausages. 'I know that. They think Madame Evangeline is just a figment of my imagination. They are probably right. It doesn't detract from the fact *I*, whichever personality that is, am a raving psychopath. *I*, whichever personality that is, killed my son. *I*, with the personality I am now, doesn't have a clue how that happened.' She was getting agitated as she spoke, still chewing, but now on her bottom lip, a drip of blood slipping down her chin. Her arms were shaking and her knuckles where white as she gripped the cutlery in each hand tightly and started to bang the base of each against the arms of the chair.

'I. Still. Killed. Him.' she pronounced, spitting each word, banging the cutlery in time. Then she stopped, suddenly, tension flowing from her body, and took the last piece of bacon from the plate, speaking as she chewed, in a convivial manner. 'Now, stop changing the subject. Tell me why we are here. Where the hell is here?'

Dr Hanlon laughed, a huge guffaw and threw himself back into his seat. 'Rebecca, Rebecca, Rebecca. I am really not avoiding the subject. I am a psychiatrist. You know what we are like, we always answer a question with a question. By the way that was impressive, truly impressive self-restraint. Which only strengthens my belief that you are far from psychotic. Right. Straight answers. We are in Broadmoor, in an older part of the hospital, well away from the wards. I have been trying, unsuccessfully I may add, to bring out Madame Evangeline. In the past two weeks you have been weaned off your sedatives and have had various sessions of hypnotherapy to try and break down the mental barriers between your personality and Madame Evangeline's. Nothing, absolutely nothing I have tried either psychologically or physiologically has found even a glimmer of a suggestion that she is inside you. She is real Rebecca. You are not delusional, you do not have DID and in my informed medical opinion you are perfectly sane, cognitive and rational, if ever so slightly OCD.'

'But I still killed my son.' she answered, softly, yet intently, finishing off the last of the egg on her plate.

'You may have been involved in his death, but that doesn't necessarily mean you killed him. We have to try and fill in the blanks of your recollection. You told me certain things under hypnosis. We need to try and get you to remember them while you are conscious and yourself. Some of the things you told me have to do with your care, how you were treated at the Fielding Institute. That's one of the reasons I brought you to this part of the hospital, away from the main body of staff, away from anyone else who might feedback to Dr Ennis what you have already told me about him and his team, and other things you might not have remembered yet.'

He handed her a napkin, taking the empty plate from her. She wiped her lips, wiped the blood off her chin and started to play with the edge ply of the napkin between her thumb and forefinger, the rest balled into her hand. Her eyes were welling up with tears, and she dabbed them away with the napkin. 'I want to understand why, I want to understand how. If you have found out things in my subconscious that can help me make some sense of this, give some credence to the madness of it all, then I want to know. I promise, I will not try and harm myself: at least, not until we have worked out what happened. After that, I can't promise anything.'

He reached over and cupped both of his hands over her balled fist holding the napkin and squeezed. She didn't pull away, she looked down with the saddest smile on her lips as he said, 'I will do everything in my power to help you remember, to help you get to the truth, to help you understand: I promise that. After that, hopefully we won't need promises, hopefully you will see a light that's worth following.'

'Thank you Doc.' she said, putting her free hand over his. 'One thing I do remember, one thing I always knew, but never told anyone. I didn't think it was important and to be honest, given what even I thought about my state of mind, it could have been just one of my own delusions. Now I know it wasn't. It's about Dr Ennis.'

'Go on.' encouraged Ben.

'When I told you earlier that I knew what he was like, how I knew all about his voyeuristic tendencies. It wasn't just what happened in the hospital, it wasn't just that I have lived those tendencies too. After the first time I went to the lap dancing club, on the hen night, I went back many, many times afterwards. To that club and many others. As a voyeur, you like to keep your anonymity. Going back to the same place too many times gets you known, it takes the edge of the thrill. However, you do start to see regulars, people with the same fetishes. I started to go to straight as well as gay clubs, to be honest, anywhere I could watch. It was in one particular S&M club I had visited a few times that I saw him. He was there every time. I didn't know who he was and never spoke to him. I just saw him. It was only the very first time I was being fingered by a guard at the institute, and caught the sight of him staring at me through the door, masturbating, that the memory of him came back to me. It was Dr Ennis, he used to frequent the S&M clubs in Edinburgh.'

7:30 am

The deep resonating thrum of a yellow Air-Sea Rescue helicopter rose above the background noise of early morning traffic driving past on the A1 trunk road next to the Services that Saul was parked up in. He was leaning against the boot of his SLK, still in his Tux, drinking a coffee. He watched the helicopter fly overhead and out towards Holy Island, the Castle on the Island just coming into silhouette as the dawn broke in talons of ruddy orange on the horizon out to sea behind it. A filthy, scratched and dented grey Volvo, the driver's wing mirror held in place with gaffer tape, pulled off the main road and parked up beside him. A few seconds behind it, wailing sirens announcing its arrival before it could be seen, a police car sped by and took a right turn onto the road towards the Island.

Saul stood and picked up another coffee which was sitting on the boot of his car and watched as a burly, broad, blonde haired man stepped out of the Volvo. He was wearing a Mac that was covered in dog hair. Barking could be heard as he shut the car door, shouting, 'Shut yer yappin, Jackson.' before turning to Saul, looking him up and down.

'Do I need some secret passcode to talk to you then? The pheasants in Lothian are remarkably gamey for a chilly October, or some such nonsense?' he said as Saul proffered him the coffee.

Saul frowned, 'No, just a hello will do. It's not my usual getup, trust me. John Saul, DI Bentley I presume?' he said, offering his hand to shake as Bentley took the coffee.

'Aye, that's me, let's get the jokes over now. Names Fenny Bentley. There's nothing you can say I haven't heard before, so try your worst.'

he dared Saul, wiping his hand on his raincoat, which covered it in more dog hair, before grabbing Saul's hand and shaking it vigorously. 'What in god's name is the commotion with the helicopter and blues and two's all about. Some kind of raid going on?' he asked, looking down the road at the receding flashing lights on the police car.

'I doubt it. Someone is probably stranded on the causeway to the Island again. The tide will have come in and caught them. That's usually why the helicopter comes out. There are huge signs up warning people not to cross when the tide is coming in, but it must just be in our DNA to ignore the bloody things. They have to rescue hundreds of people a year for the same stupid mistake. It costs a fortune.' said Saul.

'Aye, there's nowt as queer as folk. Tell them not to do something and bugger me, they will. So, I hear you Sassenachs have stumbled onto one of our old cases.' Bentley said, joining Saul in leaning on the boot of the SLK, both of them watching the traffic now as it sped past on the A1, the sun rising behind them.

'I wouldn't say stumbled, more setup. We've also just found out that Rebecca Angus has gone missing, either broken out of the Institute or kidnapped.'

'Jeez, it's a bad day knowing that loon isn't locked away safely. Now if it was me, I would have strung the bitch up straight away. I'm surprised she never managed to top herself, the amount of times she tried. Would have done us all a favour.'

'Did you ever have anyone come and visit her while she was in custody, specifically an Irishman by the name of Hanlon, Ben Hanlon?' Saul asked.

'No. No one at all came to see her. She had no family. She was an orphan. Been in and out of care and foster homes. Also spent the odd spell in juvenile centres when she was a kid. She was 'married' to another dyke for a while and they had the son, Michael. Sick if you ask me. Took the egg out of Rebecca, implanted it into her missus. Bobs your uncle, fanny's your aunt, or in this case fanny's your uncle as well, and you've got a bastard baby. Her missus died in a car crash as they were going to hospital to give birth to Michael. Justice of a sorts. She never mentioned anyone of that name.'

'What about Madame Evangeline. What did you find out about her?'

Bentley smirked, shaking his head as he did so. 'There was no Madame Evangeline. If you want my opinion, she made her up so we would all think she was a sandwich short of a picnic. Worked too, kept her out of real prison and on her jollies in a hospital. We checked out every single sex club that Rebecca told us about, and believe me, there were lots, just about every single one in the Lothian area, a few I didn't even know about. No one, not one person ever recalled seeing Rebecca with anyone else. Everyone recognised Rebecca. There's a photo-fit in the evidence boxes of how Rebecca described this Evangeline tart. She's the spit of Rebecca but with red hair.'

'Yes, Dr Ennis gave me a copy of that.'

'We talked to the club owners and showed them the photo-fit. They said that's how Rebecca would come in occasionally. That's why Dr Ennis thought she was schizo. Same person, different colour hair, schizo personality.'

'Did anyone from the clubs have any kind of relationship with her?'

'You might think that. I mean, if you are going to a sex club, the least you think you would be getting is a good shag. She didn't. She watched. She just watched. Pervert. No one can even recall a conversation with her beyond a polite hello. She was a loner. A crazy loon.'

Saul took a sideways look at him, disdain on his face. 'Do you want to tone down the bigoted comments a little there?'

Bentley turned too, curling his lip in a sneer as he answered. 'Look, you arrogant twat, I just speak as I find, if you don't like it, then fuck off. I've trawled my arse all the way down that excuse of a road for the past hour to help you out. I'd welcome a little gratitude rather than attitude.' he said, coffee spilling on his hands and down onto his and Saul's trousers as he raised the cup animatedly while speaking. 'Fuck, now look what you've made me do.' he finished, wiping the spill on his Mac.

'Okay, okay, I'm sorry.' Saul began, rubbing the coffee off himself. 'We do appreciate the time you've spared us assisting in our efforts to stop a potential murderer. What about her son. What did you find out about their relationship?'

'Well now, she definitely did fuck him, and if you try to tell me that's not sick, then you are one twisted prick too.' he challenged.

Saul didn't bite. 'Anything else about their relationship.' he asked.

Bentley backed down slightly. 'Nothing out of the ordinary, other than that. They were close according to her work colleagues, even after he went to Uni. He still went home a couple of times a month and would call her regularly. He had a circle of friends at Uni. None of them were aware he was having a sexual relationship with his mother. He had been seeing a few girls but hadn't been in any long term serious relationships. He hadn't tried any kinky stuff with them. His best friend, a Joe Magnus, had no idea he enjoyed gimping up. None of the neighbours where she lived knew them that well either.'

'Did she ever talk about visiting an old, dilapidated country house out in Northumberland, either by herself or with her son?'

'No, not that I can recall. She did talk about visiting Madame Evangeline's place, or what she thought was Madame Evangeline's place, on the night of Michael's murder. That's where she claimed to have killed him, but she never described it as dilapidated.'

'Hold on, I thought she killed him in her flat?'

'She did. However, during questioning she claimed the three of them had left a New Year's Eve Masquerade Ball in a taxi and gone back to what she thought was Madame Evangeline's apartment. In another story, she has them getting into a limousine. She couldn't remember how they got there or even where *there* was. She could only describe the sick sex they got up during the journey and when they arrived. We checked out the sex club hosting the ball. They remember her and a guy all gimped up, presumably her son, but no one else with them. CCTV has them getting into a taxi, and that taxi took them back to her flat. All just part of her schizo life.' said Bentley, finishing off his coffee and throwing the cup on the floor.

'Apart from the sick sex, was there anything else that stood out about the apartment she described?' asked Saul.

'I've told you, it was her screwed up mind, it wasn't real: she wasn't really there. She was at her flat ripping the fucking heart out of her son. Look, I have to get back to a real case, where there are real murderers to catch. Get the files, and if you've got any more stupid fucking questions, look in them.' he scowled, going to his car and opening the boot. A black lab covered in mud jumped out and made a beeline for Saul, sniffing his trouser leg before pissing up against him.

Bentley laughed, 'Good boy Jackson,' he said, 'Open your boot up.' he ordered Saul, who was trying to get out of the dogs way. Saul blipped it with his key and it popped open.

'So, she didn't describe anything like a black fireplace, with gargoyles and cherubs on it. Or leather chesterfield sofas. How about a Steinway grand piano?' Saul asked, frustration evident in his tone as he tried to avoid the dog circling him.

Bentley threw the box into the boot and turned to face him abruptly. 'How do you know that?' he questioned, confusion in his chubby features. 'Yes, that's exactly how she described the apartment.'

'Then it wasn't a figment of her imagination,' Saul answered, shaking his leg as the dog started to chew on the bottom of the trouser, 'because that's where we found her son's exhumed body this morning.'

7:52 am

'These clubs don't have big flashing neon lights outside. They are a lot more discreet, a lot more private. I found out about the first one I went to from Destiny, the hostesses at the lap dancing bar. After frequenting Labia's for a number of months, I suppose becoming a regular, one evening she slipped a card into my hand as I was going into a booth to watch. She said to me, 'If you fancy something a little different, try this. Take the card and let them know I sent you. There's a lot more to watch, and to take part in.' she continued, smiling, stroking the back of her hand down my cheek as I walked by. 'You never know, you might see me there.' she finished. I flushed red immediately, with embarrassment but also with the sharp thrill of excitement that her touch sent searing through my body. The place was called 'Sodom & Gomorrah's' with the S&M's emboldened on the card. There was an address and a note about the dress code: Leather. It was only a ten minute walk away from Labia's.'

'For me, visiting a club was a night out, a once a week treat. I would spend my working hours thinking about it and spend hours after work getting myself ready. It became a routine, a ritual. I would have a lovely long bath with scented candles, usually apple wood; I love the smell of apple wood. I would then do my hair. I would try out different styles and different colours. I loved being a redhead, it always made me feel more confident, a lot more risqué.' She laughed, 'If what I was doing could ever be more risqué. I would then wax my legs and my bikini line, the feeling of being bare down there so sensual, as was the waxing. After that I would do my nails, both my fingers and toes. Finally I would decide what to wear. I would try on dozens of outfits, imagining myself as a different person...'

She had been gently stroking her arm as she talked about getting ready, her gaze distant, lost in the recollection. She stopped talking abruptly, a look of concern crossing her face as she focused on Dr Hanlon.

'I don't want you to think that was part of a Multiple Personality psychosis.' she anxiously said to him. 'It was just role playing. I enjoyed pretending, it added an extra dimension of excitement.'

'It sounds to me you consciously recognise that behaviour in yourself. It's your choice. It's not a psychosis. It's definitely not DID. We all imagine ourselves being someone else. Usually to compensate for, or to escape from, what we perceive to be the failings in our own life. That's normal. It's the point at which it happens subconsciously where you have to worry.' he said reassuringly.

The slight rise in tension abated, and Rebecca continued. 'That night I was a redhead. I wore a tight fitting strapless black leather dress which laced up at the back like a corset, pulling my waist in and pushing my boobs together and up. It was a bugger to get on by yourself. I spent ten minutes jumping up and down just to get into it, then another half an hour at the mirror to try and get it fastened! I wore no bra or panties underneath, there wasn't the room. Only black lace topped hold ups and black leather high heel ankle boots, with little silver chains dangling from a stud on the front of them. I liked the way I looked that night. I felt confident, excited, aroused and utterly terrified. I didn't know what to expect at this new club but even the terror was intoxicating.'

'It was a chilly early autumn evening so I wore a long coat over my outfit and took a taxi to the club. I arrived at about ten thirty at an inconspicuous door down a side alley off the main street. There was no sign, just a bell, which I rang. The door was answered by what you would consider to be a normal bouncer at a night club, big and broad and wearing a black suit, white shirt and shades. I handed him the card and let him know that Destiny had sent me. God that sounds so corny.' She giggled, 'But trust me, although I was trying to sound confident, I was nervous as hell and probably came across sounding like Larry the Lamb. He looked me up and down as I smiled encouragingly at him. He then opened the door wider and allowed me into a narrow dark hallway down which there was another door about five metres further on. He took my coat and hung it on a rack with many more. There was a small window in the door in front of me, through which red lights and the occasional bright white strobe flashed. As I got closer to it, the unmistakable deep bass of dance music started to pervade the corridor. I reached to door and, being the voyeur that I am, stood and looked into the room beyond for a few minutes, taking in this wholly new experience.'

'To be brutally honest, my initial reaction was one of utter disappointment. There was a fair amount of dry ice going around and to my eyes, it just looked like a normal, slightly Goth themed night club. There was a central area, where I could see lots of people dancing: or at least I thought they were dancing. There was a long bar down one wall where people were chatting, laughing, cuddling and kissing. Around the dance floor there were deeply recessed booths and from my vantage point, it was hard to see into them as they were very dimly lit. I could make out the odd movement, but that was about it. The décor was all black, with subdued red lights, the occasional strobe coming from the front of a set of decks at the far end of the central area. And the music, my god, it was 70's disco. Now I don't mind 70's disco, but it's not the kind of thing that goes with a Goth themed club and leather clad clientele. I was slightly deflated to say the least at that point: until my eyes started to get accustomed to the light and I started to see through the mist.'

'Some people were erotic dancing. Yes, they were. In amongst others who were touching, feeling, kissing, licking, fingering and not to put too fine a point on it, fucking, right there in the centre of the room! I think my jaw quite literally did drop at that point. I had expected something a little more extreme than the lap dancing club, but not as blatant as this. I did see the odd whip being used, a few slaves being led around and pulled down by reins. I'll be honest, I had a slight panic attack at the sight of it all coalescing in front of me and was about to turn and walk away. Until I saw a few single people, dotted in amongst the couples, threesomes and foursomes, just sitting casually watching and drinking. There was one woman in particular, sat at the bar on her own. I watched her for a few moments as she just took in the room, occasionally stroking herself sexually. A man in a leather G-string, and nothing else, approached and whispered something in her ear. She smiled politely at him and shook her head. He just gave her a gentle peck on the cheek and walked away. As much as it was overwhelming and totally outside of my experience, that one interaction gave me confidence that I could watch and be safe. Does that make sense?' she asked.

'It's normal when we start pushing the boundaries of our own experiences to get nervous, to get terrified even. It's what we all do. It's survival instinct. If you can see something familiar in that alien environment, it becomes a crutch to support you through learning all about the new experience. In that moment, she was your familiar. Was that Madame Evangeline?' he questioned.

'No, that wasn't her. I get where you are coming from. The lady was the crutch that made me walk through the door. The overpowering smell of sweat and leather assailed my nostrils immediately, with the pungent musky odour of sex swimming in the eddies of the dry ice circling around me, as I walked through the copulating carnal circus and found an empty seat at the bar. I ordered a drink and sat for a few minutes just taking in the rest of the room. I could now see into the circular booths a little more. They weren't booths, they were beds, sunk into the floor with cushioned partitions separating them. I looked from one to the next, sipping on my drink with a look of sheer disbelief on my face as I observed one sexual scenario after another. In one there was a man handcuffed to metal rings on the wall, a leather cowl over his head, otherwise naked. There were two women in the booth with him, one lashing his genitals with a whip while the other one was rolling a Wartenberg Wheel all over his skin. In another, a man was bound hand and foot with manacles, lying on his back with one woman sitting cowboy and riding him while the other was literally sat on his face, forcing her anus and vagina over his nose and mouth. She was facing the other lady. They were raking each other with Vampire gloves, which were leather with small spikes in them, drawing blood while kissing each other passionately. In nearly every case, right across the club, it was the men who were submissive.'

'It was the first time I saw Dr Ennis. He and a woman were in a booth with another man who was on his knees, naked. The other man had a metal collar around his neck with two thick chains attached. Both chains went down his back. The first had manacles at the end which were tight on his wrists, pinning his hands and arms into the space between his shoulder blades. The other went down to his ankles, which were pulled half way up his back. The woman was on her knees, head down into his crotch performing fellatio on him. Dr Ennis was sanding astride her and the bound gentleman was doing the same thing to him.'

'To be honest, so much gratuitous sex being carried out so flagrantly was overwhelming. I didn't find it stimulating, I didn't feel as though I was a voyeur in that environment. The clandestine thrill just wasn't there. I think the barman, a muscle bound slim young man, wearing nothing but a leather apron around his waist, must have sensed this. 'First Time at a Munch?' he asked. 'Can you tell?' I replied. 'It's the shell shocked, jaw dropped expression that gives it away.' he continued, smiling at me. 'Down the side there,' he said, pointing to an entrance at the far end of the bar, 'are some quiet, private rooms with places you can watch discreetly, if that's what you like. It's not as in your face as this.' I thanked him and headed for the private rooms, out of 'Sodom and Gomorrah' and into a quieter, more subdued corridor, the throbbing disco receding. The setup was like Labia's, little viewing areas in front of windowed rooms, curtains concealing them. I popped my head into a few, which were taken, before coming to one which was empty. I looked through the window and breathed a sigh of relief as I saw what seemed to be a normal couple. No three or foursomes, and on initial observation, no overtly masochistic things happening. These establishments really do love their chaise lounges, and I made myself comfortable on the one in front of the window and started to watch them.'

'I thought she was giving him a gentle massage. He was lying on his stomach, stretched out full length, just wearing a pair of leather braces which were clipped to a thin belt around his waist. She was sitting astride him, wearing what looked like half-length chaps on her thighs, nothing on her buxom top and black Vampire Gloves. She was gently stroking her hands from his neck, right the way down his back to the base of his spine, red weal's rising on his skin. As she moved down his back with her hands, her backside also moved down over his behind and onto his legs. I could see similar striations appear there, and saw little pins all over the inside of her chaps too. Each time she stroked or moved, he let out a low, guttural growl of pleasure from the pain, his face contorting with the agony, then softening with the ecstasy.'

'I became engrossed in the genteel intensity of the infliction being carried out in front of me. I started to touch myself in long lingering strokes, from my knees, down the inside of my thighs, over my stocking tops to the bare white flesh of my mound, occasionally digging my long, painted finger nails into the yielding flesh on the way. It was all about the skin, and I tried to stroke myself in the same places that she was massaging him, my body tingling with the anticipation of the next touch.'

'Then, I noticed a reflection appear in the window in front of me as someone popped their head through the curtain behind me. That isn't unusual, but once they see someone else is in the viewing area, they generally leave. This time, she didn't. The pale, immaculate complexion of a female head, with gorgeously well-defined cheek bones and full, pouting lips, hovered disjointedly in front of me in the window, luscious long auburn hair setting off her intensely emerald eyes. Eyes which were devouring what she could see of my reflection, of my dress raised around my waist, nails impressed upon naked flesh, a hand caressing my exposed breast. My heart started to palpitate uncontrollably, the thrill of watching being overwhelmed by the thrill of being watched. I didn't stop touching myself. I didn't take my eyes off her reflection watching me. The couple in the room in front were out of my mind now. The only thing I could see, could think of, could feel was her voracious gaze ablaze upon me.'

'She slinked in and slowly walked around the chaise longue. She was wearing a skin tight leather cat suit and thigh length leather boots. Our eyes didn't leave the reflection in the window until she knelt on the floor down by my open thighs, at which point we turned and looked at each other. She was smiling, a picture of controlled desire with a sparkle of lust twinkling in her eyes. Whereas I was not. My body was shaking, my breathing timorous: the smile I returned twitching with anticipation. Her eyes then strayed down my body, stopping for a second to devour my breasts. She bit her lip, supressing the urge to lean over and kiss my erect nipples. Her gaze moved further down, drinking in the rucked up leather around my waist, darting back and forth over the bare flesh of my hips before settling on the delicate, wet, hot and pulsing area between my open thighs.'

''Beautiful', she said, simply, looking back up at me briefly, a wicked smile on her lips, before her gaze returned down below. She leaned over slightly and lowered her head down between my thighs and I gave out a small shriek of anticipation at the thought of what she was going to do. She looked up at me again, her smile broadening before she puckered her lips and blew a breath of ecstasy ever so gently over my yearning clitoris. The sudden sensation was statically erotic, my whole being tensing with the intensity of the feeling. She continued, blowing gently around my slightly parted lips, down to my perineum and all the way back to my clitoris, my groin pulsing with the waves of pleasure that were rising from the depths of me, starting to surf on the wave of orgasm. 'She is so, so beautiful.' she said, raising her head for a second and looking at me again. I could see her sucking the moisture out of her tongue, could hear the dry barbs of her taste buds rising as she stuck it out in the cool air, going down once more and licking upward from my perineum. The second her tongue touched me, I started to come, my body wracking, panting heavily, moans getting louder and louder. Slowly, the dry, coarse buds of her open tongue smothered my hot, moist lips, sending searing pleasure coursing through me, rapturing an already flowing orgasm. Upwards she continued, rolling her tongue, reaching the top of my lips, where it engulfed my exposed, throbbing clitoris and sucked it. I exploded, my body bucking and tensing, screaming as the orgasm overwhelmed me. I grabbed her shoulders and held her tight against my vulva until the last wracking wave abated and I flopped back into the sofa, hands dropping away from her, utterly sated.'

'She looked at me, smiling, her lips glistening with my pleasure. She moved up and placed a tender kiss on my still quivering mouth as she stood up. She unzipped her suit slightly, down to the curve of her cleavage, reached inside and took out a small, white mobile phone. She leant down and pulling my leather corset forward, placed the phone against the swell of my left breast. 'That was delicious.' she said. 'I'll call you.' she finished as she zipped her suit back up and started to back out of the room, slowly. 'Absolutely delicious.'

'Wait!' I said, a little too eagerly, 'Don't go just yet. I don't even know your name?' I implored. She continued to back out of the viewing area, her body through the curtains now, only her head remaining. She smiled at me and said, 'Call me Evangeline: Madame Evangeline.'

8:33 am

Shadows slowly elongated and evaporated over the brooding Cheviot Hills as the sun started its ascent beyond dawn, dancing through the morning mists which clung to the upper slopes of the range. Dew glistened on the fading purple heather that coloured the otherwise dour brown and green landscape which was interspersed with exposed rocks and shale landslides.

The bottom of the slopes gave way to open fields, most of them sewn with winter crops which were just starting to rise through the carpet brown landscape. The odd green field, sheep or cows languidly grazing, were dotted throughout the vista. Half a mile in front of the hills sat Featherstone Hall in its dishevelled grounds, an ugly blot on the natural beauty of the surrounding countryside.

Saul stood at the window inside the MIU, looking out over view, deep in thought. The open space in front of the Hall was bustling with activity, vehicles coming and going constantly. Strange finished filling his coffee cup from the bubbling percolator on the bench beside the various officers and tech staff beavering away at the computers. He walked to the window and stood beside Saul, the two of them standing in silence for a moment, before Strange wrinkled his nose.

'You stink of piss John. If that's your aftershave, I would take it back.' Strange wryly said.

'It was that bigoted bastard's dog. Used me as a lamppost. Ripped my trousers too. It took all my self-restraint to stop myself kicking it.' Saul answered with evident anger, lifting his leg to show Strange the damage. 'Mind you, I wanted to kick Bentley even more. What a waste of space. I have no confidence at all in any evidence that he may have gathered. He's all for an easy life, and Rebecca confessing to this murder meant he didn't have to probe deeply into this case. I'm beginning to understand what our 'Unknown Caller' was getting at now. There are dozens of inconsistencies. Everyone seemed to put them down to Rebecca's condition.'

'That's as maybe John, but it still doesn't get us any closer to identifying anyone else involved in Michael's murder. We've got to focus on facts now. We don't have the luxury of time.'

Irritated, Saul replied, 'I know that Sir, and I don't have facts at the moment. But I can tell you I don't trust Bentley, and I trust Ennis even less.'

'Let's see what you do trust then John.' encouraged Strange, putting a hand up to the back of Saul's neck and rubbing it gently, 'And try and get rid of some of this tension along the way. I don't think I've ever seen you so uptight. Come on, pictures first, tell me what you think.'

Strange gently ushered him around to the table where Saul picked up the photos and photo fit Dr Ennis had given him. Saul stuck the first one, of Rebecca before she had been committed, up below her name on the board. The second photo, of Rebecca's scarred and bruised body, he put down next to the words 'Person in the Crate'. He pursed his lips, gently shaking his head. 'I don't think its Rebecca in the crate Sir. Look at her skin, just about every visible surface has some kind of lesion on it. The skin of the person in the crate looks smooth and unblemished. It makes no sense that our 'Unknown Caller' would put her in there, not when he is trying to clear her name.'

'That poor lady.' said Strange sadly. 'Whether she did or didn't kill him, whether she is mad or not, to feel so desolate, so bereft as to inflict that kind of pain upon yourself is unimaginable. I agree. I don't think it is her in the crate, but let's keep the photo there for now, until we know any different. What about her?' he asked, pointing to the photo fit in Saul's hand. 'Where do we put her?'

Saul took a marker and wrote the name 'Madame Evangeline' just to the right of Rebecca and stuck the picture under it. 'I know Ennis thinks she is just another personality inside Rebecca, but as I said, I don't trust one jot the thoroughness of his assessment. I believe we have to treat her as real. We already have the potential corroboration of Rebecca's story about this place.' he said, glancing out of the window to the Hall. 'We know there is a huge inconsistency with how Rebecca remembers leaving the party on New Year's Eve and the evidence the police found. I think we have to work on the basis she is real and figure out how we prove that, and more importantly find her.'

'True, but is that enough to go on, is that enough for us to get any evidence to suggest she is real in the next 16 hours, let alone find her?' started Strange, before being interrupted.

'Right,' said Reynolds, interrupting Saul, 'The C...C...CCTV footage is ready now Sir.'

'Excellent, thank you Steven.' answered Strange, turning and walking past the table which was covered in documents from the Evidence files provided by DI Bentley. Saul turned from the white board and followed Strange to the far wall, where one of the plasma TV's started to show a clear black and white image.

'So, you can see the high street clearly with a taxi waiting. Lots of revellers passing by, quite a few in fancy dress. It is New Year's Eve after all.' Strange said, relaying the footage. 'There, pause there please Steven.' he finished, then approached the screen.

'Okay, we have what looks to be a male in an all-black Gimp outfit being led by a woman dressed in similarly black attire approaching the taxi. She certainly looks like Rebecca. That's a very clear shot of her face.' said Strange. 'There's not another woman there John.'

'I see that!' said Saul abruptly, pondering, and moving closer to the screen. 'She's on a mobile. Can you see that?' prompted Saul, pointing to her right arm which was raised towards her ear. 'Reynolds, just move that forward a few frames. Great. Now stop. Look, you can see a white mobile in her hand. Now who is she calling?' mused Saul.

'It is New Year's Eve John, not too far off midnight, she could be calling anyone.' answered Strange.

'Yes, possibly, but she had no family, very few friends, and her son is with her. Play on Reynolds.' instructed Saul. They watched as the two of them got into the taxi and it started to drive off. 'Stop, there again.' Saul said quickly. 'Look, clear as day, she's laughing. Whoever she is talking to, she's laughing. Does that look like the face of a woman who is going to rip her son's heart out to you?'

Saul turned to the table, eyes scanning the various documents until they settled on one poking out of a small pile. 'They would have inventoried and checked any mobile phones and calls.' he said, picking up a bundle of papers headed 'Flat Inventory' and running his finger down the first page, then flipping to the second. 'There it is.' he said, looking up from the papers to Strange, his tone slightly perplexed. 'The inventory lists her mobile as a Nokia Lumia, a *black* Nokia Lumia.' He flicked further through the bundle, stopping on a page near the back. 'There's a list of calls to that mobile. The last was to her son's mobile at 4:48pm for 15 minutes. And then no calls at all after that.'

Strange was back at the whiteboard, and wrote 'White Mobile Phone?' underneath Rebecca's name. 'What does that tell us then?' he asked, turning to Saul.

'The main thing it tells me is that I am even more concerned about how thorough the original investigation was. There's no notes at all about that phone in the files.' said Saul, picking up one of the main documents at the front of the table: Rebecca's original statement.

'She makes no reference to it either. Yet it's there. Rebecca mentions being in a limousine with Madame Evangeline and her Gimp. Why didn't she refer to him as her son?' he mused, before continuing. 'She doesn't mention anything about the two of them getting into a Taxi. Reynolds, play the video of them getting out of the Taxi.' Saul instructed.

Reynolds did so, and the image changed to a Taxi pulling up on a street with a few shops, all of them closed. No one was visible apart from Rebecca and the Gimp getting out of the Taxi. They linked arms and started to walk off down the street, in a direction away from the camera. They were visibly swaying from side to side as they walked.

'What's the name of that street, can you zoom in on the sign Reynolds?' asked Saul, pointing to a blurry name plate. Reynolds did so, the words 'Settle Avenue' coming into view.

'Reynolds, bring up a map on your computer and punch in the addresses of that street and Rebecca's flat.' Saul said brusquely.

'What are you thinking John?' asked Strange, looking at Saul, whose eyes were darting from the notes he was reading, to the screens in front of him.

'I'm wondering why they didn't get dropped off at her flat. Reynolds, can you also overlay the locations of known CCTV camera's onto that as well?' he enquired, moving towards the screen as a map appeared of the Leith area.

'I'll try.' answered Reynolds as he entered the address information, two red pins appearing on the screen about a centimetre apart.

'They seem to be heading off in the direction of her flat, but it's about a half a mile away. Why?' Saul pondered, drawing his finger over the route between the two pins.

'John, they may just have wanted a bit of fresh air. If you look at the way they were staggering, there's no doubt they were intoxicated. How do you think this helps us figure out if Madame Evangeline is real? Please remember we only have sixteen hours left and we have to focus our efforts. I know you are seeing inconsistencies, but are they material in a way that will help us?' Strange stated in a soft, conciliatory tone.

A look of frustration shot into Saul's eyes as he quickly turned to look at Strange, but it abated almost immediately as he recognised the openly honest, challenging demeanour of his superior. 'Sorry Sir.' he said. 'We have a half mile trip within which we don't know what happened. What if it was Madame Evangeline she was talking too on the phone, arranging to meet up? If this woman is real, she is someone who likes to maintain her anonymity, she is someone who likes to cover their trail. It's half a mile where they could have possibly climbed into a limousine and headed here. If we can get other CCTV footage of their short trip?' Saul finished, the last words half statement, half question.

'Possibly, John, being the operative word. We still have no conclusive evidence to suggest this is the location Rebecca was talking about. It's just as likely that our 'Unknown Caller' has set this up based on openly available information in the case documentation: we have to consider that.' posed Strange.

'I understand that Sir. But either way, we were led here, in particular, *I* was led here on the basis of there being evidence which would point us to an alternate 'killer'. If that alternate 'killer' is Madame Evangeline, we have to try and find out who she is and how she was involved. We have to find a link between both this location and how they arrived here.'

'Sir,' interrupted Reynolds, 'I've managed to map all the CCTV cameras in the area.'

Saul and Strange turned back to the screen, dozens of purple pins now highlighting camera locations, the immediate radius around the red pin of Rebecca's flat clear, the nearest camera being the red pin on Settle Avenue.

'Shit.' shouted Saul in frustration, realising there were no other cameras on the trip to the flat.

'Well, I guess that rules out getting any images of the two of them closer to the flat, which is possibly where Bentley and our Leith colleagues got to in their investigation.' said Strange firmly, addressing the still brooding, calculating countenance of Saul.

On the screen just to the left of the map, Harris nervously edged himself into the empty seat in the Path Lab Video Conferencing suite. 'Hello gents. Can you hear me?' he asked, uncomfortably staring into the camera.

'Ah, Ian, what news have you got for us?' asked Strange, his tone turning jovial again.

'We've got results back on the other blood samples taken. One really odd, the other interesting. The odd one is the blood spatter. Initial tests showed it was animal blood, which subsequent tests confirmed. The odd thing is that the animal is snake. Now, it would have taken a large number of snakes, I'm talking a couple of hundred, to create the amount of blood that was splayed around the room. I would suggest checking exotic pet suppliers to see if any registered keepers have been on a buying spree recently.'

'That's promising Ian.' nodded Strange, walking to the whiteboard and writing 'Snake Blood' under 'Unknown Caller'. 'Phyllis, could you start looking into breeders and suppliers in the area please?' he asked, coming up behind her and placing a hand gently on her shoulder, smiling appreciatively down at her. She nodded, a fleeting smile crossing her stern features.

'Okay Ian, what about the interesting news?' asked Strange, looking back up at the screen.

'The interesting result is from the older bit of dried blood and hair that were on the edge of the fireplace. Interesting in that it is definitely blood and hair from Michael Angus. Given how ingrained it was in the fireplace and how much it was dried out, my opinion is that the blood has been there for a while, more than likely from the time Michael died. Darrie is currently checking the contusion on Michael's head.'

'Do you think Michael may have banged his head on the fireplace?' Strange asked, directly.

'That's what it looks like.' answered Harris.

'Which gives us,' Saul interjected, 'something concrete to tie Michael into this location. Which tips the balance of probability towards this being the place they visited on the night he died, in line with Rebecca's statement. Which also means, we have one bit of information our Leith colleagues never had.'

'Which is?' questioned Strange.

'The route they would have left the city. There are only three A roads that bring you here. The A1, the A68 or the A697. We might not have the footage from close to her flat, but we can now check CCTV for a black limousine heading out of Leith, near midnight, on one of those three roads, towards Featherstone Hall.'

8:55 am

The toilet role holder was metal, she could see the edge of it was rusting and serrated with age. She ran a thumb heavily along the uneven surface, specks of rust dropping off under the force, drawing a sliver of blood. One of the screws securing the holder to the dull white painted stone wall was slightly loose. Her eyes lit up at the sight of it and she shot a furtive glance to the cubicle door which was slightly ajar.

'It's the simple things that strip away the dignity, that make you feel worthless.' Rebecca began, her voice slightly raised, her face intent, eyes darting between her shaking fingers and the door as she slowly turned the screw. 'Wearing nappies was the worst. A grown woman, wearing nappies. Having the orderlies change me, like a baby. Not that they needed it, but giving them another opportunity to fiddle with me as they cleaned. I was never complicit in that. I hated it. I felt dirty and degraded. It was always a challenge, on medication, to keep control of my bowels and bladder, but I tried. I would sometimes hold it in for days so they wouldn't have to touch me. It was dirty. Dirty. Dirty. Dirty. This is the first time since I was committed that I have sat on a real toilet. Thank you for letting me do this.' she finished, noisily unrolling the paper as she finished loosening the screw, which she wrapped in a piece of tissue with one hand as she wiped herself below with the other. She then secreted the little parcel up inside her vagina, smarting slightly as she forced it in.

'All done.' she said loudly, flushing the chain as she stood and made her way unsteadily out of the cubicle. Dr Hanlon was leaning against one of the ceramic sinks as Rebecca approached an empty one beside him. There was a mirror on the wall behind it. She stopped dead as she saw her reflection looking back at her, her whole body visibly sagging, mouth dropping open and eyes widening with shock as she took in her damaged façade.

'Jesus.' she said, her voice trembling, lips quivering, eyes glistening with the tears that were starting to form. 'I never realised.' she continued, raising a hand to her face and stroking it gently over the scars on her cheek, letting the fingertips linger on their ridges. Tears started to meander from the corners of her eyes, following the landscape of scars to meet those fingertips. She moved her fingers down to the cracked lips, opening her mouth to lick away a ravaged tear. She physically convulsed as she saw the wizened, gnarled stump of her tongue. 'Oh God, what have I done!' she shrieked, as another convulsion wracked her body and she bent double, vomiting into the sink. Dr Hanlon stood up immediately and grabbed her around the waist as she began to sag, her body convulsing again as she emitted another spurt of vomit: most of her breakfast.

'It's okay Rebecca, it's just shock, let it flow, just let it flow.' Dr Hanlon said, consoling her, supporting her body over the sink and rubbing her back gently. She was breathing heavily, looking down into the vomit strewn bowl, the wracking now abating. She turned on the tap and started to wash away her sick, straightening her back as she did so.

She looked into the mirror once more and let out a strained humourless laugh. 'I am one scary motherfucker.' she said while trying to get control of her breathing.

Dr Hanlon's head peered over her shoulder, his reflection exuding a charming, crooked Irish smile, warmth radiating from his eyes as he said, 'I don't think it's your best look, no.'

'I'm alright now Doc, thanks, just need to clean myself up.' she said to his reflection. He nodded and took one step back from her, still keeping eye contact in the mirror. She finished cleaning the bowl, then splashed her face with cold water, letting out a huge sigh as she did so.

'Well Doc, I think I need a sit down now.' she said, turning towards him and linking his arm. 'I'll help you back to the cell, shall I?' she finished, with a sheepishly mischievous look.

'Oh, okay.' he acknowledged playfully. 'My leg is playing up a bit, so any support you can give me would be greatly appreciated.' he continued as she held his arm tightly, almost snuggling into it. They left the washroom and slowly headed back down a narrow corridor, one side covered floor to ceiling in cracked, stained white porcelain bricks, the other similar, but broken up by narrow metal cell doors every two metres.

'I don't believe anybody deserves the kind of suffering you have put yourself through.' he started, feeling her body tense as she prepared to rebuke him, adding quickly, 'Regardless of how justified you think it is. We have failed you.'

'I don't think you had much hope with a head case like me. Anyway, how can you say 'We?' You have only looked after me for the last few weeks. I've only known you for a few hours. You,' she said, poking a finger into his ribs, 'are the first person to make me care enough to want to understand. So, less of the self-deprecating 'We' please, that's my territory.'

'That's not quite what I meant, but alright, I'll stop going on about it. Tell me more about Madame Evangeline. What was your relationship like?' Dr Hanlon asked as he limped back into the cell, both of them sitting down in their respective seats.

'I was her slave to start with and she was my teacher. I would agonisingly waiting for a text or a call that would signal our next assignation. I couldn't call her. Yes, she had given me a mobile, but every time she called, the number came through as unknown. It was the same when she texted me, 'Unknown': I didn't even think that was possible.'

'How did you feel about that, being totally at the behest of someone else?'

'Honestly? When I didn't hear from her, which was sometimes weeks at a time, the anticipation, no, the frustration of the wait was exquisite agony. I felt like a lovesick teenager all over again, feeling a hollow sorrow that tomorrow was far too far away. I know it was control. I know that she was teaching me, and when that phone bleeped, or rang, it felt totally different. The exhilaration was overwhelming and the thought of our next *date* consumed me, absorbing my every thought until it happened.'

'It was the thrill of the unknown. I was never sure when she would get in touch and I was never sure where we would be going. It would usually start with a text telling me what to wear. It would either be something she knew I had, or an order to go to a particular shop and buy a specific outfit. From then, through the rest of the evening, usually until about ten o'clock, I would receive dozens of messages. Some would be instructions on what I needed to do next while getting ready. Some were seductive teases asking me to think about particular moments on our previous encounters, asking me to relive where she laid her hands on me.'

'But you didn't have any say in that, any choice in how a *date* would go?' Dr Hanlon probed.

'I always had a choice, when you come down to it. I could have thrown the phone in the bin and just got on with my life. It was my choice to get involved, to live through each and every enlightening encounter we experienced together. It was only the last...' she paused, her lip starting to tremble as she talked, hands crossed on her knees, one fingernail rubbing the strap weal on her wrist momentarily, before she regained control and continued. 'Let's not think about the last time, just yet.' she finished, looking deep into Dr Hanlon's eyes with a haunted smile on her face.

He reached over and placed one of his hands over hers and squeezed, smiling reassuringly back at her. 'At your own pace.'

'It's sad, I know, but I could produce a distribution graph of the times she called. It was always between ten and ten thirty. Ten thirteen was her favourite time. Twenty times she called at ten thirteen. It's irrational, I know, but once it got past ten thirteen, I would start to panic slightly, concerned that she might not call. There was never an occasion, once I started to receive texts that she didn't call: but the closer it got to ten thirty the more fractious I would become.'

'Once she did call, whatever the time, the relief I felt at hearing her voice again was palpable and my body would quite literally swoon at the deep seductive timbre in her tone. She was always playful. It was never as simple as getting an address to a club or some other location and turning up. Sometimes it would be a trail of calls and instructions to go to places and do things before we would eventually meet up. It was fun, it was thrilling and she played on my voyeuristic tendencies, always pushing my preconceptions and moral boundaries.'

'In what way?' Dr Hanlon enquired.

'Lots of ways. On one occasion she had me dress in nothing but high heels and a knee length leather coat and get onto a busy bus. Once on, I had to stand in the middle of the aisle and slowly unbutton my coat, letting it open up about a centimetre, exposing my nakedness underneath. I then had to watch the reaction of the people on the bus. It was enlightening. Most didn't notice. They were absorbed in their own world of everyday, unfocused eyes lost in the strobes of streetlights flitting by. Some glanced my way and looked me up and down and didn't even see the flesh on show. It's the way the mind works for some people. You would know all about that.' she said, smiling at him. 'They saw a lady in a coat. A centimetre of skin wasn't enough to register in their conscious mind. Then there were those who did see. You had your furtive glances from those, mainly men, who didn't want you to know that they had seen and would never, ever make eye contact. You had couples who would giggle under their breath to each other, even the older ones. No one, not one person ever showed an ounce of indignation or outrage. At the worst, they simply didn't acknowledge me, even though they had seen my teasing flesh. The most interesting, and the ones I had to tell Madame Evangeline all about, were the women who watched and drank in every last sliver of my skin, the women who looked achingly into me: the women who were at my behest.'

'Interesting, very interesting. And how did she use the information you gave her, about these women?' Dr Hanlon delved, leaning forward in his seat and listening intently.

'To play, to pretend. I would tell her what they looked like. I would tell her how they dressed. I would tell her how they wore their hair. I would tell her how their dilated eyes devoured me. I would tell her how their lips traced elation on the echoes of my flesh. I would tell her where their hands caressed their curve and swell. I would tell her how I could feel their simmering sensuality tingling in the rhythm of my skin. She would tell me to imagine I was them. She would tell me to do all the things to her, that I imagined they wanted to do to me. She would tell me to live out their fantasies on her. She would say: dominate me.'

9:22 am

A shaking slender hand, three false nails now missing from it, snaked out from beneath a deep burgundy silk duvet cover which was pulled right up to a black wrought iron bedhead. It ungraciously patted over the top of a bedside table, which was carved out of a solid piece of oak, until it hit upon the Bose Clock Radio sitting there displaying the time. The hand yanked it under the duvet, the power cable being pulled taught which knocked an empty wine bottle onto the floor in the process with a loud clatter, spilling the remnants within.

A mumbled 'Shit!' could be heard, which was quickly followed by the duvet being unceremoniously thrown off the rising figure beneath, onto the sheepskin rug which covered exposed oak floorboards. Floorboards now stained with the dregs of her last tipple.

Sarah sat up too quickly, her torso and head spinning as she tried to gain her balance, her eyes blinking furiously as they tried to adapt to the light that was streaming through the open curtains into the bedroom. She was still in her red dress and dressing gown. Her mobile was impressed into the mattress underneath where she had been lying. There was a trail of dribble mixed with sick and red wine on the pillow where her head had been sleeping. That trail continued on her cheek and chin. In her left hand she had a worn and smelly faded green taggie, three of her fingers through tags on the outer edge. She lifted this to her face, covering her mouth and nose with it and breathed its odour in deeply, letting it fill her lungs. She exhaled, then used it to wipe the sick off her chin.

'Jacob, my gorgeous baby boy.' Sarah said, drinking in the scent of the taggie again, 'I'm sorry.' she jittered as she burst into uncontrollable tears. For a moment she sat there on the bed, weeping, staring blankly ahead of her, until her gaze started to focus on a painting on the wall, another one of John's original compositions, an abstract she hated. It was so abstract, even John couldn't explain what it was meant to represent. A steely resolve started to course through her with that thought, quickly followed by a spasm of pure anger. The radio was still in her right hand and, yanking the power cable from the wall in the process, she hurled it with palpable hatred at the canvas, screaming the word 'Bastard!' at the top of her croaky voice as she did so. The radio hit it, smashing on impact, fragments flying in every direction, ripping a huge hole in the centre of the picture.

The fury dissipated from her in a second as she took a deep breath and regained her composure before saying 'Right.' firmly, standing up with conviction: then immediately sinking back to the bed as the quick change of altitude befuddled her head. 'Okay, perhaps not so quick.' she said, admonishing herself, slowly standing this time, reaching down to get her phone as she did so.

Sarah started to slouch slowly out of the bedroom, checking her phone as she went. 'Nine missed calls, seven texts and three voicemails.' she mumbled as she shuffled, opening the call list to see that five were from John, her mumble changing to a growl, and four from Rob, at which point her voice rose in a panic, 'Holy Cow!' she exclaimed, stabbing the call icon next to his name and pushing the phone to her ear as it started to ring.

She started to pace up and down on the landing, forcing one of the false nail-less fingers through a tag on the taggie, straight into her mouth, and nervously began chewing the small amount of real nail that was left.

'Rob!' she squeaked through gritted teeth as the call was answered, the finger she was chewing joining its brethren in a fist which she curled up under her chin. She stopped pacing at the same time and stood up on her tip toes as she began to speak.

'I am so, so sorry. Truly. I am just so disgusted with myself for getting that drunk and leaving all of those messages. I'm mortified too that I kissed you. You must think I am a total bunny boiler. I know I left a message saying I was sorry, then another saying I wasn't, but I am.'

As Sarah paused for breath, Rob took the opportunity to speak. 'Whoa, slow down there. Deep breaths please: and shush....' he said jovially, replaying words he used to calm Sarah on the odd occasion she would have panic attacks when Jacob had particularly bad fits.

'Sorry.' she said, taking in the instruction and physically forcing herself to shush: to breathe in deep and let the whispered word elongate on the wave of the exhale.

'How's your head this morning. From your messages I'm guessing you had a glass, or two, or three and that John didn't come home.'

'Three bottles, I think. My head doesn't quite know what to do with itself yet. It's already had to cope with anger, frustration, hate, embarrassment, trepidation, excitement, loathing and panic and that's just in the last five minutes. The anger, frustration, hate and loathing were all for John, by the way. Well, mostly. There was a bit of self-loathing in there. And the rest: they were for you.'

'I'm sorry I didn't get back to you last night. I wasn't with a girlfriend, and no, before you ask, I don't have one. I volunteered for a locum stint at the RVI until five. I've had a few hours sleep and I'm off into the office shortly. Don't beat yourself up about the kiss, or the messages. I do like you, but I know you have a lot going on at the moment and your emotions are all over the place. How you think you feel about me is probably getting exaggerated out of all proportion and seems to be the antithesis of how you feel about John. You need to talk to him.'

While Rob had been talking, Sarah had walked into Jacob's bedroom and was distractedly running her free hand up and down the soft cotton sheet in his cot.

'I know I do. And if he ever comes home, I will. Jacob is at the centre all day, so hopefully we will get a chance to talk later. Thank you for understanding. I miss that, I miss that so, so much with John. I just....' she paused, welling up with tears, her lips trembling before she continued. 'I just don't know if we can ever get it back.'

'You never will if you don't talk about it. Are you going to see how Jacob is?' Rob enquired.

'No. That's my commitment, you know that. A full break for 24 hours. No fretting, no stressing, no constantly calling to see how he is doing. Proper respite, just as we agreed. I can be a good girl you know.' she said playfully, a warm smile on her tear, makeup and vomit stained face.

'Yes, but I bet you are in his bedroom in that stinking dressing gown with that tatty old taggie in your hand.' he teased.

'Pah!' she laughed. 'And I thought you knew me.' she answered. 'Thank you again, let's talk tomorrow when you are around.'

'Tomorrow, I will burn that bloody dressing gown. You take care, and please, talk. I'll see you tomorrow.' he finished and hung up.

Sarah looked at his name on the phone for a few seconds and let out a deep sigh, saying 'And shush.....' under her breath.

She flicked onto the text messages, all from John, and read through them with a resigned, almost hollow stare. She then listened to the voicemails, pushing the Pinocchio mobile above Jacobs cot gently around as she did. They were all from John, all reiterating what the text messages said. That he was sorry, that he was tied up on a case and that he didn't know when he would be home but would call her later. 'Nothing new there then.' she grumbled as she hung up, staring at the spinning mobile until it came to a stop.

When it did, she flicked through names on her phone until she came to 'Allie McNeil' and pressed the call button, raising the phone to her ear once again.

'Magic Mike's Meat Munching Massage Parlour, this is your Dish of the Day Joanna speaking, how may I spank you.' came the reply when the call was answered.

'Morning Allie, are you fantasising about Matthew McConaughey again.' smirked Sarah as she left Jacob's bedroom and wandered back into her own, a lot steadier on her feet now. She started to take some clothes from the wardrobe as they spoke.

'Ah, he could have been mine Baby Girl, he could have been mine. If my agency was on the other side of the Atlantic and not in Newcastle. If he was X-list calibre and happy with satellite TV commercial fodder rather than being an A-List celeb who makes Hollywood blockbusters. I know he'd love my breasts, I had them made to the exact specification Wikipedia said he liked.'

'You do know people can put whatever they want onto Wikipedia, don't you. It's not all factual.'

'Hey, factual or not, even I love these boobs. Why are you calling me this morning Baby Girl? I though last night was date night. I wasn't expecting you out of your love shack for hours yet?'

'He didn't turn up. Called out on a case. I got smashed on my own, a three bottler.' Sarah answered, cradling the phone in her chin as she took matching underwear out of the solid oak dresser at the side of the bed.

'Oh, sorry to hear that Baby Girl. Are you suffering?'

'From the drink, no. From everything else, I am feeling pretty messed up at the moment. Are you free this morning to grab a coffee and have a chat, I need my girlfriend.' she asked, slumping onto the bed next to the clothes she had collected, finally taking the taggie off her hand and laying it precisely on her pillow.

'Of course, what's bothering you?' asked Allie, the light-heartedness replaced by concern.

'Well, if I tell you the least of my problems is that I made a pass at Rob last night, does that give you a feel for how bad the worst might be.' offered Sarah.

'No way! Gorgeous Rob the Doc? You are kidding me, you sly bitch. He was my Matthew stand in.' she answered in surprise, light-hearted all over again.

'Way. I have talked to him this morning and apologised profusely. He was so nice about it, so understanding. Everything John used to be.'

'I guess the worst is John then: again.'

'You guessed right, but you don't know the half of it. I just don't know what to do. I don't know him anymore. The best I feel is animosity, the worst I feel is nothing, absolutely nothing.'

'Jeez Sarah, they are strong words, I didn't think things were that bad?'

'It's been simmering, but recently some of the things he has said, some of the things he has done are off the map.' she paused, shaking her head, ripping another false nail off with her teeth and feasting on the real one below.

'I don't like him anymore. I don't want him around me and I *certainly* don't want him around Jacob. To be absolutely honest, I think I want a divorce.'

9:39 am

'We have made good progress.' relayed Saul, looking towards the camera concealed in the bookcase. He was standing beside the small table with the phone on it, opposite the door into the Drawing Room of Featherstone Hall and looking between the bookcase and the plasma screen above the fireplace. Strange was standing in the corridor just outside the room, looking on encouragingly.

'I'm sure you will know that Rebecca Angus has gone missing. She was last seen being taken from the Fielding Institute by someone purporting to be Dr Hanlon. We have reason to believe that you and he may in fact be the same person.' Saul waited for a second to see if the telephone rang, wandering closer to, and staring intently at the bookcase. It didn't ring, the only sound the constant background beep, beep, beep from the heart monitor on the TV.

'Every Police Force the length of the country has an image of Dr Hanlon and of Rebecca Angus and are on high alert for anyone matching their description. You may find that movement in public will become difficult.' Saul suggested, calm and measured in the delivery. He waited again, walking away from the bookcase and sitting down at the piano, lifting the lid over the keys. He plinked a key in time with the heart monitor, gazing over to Strange as he did, who frowned, and shaking his head, raised two fingers and mouthed 'Plan B'.

'We have confirmed that Michael was in this room, probably on the night of his death. After reviewing the case files, we can also confirm that Rebecca Angus stated that she was also in this room. I am sure you know that Dr Ennis felt this location was part of Rebecca's DID.

We now know it wasn't. We are also assuming her assertions about Madame Evangeline are true. We are trying to find some evidence of her existence. Based upon Rebecca's statements, if she is real, then either she was involved in Michael's death, or knows something about it.' He stood up from the piano and walked towards the crate in front of the fire, running a hand along the top of it, then tapping a finger slowly on the side. He shot a challenging glare back at the bookcase as he did so.

'We did think it might be Rebecca in the crate. But we have pictures of how she looks now. They are harrowing.' he said as he leant against the crate. 'I can fully understand why you are so furious, if that is what has happened to her as a consequence of a miscarriage of justice. I can see why you would want to help her in any way you can. I can see why you want whoever is responsible for the atrocities exacted upon her brought to justice. We feel the same. I feel the same.' he stood up from the crate and walked towards the plasma screen, positioning himself in front of the right hand side of it, which showed the arms of the person in the crate.

'What I can't understand, of someone who is so passionate in their convictions of Rebecca's innocence, of someone who is so forthright in wanting to see justice done, is why they would threaten the life of someone else to reach their goal. Does that make you any better than the person who killed Michael and let Rebecca be convicted?' he posed, running a finger down the image of the arm on the screen as he spoke.

'There have been twelve people reported missing in the past forty eight hours in Northumberland and the Scottish Borders. Their families are distraught, each and every one of them frantically wanting to be reunited with their loved ones. They want to know where they are and what has happened to them. One of them could be in that crate. One of those families could have their minds put at ease. One of those families could be reunited with their loved one. You could make that happen.' he turned back to the bookcase, imploringly, the beep, beep, beep of the heart monitor the only sound in the room as he waited patiently for about thirty seconds.

The beeping continued as Saul sighed dejectedly. 'We are doing everything we can to try and get a resolution to this case in the next fourteen hours. I will do everything I can. I would just ask that you work with us. Please.' he shook his head disconsolately as he started back towards the door into the room. He paused before he went through it, looking at the 'Basket Of Apples' picture for a moment, taking in the different perspectives in the painting before continuing out.

'It was worth a try John.' consoled Strange, falling in behind Saul as he headed off down the corridor, patting his back as he passed by. 'We have to try and open some kind of communication channel with him, see if we can negotiate.'

'I don't think that's going to happen Sir. He has a plan and he is sticking to it. We've got until midnight to find the killer, or to find him: that's not going to be negotiable, no matter how much we find out along the way.'

Corporal Garry was striding towards them from the MIU, a look of thunder on his face. Strange took a stride in front of Saul and put a hand up to pause the verbal onslaught he could see rising in Garry's expression.

'I know Gaz, we shouldn't have gone into the room until you had cleared it, but I am in overall command, and we just needed to quickly see if we could open a line of communication with our 'Unknown Caller'. We are running out of time and we have to try and see if we can negotiate some kind of extension or at least some compromises. I take full accountability for that action and the consequences.' he said firmly, Garry fuming a foot away.

'With respect Sir...' Garry started, but Strange interrupted him.

'In my experience Gaz, sentences that start with that phrase always end up disrespectful. I know you don't agree. That's fine. Arguing about it is not going to change what has happened and will just lose us valuable time. Are you any further forward finding out about the bomb? Thoughts on the trigger mechanism?' asked Strange, walking forward and putting a hand on Garry's shoulder, gently directing him to walk beside him towards the MIU. Saul joined the line on the other side of Garry.

'My last word on it Sir: You were bloody stupid.' Garry said.

'Noted, and agreed. News?' Strange pressed.

'You were bloody stupid because we have found out that there is an active trigger on that bomb. We have managed to break the security key on the Wi-Fi in the room and can see the traffic streams. There are three thousand two hundred and fifty encrypted channels going into that crate. Then there is one unencrypted. I think it has been left unencrypted so we can get an idea of what the rest are doing.' started Garry.

'Which is?' asked Strange as they approached the MIU and started climbing the steps.

'The IP packet information suggests that a heartbeat signal is being sent to the trigger device in the crate. The heartbeat is a time, 12:00 am tonight. The coding suggests that if the trigger doesn't receive at least one heartbeat message in a millisecond period, it will explode. Anything that disrupts the signal to that crate, literally anything, will blow it up.'

'Okay, so what does that mean for us? Can we hack into these encrypted channels and change the time, change the commands?' asked Strange as they convened around the table.

'Reynolds is looking at that. Have you seen anything?' Garry enquired, walking up behind Reynolds.

'Only that the majority of the c...connections are very small. Just a c...couple of Kilobits a second being sent. I think these are all the heartbeat c...connections. Then there are about a dozen which are large, a c...couple of Megabits at least. I think these are the video streams. The worrying thing is the source IP address of the unencrypted c...connection.' said Reynolds.

'Why is it worrying Steven?' asked Strange.

'It is c...coming from a government c...computer system. I've looked up the IP on Whois and it is registered to a Department Of Health Office in London. I would guess that the c...computer has been hacked and a Bot is running on it.'

'A what?' asked Saul.

'A Bot is a small c...computer program. They are generally used illegally, to hack into c...computers, to carry out Denial Of Service attacks or to surreptitiously spy or steal information from organisations. Lots of them together, as we have, are called a Botnet. All the other heartbeat connections are probably c...connecting in from hacked locations too.' informed Reynolds.

'That doesn't sound good at all. It is worrying, very worrying. Do we have any contact information for that Department Of Health office Steven?' enquired Strange, a pensive expression on his face.

'Yes we do.' answered Reynolds.

'Good. Could you get in touch with them and see if you can talk to someone technical and find out some more about that Bot. Please stress to them the importance of not switching it off at the minute. If that is going to be a problem for them, please pass them back to me. Is that clear.' asked Strange.

'Yes Sir, no problem. Just before I give them a call Sir, I have some information back on the CCTV search for Limousines. We have identified fifteen black limousines coming out of Edinburgh on the three roads identified on the night in question. We have carried out PNC checks and have names and addresses for them all. DI Munro is chasing up the contacts now.' said Reynolds.

'Great work Steven.' Strange started, patting Reynolds on the shoulder, before walking towards the whiteboards and noting the information about the Wi-Fi connections under the crate. 'Steven, did we get any information from the Telco's about where our 'Unknown Caller' was calling from?'

'No Sir, they couldn't pin down a specific cell unfortunately.' answered Reynolds.

'Sir, given that we now know it is an active trigger on that crate, I think we need to keep everyone out of that room. It is quite literally a time bomb. Any one of those connections dropping could set it off.' stressed Garry.

'Point taken Gaz. I promise, if we need to go back in there again, I will run it past you first. Just bear in mind we may have to, so if you have anything you think can protect us, or if there are any other things you can check to see if you can disarm it, please, please be my guest.' said Strange.

'It's going to be difficult to find anything, but we will keep trying.' Garry answered. 'I'll get back to it now.' he finished before leaving the MIU.

Saul joined Strange at the whiteboard and the two of them looked intently at the information in front of them.

'Who are we still waiting updates from?' asked Saul.

'Well, we know who all the local missing persons are now and have made contact with all of the relevant parties. Nothing obvious there at present. To be honest, that is going to be a dead end unless we can see any more from that crate. Hopefully Steven can get somewhere with those video feeds once he has talked to the DoH. Companies? We haven't had an update on companies yet.' Strange said poking a pen at the note 'Who owns this house?'

'Phyllis, have we managed to find out who the owner of this house is yet? Have companies house come back about Axiom.' asked Strange, turning back to the bank of computers where she was sitting.

She was on the phone but put her call on hold and quickly said. 'Just confirming that now Sir, give me another minute and we will have the information.'

'Excellent.' smiled Strange reassuringly, before turning back to the board.

'We still need Darrie to let us know if he has seen anything untoward on Michael's skull. Then there is confirmation on how the other Dr Hanlon managed to intercept Dr Ennis's phone calls and e-mails. I'm still not sure about Dr Ennis. My gut tells me he is involved in some way.' Strange said, turning to Saul, whose eyes were darting around the wealth of information on the board in front of him, deep in thought. 'What are you thinking John?'

'Just about pictures.' he replied, after a few seconds in silence. 'There's a Cezanne in that room over there. And there's a Cezanne in Ennis's office. Could be a huge coincidence and I have no idea at all how that could be of any significance, but it just makes me very wary of him.'

'Sir?' said Phyllis, interrupting firmly. 'I have the company and contact information for the owner of the property now.'

Strange and Saul turned and approached Phyllis, Strange speaking. 'Great news Phyllis, who do we have then?'

'It's a very convoluted chain of companies, with offshore title and holding companies all under the umbrella of a group company called Pison Properties. Its registered office is on Grey Street in Newcastle.'

'Sorry.' interrupted Reynolds, putting his call on hold. 'Did you say Pison?'

Phyllis looked at him sternly. 'Yes Mr Reynolds, I said Pison.'

'It's Okay Steven.' interjected Strange, placing a hand on his shoulder, 'Do you have anything to add before Phyllis continues?'

'Really sorry for interrupting Sir, Phyllis. It's just that one of the PNC checks we did earlier came back with a company of the same name, registered office Grey Street, Newcastle.'

'Which means,' started Saul. 'That the company who own this property also own a black limousine seen leaving Edinburgh on the night Michael died.' he finished, looking at Strange.

Strange nodded his head, looking around the room as he did. 'Great work everyone, we might just have found a link to prove the existence of Madame Evangeline.'

10:00 am

'I could end up anywhere. On the night I took the bus trip, the final destination was near to the Scottish Parliament Buildings at Holyrood. There are flats next to the main parliament buildings which the politicians stay in when in session. I had to wait for her on a park bench down from the flats, in Holyrood Park, with King Arthur's Seat, the large hill right in the centre of Edinburgh, just in front of me. I had no idea what she had planned for us that evening. It was about eleven, so very gloomy, but there was a gibbous moon that evening, high in a cloudless, crisp sky, its stark glow defining the hills in front of me. That glow also invaded the shadows, making the darkness at the base of the hill penetrable if you sat and watched long enough.'

'I sat there for about twenty minutes waiting for her. The first few minutes were spent watching night time revellers walking by on their way home, or onwards to parties. In the gaps between watching passers-by, my eyes became accustomed to the gloom and started to see into the shadows at the base of the hill. Behind the bushes I saw the odd movement, the odd flash of flesh. I concentrated on one particular area for a while and eventually made out what was happening. There was a couple to the side of one particular bush, and from what I could make out, they were having sex, with her on top, her breasts bouncing up and down as she rode him. There was man in a suit on the other side of the bush. I could tell he was masturbating while watching them. There were at least another half a dozen such encounters taking place in amongst the bushes, under the mesmerising glow of moonlight. I surreptitiously snaked a hand inside my coat and started to stroke my tingling skin as I watched, waiting for Madame Evangeline to arrive.'

'I was so engrossed in what was happening in front of me, it took me a few seconds to realise the warm breath on my neck wasn't as a result of my voyeuristic fantasising. I turned and she was there, kneeling down behind me and gently blowing on my neck. 'Mmm.' I said, 'Don't stop that.' She didn't, her lips moving closer to my neck, tenderly kissing my tingling skin.'

"Have you recognised anyone in the bushes?' she asked, pulling the collar of my coat down, little kisses coursing down my neck and onto my shoulders. She slid a hand inside the front of my coat and cupped one of my breasts, caressing the curve, stroking the swell. People passed us by, some smiling in acknowledgement, some looking away. I was oblivious to them. She just stared them out. 'They are too far away to make out any faces.' I said. 'I wouldn't expect to know any of them anyway.' I continued, raptured by her touch.

"Oh, you do. Let's take a walk.' she said, standing up and coming around to the front of the bench. She stood in front of me, wearing a knee length leather coat, exactly the same as the one I was wearing. She put her hands in its pockets and tantalisingly opened it, exposing her naked body underneath. I could see the luscious shadow of her cleavage, part of her breasts visible, just stopping short of exposing her nipples. Her toned, flat stomach rippled as she fervidly breathed in and out. My breathing echoed hers, simmering with excitement. My eyes strayed down from her stomach. She was standing with her legs slightly parted, and from where I was sitting, her gorgeously shaved vagina was right in my eye line.'

Rebecca looked up at Dr Hanlon. One of her hands was gently stroking her breast as she relived the memory. She pulled it away quickly. 'Sorry. I get so engrossed in the memories of her, they are so vibrant and vivacious.'

'It's alright Rebecca, you don't need to apologise. The more you can relive the intensity of the memories, the more you will remember.' Dr Hanlon replied reassuringly.

'It's working. I'm remembering things. Madame Evangeline had the most beautifully dark and delectable tattoo. It was right at the top of her vulva, coming out on either side of the skin covering her clitoris. It was a forked tongue, quite literally snaking up around three centimetres from her clitoris towards her belly button. It was coloured a deep cherry red. She called it 'Her Temptation.' I put a hand forward as she stood in front of me, tracing one of my fingers down from the fork of the tattooed tongue, all the way down to the skin covering her pulsing button. She laughed and took a step back. 'Patience, my darling.' she teased, turning to her left just as two men coming from the field passed on her right, one staring straight at me with a lewd, penetrating glare. It was Dr Ennis, his gaze staying on me as he and the other gentleman passed by. I didn't think anything of it at the time, but now I wonder if he also saw Evangeline?'

''Let's go and see who's in the bushes.' she said. We linked arms, looking like twins, dressed in the same coat and boots, hair done the same. She kept leaning over and kissing me deeply, her tongue exploring my mouth as we approached the line of bushes.'

'That gentleman there, wanking,' she whispered into my ear, nibbling the lobe as she did, 'Is the one of the Under Secretaries for Transport. He is the SMP for Renfrewshire.' I was swooning as she was sucking my lobe, but managed to take a look at the gentleman in question and did recognise him. 'Jesus!' I cried under a whisper. 'It's a bit open here isn't it, a bit close to home.' I said, motioning back to the parliament buildings behind us. 'That's part of the thrill, isn't it?' she said, a wicked glint in her eye. 'The possibility of getting caught just heightens the already euphoric state of voyeurism.' she finished, stopping and turning to me face on.'

'We were standing out in the open, albeit in the shadows, and she asked me, 'What did you imagine the women on the bus wanted to do to your naked body?' her eyes simmering with an urgent desire. 'I think they wanted to play with my hot wet cunt!' I replied, my voice deep and sensual. She grabbed one of my hands and pushed it between her thighs. 'Show me!' she instructed, her smouldering gaze overflowing with passion as she leant forward and started to forcefully kiss me. She put one of her hands between my thighs and started to vigorously stimulate my clitoris, her other hand behind my head, forcing it onto her wanton lips. I did the same, and for the next few minutes we kissed rapaciously, hands below gratifying each other. We both moaned and groaned as we kissed, the growing crescendo of orgasm causing us to bite lips, to scratch necks, to slide fingers inside and to hug tightly as we erupted. She looked at me with an iniquitous smile, beads of sweat evident on her forehead and surreptitiously whispered. 'They are watching us, take a peek and give them a wicked grin.' I did, noting the incorrigible stares, the frantic wanking hands. 'Now.' she said. 'That is control, that is real control.''

'Is that how you felt, in control?' asked Dr Hanlon.

'I certainly felt emancipated. I did feel a certain kind of power. It was more influence than control. It was liberating the think that I could do that, and people would be even remotely interested, would stop what they were doing and watch me: watch us.' she reflected, a yawn escaping as she finished the sentence.

'It might be time to take a break now. We have been going since midnight.' he said, standing up and plugging the drip tubes back into her cannula and switching the drip on again. 'Don't worry, this is just a light sedative to help you sleep.'

'It's alright Doc, I trust you. Mind you, a nice soft bed with clean sheets and a big fluffy duvet would be the ticket right now. Do you think if I let you watch me, I could control you into getting that for me?' she said, smiling, her eyes getting heavier.

'Rebecca, I can honestly tell you, trying your feminine wiles on me will definitely not work. I'll see what I can do on the bedding.' he finished as her eyes closed in front of him, her body gently slumping into the chair.

'Sleep tight Rebecca, we will talk again later.'

He rearranged Rebecca into a more comfortable position in the chair. He then took off his cardigan and placed it over her torso. He placed a gentle kiss on her forehead and then limped out of the cell, locking the door behind him as he left.

As he walked down the empty corridor, his footsteps echoing off the parquet flooring in the silence of the building, the limp seemed to ease, and by the time he had reached the end of the corridor, it was gone completely. He passed a number of cell doors and then came to a normal office door, opened it and entered the room.

There was a bank of monitors on one wall as he entered the room, different images playing on them, some moving, some static. A single desk sat in front of the monitors with a keyboard and mouse and two mobile phones on its surface. He sat down at the only chair in the room, which was in front of the desk.

'Now, Rebecca, what did you get up to in that toilet?' he asked rhetorically as he altered some video controls via the keyboard, and one of the screens in front of him started to rewind. He stopped the video when he saw her in the cubicle, then set it to play, watching as she undid the screw from the toilet roll holder. He smiled and said 'That's my girl.'

One of the screens had a red light flashing on its bezel. The image on the screen was a room. The angle of the camera took in a piano in the forefront behind which were some sofas. On a wall at the rear of the image, above a fireplace, could be seen a plasma TV showing the same video feed that was on this screen. He rewound the image, watching in reverse as a man entered backward and started to move around the room. He stopped it just as the man was about to leave the room backwards and let it play. He listened as DI Saul talked into the camera. He watched him intently as he sat at the piano, nodding his head gently and smiling as Saul moved to the crate and started to talk again.

He picked up one of the mobiles from the desk in front of him, a silver iPhone which was sitting next to a white phone, and called a number at the top of the call list.

'She's asleep now. She trusts me, at the moment. There may come a point when she tries to gouge my eyes out with a screw, but not just yet. How are things at your end?' he asked, listening intently to the reply.

'I don't think it will be long. John has just been back into the drawing room. They have found the evidence linking the Hall to Michael's murder and they are working on the premise that Madame Evangeline is real. I don't think it will take too long to find out who owns the property.' he continued.

He nodded as he listened, watching Saul pause at the 'Basket Of Fruits' picture before leaving the room on the screen. 'I should be there in about an hour. I'll take over from you then. Be careful.' he finished, then hung up.

He dropped the iPhone into his pocket and picked up the white phone, toying with it in his hands for a few second before placing it next to the keyboard. He looked around the small room, pointing to the various contents one after another until he seemed satisfied with everything that was in there.

'Right.' he announced. 'Lets' see if we can't find you a nice crisp, clean comfy bed Rebecca. God knows you deserve it.'

10:37 am

The silver spoon irritatingly clinked off the side of the half empty coffee cup over and over again. Sarah was lost in her own thoughts as she absentmindedly stirred the triple shot Americano, gazing through the window and gazing through the people who passed by on their way to the important things in their lives. Her pupils reflected the frosted windows in the Georgian sandstone buildings on the opposite side of Grey Street to the café she was sitting in, her eyes tracking the shadowed silhouettes moving on the other side of them. Everyone apart from those silhouettes were background noise to her, as was the spoon clinking, as was her friend, who had just entered the coffee shop and was standing beside her, trying to attract her attention.

'Earth to Sarah, come in Sarah.' Allie said in a raised voice, waving a hand in front of her friend's distant eyes and putting a concerned hand on her shoulder. 'Are you okay Baby Girl?' she asked.

Sarah looked up toward her, but her eyes still didn't show any sign of recognition, still lost in their own world of contemplation.

'Sarah?' Allie questioned in a concerned tone. 'Are you alright?' she finished, sitting down in the empty seat next to Sarah and grabbing her friend's hands. Sarah's bottom lip started to quiver and Allie could feel her hands shaking. Sarah's bloodshot, red rimmed eyes started to glisten with the tears that were welling up. She looked down at Allie's hands over hers and took a deep breath, then turned back to Allie, a smile forced on to her face as she clasped her fists together hard.

'Sorry Allie. Just lost in a dark place there. Thanks for coming.' she said in a pained voice. Sarah reached over and gave her friend a huge hug, pulling her in tight, taking solace in the intimacy of the embrace, in the intimacy of their friendship.

'It's alright Baby Girl, that's what I'm here for.' Allie replied, letting Sarah hold the embrace as long as she needed, feeling the tension in her ease slightly until she let go and sat back, a more composed expression on her still fraught features.

'Well, you are the first woman to have a good snuggle up to my new boobs.' Allie said, rearranging her breasts in a low cut top under her silver Jacques Vert jacket. 'What do you think?' she finished humorously, sticking her chest out, pulling her shoulders back and posing with her head to one side while pouting her collagen filled lips.

A genuinely warm smile broke through the pain ingrained on Sarah's face as she looked down at the ample cleavage. 'A little big and far too hard for my tastes, but I'm sure the men will love them.' she answered.

'Oh they do.' Allie retorted playfully. 'Watch this.' she added, turning around and attracting the attention of a waiter who had just finished at another table. She looked at his name badge as he came over, his gaze immediately drawn to her thrust out chest.

'Hi Philippe, how are you doing today? Could I get a double shot caramel macchiato, with a double squirt of cream, please?' she teased.

'Of course madam.' the waiter replied in a faux French accent, blushing as he tried not to look at her breasts, failing miserably. 'Is there anything else I can get you?' he asked, slightly flustered.

'Not for now Philippe, but maybe later.' she answered, winking as she did.

He turned quickly, taking his eyes off the temptation as fast as he could. Sarah let out a quiet chuckle under her breath as he left, enjoying the distraction Allie was orchestrating, and leaned over to Allie surreptitiously. 'You are a whore, a brazen, unadulterated whore.'

'Hey, less of the unadulterated, there's been plenty of adultery in my life, I'll have you know.' she corrected, playfully petulant.

In an instant, the joviality was gone from Sarah, the introspection invading again. 'Yes, I know.' she quietly said, reaching out her hands and placing them on top of Allie's.

'It's a mess Allie. I'm a mess.' she said, looking at her friend imploringly.

'I can see that. I can see it's not just from one three bottler either.' Allie looked down at Sarah's hands, and lifted them up to eye level, stroking the bitten nail on one of the fingers. 'I haven't seen you bite your nails this bad since we were at high school and that thing we don't talk about happened with that trampoline coach we don't mention. What has John done?'

'It's about a lot of things. What he has done, what he hasn't done and what he has stopped doing. You know John, you know how he reads people. He just doesn't do that with me anymore. He always used to instinctively know my moods and what I was thinking even before I knew myself half the time. That's gone, totally gone. All I get now is indifference. For such a long time now it's just been indifference.'

'Have you talked to him about it?' asked Allie.

'I've tried. On the odd occasion he is around. And that's what he hasn't done: be around. I know it's mainly to do with Jacob. No, sorry, that's not fair on Jacob. I know it's to do with the circumstances of Jacob's illness. I know John can't cope with the lack of responsiveness from Jacob. I know that. But try and talk to John about it and he shuts down. He becomes less emotionally responsive than Jacob. I know he can be like that, he has always reacted the same when I have probed him about his past. He just shuts off and there is no talking to him.'

'But you guys have been battling with Jacob's illness for years. What's so different now, what has changed?'

'We used to argue, we used to fight like wailing banshees. We used to be up all night sometimes, battling, disagreeing on the best way to try and help our beautiful little son. We both had hope, we both had an unwavering conviction that there *was a best way* to help, that we had choices. Time moved on and the choices became less and less. John doesn't think there is any way to help him now.' The tears were back in Sarah's eyes, gathering in the corners, ready to fall.

'Oh Sarah, he can't think that. Look at everything he does to raise funds for Jacob. If he thought that, why would he do it?' Allie encouraged, holding Sarah's hands tightly.

Sarah shot Allie a scathing glare, her next words fiercely whispered. 'He does that to distract himself. He does that so he doesn't have to come home. He does that so he doesn't have to spend time with me. He does that so the outside world thinks he is a caring, considerate father who would do anything within his power to help his son. He does that because he can't stand being around Jacob.' The sentence ended sibilant, the hiss dissipating on the echo of her hostile breath.

'Baby Girl, it's not me you are angry with, remember that. I'm here to listen, but less of the attitude. I will ask questions, not because I don't believe you, but because I don't understand.' Allie replied with a firm voice married to sympathetic eyes.

Sarah visibly wilted in her seat, the ferocity ebbing from her body as diffidence descended upon her. 'I'm sorry. I know it's not you.' she apologised, stroking Allie's hand affectionately as she regained a little composure.

'It's John and the things he has done. He came home the other night and wanted to talk. He wanted to talk about Jacob. He said...' a sudden single sob caught in her throat, making her pause to catch a breath.

'He said that we should start to think about the possibility that there may be no cure for Jacob's illness. He said...' this time her chest started to wrack, sobs making her words a shrill sing song.

'He said that if there was no cure, we should think about, we should at least consider the possibility of...' she was taking deep inward gulps of air with each sob, lungs burning with the intensity, finding it almost impossible to say the word: almost.

'The possibility of euthanasia.' she blurted out, letting the final word ride on the exhalation of her collected breath, adding a whispered 'Shush...' as she finished.

'Fuck. Did you just say euthanasia?' Allie said incredulously. 'John wants you to think about killing your son!' her mouth opened and closed as she looked for something else to say, shock side-lining speech.

'Madame, your double shot Caramel Macchiato.' said Philippe, breaking the silence as he placed Allie's drink on the table in front of her. His false smile changed into a rictus stare as he saw the salty tear trails flowing from Sarah's puffed up eyes.

'Yes. Could you leave please, we are having a private conversation.' Allie replied curtly, waving him away with her hand.

'Okay, now I understand. Jesus Baby Girl, what did you say?' asked Allie, shock still rumbling in her tone as she spoke.

'Just about every expletive I know. It was a very one sided argument. I swore at him for half an hour, screaming and shouting, then threw him out of the house.'

'Where the fuck did that come from?' Allie asked, still shaking her head.

'I have no idea. But I want to find out. I've only seen him for about an hour since then, what with the shift he was on and him being away this weekend. I was hoping that we could have a civilised conversation about it last night, or perhaps today, when we had time to ourselves, so I could understand why he has given up on us.'

'God, you really need to talk to him about this. It's just....it's just fucking mental. I can't get my head around it.' said Allie, gulping down her drink to calm her nerves.

'When I see him, I will. And not just about that. About the other thing I have found out as well.' Sarah said, reaching down and removing an A4 size brown envelope from her Louis Vuitton bag at the side of their table. She took several black and white photographs out of the envelope and handed them to Allie.

'What are these?' Allie asked, perplexed, flicking through them. 'It's John.' she added. 'With a woman?' she continued. 'Kissing a woman!' she finished, dumbfounded once again.

'I had him followed. I got these yesterday. She is called Jessica. Jessica Seymour. She's beautiful, you can see that. A very successful business woman in her own right, but has also inherited her dead husband's business empire. No children, no immediate family. They met running, apparently. Her offices are over there, third floor up.' Sarah said, looking out of the café, past the passers-by, to the building opposite: to the silhouettes moving behind the frosted windows.

'That's just a few of the details the Private Investigator found out. The most devastating thing he uncovered, is that they have been having an affair for more than two years.'

11:01 am

Saul stood at the top of the circular car park in the middle of Newcastle and looked out over the city, losing himself in the surrounding normality of the everyday. The sun was shimmering, high in the cloudless blue sky, reflecting off the glass cover over the main stands of St James Park, the football stadium looming large over the city centre. The city was buzzing with everyday life, people parking up and heading off into the main shopping centre, Eldon Square, or off to the main shopping streets nearby. It was approaching lunchtime, so a steady stream of students could be seen exiting the University Buildings opposite and heading off to one of the many pubs in the Haymarket area.

A ten year old, immaculate blue Vauxhall Corsa pulled into a spare parking bay next to his SLK and DI Saxon got out of it.

'Sorry to keep you waiting Sir, the traffic coming in was heavy.' said Saxon, coming up alongside him and taking in the view too.

'No problem Saxon. Newcastle at lunchtime can be a bit gridlocked, especially around the Haymarket. It's where all the buses terminate. It's easier to get down to Grey Street from here. Do you have the address?' he asked as he started walking down the spiral road of the car park.

'Yes Sir, number fifty seven.' she answered, following on slightly behind him as there wasn't enough room for two people to walk side by side.

'Do you think anyone at Pison is involved in this Sir?' she asked.

'It's difficult to say at the moment. Certainly the company own the property and seem to own a limousine that may have been heading toward that property on the night in question. We have to find out if there's anyone within the company that matches the description of our suspects; either our 'Unknown Caller', Dr Hanlon or Madame Evangeline.'

'Do you think she is real? Madame Evangeline?' Saxon asked with an excited expectation, coming alongside him as they reached the bottom of the car park and headed off in the direction of China Town.

'I know that I don't trust Dr Ennis. I know that DI Bentley is a prick and from the evidence I've seen has done a piss poor job during the initial investigation. Is she real? There is certainly enough doubt in the evidence to make us have to think she is real. Personally, I think she is, but that's just my gut telling me that, not evidence. Otherwise, there is no other obvious suspect. And our 'Unknown Caller' was adamant that someone else was responsible for Michael's death.'

'Why don't you trust Dr Ennis? Do you think he might be involved in this? It certainly seems very strange to me that a patient initially in his care should go missing. Have you considered that he could be our 'Unknown Caller', that he could be Dr Hanlon and that it could be him that has set this all up?' asked Saxon as they turned left into Eldon Square Gardens and headed off down towards Grey's Monument, a large sandstone pillar in the middle of the city on top of which a Statue of Earl Grey, a former Prime Minister, stood proud.

Saul shot her an appreciative glance. 'Yes, it's definitely crossed my mind. I don't trust him because I know he is a sadistic bully who preys on the vulnerable people in his care and hides behind the law and 'process' to justify the atrocious things that he has done. Trust me, if I find even the tiniest shred of evidence that he is involved in this, I will crucify him.' Saul answered harshly, venom in his last words.

'That's one thing that I am struggling with on this case Sir, people's motives. I know that is investigation basics. What's the motive? Why did Rebecca kill her son? Was it really just madness? And why is our 'Unknown Caller' doing this? What's in it for him?' They passed the steps of Greys Monument which were filled with people sitting having their lunch, listening to and watching the menagerie of buskers, jugglers and clowns all vying for the odd piece of silver.

'How long have you been a DI?' Saul asked inquisitively.

'Three weeks Sir, this in my first real case. So far I have just been shadowing DI Munro, doing lots of paperwork.' she answered eagerly.

'Lucky you. Don't, whatever you do, take much advice from him. He is old school cynical, old school method. It doesn't work in the world today. I would agree with you, the motives are elusive at the moment. Investigation basics should also teach you to work out the 'how' first and nine times out of ten, that will point you to the why. Sometimes both are blatantly obvious, but if they aren't, always focus on the facts. What does the evidence tell you?' he said, smiling reassuringly at her. They were heading down Grey Street now, leaving the main shopping streets behind and heading into a hubbub of office workers going about their business or heading out to lunch. They passed the neoclassical façade of the Theatre Royal on their left, building height banners dropped between six tall pillars at its front, advertising the latest stage show.

'Right, number fifty seven, where's number fifty seven?' Saul asked rhetorically, looking up at the numbers above the ground floor level shops and café's as they continued to walk. 'It looks like this side is even, there's number sixty.' he said as they walked past Iguanas, one of the cafés on the street. 'That would make number fifty seven just over there, beside Browns.' he stated, walking across the road between cars, Saxon following him.

They stopped outside the door to number fifty seven and read the labels against the intercom on the side wall. Axiom and Pison Properties were on floor three, along with a company called 'Equity Investments'. A quizzical expression crossed his face as he read the name and he went silent for a few seconds, deep in thought.

'Is everything alright Sir?' asked Saxon, standing behind him.

'Pardon?' he said distractedly, then added, 'Yes, everything's fine. I just recognise the other company name, that's all.' he answered brusquely, as he buzzed the intercom.

'Hello, Pison Properties, this is Janice speaking, how may I help you?' asked a tinny female voice from the intercom.

'Hello Janice. I am Detective Inspector Saul from Northumbria Police. My colleague, Detective Inspector Saxon and I would like to talk with the owner of the company if that is convenient. Could we come up please?'

'If you push the door Sir when you hear the buzzer and come up to the third floor. The owner is in a meeting at the moment, but I will see if she can make time for you.'

They entered when the buzzer sounded and started up the ornate oak staircase, Saxon following Saul. The building still retained a lot of its original features. The high ceilinged rooms had sculpted plaster coving and ornate ceiling roses above crystal chandeliers. Original oil portraits of different gentlemen dressed in period finery hung from picture rails up the stairway as the ascended. Saul looked at the names on the small plaques below each as they passed them, a bemused expression crossing his face.

'There's a long line of Seymour's in this company.' Saxon commented as she took in the names too.

'Yes, there are.' Saul said, his tone thoughtful.

They were greeted by a slightly nervous but smiling Janice when they arrived at the third floor. 'Detective Inspector Saul, Detective Inspector Saxon, if you would like to follow me, I'll take you into Mrs Seymour's office. I have told her that you are here and she will be with you in five minutes.' she said, turning and walking through into the main offices.

Saul followed her silently, taking in his surroundings, eyes darting over the faces of the dozen or so people working at desks in an open plan area. Janice led them into a large room off the main office and invited them to take a seat in some comfortable leather chairs in one corner of the office. They both sat down.

'Can I get you a drink while you wait?' asked Janice as they sat down.

Saul didn't answer for a moment. He was looking around the room intently and his gaze had stopped on a picture on the side wall behind the door they came in through. Saxon looked at him perplexed for a split second, waiting for him to answer. When he didn't, she did. 'Nothing for me thank you. Sir?' she questioned, irritation evident in her raised voice.

Saul looked back at Saxon abruptly, frustrated. 'Yes Saxon.' he said.

'Janice asked if you would like a drink Sir.' she reiterated, calmly.

Saul looked at Saxon, bemused, then at Janice, his expression not changing. 'No thank you.' he said dryly, turning back immediately towards the picture.

'No problem. If you do need anything, I'm just outside.' Janice said with a strained smile towards Saxon.

As she left the room Saul stood up and approached the painting on the wall that had caught his attention. Saxon followed him.

'What is it Sir?' she questioned, taking in the picture.

'It's a Cezanne. It's called 'Nature Morte Au Crane' or 'Still Life With Skull' he answered, running a finger down the canvas which showed a table with a white cloth half covering it, on top of which sat a number of apples with a skull sitting just behind them. 'It's an original. The third Cezanne original I have seen today. Why here, why the hell is it here?' he posed, shaking his head as he stared at the painting, chewing his bottom lip with a visible frustration.

'Saxon, could you go to the desk please, tell me if there are any photographs on it?'

'Sir?' she questioned, perplexed.

'It's not hard Saxon.' he raised his voice abruptly. 'Go to the desk and tell me if there are any photographs on it!' he repeated, louder, turning and glaring at her.

'Okay Sir, I'll go and look.' she answered nervously. She walked behind the desk and saw three photographs on its surface. The first was of an older man who had a striking resemblance to the portraits hung on the stairway. The second was of a dog, a Border collie leaping into the air and catching a ball. The third. She looked at the photograph. She looked up at Saul. She looked back at the photograph, astonishment overtaking every sinew in her face.

'It's you Sir. There is a photograph of you on the desk.' she said, in shock.

'Fuck.' Saul said, running his hands through his already bedraggled hair and grabbing it hard. 'Fuck, fuck, fuck!' he hissed. 'Some motherfucker is playing with me.'

'Sorry Sir, I don't understand. Why is there a photograph of you here?' asked Saxon, confusion evident in the question.

'Because the person who works from that desk is a friend of mine, a good friend of mine.' he answered curtly, while pacing back and forth in the few metres between the painting and the sofas, deep in furious contemplation.

'Surely if you know this person Sir, you would know that they would be working here?' Saxon said, bemusedly.

'I knew she worked for a company called 'Equity Investments', I knew it was on Grey Street. What I didn't know was the specific building, or that there were other companies in the group. Now that I do know those things, it opens up a whole other level of complexity. I can't interview her. I know her. It compromises her, it compromises me and it compromises the case.' he spat harshly, still pacing back and forth.

'Sir, I'm still confused. Okay, so you didn't know she worked here, but how can knowing her compromise the investigation?' Saxon asked.

Saul stopped pacing and put his head in his hands, rubbing them over his face rapidly for a few seconds, before breathing out heavily as he stopped the frantic action and slowly drew the tips of his fingers down from his forehead to his chin, sinking the nails in slightly on the descent.

The door opened and a tall, slim woman wearing a black shift dress, black suede high heels shoes and a simple set of pearls around her neck, entered. She had a short blonde bob, perfectly straight, cut around her elfin ears which were pierced three times each side, simple pearl studs in each piercing. She wore very little make up, save for some eyeliner under her striking green eyes, and a rich cherry gloss lipstick. Her face exuded a natural radiance with a slight blush in the cheek. There was also a slight furrow in her otherwise smooth brow as she looked inquisitively at Saul, then over to Saxon.

'John?' said Jessica Seymour, walking up to him and placing a friendly kiss on his cheek. 'What are you doing here?' she asked as he received the affection stoically, stepping back from her slightly.

'I'm sorry Jess. We are here investigating a potential murder. The case I told you about earlier.' he said curtly, taking a slight step further back. Saxon gave a quizzical look on hearing Saul's last comment, but said nothing.

'John, what has that got to do with me and why are you being so abrupt? Surely if you have some questions, you can just ask them?' Jessica said, perplexed, crossing arms in front of herself and taking a step back from Saul.

'Shit.' Saul cursed, banging his fingernails off his trembling lips. 'I'm sorry Jess, I didn't know we were coming here to question you. It's going to get complicated and it is going to get messy. Sorry. Let's take a seat. Saxon, could you come over too. DI Saxon, this is Jessica Seymour.' he said as they all sat down on the sofa, Saxon shaking Jessica's hand as they did.

'Right. In summary, last night we found a dead body at a property owned by Axiom, your company. We are treating the circumstances as suspicious. One of the lines of enquiry we are pursuing relates to a black limousine seen heading towards the property on the night of his murder. That limousine is also registered to your company. We are also looking for a woman who was in the Edinburgh area on the night of his murder and subsequent to his murder.' Saul said, looking Jessica directly in the eyes with a concerned expression and pausing for a second, glancing at Saxon momentarily also.

'This is where is gets a bit complex. I know that you have a passing resemblance to the woman that we are looking for. I know that you were in Edinburgh around about the time the murdered took place.' he added pausing again as surprise surfaced on both Jessica's and Saxon's face simultaneously.

'I know that you were there, because I was with you. It was New Year's Eve, 2012 and we were there for a half marathon. At this point though, it doesn't matter that there is a reasonable explanation for you, or I being there. The fact that you own this company, own the car and were in the same vicinity as the victim means that you will need to help us with our enquiries. I can't question you about it because I was with you. Do you understand?' he asked, eyes darting between them pensively.

'I understand the information you are giving me, but...' Jessica started, still startled. 'But it sounds incredible!' she added, nonplussed for a second, staring wide eyed between the two officers. She regained her composure remarkably quickly, sitting up straight, pushing her shoulders back and straightening out her dress over her knees.

'But, if you need to question me, that's not a problem. Just let me know what you need me to do.' she asked, calmly and politely.

'I need you to go with DI Saxon, up to Featherstone Hall. The team will then interview you with regard to this matter. Unfortunately I can't be involved in the investigation now.' he was sat beside her, and gently placed a hand on her knee. 'I need you to tell them the truth about that day. I need you to tell them the truth about us. Everything about us.'

'Sorry Sir.' interjected Saxon. 'I'm not quite sure why you can't be involved in this now.'

'No need to be sorry Saxon. I know Mrs Seymour well. Very well. We have been having an affair for a very long time. I can't be involved in the investigation because by association, I am implicated in the events leading up to the victim's death. At this point in time, I am also a suspect.'

11:40 am

'How many!' Strange asked, incredulously. He was leaning down, arms pressed against the surface of the desk in the MIU, taking in what DI Munro has just told him.

'They have counted more than two thousand at the minute. There are tanks lining the walls of the warehouse with thousands more live ones inside. Apparently the stench from those two thousand dead snake carcasses was a bit unpleasant. One or two of the guys vomited. It was the stench that someone complained about. One of the local PC's went to investigate, called it in and it flashed up on our 'Has anyone seen a shitload of snakes' radar.' Munro finished, wryly.

'Are SOCO there yet? Have we got any Detectives on the way?' Strange asked.

'The location is secured, SOCO have started to process the scene. DI Cummings is on the way. It's in a row of other leased warehouses down in the old dockyards in Wallsend. The PC who arrived first questioned the other warehouse owners. The unit had been empty for a long time and no one can recall any recent activity from it. One very important thing that's come to light. While the units are all leased, the owner of the warehouse complex is a company called Pison Properties. The same Pison Properties that owns Featherstone Hall.' Munro finished, smugly leaning back in his seat, the front legs of it off the ground.

'Interesting.' Strange answered, a glint in his eye as he turned and marked up the white board under his notes on 'Snakes' with the owner and location of the warehouse.

'Keep an eye on that and feedback anything of note from either SOCO or the investigating officer immediately. Phyllis, keep checking with those suppliers. They had to get those snakes from somewhere. Anything else on Missing Persons?' Strange asked Munro, turning back from the whiteboard.

'Three people have turned up and been reunited with their worried families. No leads relevant to this case coming from the other investigations at the moment.' Munro said, rocking back and forth on the seat.

The conference phone on the desk started to ring. Strange checked the number then answered it.

'John, how are things going at Pison?' Strange asked.

'Saxon is bringing Jessica Seymour, the owner of the company, in for questioning. They are on their way up to you now.' Saul said, his voice distorted, the call fading in and out.

'Why are you bringing her in for questioning? What have you found out?' asked Strange inquisitively, leaning closer to the conference phone. Munro stopped rocking on his chair and leaned in closer too.

'Sir, do you recall the conversation we had about Personal and Professional. Well, this has just got very personal. I know Jessica. She owns the company. She owns the limousine. She looks a little like the photo fit of Madame Evangeline that we have. She was in Edinburgh on the day in question. She is most definitely a suspect, and because she is a suspect, so am I.' Saul said, his voice breaking up.

'Are you driving John, the connection isn't great. Explain to me what you mean by that. Why are you a suspect?' Strange asked, perplexed, standing upright and putting his hands into his trouser pockets. Munro raised his hands in a quizzical gesture too.

'Yes, I'm driving. I don't have time to explain at the moment Sir, Saxon will bring you fully up to speed when they arrive. I have to go and check some..in. .ut.....' A loud beep came from the phone as the call cut out.

'Curious.' Strange mused, poking the redial button on the phone. It rang dead, out of signal range. He turned back to the whiteboard and wrote the name 'Jessica Seymour' under the heading 'Axiom/Pison'.

'Well, let's wait to see what comes of that. It sounds as though we may have a suspect at last.' Strange said to the room in general, his tone slightly dubious.

'OK, Steven, is there any update on your connection machinations?' Strange asked, abruptly changing the subject, walking up behind Reynolds and placing hands on his shoulders.

'The IT Guys at the Department Of Health Offices are still c...checking the c...connection at their end. They have found that as well as it talking out of their network to this location, it also has active c...connections going into their internal network. They are trying to figure out what those c...connections are doing. In the meantime I've been trying to decrypt the encrypted c...connections. I have managed to do three of them. It's the same type of traffic, all heartbeat messages. All c...coming from some type of government or public sector organisations. I am getting in touch with the relevant IT Teams as soon as I know who the organisations are. Whoever this person is, they sure know how to hack c...computers.' Reynolds said.

'What about the larger connections, the ones you think are carrying the video streams, any joy with them?' asked Strange.

Reynolds shook his head. 'Not yet Sir, they are going to be harder. They are using a stronger level of encryption. It could be a few hours before I manage to get anywhere with them.'

'Okay, keep up the good work.' Strange said positively, patting Reynolds shoulders as he did.

'Georgie, are you there!' Strange said loudly, looking up towards the screen showing the autopsy room.

Darrie could be seen on the screen, deep in active concentration, working on the cadaver which was just below the camera angle, out of view of Strange as he watched.

Darrie raised his head, then a blood stained gloved hand with which he mopped his sweating brow. With the other hand, he lifted Michael's brain into view.

'I've just removed his brain Jerry. I have to say, the initial autopsy was a Pigs Ear. I know the chap who carried it out. Met him at a convention a few years back. Think I might even have buggered him a couple of times while we were there. I'll be buggering his career now. I would guess due to the damage of the chest cavity and with having a confession from the killer, he didn't put much effort into other possible injuries. He certainly didn't do a full autopsy on the head. Mind you, that may be me being a little disingenuous. From the outside, there really isn't any physical sign of injury to the scalp. There is a very slight graze with some light bruising. No real external bleeding to speak of and it's all hidden under his hair.'

'So there is something there then?' asked Strange.

'Oh yes, most definitely yes.' Darrie answered, angling the bottom rear of the brain to the camera. 'Do you see that red swelling, about a centimetre across, there?' he said, pointing at a slight mound sticking out from the Occipital Lobe. 'That is internal haemorrhaging. This is what happened. Young Michael here has had a light bang on the head. A bone has splintered off on the inside of his skull and pierced an artery in his brain. That has caused the haemorrhage. He would have died within thirty seconds of the blow. Young Michael didn't die from having his heart ripped out. All of that was done post mortem. He died due to a blow on the head. From what Harris found at the Hall, my professional opinion would be that he knocked it on the fireplace. How, I can't tell you, but he didn't die at Rebecca Angus's flat. He died in Featherstone Hall.'

12:15 pm

'It's me again Sarah, please call me back when you get this message, I need to talk to you urgently.' Saul huffed into his phone as the call went to voicemail. He was striding towards the Reception of the Fielding Institute from the car park. He thrust the phone back into the inside tuxedo pocket with such force, the lining ripped.

'Great.' he mumbled under his breath as he entered the Reception and approached the desk, the same young lady as earlier behind it.

'Good afternoon Detective Inspector Saul, are you here to see Dr Ennis again?' she asked, smiling politely at him.

'Is he in his office?' Saul asked tersely.

'Yes, would you like...' she started, but Saul was already walking away, down the corridor towards Dr Ennis's office.

'Sir, Sir, could you wait until I ring through.' she called ineffectually, Saul ignoring her. She stabbed a button on the phone, the call answered quickly. 'Dr Ennis, DI Saul is coming to your office now, he doesn't seem to be at all happy.' she relayed, looking anxiously down the corridor as she spoke.

Saul barged his way into the office, pushing the door open hard, where it swung fully on its hinges and banged off the wall with a loud thud. Dr Ennis stood up as Saul thundered across the room, blood rushing up his neck and into his cheeks as fast as he stood, his own expression starting to fume with anger. Dr Ennis moved quickly to the side of his desk, right into the oncoming path of Saul, where he stood defiantly, arms slightly raised in a defensive position in front of him. Saul's hateful glare didn't leave Dr Ennis's fiery eyes for one second as he covered the last few feet over the office and stopped directly in front of him, their faces mere centimetres apart. Their gaze was locked, for a moment both of them just standing there, features twitching with the pent up anger bubbling inside. Saul's fists were balled tight, ready to punch, knuckles red raw with the pressure he was applying. Dr Ennis's hands were one above the other, trembling in anticipation of action.

Saul's lip started to twitch as he took in the furious glare of Dr Ennis. He started to shake his head slightly, releasing the pressure in his fists a little, taking a step back. 'It would give me great *personal* pleasure, great *personal* pleasure to beat you to a pulp.' Saul whispered, the words full of vitriol.

A derogatory sneer curled its way onto Dr Ennis's countenance as he also took a step backwards, the immediate tension of the encounter dropping slightly. 'The feeling is mutual, believe me. If that's what you have come here for, then by all means have a go, as they say.'

Just then, two Security Guards jogged into the room, short handled batons out tight against their forearms, ready for action. Dr Ennis raised a hand as he saw them approach Saul, who was turning ready to engage them. 'It's alright gentleman, DI Saul is just here to ask me a few questions, there's nothing for you to worry about. Thank you for coming so promptly.'

'Are you sure Sir?' one of them asked as they both slowed to a stop beside Saul.

'DI Saul, you are here *just* to ask me a few questions, I presume?' Dr Ennis said, the question heavy with intent.

Saul looked from Dr Ennis to the guards, then back to Dr Ennis. 'At the moment, I am here to ask a few questions. At the moment.' he finished curtly, sitting down in the seat in front of Dr Ennis's desk, crossing the legs of his tattered trousers and relaxing right back into it, still staring at his host.

'I am sure gentleman. You can leave us now.' Dr Ennis said, motioning them out with a flick of the hand. He straightened his jacket, then sat down in his own seat, leaning forward and resting his elbows on the desk, steepling his hands in front of him.

'I see there is an anger inside you after all Saul. You aren't the stoic automaton everyone makes you out to be.' he stated, snidely.

Saul shrugged his shoulders, the earlier anger dissipated through his frame, his demeanour now relaxed and calm once again. 'Whereas you are the aggressive, sadistic bastard I always knew you were.' Saul replied, his tone challenging.

Dr Ennis visibly smarted at the words, sitting upright and clasping his hands together tightly, the ruddy hue of anger flushing up his neck once more.

'But I haven't come here to goad you.' Saul added quickly, smiling at the reaction, seeing Dr Ennis just about to burst. 'I have a few more questions for you following our meeting earlier.'

Saul looked past Dr Ennis, to the picture hanging on the wall behind him. 'You mentioned that the Cezanne was left to the Institute. Could you tell me who left it?' Saul asked.

'Back to the picture again. I know that you are an artist Saul, but I don't know why on earth that thing interests you. What does it have to do with Rebecca Angus?' Dr Ennis asked brusquely.

'That's what we are trying to ascertain. We are reviewing every lead and every piece of evidence again. It looks as though the initial investigation wasn't as thorough as it should have been and there are glaring holes in the evidence. For example, we have already found out that Madame Evangeline's residence, which Rebecca states herself, Michael and Madame Evangeline visited on the night of his death does, in fact, exist. I believe you concluded that her recollection of that location was part of her DID.' Saul paused as he finished the sentence, observing Dr Ennis's expression.

Dr Ennis was still simmering, clasping his hands tightly in front of him. He raised an eyebrow and said. 'That is correct. Based upon the evidence that was presented at the time, yes, that was the conclusion.' he answered, evidently squirming in his seat, but keeping his frustration in check.

'We have also found the limousine that Rebecca states took them there. Again, I believe you concluded that her recollection of that vehicle was part of her DID.' Saul added, still watching Dr Ennis intently.

'Again, that is correct, based on the evidence that was presented at the time. Neither of those things fundamentally changes the diagnosis of Rebecca's condition. If anything it just clarifies the disjointed state of her mind and that reality and fantasy to her were inextricably entwined.' Dr Ennis answered firmly, the main arteries in his neck throbbing with tension.

Saul shrugged, leaning forward in his seat. 'Possibly. However, we have also just taken a woman in for questioning. A woman who owns the property Rebecca and Michael Angus visited on the night of his death. A woman who owns the limousine they travelled to that location in. A woman who we know was in Edinburgh at the same time they were. A woman:' Saul paused for a second, watching every single twitch, tickle and tick on Dr Ennis's face as he delivered the statements, before finishing. 'Who looks remarkably like the description of Madame Evangeline.'

Dr Ennis banged his hands on the table suddenly, the simmering frustration inside spilling over as he shouted. 'Once again, Detective Inspector Saul, based on the evidence we had at the time, it is my professional opinion -it *still* is my professional opinion- that Rebecca Angus suffers from DID. If you have any specific questions you would like to ask me, then please, ask them. However, if all you want to do is laud your Pyrrhic victory over me, then I would ask that you leave immediately.' he finished, nostrils flaring and eyes bulging with anger.

'What I would like to know Dr Ennis, is who left you the Cezanne. It is important to this case.' Saul asked calmly, relaxing back into the seat again.

'It was bequeathed to the Institute by one of our patrons on his death, along with a large cash donation. As I mentioned previously, we do have all the relevant paperwork.' said Dr Ennis, still visibly frustrated.

'I am sure that you do. What I want to know is, who was that patron?' Saul reiterated.

'It is no secret Saul. It was Henry Seymour. He was one of the original founders of the institute and its main financial benefactor at the time.'

Saul tensed in the seat where he sat when he heard the name, gripping its arms firmly. 'And was there any particular reason why Henry Seymour was such a prominent benefactor of the institute?'

'I'm afraid I couldn't possibly comment.' Dr Ennis answered, his demeanour changing as he noted the tension in Saul's voice.

'Dr Ennis, Henry Seymour is dead. Any professional confidentiality that may have been in place whilst he was alive has lapsed. I could get a warrant to make you divulge that information, but I would like to think that you would be co-operative with our investigations.' Saul stated, his tone curt.

Dr Ennis ruminated on the request for a few moments and then spoke. 'Do you recall the gentleman I mentioned earlier, who painted the picture in the reception area?'

'Yes, the psychopath.'

'He was an ancestor of Henry Seymour. It was his great, great grandfather. The Seymour family over the course of the last few generations have been beset with a much higher than normal level of mental illness. There are some reasons for this. Interbreeding being the most pronounced. Henry wanted to understand if there was anything else in the genetic and mental makeup of his family's bloodline that could be causing the aberration. He paid us to research the family 'Curse', as they called it.' Dr Ennis relaxed back into his chair as he spoke, some of the rouge draining from his complexion as he calmed down.

'What did the research involve?' Saul asked.

'For those family members that were deceased, it involved going through any case notes that were available from their touch points with the medical establishment. There were many. Ninety percent of the Seymour family had been in touch with mental health professionals from the records we have. It also involved providing care and counselling for living relatives and proactively researching the families conditions. With Henry's death, the last of the known Seymour bloodline ended. Unfortunately we never came to any conclusive outcome before his death. It was a shame given the amount he had invested in the research.'

'What living relatives were you involved with?'

'He had a brother, a recluse, who lived in Northumberland. He was bipolar. It was very rare he wasn't in a state of deep depression. He passed away about two and a half years ago. He had a sister who lived in Italy. She was autistic and dyslexic. We only met a couple of times during the early inception of the Institute. She died about eight years ago.'

'No other relatives.'

'None that I was aware of. Henry spent a large amount of time of the family's genealogy and couldn't find any other living relatives.'

'Given the relationship you had with Henry Seymour, I would surmise that you also knew his wife.' Saul imperceptibly tensed as he asked the question, leaning forward just a fraction in his seat.

'Jessica. Yes, I know Jessica.'

'And what type of relationship did you have with her?'

'Platonic on a personal level. We would often meet at fundraisers or dinners that she attended with Henry.'

'What about on a professional level.' Saul was leaning further forward now, scanning every movement of Dr Ennis's face.

'That is where I have to stop answering your questions as she is still alive. I cannot possibly divulge any information regarding my patients.' Dr Ennis answered, slightly smugly.

'So she is your patient.' Saul pushed.

'Yes, she is.'

12:53 pm

Strange held a bundle of case notes in his hands, on top, the artist's impression of Madame Evangeline. He looked through the one way glass into the interview room at the far end of the MIU, to the sitting figure of Jessica Seymour. He put a hand over the hair in the picture, obscuring it from view, emphasising the facial features. He took in the green eyes of the picture, then looked to the green eyes of Jessica. He took in the high, angular and defined cheek bones in the picture, and the high, angular and defined cheek bones on Jessica. He took in the small, slightly rounded button nose on the picture, and the same nose on Jessica. The full bodied lips on the picture. The same on Jessica. The elfin ears, the same on Jessica. The narrow chin, the same. He watched her for a moment, taking in the precise way she held herself in the chair. Her spine was straight, shoulders back and head held high with perfect deportment, legs and feet parallel and angled to one side, with hands clasped together in her lap, immaculate etiquette for a seated lady. She took the occasional sip from the glass of water on the table in front of her, but otherwise sat calmly and patiently. He sighed to himself, then left the small observation room, coming out into the main room of the MIU again, before going into the interview room.

Jessica stood up as he entered, straightening her dress down as she did. She held out a hand to shake as Strange approached the table.

'Jessica Seymour.' She said politely, leaving a question in the tone for him to reply.

'Hello Mrs Seymour. I am Detective Chief Inspector Jeremiah Strange. I am leading the investigation into the discovery of a body at Featherstone Hall. Thank you for coming in today. I take it DI Saxon has given you a little bit of background to the case? Please, do sit.' Strange finished, waiting for her to take up his offer before he too sat down.

'Yes, she has given me a background to the case. I have to admit to being somewhat shocked and taken aback at what is going on, but please be assured, I am here to co-operate in any way I can.'

'Thank you Mrs Seymour, I appreciate your candour, especially given the circumstances. I would just like to mention before we start the questioning formally that you are not under caution. You are simply here at this point to help us with our investigation. If at any time you feel that the questions I am asking become difficult, or you feel that you should be taking advice, please let me know and I will stop immediately. Are you happy to continue on that basis?' Strange asked, smiling encouragingly.

'I understand Chief Inspector and I am more than happy to continue.' she replied, returning the smile confidently.

'Right.' Strange said, starting the tape at the side of the desk. '12:35 pm Monday. Interview with Jessica Seymour. Interviewing Officer DCI Strange. The interview is not under caution.' He finished, looking down at the file in front of him for a second before he continued.

'Mrs Seymour, could you please confirm if you are the owner of the following companies, Axiom and Pison Properties?'

'I am the Managing Director of the companies and the largest shareholder. Sixty percent of the company is in trust, but yes, fundamentally I am the owner and run the company with a board of trustees.'

'We have information from the Land Registry that show the deeds for Featherstone Hall belong to Axiom. Is that correct?'

'Yes, we own Featherstone Hall.' she replied, gently rubbing the thumb of one hand against the palm of the other in her lap.

'Could you explain how and when you acquired the property and why it was registered with an offshore company?'

Jessica smiled at the question. 'It may look slightly Machiavellian Chief Inspector, but there is a simple explanation. My husband's brother, Cecil Seymour owned the property until his death. He was Lord Featherstone. The Hall has been in the Seymour family since it was built. On Cecil's death, the property passed back to Henry, as did the title. Henry relinquished the title and he didn't want to live in the Hall so planned to have it developed. It was put under Axiom, which is our offshore holding company for assets we are not actively exploiting. It saves the company paying various taxes while the property is empty. The company has not been able to progress the development of the estate, in the main due to Henry's death and the time it has taken to sort out his affairs.'

'The Company is not renting the property out then? As far as you are aware there is no one living in it?'

'No, there shouldn't be. The house was emptied and mothballed when Cecil died. The last time I was here was a few days before he died, when he was seriously ill.'

'One of the rooms in the house, the main drawing room, looks to have been recently decorated. It was the room we found Michael Angus's corpse in this morning. Did the company at any point carry out that work?'

'No. I have no knowledge of that work being carried out.'

'As the owner of the company, of a large company, would that be the kind of thing you would know about?'

'In the general day to day running of a large company, perhaps not. However, having only recently gone through probate, we have had to be very vigilant on everything we spent, so every item of expenditure had to be approved by the trustees. I cannot recall seeing anything to do with development work at Featherstone Hall.'

'And yet, we have a room which has been decorated with a number of very expensive items in it.' Strange posed.

'I am sorry Chief Inspector, I can't explain why that would be.' she offered, apologetically.

Strange nodded and jotted some notes on the file in front of him. He then took some sheets from inside the folder. He placed the first one in front of Jessica.

'For the tape, I am placing a photograph of Rebecca Angus in front of Mrs Seymour. Mrs Seymour, this is a picture of Rebecca Angus, the person who is currently incarcerated for the murder of Michael Angus. Do you recognise her at all?' Strange asked.

Jessica shook her head. 'No sorry, neither the name nor the picture ring any bells.' she answered.

'How about this one: and for the tape too, it is a picture of Michael Angus?'

It was a post mortem picture of his face, lifeless and cold. Jessica looked over it intently, her brown furrowing, a tinge of sadness in her voice as she answered. 'No, I don't recognise him either, sorry.'

He placed a third picture in front of her. 'For you and the tape, this is an artist's impression of a woman Rebecca Angus claims was with her and Michael on the night of his death. She is called Madame

Evangeline. Do you recognise her or the name?' Strange asked, paying particular attention to her face as she looked down at the picture.

Once again, she took her time viewing the image, a slight look of concern fleeting into her demeanour. Her thumb started to circle in her palm just a little faster. 'I have never heard of anyone called Madame Evangeline. However, the picture does have a lot of facial similarities to myself, although I have never had long red hair.' she replied, wearing a worried frown as she did.

'I know this must be difficult, so thank you for your openness Mrs Seymour. Could you tell me where you were on the day and evening of the 31st December, into the early hours of the 1st January 2012 please?'

Jessica took a sip of water, her whole body becoming uptight at the question. She put the glass down and her hands returned to the rhythmical circling. 'I was in Edinburgh. I was there running a half marathon. I was staying in the Old Waverley Hotel, at the end of Princess Street. I was there until the morning of the 1st January, until checkout time, about 10:30 am.' she paused, taking another sip of water as her mouth dried out. 'I was there with John Saul.' she finished, the last few words rushed out. She sighed heavily, releasing some of the tension that had overcome her.

'Thank you again Mrs Seymour. I know that we are going to be talking about your private life and about an Officer involved in this investigation, so if you do need to take a break at any time, just let me know.' Strange empathised. He looked down at his notes, gathering his own thoughts for a second, then asked. 'Could you tell me how you travelled to Edinburgh on the 31st?'

'My chauffeur drove me up in the company limousine. He picked me up from home at around 7:00 am and we arrived at about 9:00 am. He went home after I booked into my hotel.'

'Did he not stay around to take you home?'

'No, the arrangement was that I would be going home with John.'

'Who is your chauffeur?'

'His name is Ewan Jones. If you need to talk to him you can reach him via the office, he is at work today.' Jessica offered.

'Thank you, we will do that.' Strange took out another photograph from the folder and placed it in front of Jessica. 'For the tape, I have just placed a CCTV still of a limousine on the table. Mrs Seymour, could you confirm if that is your company limousine please?'

Jessica looked at the number plate clearly visible on the image and over the body of the vehicle. She nodded her head affirmatively as she continued. 'Yes, that is the registration of our limousine. It is the vehicle as well. Ewan keeps a Woody Woodpecker toy stuck to the window just above the tax disc. I can see it.'

'Could you read the date and time from the image please?' Strange asked.

She scanned the photo quickly, eyes finding the information in the bottom right corner. '12:35 am 1st January 2012.' She relayed, a surprised expression crossing her face as she looked up at Strange.

'That picture was taken by a CCTV camera at the Portobello junction on the A1 out of Edinburgh. Do you have any idea why the vehicle would still be in Edinburgh at that time, when you thought it was back in Newcastle?'

The surprise morphed into astonishment as she shook her head from side to side, staring intently at the CCTV image. 'I really have no idea. As far as I was aware, Ewan took the limousine straight home.'

There was a knock on the door as she continued staring down at the image. DI Saxon poked her head around it as she opened it. 'Sir, could I have a word please.' a high level of gravitas in her tone, 'It is important.'

'Yes, no problem,' he started, shooting her a perplexed glance. 'Sorry Mrs Seymour, I will only be a minute, is that alright?' he asked apologetically.

'Yes, no problem.' she answered distractedly, still looking at the picture.

'Thank you. Interview suspended at 12:54 pm.' Strange said into the tape, pausing it as he did. He picked up the bundle of files from the table and quickly left.

Jessica picked up the CCTV still from the table and ran a finger over the number plate, then up to the Woody Woodpecker toy, all the time shaking her head dejectedly, her countenance pensive, concerned and scared all at once. She put it back down, arranging the other photographs and picture in a line in front of her, gingerly touching the faces of the people in the other three, Madame Evangeline first, then Rebecca and lastly Michael, fingers lingering on his empty eyes.

The door opened again and Strange re-entered the room. 'Thank you for your patience Mrs Seymour.' he started, his tone a little curt and his mannerisms slightly more abrupt. He pressed the start button on the tape before continuing. 'Interview recommenced at 12:57 pm.' He continued, taking a couple of photographs from the top of his files. 'Mrs Seymour, could you tell me where you were at 12:35 am on the 1st January 2012 please.'

'I was at the Old Waverley Hotel, in my room.'

'And where you alone at the time?' he asked.

'No, John was with me. We had been there since around 7:30 pm the previous evening, after returning from an early dinner.'

'Was there any point during the evening that the two of you were apart?' Strange queried.

'No. We were asleep some of the time, but awake for long periods of the night. I can't recall exactly when we slept.' she answered with a tinge of embarrassment.

Strange took the top photograph from the two he held in his hands and placed it just above the one of Rebecca that Jessica had lined up.

'For you and the tape, this is a photograph of the limousine captured at another set of traffic lights, five minutes earlier than the one I showed you earlier. The image is much clearer. Could you tell me who you can see looking out of the lowered rear window?' he asked.

Jessica leaned forward to take in the image on the table. Her eyes darted from that to the picture of Rebecca below. 'It looks like Rebecca Angus.' she answered, the words croaky as her throat dried out. She took a sip of water from the glass, her hand shaking as she did so.

'Would you like to take a moment Mrs Seymour?' Strange asked.

'Sorry. No. I'm alright. This is all just a bit of a shock, to be honest.' she answered.

Strange nodded. 'I can appreciate that.' he said, as he laid a second photograph on the table over the picture of the limousine. 'This is another picture at the same lights, showing a clearer image of the limousine driver. Could you tell me if that is your regular driver, Mr

Ewan Jones please?' Strange asked, folding his hands on the table over his file.

Jessica took in the slightly blurry features of a man wearing a chauffeur's cap, dark hair evident just below the brim line. In an instant her expression turned from inquisitive, as she looked over the features, to incredulous, as the blurred elements started to coalesce in front of her eyes into someone she did recognise. She looked at Strange in utter astonishment, her mouth agape as she sought words to answer his question.

'Mrs Seymour, is that Ewan Jones?'

She shook her head slowly, the sideways motion stuttering as her body shook, her lips trembling and the words timorous as she said. 'No, it's not Ewan.'

'But you do recognise the driver?' Strange prompted, firmly.

'I do.' she barely whispered, disbelief screaming from the near silence. 'It's John. It looks like John.'

1:35 pm

'Now that's what I call retail therapy.' Allie said, sinking backwards into her seat in the restaurant, dropping the dozen or so designer label bags she was carrying to the floor around her. They had left the coffee shop earlier a couple of minutes after Sarah had dropped the bombshell about John having an affair. Allie had seen the distress it was causing her friend and ordered Sarah out on the shopping trip to distract her mind.

Sarah sat down opposite, placing her three bags on the empty seat next to her. She smiled at Allie. 'It was fun finding clothes to best accentuate your new assets, I have to admit.'

Allie faked shock, clutching a hand to her new chest. 'I'm offended. It wasn't just about me. We did go into one shop for you too.'

'For Jacob, I think you will find.' she corrected, opening her handbag on the table and taking out her phone. The modicum of joviality that had managed to work its way into her mood suddenly left as she took in the notifications on the front of the phone. She looked up at Allie, all of her previous tribulations tattooed in her expression. 'Ten missed calls from John. Five text messages from John.' she stated with a heavy sigh.

'Well, he can just wait. If he couldn't be bothered to haul his scrawny ass away from work to celebrate your anniversary, he can damn well wait until after lunch before you call him. Be strong Baby Girl.' Allie ordered, leaning over the table as her eye was caught by something in Sarah's handbag. She pulled the small piece of cloth out and shot

Sarah a surprised look. 'Tell me this isn't what I think it is?' she asked, holding the cloth up in front of her.

Sarah leaned over and grabbed it off her petulantly, another one of her false nails flying off as it caught in one of the tags on the taggie.

'It's Jacob's taggie, that's all. It's just nice to have it close when he's not around. There's nothing wrong with that.' she defensively answered, hiding her hands and the cloth under the table.

'That's the same taggie you had during the thing we don't talk about, isn't it.' Allie challenged, all joviality gone from her tone.

Sarah's demeanour was resolute for a few seconds, fronting up to her friend, but under Allie's stern consternation, she cracked, lifting the taggie onto the table. 'Yes, it's the same taggie. It is Jacob's now.' she answered contritely, twirling the piece of cloth through her fingers, slipping the tags over a few of them.

'I didn't realise you still had it. I certainly didn't know you had given it to Jacob. Why the fuck have you done that, after everything you went through. It can only bring back bad memories, surely.' Allie chastised.

Sarah didn't look up from watching her hands playing with the taggie as she spoke quietly. 'It's not this tatty bit of cloth that brings back bad memories. It's watching Jacob every day. It's the realisation that every decision I made back then almost certainly caused Jacob to be the way he is. This is my comfort. My link to keep some sense of the nonsense that happened. It's a way of letting Jacob know that for the briefest of times he had a sister. It's my way of keeping the promise of them alive, in the touch of something they both held.'

Allie sighed heavily, shaking her head. 'You cannot possibly know that Baby Girl. No one knows why Jacob is the way he is. No one.' she stated.

'It's not a case of knowing, it is how I feel. Every day it's how I feel.' Sarah retorted.

'Have you ever told John about this?' asked Allie, concerned.

'About how I feel, or about what happened?' Sarah queried.

'Both.'

'He knows a little bit about the thing we don't talk about. He doesn't know about the pregnancy. There's only you, me and my parents that know about that now. As to the aching guilt I feel every second of the day, knowing that I caused Jacob's condition, no, he doesn't know about that.' Sarah answered, twirling the taggie over and over.

'Don't you think it is something you should talk about? If he is hurting and you are hurting and neither of you are talking, is it any surprise you are drifting apart.' Allie stated.

'Good afternoon ladies, could I get you anything to drink while you are looking at the menu.' asked a waiter arriving on their blindside at the table.

Automatically Allie said. 'Could I have a bottle of your 66 Chateau Lafaurie and two Caesar Salads as well thank you.' she finished abruptly, flashing him an emotionless smile.

'I think it is way beyond talking. He is having an affair Allie, have you forgotten that!' Sarah retorted angrily in a whisper as the waiter left.

Allie paused for a moment, taking in her friend's troubled countenance. 'The first time I saw that taggie was when your parents thought you had been abducted. It was just after they had arranged the appointment for your abortion. You went missing, *he* was away and they put two and two together, coming up with five and thought *he* had snatched you. I knew *he* hadn't and I knew where you would be. I found you at the bottom of old Professor Langley's orchard, half a mile down the country lane from your parent's farm. You were sitting under our tree, the daddy of the orchard, right in the middle. The place you always went when you were scared, ever since we met, when you were five and three quarters and I was six. Not that we weren't kids on that evening. God, it's scary to think you were only thirteen.'

'Allie, we don't talk about it, that's the whole point of calling it the thing we don't talk about!' Sarah chastised, a little fire in her eyes.

'In this case I think we need to. I found you, taggie in your hand, sitting there with the evening dew settling on your coat, mingling with the tirade of tears you were shedding. Your Bros holdall was leaning on the tree next to you. I seem to recall you had packed only one pair of clean knickers and the rest of the bag was filled with makeup.' Allie smiled at Sarah as she relayed the memories.

'I know you didn't agree with what they did at the time. I know that's why you ran away. I know you hated them for it for a very long time afterwards. But you do know that they only ever had your best interests at heart. They did what they did because they loved you, not because they hated you, or hated him. We spent a long time talking about that into the early hours of the morning. Perhaps it's the same with John. Have you considered that what he really wants, when he is talking about euthanasia, is to have a plan in place should things take a turn for the worse with Jacob. Just think about the tough decisions your parents had to make on your behalf. I'm not saying it is right, I'm just asking you to think about it.' Allie finished, somehow managing to convey concern on an immovable face, in spite of the Botox.

The fire left Sarah's eyes and she looked back down at the taggie. 'I remember. I know what you are saying. Some days I think they were right. Most days I think they were wrong. But I don't blame them anymore. I put myself into that situation. I was a minor and they had to look after me. It was all because of the choices I made, the forbidden fruit that I partook of. I know I need to understand where he is coming from. I never gave him the chance to explain, I just flipped.'

'Not out of character then!' teased Allie, before continuing. 'Do you remember one of the other things we talked about that night, about his wife?'

'I remember. I remember I blamed her for not understanding her husband and for not giving him the things that a wife should. I blamed her for pushing him away from their marriage, into the arms of someone else; into my arms. None of it was my doing, none of it was his doing; it was all her fault.' she recollected.

'You are in her shoes now. Do you think you understand John? Do you think you give him the things a wife should? Do you think you are pushing him away from your marriage? Are you pushing him into the arms of someone else?' Allie challenged, opening and pouring the wine that arrived at the table, pushing a full glass over towards Sarah as she took a huge gulp out of her own.

'I was very young and very naïve. I knew nothing about relationships. I know it didn't stop me thinking I knew everything and putting everyone through hell. It's different now. John and I made a vow, shortly after we met, that if either of us didn't want to be with the other, we would say so. If we met someone else we wanted to be with more, we would say so. What we wouldn't do was lie or deceive each other. That was our scripture, our simple honesty, and he has abused it.'

'Well, Baby Girl, it's a very romantic thought, but you are still naïve if you think that was ever going to happen. You have secrets. He has secrets. Neither of you ever had a relationship where you could be totally honest with each other, so how the hell do you think you were going to keep that little promise. Don't get me wrong, I love you both to bits and I am certainly not condoning what John has done. I am one hundred and ten percent behind you. I'm just asking you to be honest with yourself before you talk to him. Ask yourself the question. Have I given him any cause to stray? For pity's sake, you made a pass at Rob last night, so bear that in mind too!'

Sarah cringed and lowered her head into the taggie as Allie said the last sentence. 'Oh god, did you have to remind me of that. It was so embarrassing.'

'Yes I do. You are having a mare about John having an affair and there you are playing tonsil hockey with someone else. It is all down to the two of you not talking. It is all down to the two of you not being honest and open about how you feel. If you really believed that shite trite promise you made, you would take the pain of realisation and split the fuck up without any blame, any animosity or any repercussions. Just accept bad shit has happened and that together, the two of you are toxic.' Allie extolled, floridly.

'Christ Allie, tell me what you really think, why don't you.' Sarah answered in surprise.

'Well, it's just fucking relationships, it's not like it's anything important, like Botox.' Allie retorted, a wily grin on her face. 'Consider that a verbal slap.'

'Ouch.' Sarah joked, contorting her face in contrived pain.

'I love you to bits Baby Girl and trust me I do know how hard it is for you, but you don't help yourself, letting the baggage of yesterday...' she began, reaching over and shaking the taggie in Sarah's hands. 'Cast it's shadows on the life you have today. Never forget her. Never ever forget her. But that's not why Jacob is the way he is and that certainly isn't why you and John have problems.' she finished, grabbing one of Sarah's hands and squeezing it hard.

Sarah's eyed began to well up, with tears of relief, her face relaxing as she looked at her best friend. 'Thank you, for listening. You always know how to help me get over myself. You always seem to have the answers.'

'I don't have any answers, just perhaps the right questions. It really does help that I don't give a shit.' she winked.

'Yes you do, behind that plastic chest of yours, there is a heart of gold.'

'No there's not, it's plastic too, and full of collagen. I had that done two weeks ago. You should call John. Get yourself home and talk. After lunch though. He's still a bastard for hurting my Baby Girl, so let him sweat for a little while longer. Now, where's that Caesar Salad. Waiter!'

2:20 pm

Saul's black SLK came careering down the overgrown gravel driveway of Featherstone Hall, throwing up stones in every direction, a policeman patrolling the perimeter having to jump out of the path of the oncoming vehicle. The car skidded sideways to a screeching halt just outside the MIU, a wave of gravel surfing out from the tyres, peppering passers-by and other vehicles. Shouts of admonishment greeted Saul's ears as he leap out of the car and rushed to the open door of the MIU.

DI Munro was in the doorway watching his approach. 'Slow down Saul, you can't...' he started to say, the sentence ending in a wheezy whisper as Saul's oncoming fist connected with his stomach, winding him, forcing him to bend double in the doorway. Saul pushed through the opening to one side of him, stepping over his groaning poleaxed torso. Munro stuck out an arm as Saul got inside the MIU and grabbed his foot, causing him to lose balance and stumble headlong onto the floor.

'What the hell is going on here!' shouted Strange, quickly coming out of the interview room to the right of the MIU entrance, Jessica's concerned expression fleetingly glimpsed before he pulled the door closed. He saw Saul spread-eagled, starting to get up and Munro doubled up. In an instant Strange leant down, grabbed Saul's left arm and thrust it up his back, suppressing his movement as he sat astride him and secured the other arm in a similar fashion.

'Jesus John, what the fuck do you think you are doing? It is absolutely unacceptable to strike a fellow officer like that.' Strange shouted, grappling to control Saul who was trying to wriggle free from underneath him.

'I need to talk to you urgently Sir, there are some things I have found out at the Institute.' Saul retorted in a frustrated, raised voice, still endeavouring to break free.

'John, calm the fuck down or I will have you thrown into the mobile cell. Do you want that? I don't know what's wound you up but taking it out on us is going to get you nowhere.' Strange ordered, his slight form still pinning Saul to the ground, sinews on his bare forearms raised with the effort he was putting into the restraint. Saul slowly stopped struggling, letting out grunts and sighs as he did so.

'Okay, alright. I'm calming.' Saul replied, his body becoming inert as he said the last words.

'Good. Leigh, could you see to Mick please, see if he needs any treatment. Buglass, pop in and apologise to Mrs Seymour, offer her a tea and let her know I'll be back as soon as I can. Tell her John is alright too. You are okay, aren't you John?' It was a statement, not a question.

'I'm okay. I'm sorry.' Saul replied, frustration still evident in his tone.

'Well, your tone doesn't quite marry up with the words at the minute, so here's what we are going to do. Buglass is going to put a pair of cuffs on you and then the two of us are going for a refreshing walk around the estate to clear your head of the rage that's descended on it. Is that clear!' Strange stated.

'Crystal.' Saul answered as Buglass leant over sheepishly, an apologetic expression on his face as he handcuffed him.

'Right.' Strange stated, standing up off Saul's back, pulling him upward by the handcuffs and grabbing the neck of his jacket tightly to control his movement. There was a loud rip as the stitching on the collar came away under the force Strange put into the grip. Strange angled him back around to the entrance of the MIU. DI Saxon was helping DI Munro back to his feet and supporting him to a seat around the table. Munro glared angrily up towards Saul and spat through the pain. 'Bastard!'

Saul looked down at him with disdain as Strange frog marched him down the steps of the MIU and out into the sunny, crisp autumn air of the Northumberland countryside. He led him out to the left side of Featherstone Hall, away from the main buildings and off to a stable block which lay about five hundred metres away. At a safe distance from the MIU, he released his grip on Saul's jacket and came alongside him.

'So, are you going to tell me what that little tantrum was all about?' Strange questioned, annoyance resonating in the timbre of his gentle voice.

Saul looked sternly ahead, his furious gaze locked in the distance, its ferocity rebounding of the spectacular flashes of purple heather on the hills behind the Hall. 'Ennis is playing me, he is fucking playing me and he is using Jessica as a pawn to exact his warped idea of revenge. I really need to talk to her.' he growled through gritted teeth, turning his fiery glare towards Strange.

'Not going to happen. Not at the minute. Not until you have calmed down. Not until we have talked.' Strange said firmly. 'Focus John. You are angry. You are angry with Dr Ennis. He isn't here. I am. What I need to understand are the facts. What I need to understand is why you think that of him. What I need to understand is how I can help you. Being angry with me isn't going to help us achieve that, is it?'

Saul stopped dead, his frame visibly sagging as he did, an enormous sigh escaping his lips, every bit of frustration escaping with it as the adrenalin drained from his body. He shut his eyes, to stop the escape of frustration turning into tears.

'I'm sorry Sir. This has got very personal, very, very quickly. A few hours ago I was looking for a killer. All the evidence suggests that killer may be someone I know. That someone I know is a patient of Dr Ennis. Rebecca Angus was a patient of Dr Ennis. I don't have any evidence at the moment. Just a theory.' Saul finished, raising his head to the cobalt blue, cloudless sky and opening his eyes with a sigh.

'I agree with you John. A lot has happened in the last few hours. A lot of evidence has come in. A lot of leads are coming to fruition. Probably the most surprising having to do with you. It's not just *someone you know* John. It is your lover. It is the woman you are having an affair with. I applaud you for recognising that you are compromised because of that and getting Leigh to take over. It would have been even better if you had talked to me about it earlier, when I gave you the opportunity.'

'I didn't know she was involved earlier.' Saul replied, looking at Strange quizzically.

Strange looked at Saul and shook his head disconsolately. 'Let's walk.' he said, heading off towards the stables once again, Saul dutifully doing the same. 'This all started with someone wanting you on the case John. It started with you leaving your wife alone on her wedding anniversary to come here. It started with us having a conversation about the blurred lines between personal and professional. They aren't so much blurred as bled through right now. I can only help you if you are open and honest with me: and that's the only way you can help yourself. Focus. Someone has got it in for you. What are they going to try and exploit? Things in your life that are exploitable. Such as an affair. Think John. Think. And not just with your dick.'

They walked in silence for a moment, Saul ruminating on what Strange had said, before he responded. 'I was going to tell Sarah last night. I was going to tell her all about Jessica. I am going to leave her.' he paused, smiling ruefully as he turned to look at Strange. 'And that's not just my dick talking. We haven't been right for a long time, way before Jessica came along. There is no point in ignoring the obvious. We started to fall apart the day Jacob was born.' he fell silent again as they ambled through the unkempt grass.

'I am sorry to hear you say that John, genuinely. I can't even begin to imagine what it is like bringing up a child with an illness such as the one Jacob has. The strain it must put on everyone involved has to be intense. Did you ever consider just quitting, jacking the job in and concentrating on the family? I know you don't need to work.' Strange asked.

'Depends what you mean by need. No, financially, I don't need to work. I thought about it long and hard in the first year. But as the months went on and there was no improvement in Jacob's condition, I found it harder and harder to cope. I haven't drawn or painted anything new for over three years now. I can't. Every time I try the paper ends up black: pitch black. The emptiness of forever. It's what I see every time I look into Jacobs eyes. So what I need is something to distract me. What I need is something to fill that emptiness. What I need is this.'

Strange raised an arm and put it around Saul's shoulder, pulling him in tight to his side. 'My friend, today is a day you definitely do not need this. We have some things we need to talk about, professionally, but then I think what you need is to talk to Jessica and to talk to Sarah, especially to Sarah. You do not want her finding out about Jessica from anyone else.'

'I have tried calling. I popped home quickly before I went to the Institute. She wasn't in. She is pissed with me. We don't really have time though. There is so much to do here.'

Strange stopped abruptly and turned to face Saul. 'John, stop. Focus. Listen to what I have been telling you. You cannot be involved in this case now. You know you are a suspect. You know I need to question you. Look at what you did earlier. You are far too involved personally in this to even think about playing a professional part.'

Strange saw the anger flash into Saul's eyes again and continued on, not giving him a chance to respond. 'John, there are things that have come to light while you have been away which involve you. We need to investigate them. They implicate you directly with the events on the night that Michael died.'

The anger abated from Saul's countenance, to be replaced by concern. 'What do you mean? How could there be anything to implicate me? What has come to light?'

'We found, when checking the CCTV footage of the limousine leaving Edinburgh, some clear images of the occupants.' said Strange.

'You have found a definite link between Rebecca and Madame Evangeline?' Saul asked, surprised.

'Rebecca, yes. Madame Evangeline, no. We have another image. An image of the driver. An image of the driver, who looks remarkably like you, John.'

Saul stood there dumbfounded, the slow shaking of his head turning ever more rapid. 'No, no. That's not possible. I never went near a limousine that night. I was with Jessica. I couldn't....' he started to ramble.

'John!' Strange shouted. 'Focus. You know how this works. At the moment I am gathering facts and the facts in front of me potentially put you in a limousine with at least one of our key suspects. I know you will tell me that you were with Jessica when I question you, because that is what she is telling me. Clear?' he paused, Saul nodding his head, still obviously bemused.

'You know what I have to do John. You would do the same. What I have to work out now is: are you an alibi or are you an accomplice.'

2:55 pm

Strange entered the Interview Room, smiling over to Jessica as he clipped the door closed.

'My sincere apologies about the interruption.' he said as he sat down, adding, 'It was John. He is alright now and when we have finished our interview, I think it would be good if the two of you had a chat.'

'Are you sure he is okay, there seemed to be an awful amount of shouting.' asked Jessica, concern evident in her tone.

'A lot has happened in the past few hours. A lot that John needs to get his head around. Let's just say emotions are running on nitro at the moment. He has calmed down now.' Strange answered reassuringly. 'Now, where were we?' he asked rhetorically, flicking through the papers in front of him.

'Right. So I have the timeline for your whereabouts that evening and the people you interacted with. The only other thing that would be useful are any receipts or bank statements that could confirm the times that you mention having dinner and drinks. Can you provide them?' Strange asked, running a finger down his notes as he did.

'Not a problem Chief Inspector. If I haven't got a record, I am sure the hotel will.' Jessica answered.

'Good. Thank you.' he said, slightly distracted as he mulled the next question over in his head.

'John has just been to interview Dr Ennis at the Fielding Institute in relation to this case. Do you know him?'

A visible alertness entered Jessica's demeanour, her frame stiffening slightly, head tilting to one side and eyes widening. 'Yes, I know him.' she said, her voice inquisitive, without asking a question.

'How do you know Dr Ennis?'

'My late husband was a patron of the institute. We met numerous times at fundraising events and social occasions. He is a platonic acquaintance.'

Strange looked at her as she answered the question, leaving a silent gap for a few seconds before continuing. 'Were you aware that Rebecca Angus was one of his patients?'

'No. As I have said, I don't know who Rebecca Angus is. I never had cause to discuss any of Dr Ennis's patients with him. Any conversation we had at events tended to be polite chit chat.' she answered.

Strange could see that her eyes were still filled with unasked questions as he paused again, gathering his thoughts.

'One thing Dr Ennis mentioned to John was that you are a patient of his?' Strange stated, not taking his eyes off Jessica's face.

Her composure wobbled, eyes dilating in surprise, her bottom lip trembling slightly. She raised her hands from her lap and took a quick sip of water before resting them on the table, digging her thumb nail onto her palm.

'I used to be a patient. That was a few years ago now. I'm not sure how that would be relevant to your investigation Chief Inspector.'

'It may not be Mrs Seymour. I am just trying to understand the facts and the dynamics of the relationships that are at play in this case. If there is anything you are uncomfortable answering, please do say. At this point,' he stressed. 'You are helping us voluntarily, which I appreciate immensely.'

'I'm sorry Chief Inspector. If I am coming across as being evasive, I don't mean too. I am just surprised. Something happened a few years ago which I would rather not talk about. As a consequence, I needed some support, some counselling. Dr Ennis provided that. It was a number of consultations, just talking through what had happened, helping me make sense of it. There was no treatment, medication or incarceration involved. If my husband hadn't had a professional relationship with Dr Ennis, I would probably have just gone to a normal psychiatrist to be honest.'

'Thank you for your candour Mrs Seymour. Were you aware that John was involved in an investigation into events at the Fielding Institute?'

'I was aware, yes. However, John doesn't talk about the cases he is working on. He is very particular about that.'

'Since your husband's death, has your company maintained any kind of relationship with the Institute?'

'The company never had a relationship. It was Henry who had the relationship. He bequeathed an amount of money and various paintings to them in his will, but other than that the company had no involvement with the Institute.'

'What about yourself. When was the last time you saw Dr Ennis?'

'It's been over three years since I have had any contact with him.'

'Do you know if Dr Ennis was aware of the relationship you have with John?'

'I doubt it. I wasn't involved with John when I was seeing Dr Ennis for counselling, and I haven't seen him since, so he wouldn't have known that from any conversation with me.'

'One last question for the moment. What was your opinion of Dr Ennis?'

'In my dealings with him, he seemed to be a competent psychiatrist. He certainly helped me come to terms with the things I was having problems with. I do know he is a very volatile character and both from observation and from anecdotal conversations, he can be brutish in his treatment of other people. I have to say that was never exacted upon me. Personally, I don't particularly like him. I find him arrogant, manipulative and malicious.'

'Thank you Mrs Seymour for coming in to answer these questions. As you have seen, things are developing quickly and there may be more questions we need to ask. Are you in a position to stay fairly local just in case? I fully understand if you are unable to.'

'It's quite alright Chief Inspector. I would like to stay close. My company seems to be intrinsically involved in this. I seem to be implicated. More importantly, John appears to be at the heart of it and I want to be around to support him. I am aware you are under a deadline as well so whatever help I can offer, even if that is just making the coffee, please allow me to assist.'

'I appreciate the offer Mrs Seymour. Unfortunately I can't let you stay on the command deck here during the investigation. We do have a Visitor Unit out the back that has refreshment facilities in it, or if you want a bit more comfort, there are Café's and Bar's in Wooler, which is about fifteen minutes down the road.'

'Thank you Chief Inspector. Is it possible for me to have a chat with John now?' she asked politely, the last vestige of nervousness vacating her bearing as she sat with elegant poise once again.

Strange nodded in acknowledgement. 'Of course Mrs Seymour. I will just go and get him. Please bear in mind we are in an active investigation and I still have some questions that I need to ask John about the evidence we have found, so I will have to insist on standing just outside the door and I will be listening, is that alright with you?'

'Certainly Chief Inspector, I have nothing to hide. I just want to see how he is.'

'Good.' Strange said, standing and leaving the room, returning a few seconds later with Saul in his wake. 'Please talk about anything you feel you need to: anything!' Strange said sympathetically as he walked out of the room and pulled the door to, leaving the tiniest of gaps.

Saul was dishevelled. His tuxedo was ripped in multiple places, dust and dirt dotted over the jacket, especially visible on the once white shirt which was now grubby and torn. His hair was unkempt, bits sticking up everywhere from where he had been agitatedly pulling it. His complexion was pallid and drawn, that and the dirt on his face making his designer stubble look neglected and tramp-like. His posture was withdrawn, shoulders hunched, head drooping, back arched: browbeaten.

Jessica stood immediately Strange left the room and rounded the table, throwing her arms around Saul's neck and cuddling him in tight to her body. For a second he didn't respond, but then slowly raised his arms and snuggled her into him in the same way.

'John, you look absolutely terrible, my darling. I can see this is draining you.' she whispered into his ear, her head resting on his shoulder, ever so slightly looking up to his face.

'Ennis told me that you were a patient of his. I don't need to know the why's of that right now, I just need to know if he ever hurt you.' Saul asked, kissing the top of her head.

'No John, he never hurt me. I don't like him, but he never hurt me. I'm sorry if you think I have been keeping things from you. That was never my intention. I saw him after the abortion, when I was struggling to cope.' she said, nuzzling into his neck.

'There is no need to apologise. I'm sure there are hundreds of things we still don't know about each other. What I do know is that I am so, so sorry that you have been drawn into this. I think Dr Ennis is at the heart of it and I think he is using any means and method at his disposal to exact his own type of warped revenge upon me. He doesn't care about the collateral damage his is causing along the way. How are you coping?' he asked, relaxing his embrace and leading her to sit down at the table. Saul grabbed the chair from the opposite side of the table and the two of them sat down facing each other, Saul's legs either side of hers. He leant over and ran a hand through her short hair, letting his thumb trace a tender caress down her cheek.

Jessica smiled sadly, and leant into the caress. 'I am flabbergasted John. There's no other word to describe it. It is all just so incredible. Two hours ago I was worrying about what Sarah was going to say when you told her about us. I was worrying that you wouldn't be able to do it and would want to break up with me. I was worrying what would happen to Jacob in all of that. I thought the angst I was feeling because of that was bad enough. But this. I am trying to keep calm and composed but honestly, my mind is screaming at me. It doesn't know what on earth is happening. I am implicated in this, my company is implicated in this, you are implicated in this and these are people I have never even met!' Jessica said, her tone tingling with the terror that was washing over her wide, panic stricken eyes.

Saul's hand circled behind her neck and started to gently massage the tension he could feel there. He leant even further into her, pulling her head forward delicately, kissing her quivering lips softly first, then kissing the tip of her nose tenderly before leaving his lips impressed upon her forehead for a moment. He pulled his head back a few centimetres, bringing his gaze level with her startled, sparkling emerald eyes.

'This has nothing to do with you. I know where you were on the night that all of this happened. I know where I was. That's what matters, that is what you have to keep reminding yourself. I know that is not easy, but please, try.' he said quietly, warmth emanating from his tired, bloodshot eyes.

'Et Tu, my darling, Et Tu.' she whispered, leaning forward and kissing him hard, lips lingering.

Their lips parted, the kiss bequeathing each a smile. 'I am trying, and it is hard. Poor Munro is feeling the worst of how hard I am finding it.' Saul said. 'I also need to go and talk to Sarah. She still doesn't know about the two of us or about any of this and I don't want her finding out from anyone else. After I have been interviewed I am going home to see her.'

'You need to. You have a lot to talk about.' Jessica replied, her eyes turning away from Saul as she spoke.

He saw the concern in her gaze before she broke contact. He moved his hand from the back of her neck and placed it under her chin, lifting her head back in line with his. 'I will be telling her that I am leaving. I will be telling her that I have met someone else. I will be telling her that I love you. You,' he said, intently staring at her concerned expression, 'have nothing to worry about on that count.'

She smiled. 'When you have, I will be waiting. I'm not sure where.' she said, in her low sultry tone. 'But I will be waiting.'

'I'm might be off the case but once I have seen Sarah, I will be coming back here. I have no doubt they will need to interview me further.'

'I will be waiting here then.' she finished, leaning over and giving him a huge, encompassing hug which ended in a gentle kiss on his lips. She then stood up, straightening her dress down, picking up her Cartier Handbag, her Vivien Westwood coat and left the room, letting her arm trail up Saul's chest and over his shoulder as she went. He held onto her arm, letting it slip through his grip, all the way until the tips of their fingers parted.

As she left, Strange smiled towards her. 'Leigh, could you assist Mrs Seymour please.' he asked as he came into the interview room, closing the door and leaning up against the back of it. Saul had his back towards him, sitting hunched over in the chair.

'She seems to be a very sincere person John. It's obvious that she cares a lot about you. I can see that the feeling is mutual. I need to ask your view on something though. If you didn't know her, and had the evidence we have, would you think she was involved in this?' Strange asked, watching Saul as his hunched spine straightened up and his head raised from the nothing it was looking at on the floor. Saul stood up and took the chair he had been sitting in, and walked around the table, looking at Strange as he passed.

'I'm a suspect now Sir, let's do this by the book.' he said, placing the chair and sitting down in it. He pressed the start button on the tape and said into it. '3:15 pm. DCI Strange interviewing DI Saul. Would you like to ask that question again Sir?' Saul said, looking up towards his superior in a calm and open manner.

Strange nodded, impressed. 'Good focus John, good focus.' he started, leaving the door and sitting down in the chair Jessica had vacated, pulling it under the table and facing Saul.

'If you didn't know Mrs Seymour, but knowing the evidence we have about her in this case, would you think she was involved?' Strange asked again.

'Yes Sir, I would.' Saul simply stated.

Strange took a photograph off the file in front of him and placed it in front of Saul. 'For the tape, I am showing DI Saul a CCTV image of a limousine, with the driver of the vehicle highlighted. DI Saul, do you recognise the driver?'

'The person has a passing resemblance to me.'

'And where were you at the time identified on the image.' Strange asked, pointing to the bottom corner of the picture.

Saul looked down at where Strange was pointing. 'At that time, I would have been in the Old Waverley Hotel, in room number 389 with Jessica Seymour.'

'What was the last time you can recall being with anyone other than Mrs Seymour on that evening?'

'We ordered room service, Champagne and Ice Cream just before midnight. I called home and talked to Sarah for about ten minutes, just after midnight from the hotel telephone. Room Service was delivered at around 12:10 am. I signed for it. That was the last time I saw anyone else other than Jessica until we went down for breakfast at 8:30am. I would guess we fell asleep around 12:40 am. We were awake a few times after that but I have no idea what the times would have been.'

Strange was looking at his notes from Jessica's interview as Saul relayed his version of events. He looked up as Saul finished. 'For clarity, between 12:10 am and 8:30 am on the 1st January 2012 you and Jessica Seymour were alone in your hotel room and did not see another person during that time?'

'That is correct Sir.'

'Do you feel that Mrs Seymour could have left the room without your knowledge during that time?'

'That is a possibility Sir. However, on the couple of occasions I did wake during that period, she was there. She also woke me on one occasion. I have no reason to believe that she wasn't sleeping next to me the whole time.'

'Right,' Strange started. 'Interview terminated at 3:25 pm.' he finished, stopping the tape recorder as he did.

Saul looked up at him quizzically. 'Is that it Sir. Don't you want to corroborate my movements with Jessica for the rest of the day?'

'There's no need John. My focus is on that evening and what happened. Your version of events ties in exactly with Mrs Seymour's and I am sure when we check with the hotel, they will confirm the timings that you both state. However, I am sure that in the next few hours, more evidence will come to light which will implicate either one or both of you. I have exactly the same feeling as you John, I think you are being played. What I don't know, is if that is because you are really guilty and someone is exposing the evidence to prove that, or because you are being setup.'

'My thoughts exactly Sir, although knowing what I know, it's the latter.'

'I can't and won't assume that John. The two of you are still my Prime Suspects. The only reason you aren't under caution at this point is because all of the evidence so far is circumstantial. The second any concrete evidence is unearthed, I will arrest you.'

'I know Sir and that is absolutely the right thing to do. Sir, I know I am off the case now, but could I offer a thought?'

Strange smirked sardonically and leant back in his seat. 'Do I have a choice John?'

'No Sir, not really. You need to get Ennis in and question him. There are too many things that tie him to this case. I keep mulling over why someone would want Rebecca Angus out of the way. Surely if you wanted to clear her name, you would want her around to prove any new evidence. She would be able to say if Jessica were Madame

Evangeline in a second, or if I was driving the limousine. She would be able to confirm this is the place they visited that night at the drop of a hat. I think Ennis has set this all up and hid her away so that he can play his sick game.'

'I appreciate where your theory is coming from John and I think you are right, we do need to question him further. In return, could I ask you to consider something for me?'

'Certainly Sir.' answered Saul, looking intently at Strange, who had a pensive look on his face.

'Just remember the old adage, keep your friends close and your enemies closer. I know how you feel about Jessica but bear in mind the relationship she has had with Ennis in the past and how much evidence, albeit circumstantial, that we have on her. There may be more than one person playing you John.'

3:30 pm

Strange leant against the frame of the open door to the MIU, hands pushed deep into his trouser pockets. He watched the intimate and tactile body language of Saul and Jessica as they embraced each other goodbye just at the side of the Mercedes, before Saul climbed in and drove off, more sedately than when he had arrived. Jessica folder her coat and arms around herself and stood for a moment longingly watching the receding vehicle, before turning and casting an aporetic gaze over Featherstone Hall, taking in the tired, lifeless orifices of each boarded up window in turn. She visibly shivered, then turned and started walking back towards the Visitor Unit, casting a nervous smile in Strange's direction as she passed.

Strange returned the smile, his eyes not leaving her otherwise elegant, composed stance, until she walked out of his line of vision. He leaned up from the door frame and turned back into the main MIU room, coming up behind the still sitting Munro.

'How's the stomach now Mick?' Strange enquired, placing an arm around his shoulder and kneeling down on his haunches beside him.

Munro looked up at him and snarled with a grimace of pain and anger. 'I want that bastard charged with GBH.'

'I understand that Mick, and you should. What I need to understand from you now is, can you hold off on that until tomorrow and are you in a fit state to continue with this investigation?' Strange asked, politely but firmly.

Munro grumbled under his breath, imperceptible profanities an undercurrent to the audible, 'Yes, Sir, I can wait and I am okay to continue.'

'Spot on Mick. Really appreciate your commitment.' Strange answered, without a hint of condescension, every single word genuinely meant as he tightened his embrace around Munro's shoulders.

'Right everyone.' Strange stated, standing up and walking towards the whiteboards. 'We have a lot of new evidence, one less detective, who now happens to be a suspect, one more new suspect and less than nine hours to figure this conundrum out. We need to focus on two lines of enquiry. Is Jessica Seymour really Madame Evangeline and was John Saul complicit in assisting her during the murder of Michael Angus. Secondly, is Dr Ennis involved in the setup of this scenario to either A: uncover the truth about Jessica and John's involvement or B: frame them.'

'Sir, do you think Saul is really involved in this?' DI Saxon asked.

'The evidence suggests he might very well be Leigh, yes. So what we need to do is chase down the evidence. Jessica Seymour and John Saul are our Prime Suspects. Leigh, I need you to dig into the stories of their whereabouts that night, check the hotel, the bills, the room service. Can you also talk to Mrs Seymour's chauffeur about his movements that day and get Forensics to search his vehicle, see if there are any prints, any hairs, anything that can give us proof of who was in the limousine.' Strange asked, noting actions under the names 'Seymour' and 'Saul' on the whiteboard.

'No problem Sir, I will start checking straight away, but I can't believe Saul is involved. Most of the things we have found out, such as the limousine, were down to things Saul suggested we check. Why would he incriminate himself like that Sir?' Saxon asked, still puzzled.

'Leigh, I appreciate that you are finding it difficult to fathom his motives, but as Detectives, what do we do? We look for facts, we look for evidence. At this point in time, the evidence suggests he is involved. That is what we need to focus on.' Strange answered firmly. Saxon lifted a thumb in acknowledgement.

'We also need to start figuring out how Dr Ennis is involved in this. Mick I need you to bring him in for questioning. We need to delve deeper into what he has found out from Rebecca Angus during the time she was incarcerated. See if we can discover if he knew anything about John being in the limousine. It still stinks to high heaven that Rebecca has gone missing and he knew nothing about it. Mick, get yourself straight away.' Strange directed Munro.

'Will do Sir.' Munro answered, tentatively rising from his seat and gingerly supporting his stomach as he left the MIU.

'Sir.' Strange directed to the plasma screen with the head of the Chief Superintendent on, who was looking down at paperwork on his desk. He looked up as Strange addressed him. 'Have the press been in touch about this at all?'

'No. At the moment this is going completely under the radar and I would like to keep it that way. We don't have a lot of time and we don't want your team distracted.' he replied.

'Good news. Now, Phyllis, have you found out anything from exotic pet dealers in the area at all.'

'Sir, I am about fifty percent through a list of three hundred. So far, not one of them knows of any individual deals the size we are looking for. The general consensus from the ones I have talked to so far is that the snakes haven't come in through a dealer. These shops tend to be working on a few dozen a year. They think it may be black market activity.' she relayed back to Strange.

Strange ruminated for a moment, then said. 'Stop calling around Phyllis. I don't think we are going to get any further on that track. Could you take over looking at the evidence coming out of the warehouse from Leigh please?' Phyllis gave a perfunctory nod of acknowledgement.

'Now, Steven, how are you getting on? Have we heard anything back from the local forensics regarding the real Dr Hanlon's e-mail and telephone calls?' Strange asked.

'We have Sir. Any e-mail or phone c...call being made to the real Dr Hanlon from Dr Ennis was being redirected. Someone hacked into the Broadmoor e-mail system and the mobile network provider. That's not an easy thing to do. Especially to a mobile network provider. It's similar to what we are seeing with the feeds from the Hall. We have decrypted about twenty percent of them now. Most are from bots on systems that have been hacked. Whoever this person is, they have a level of technical skills I haven't come across before. They are hacking into systems with the strongest defence in depth perimeter c...countermeasures in place anywhere in the world. They c...could be taking anything from these systems. Or leaving anything.'

'What do you mean by that?' asked Strange.

'False Identities. The fake Dr Hanlon being the c...case in point. This person has access to the systems which would let you make a new identity. A new NI Number. A new NHS Number. A new Passport. With the access they have, they c...could make themselves become anyone they wanted to be.'

'Jesus.' Strange exclaimed, is astonishment, a sudden thought breaking through immediately. 'Does that mean they could potentially change things, such as CCTV images?' he questioned.

'It means they c...could do anything Sir. Absolutely anything.'

4:15 pm

Saul pushed a button on the dashboard of his SLK and the black wrought iron gate to the entrance of his property slid to one side, allowing him passage into the mature landscaped bushes, trees and shrubs that lined the long driveway up to the front of the house. He pulled the car up in front of a large, separate garage block, next to a deep red Range Rover Evoque, Sarah's car, and then walked the short distance to the front door.

One of the double doors was open slightly, just off the latch. He pushed it open and stepped through into the oak floored, wide entrance hallway. Just to the left of the door were a number of designer shopping bags dropped untidily on the floor, their contents – various colourful tops and trousers- spilling from them. He threw his car keys into a bowl on top a long telephone table as he passed it, heading towards the living room.

'Sarah.' he called, walking into the room. There was no answer and there was no one in the room. His attention was attracted to the sketch above the fire and he slowly walked towards it. He ran a finger down the blotted, watermarked parchment where it now contorted Sarah's face into a blur of deformity.

'What have I done to you?' he whispered quietly to himself, as he took in the drawing, lips becoming pensive as his head slowly turned to see the other water spattered photographs and pictures on the walls. He turned around and saw an empty wine bottle and glass on the table in front of the sofa, next to them, ripped up pieces of photographs festooning the table surface, spilling over onto the floor. He picked a few of the remnants up and looked at them, eyes widening in disbelief as he did. There were fragments of his face, fragments of Jessica's face: fragments of the two of them in an illicit embrace.

'Oh god, Sarah.' he murmured, the words full of concern. 'Sarah.' he then repeated, louder, as holding the scraps of photo in his hand, he walked purposefully from the living room. He was about to go over to the other side of the hallway, into the dining room, when he noticed further scraps of photograph on the hall floor and on the first few steps of the ornate circular stairway to the first floor. He changed direction and climbed the stairs quickly, noting the occasional feature of his face glaring back at him from the ripped photographs discarded on the steps.

'Sarah.' he repeated when at the top, listening intently for a reply. There wasn't one. Only silence. But in the silence, in the overwhelming silence of his large, empty house, he heard the most delicate of whimpers coming from Jacob's room. He approached it and slowly pushed the door that was ajar fully open.

Sarah was sitting on the floor in front of Jacob's cot, wearing her old tatty dressing gown and Uggs. There was an open bottle of wine next to her, the contents half drunk. No glass. Surrounding her was the confetti of adultery: a dispersed collage of torn eyes, ripped noses, riven lips and shredded encounters. The taggie was in place over the fingers of one hand while the other hand held another photograph that was being decimated. There was only one false nail left, on the little finger of her left hand. She looked up at Saul as he entered the room, the dark shadows around her eyes glistening with the tears of her torment, snot dribbling from her nose to join the salty flows from her eyes and moisten her quivering lips.

Saul didn't say a thing, he just held her anguished gaze as he sat down on the floor next to her and wrapped an arm around her back, pulling her close into his chest. The second he touched her, the timorous whimpers coming from her quivering lips turned into deep, shaking sobs emanating from the pit of her stomach, wracking her body as she willingly sank into his embrace, consumed by the wails of her lamentation.

They sat in that position for more than ten minutes, the only movement the stuttering of Sarah's body as she cried and Saul rhythmically running a hand through her hair, over and over again. Eventually, her sobs began to subside.

'You stink of piss.' Sarah said, her words quivering and phlegmy.

'Run in with a dog. It chewed my trousers.' Saul replied, moving the offending leg slightly to show her.

'Should have chewed your fucking cock off.' she answered, a slight bit of bite in her delivery.

'I'm sorry.' Saul answered, simply. Sarah stiffened as he said the words, and lifted her head out of his chest, pulling back from their embrace. She sat up next to him, grabbed the bottle of wine and took a long deep swig.

'Sorry for what, exactly John.' she asked, wiping her sodden mouth with the arm of her dressing gown. She didn't let him answer.

'Sorry for missing out wedding anniversary. Happy Anniversary by the way, dear!' she spat the last word sarcastically.

'Sorry for fucking another woman. Sorry for having an affair. No, scratch that. Sorry for having an affair for more than two years! Sorry for wanting to kill our son!' she shouted, leaning forward right into his face, glaring ferociously into his eyes.

His glistening eyes didn't flinch, not even when the spittle from her screams peppered them, just forlornly returned her glare. 'I'm sorry I broke our promise, and didn't have the guts to be honest with you.' he replied quietly, his words resonating with remorse.

Sarah sagged back, the fury that had quickly built up being knocked out of her by what he said. 'Now, you can read me again.' she said with an ironic laugh. 'When we are broken beyond repair, that promise of honesty betrayed, you start to read me again.'

Saul reached over and tenderly placed a hand on each of Sarah's tear stained cheeks, gently rubbing their salty coarseness with his thumb, holding her head steady and looking deep into her eyes. 'I never stopped reading you Sarah. I just couldn't cope with what I saw and I didn't know what to do.'

'What did you see John, what did you see that was so hard to cope with.' she asked, wide eyed, challenging.

'Guilt. All I ever saw, from the day Jacob was born, was guilt. It's there now.' he answered, holding his gaze steady as she quickly looked away and pulled his hands off her face, startled.

'Well,' she started, taking another swig of wine as she did. 'Perhaps I had lot to feel guilty about. But what I feel now, well, to be honest, that just isn't your concern any more. I think on the guilt stakes, lately, you have been racking up a crime or two more than me. Do you feel guilty at all about having an affair? Do you feel even the slightest amount of remorse over wanting to kill our son?' she vehemently asked, fire in her movement once again.

Saul returned her glare for a moment, anger rising through his previously solemn façade. He stood up abruptly and grabbed one of Sarah's arms, yanking her up too. 'Come with me.' he instructed, striding out of Jacob's room and across the corridor, opening the door to his studio, Sarah sidling behind him, taking another gulp of wine.

There were paintings and sketches all around the walls, of every type of scene, some still life, some landscape, some portrait, all done with skill, craft and dexterity. There were a number of easels in the room, none of them with pictures on. Underneath a window on the far wall was a set of deep drawers on top of which were dozens of paints, brushes, charcoals, pencils, crayons and chalks. Saul headed for the drawers, opened the top one, and pulled out an A2 size portfolio binder. He unzipped it and took a large pile of papers from within, placing one on the nearest empty easel and then circling the room to fill each easel with a picture. He threw the remainder on the floor and stomped back to the first one he had placed.

'What do you see Sarah?' he asked her, his tone frustrated, his actions animated as he poked a finger at the picture.

She looked at the picture, then to Saul, bemused. 'Nothing John, it's just black.'

'Exactly.' he pronounced, moving on to the next easel, stabbing the picture. 'And this one, what do you see?'

'It's the same. Nothing.' Sarah said, confused.

'Nothing, precisely nothing.' Saul replayed, moving around to the next and poking it. 'And on this one there's nothing.' Before moving onto the next. 'Just as this one, is of nothing.' he continued, walking to the middle of the room and scuffing his shoes over the ones he had dropped on the floor. 'Just like all of these. Nothing, nothing, nothing!' he screamed, eyes bulging from his head as stared at a terrified Sarah.

'And do you know what all this nothing is, Sarah? Do you?' he whispered angrily, coming close and standing by hear ear.

Sarah was quivering again, this time in obvious fear. 'No.' she replied, timidly.

'It's what I read, when I look into Jacob's eyes. It's what I fear, every single moment of the day, his life is like. It's what I feel is his suffering: utter, absolute, nothing.'

4:45 pm

'Sir,' shouted Reynolds excitedly across the MIU room, turning in his seat to face Strange, who was updating notes on the whiteboard. 'We have decrypted one of the video feeds.'

Strange turned from the board and came up behind Reynolds, placing his hands on his shoulders as he did. 'Great work Steven. Now, what does that mean for us?' he asked.

'Well, first off, we will be able to see where the video is being streamed to.' Reynolds answered, frantically tapping on the keyboard in front of him. 'The IP is 10.203.56.123 which is registered to,' he continued, bringing up another webpage and launching Whois.net. 'The First C...Church of The Latter Day Saints, C...Clareville, Wyoming.' He finished, the initial excitement ebbing from his tone.

'I take it that's not good news?' Strange asked, picking up on the tone.

'Not brilliant Sir. But not bad. It just means that they have hacked another c...computer and are using it as a video relay. It doesn't give us a smoking gun as to where the images are really being viewed from. I would guess, now I know the address, I will be able to get to the image via any standard web browser.' Reynolds answered, putting the address into Internet Explorer.

'There you go.' Reynolds said, as an image of the Drawing Room and the inside of the crate appeared on the screen in front of him. 'Now, what we might be able to see in the packet information, are any c...control c...commands being sent to the c...camera.' he finished, opening up a screen of hexadecimal coding down one side, with plain text interpretation on the other.

'What could we use that for?' Strange asked, inquisitively.

'Well Sir, if the c...camera is movable, we might be able to reposition it to show who is in the c...crate. There!' he pronounced, the excitement back in his voice once again as he pointed to a nondescript piece of text on the screen. 'Now, if I append this bit of c...code to the end of the web address URL like this,' he continued, carrying out the action as he talked. 'The c...camera should move to the left.'

On the screen in front of them, the image started to move, showing more of the forearm of the crate's occupant.

'Steven, you are a genius.' Strange said with enthusiasm, squeezing Reynolds shoulders and shaking them with an obvious excitement. He moved to the side of Reynolds and sat down in a seat next to him, getting a closer view of the screen. 'Now, can you move it up to where the head should be?'

'I should be able to Sir, the last instruction was to move it ten c...centimetres to the left. I think if we move it another fifty c...centimetres, we should be roughly where the head should be.' Reynolds answered, changing a figure at the end of the URL and pressing enter again.

'Excellent.' Strange said, smiling as the image started to pan further up the arm.

'It looks like they are wearing a T-Shirt.' Strange commented as a ring of material appeared around the scrawny, still, bicep of the occupant.

The camera panned still further, exposing the shoulders and neck of the occupant.

'Definitely a V neck t-shirt. The thin neck and arms and hairless smooth skin suggest to me that they are young.' Strange added, tracing the movement of the camera with his finger as more of the occupant came into view.

The head slowly started to appear from the left of the screen, first a chin, then thin, slightly parted lips, and a slight button nose. Strange's finger stopped moving on the screen at the same moment the occupants closed, lash-less eyes came into view. His own eyes opened wide in surprise, his body moving back involuntarily with a startled shock. 'Jesus H fucking Christ.' he blasphemed, mouth agape in astonishment, his body prone for a moment.

'What is it Sir?' asked Reynolds, concerned. 'Do you recognise who it is?'

'Leigh!' he shouted, standing up quickly and awkwardly, banging his leg as he turned back to the table where she was sitting. 'Get John on the phone.' he ordered abruptly. 'Get John on the phone now!'

4:55 pm

Sarah walked up to one of the easels and ran her fingers over the black painting sitting on it. Momentarily, they started to trace out a line, a form in the darkness.

'It's not utter nothingness.' she said quietly, taking a step back from the easel and looking around to Saul, beckoning him. 'Come and look.'

Saul was still fuming, his fists clenched as he came along side Sarah. 'It's nothing Sarah, the emptiness of forever.'

'Not quite.' she said, taking his hand and teasing out a finger, raising it and running it over the painting in front of them. 'Do you feel that?' she asked.

It was Saul's turn to look bemused now as his finger traced the same journey Sarah's had moments earlier.

'Do you feel the indentation? Take a step back.' Sarah instructed, taking the step with him. 'Look at it. Can you see it in the nothing, the original outline of your sketch?' she asked.

'Yes, I can.' Saul replied, all the anger leaving his countenance instantly, to be replaced by a wistful, tentative grin. 'He's got his bum in the air, kicking his legs and wriggling his arms. He's lying on your chest having Tummy Time.' His eyes were filling with tears as he replayed the image to Sarah. She still held his hand and walked him around to the next easel.

'And this one?' she asked.

'You are sitting on the floor against his cot, your knees pulled up and Jacob is lying against your knees, his feet tickling your stomach. You are doing 'Round and round the garden' on his stomach and he is smiling. My god is he smiling.' His voice broke on the last words as a sob escaped with them, a solitary tear tricking down his cheek.

Sarah squeezed his hand tightly, reached up and kissed away the tear. 'I am pleased you got angry.' she said. 'I had a horrendous feeling you had given up on him.'

He was still looking at the outline in the darkness of the picture in front of him and shook his head. 'I may have given up on us, but I will never give up on Jacob. I don't want to kill him. I just want us to think about what we would do if we knew, without a shadow of a doubt, that he was suffering. Some days. Most days,' he corrected. 'When I feel his emptiness, I struggle so, so much. I just feel so inadequate, so powerless to help him. I am sorry that I even thought about it. It's not what I want for him. I want to try and help find some kind of way for him to...just be a little boy.'

'I know you do.' she said softly, joining him in silence for a moment, taking in the image.

'Did I tell you that we are trying controlled dilation now?' she asked, after the brief contemplative silence.

'No. What does that mean? Sounds like a birthing technique.' he asked inquisitively.

Sarah smiled. 'No, it's an optical technique. Jacob's eyes react to light normally, which suggests the iris dilator muscles are working. If you train these muscles, you can control their contraction. Rob is trying to teach Jacob how to do it.'

'How is he training him?' Saul asked.

'Just talking to him, over and over again, suggesting the things Jacob needs to do to control the movement. It's something to do with using the parasympathetic rather than the sympathetic or enteric nervous systems, which are the ones that don't work in Jacob.'

'Shit.' she added, before Saul had a chance to respond further. 'I have something to tell you, and not because I am trying to make you jealous, but because I, for one, believed in our promise. I made a pass at Rob last night.' she said with a pained look of embarrassment on her face.

'I don't think I have any right to judge you for that, after what I have done.' Saul answered sadly. 'Do you like him?'

'I like him, but I don't know how I feel about him. My emotions have been erratic for a long time now. You know that. From the day Jacob was born. You're right, I feel guilty.' she said, lifting the nearly empty wine bottle she still held in her left hand to her mouth and taking a sip. She offered it to Saul, who accepted on this occasion, taking a swig himself.

'Allie is my barometer to normality. She grounds me. She asked me earlier to consider if I thought you jumped or were pushed, figuratively speaking, into having an affair.' Sarah continued, sadness injected into the inflection.

'Sarah.' Saul interjected, turning to face her as he spoke. 'Me having an affair is not your doing. It is my doing.'

'No John, listen, please. You have to know that I understand. I am mightily pissed off that you didn't tell me, but I do understand.' she raised a hand, the one with the taggie tied to the fingers, and stroked his cheek with it. She cast her forlorn gaze between Saul and the Taggie as she spoke. 'There are things that happened in my past, things I don't think I will ever come to terms with. They still haunt me now and they have always cast a shadow over you and I. They cast an even longer shadow over Jacob. It's why I will always feel guilty, no matter what.'

'Now it's me who doesn't understand. Why are you being so understanding?'

'Oh John, you silly bugger. It's because, despite all the fucking shit you are putting me through, despite not liking you much at the moment, I still love you. It's because I want you to be happy. I know I can't give you that. I know I have already pushed you away from my broken heart. It's a relief. I don't have to pretend anymore, I can drop the pretence of the dutiful wife. I can focus on Jacob. There is no point in making either of us suffer any more. I am happy to get divorced. I am happy that you have found someone else and I am happy that you are in love. Are you in love?'

'I am.'

She smiled a huge wide grin, tears flowing from her eyes as she leant forward and kissed him fully on the lips, pressing hard and firm for second after second, until she parted, smiling once more. 'That's what I want for you.'

She took a step back from him, letting her hand slide out of his, playing with the taggie as she did, casting a wistful look around the room at the hidden images of Jacob in the darkness of Saul's creativity.

'Shit,' she announced. 'What time is it?' she asked, her eyes suddenly animated and alarmed.

Saul took his phone out of his pocket and looked at the clock. 'It's 5:30. What time are you due to pick Jacob up?'

'Right about now.' she said, scrambling in her dressing gown pocket for her own phone. She found it, quickly flicked to the hospice number and called it.

Saul looked at his own phone again, noticing the twenty one missed calls and fifteen voicemail massages. He dialled the voicemail while Sarah was on the phone.

'Hi Amy, it's Sarah here. Really sorry, but I'm going to be about twenty minutes late picking Jacob up. I've got until six, right?' Sarah began.

Saul started listening to his first voicemail. 'John, it's Strange. I need you to call me back urgently. We know who the person in the crate is. I don't know how to tell you this,' the message started. Saul was distracted as he listened, Sarah suddenly raising her voice.

'What do you mean he's not there? He was dropped off last night. Dr Adams dropped him off last night.' she said, her face full of concern as she looked at Saul.

'So I am just going to have to call it straight.' continued Strange on the voicemail. 'It's Jacob. The person in the crate is Jacob.'

5:45 pm

Rebecca slowly, sleepily began to open her eyes. Through a drowsy fug she started to focus on the soft plump pillow her head was resting in, breathing in the crisp aroma of freshly laundered cotton. She stretched out, the floral cotton quilt covering her shifting topology moving, but still cocooning her in comfort. She raised her torso up on her elbows, peeking out over the cover of the quilt to take in the room she was in.

It was a bedroom. Her waking eyes started a slow scan of her surroundings. There was a small bedside table to her left, a glass of sparkling water and some headache tablets sitting on its surface. On the wall behind it was a long, low dressing table, with a large mirror in the middle. On top of the dressing table were baskets with numerous bottles and tops of cosmetic containers sticking out of them. There were three dummy heads, different colour wigs sitting on each. On the wall opposite where she was lying there was the closed door of the room and beside that a white, rattan chair. Dr Hanlon was sitting in it, smiling at her. She gave a dozy smile back, her eyes still scanning. Above his head was a Cezanne painting, 'Nature Morte', with a Compotier, Pitcher and different fruits laying on a table covered in a white table cloth. On the wall to her right, against which the bed was resting, was another large mirror reflecting the room, giving it an added sense of depth.

'This is unexpected.' Rebecca said, her gaze returning to Dr Hanlon.

'Well, you did say you would love to go to sleep in a nice clean bed, and I am nothing if not obliging. How are you feeling?'

'A little fuzzy, my head is pounding.'

'That's the sedative wearing off. There are some tablets on the side. Take them.'

Rebecca leaned over and picked the tablets up, and popped one after the other in her mouth, sipping the water to wash them down.

'Where are we?' she enquired.

'Take a look.' Dr Hanlon said, gesturing with both hands to the windows behind the head of the bed. Rebecca swung her legs over the bed side. She looked down at the cotton pyjamas she was wearing. 'Pretty. Much nicer than the ones in hospital. Less of a draft up the back.' she said, standing and pulling the closed flowery curtains open.

'Newcastle?' she queried, taking in the wide stretch of water that was the River Tyne visible outside the window. The Millennium Bridge was directly in her line of sight, with the large span of the Tyne Bridge just to the right. Over the top of that bridge, the sun was slowly setting, painting the thin streaks of clouds that intermittently tram lined the deep blue sky a pale pink.

'It thought we were in Broadmoor, what are we doing here?' she questioned, turning from the window and taking in the contents on top of the dressing table.

'Well, that would be another little lie I told you. We were never in Broadmoor. We are here for you to recuperate.' Dr Hanlon answered.

Rebecca was looking down at something on the dresser top. There was a long kitchen knife lying there, beside which was a small, tightly wrapped piece of toilet paper. She picked the toilet paper up and unwrapped it, exposing the rusting screw contained within.

Holding it out in front of her, she addressed Dr Hanlon curtly. 'Did you take this out?'

'I did. Now, before you get all stressed, that is all I did. It's dangerous to have a rusty object like that inside you. I did bathe you too, and dress you, but I did not touch you in any way inappropriate while doing those things. I did what was necessary to make you comfortable. So, could you please throw the screw in the bin? If you are intent on killing yourself, please use the knife.'

Rebecca smiled at him with a bemused, lopsided half grin. She threw the screw into a waste bin under the dresser, then pulled out a seat next to it and sat down, still looking at Dr Hanlon. 'I take it you aren't really a Doctor working for Broadmoor?'

'I am a Doctor, but no, I don't work for Broadmoor.'

'So why am I here?' she asked, turning her legs under the dresser and looking at her reflection in the mirror. Dr Hanlon had cleaned and dressed all the cuts and abrasion on her face, arms and legs. While her skin was still ravaged with scars, it looked a lot less grotesque than when she had seen it for the first time earlier.

'To be guided along the path of redemption?' Dr Hanlon posed with mirth.

Rebecca opened and closed her mouth, watching the stub of her tongue moving. In the reflection, she caught sight of the back of her head from the mirror behind and saw the intermittent clumps of what hair was left. She picked up a brown short bob wig off one of the heads in front of her and positioned it on her head.

'I think I told you Doc, I am beyond redemption. No one can change what has happened. Not you, not the almighty, not anyone.' Rebecca answered, fiddling with the wig until it was in a position she was comfortable with.

'That supposes what you think you have done, is in fact what you actually did. I know it wasn't. It's time for you to face up to that truth.'

'What do you think?' she asked as she turned to him, running her fingers through the fine strands of the wig.

'You look beautiful.' Dr Hanlon answered, smiling.

'Your Irish charm won't work on me Doc, I look more human, but hardly beautiful.' she lowered her eyes to the bandages he had dressed her wrists in. She circled a thumb and forefinger of one hand over the bandage of the other and gently squeezed, a tinge of pain evident in her expression. She looked up at Dr Hanlon once more, picked up the knife and rested the sharp blade against the dressing on her wrist.

'I could demand that you tell me who you are.' she said, rocking the knife gently to and fro, with just enough pressure to splice threads on the bandage.

'You could, but psychological blackmail won't work on me. If you slit your wrists, I will just sit here and let you bleed to death, if that is really what you choose to do.' he said simply, crossing his legs as he responded.

Rebecca continued slicing the bandage, staring intently at him. 'I believe you would too.' she said, then put the knife down on the side.

'I won't interfere with your free will. I will just ensure that you know where that has been manipulated beyond the bounds of your freedom. After that, it's down to you.'

'Okay. Let's see if we can find the truth then.' she said, wearing a nervous smile.

'Tell me about the night Michael died?' asked Dr Hanlon.

Rebecca turned back to the mirror and started to look into the baskets of make up on the table, pulling out tubes, bottles and jars as she started to talk.

'It was New Year's Eve. I had been on shift that day and finished at about three in the afternoon. I didn't know if I was going to see Madame Evangeline that evening, I hadn't had any messages from her. I knew that I wasn't going to see Michael that night. He had already told me he was going to be out at a party. So at that point I was contemplating either a quiet night in, or a trip on my own to somewhere like Labia's. I got my first text message on the bus going home.'

''Tonight, I want you to fulfil one of my fantasies.' it read. The second I read it, my heart began to palpitate. Firstly because I was going to see her and secondly because it was going to be an evening of intrigue. What fantasy of hers would we be exploring, what games would we be playing to entice and excite. All the way home I willed another text message to arrive, to give me even an inkling of what was in store. Nothing. So I went home, tingling with anticipation, and started my ritual.'

Rebecca had opened a tub of foundation and was applying it to her face as she talked, covering up the visible scars, softening her harsh complexion.

'I bathed, a long luxurious soak where I relaxed into day dreams of what my night time reality might be. I stroked myself, letting the soft sensuousness of the bubbles and the warm rivulets of water caress my body. As I was drying, another text arrived. 'Wear your black leather cat suit, your thigh length patent boots and your cat mask. Nothing on at all under the suit. Red, long hair tonight and bring your whip.' I smiled, an enormous childish grin and did a little foot dance of excitement standing half wet and naked on the bathroom floor.'

'I continued my ritual, applying false nails to my fingers, painting them and my toes a deep, deep purple, impressing small diamond beads into the varnish. I would always get ready naked. I enjoying the freedom of the air flowing over my body as I moved around my bedroom, sitting down at my dressing table to apply my makeup.' she said, applying a thick black eye liner.

'The next text arrived and it took me by surprise. 'Look in your letterbox. Be there at eight. Go inside and mingle.' I went and looked as directed and found an invitation to a Masquerade Ball at a club called 'Delectable'. I had been there before. I was surprised because we didn't generally meet until much later. I finished my makeup, walking around the room for a minute or so to let it all dry. I had a full wall of mirrored wardrobes in my bedroom, one quarter with my normal clothes in and the rest with my evening wear. I opened the wardrobe and took out the outfit, placing it on the bed in the order I would put it on. I got dressed, enjoying the feel of the cold leather on my naked flesh as I did, putting on the cat mask, which sent a shiver of anticipation down my spine. That left only one more thing to put on, which I always left until last. I took the long red wig off a stand of a dozen different wigs, and put it on my head, positioning it and clipping it tight to my real hair. I was ready. I felt like a goddess as I took in my reflection in the mirrors.'

Rebecca took the top off a cherry red lipstick and painted her lips with it, padding and pouting into the mirror in front of her as she finished. She turned to Dr Hanlon and smiled. 'What do you think?' she asked. You could hardly see any of the scars or lesions on her face, the foundation virtually covering them all. There was a little blusher on her cheeks, giving life to her still thin face and her eyes were shadowed with a subtle pastel lime, accentuating her emerald eyes. Her lips looked voluptuous.

'Well, now I'm not being a charmer. You do look beautiful. The face of an Angel.'

Angels Bleed　　　　　　　　　　　　　　　　　　　Max Hardy

She smiled, observing her countenance in the mirror once more. 'A fallen Angel, perhaps.'

'I caught a taxi to the venue and arrived there a few minutes early. The streets outside the club were already busy with revellers, early shouts of 'Happy New Year' ringing out all around. It was a club I had been to before, just off the main street. I knocked on the nondescript door, which opened, and handed my invitation to the doorman who let me in. Surprisingly for so early in the evening the bar area was already full of people in their masquerade outfits. It wasn't a hard core sex club so there weren't people making out in front of everyone and the initial atmosphere was more cordial that carnal, with a string quartet in one corner, playing soft, gentle classical music. There was plenty of flesh on show and a lot of seductive stroking and caressing taking place however. I walked through the crowd, enjoying the subtle anonymity my mask bestowed, feeling sassy and sexy. As I passed people, I stroked my wandering hand over a buttock here, a bare shoulder there, staring in what I thought was a passionate way at the ladies I was caressing. They all smiled back at me, before returning to whatever conversations they were involved in. I arrived at the bar and ordered a wine, checking my phone as I was waiting. No more texts. So I mingled. I spent time with a beautiful woman in a red shimmering cape over a skin tight black latex dress, Little Red Riding Hood. Although this Red Riding Hood had her nipples poking through holes in the latex. She wanted me to whip her but settled for a conversation and a deep, passionate kiss on each of her nipples. She dropped a pill into my wine and smiled as I left her to mingle some more. As I sashayed through the ever growing crowd, my phone bleeped. A text. It said 'A Dominatrix with a whip should have a slave. By the band is a Gimp. He is your bitch. Treat him that way.' I looked through the crowd toward the string quartet and saw him, all in black, head to foot, standing motionless, head facing forward, not moving an inch. The only area of him that wasn't black was the hole around his crotch, exposing his flaccid penis and dangling bollocks. He was shaved bare down below. I approached him and, wrapping the end of my whip around the base of his penis, pulling it tight, I leant into his ear and whispered. 'Tonight you are mine, bitch, and you will do whatever the hell I want. Understood?' He nodded slowly. 'Good.' I said, grabbing his reins and tying them and the whip together, wrapping their ends around my hand. I tugged hard, pulling the bit in his mouth and his bits down below forcefully, causing him to stagger slightly as we walked back into the crowd, mingling. I had no idea. No idea whatsoever that my Gimp for the night was my son, Michael.'

6:30 pm

Sarah dived out of the car, stumbled and grazed her knees and palms on the harsh gravel driveway before she scrambled back to her feet and started to sprint towards the taped off area around the entrance to Featherstone Hall. Saul got out of the car just as fast but was a few seconds behind her as he came around from the far side of his SLK. Buglass was standing at the tape and started to raise a hand to stop Sarah from passing, but she simply sidestepped him and ran straight through the tape.

'Stop Sarah.' Saul shouted.

'You can't go through there!' Buglass shouted at the same time, turning and heading after Sarah too as Saul sped past him. She reached the entrance of the house and barged through the half open door into the corridor, the exertion of the sprint mingling with her blind panic to cause her to pause a moment against the door to get her bearings and decide on her next direction.

Her next direction was to head down the corridor towards a wheeled contraption with many metal protuberances sitting outside an open door with a light shining from the room beyond. She left the front door in another sprint a split second before Saul hit it in a similar fashion. He didn't stop, but headed off directly after her, only a few feet behind. She kicked the wheeled contraption out of the way as she ran into the doorframe at an angle, turning into the room, Saul mere centimetres behind her now. Once in the room, her arms started to reach out towards the crate that was in front of her, opening up to embrace it as she cried out, 'Jacob!'

Saul leapt the last small gap between them, grabbing her around the waist and pulling her to the left of the crate as he fell with her. Her right hand brushed against the wood, causing it to shudder slightly. They both landed on the floor with a heavy thud, Sarah immediately trying to escape Saul's tight embrace.

'Let go of me you fucking bastard.' she screamed, her legs and arms animatedly trying to dislodge Saul. 'We need to get him out!'

'You can't Sarah, there's a bomb in there. If you try and tamper with that crate it will go off and he will be dead. We will be dead. Just calm down.' Saul shouted above her screaming as she kicked animatedly. Buglass blundered into the room, a startled expression on his face as he took in the two of them struggling on the floor.

'Do you need any help Sir?' was all he could manage to say, weakly.

'We've got to get him out John, we've got to get him the hell out!' Sarah shouted, still fighting.

'We can't Sarah, not at the moment. Look at the screen.' he said, trying to lift her head in its direction. 'You can see him on the screen and if you stop your bloody squirming and screaming, you will hear his heartbeat.'

Sarah looked up to where he was directing her head and saw her son's face filling the right hand side of the screen. He looked serene: peacefully prone with no sign of any discomfort or injury. She heaved a heavy sigh, a harrowing sob escaping her lips. 'Oh Jacob, my baby, baby boy, Mummy is so, so sorry.' she cried, the rhythmic beep of the heart monitor invading the decreasing resonance of her screams.

Saul lifted her body slowly up from the floor as she stopped squirming, still holding her waist tight as he managed to get both of them onto their knees. Sarah's concentration was intent on Jacob's image as Saul raised her from her knees and walked them back a step, sitting down on the Chesterfield Sofa.

There was a clatter of footfall in the corridor outside followed a second later by Corporal Garry and then DCI Strange coming into view in the doorway. 'John, Sarah, are you OK?' Strange asked, concern in his voice as he strode across the room and sat down next to them, resting a hand on Sarah's arm as he did.

'We will be Sir. It's just the shock.' Saul answered, looking towards Strange, his face beaded with sweat and dirt, his expression pained and haunted. Sarah was still staring at the TV, her body quivering with emotion, her voice still frantic as she asked. 'Get him out. Can we get him out please? How can we get him out?'

Strange reached down and cocooned her shaking hands, edging himself closer as he addressed her softly. 'Sarah, we are doing everything in our power to get Jacob out of there as quickly as we can. I can see that you are distressed and I fully understand that you want to be close to him while he is in there. But it is not safe in this room. Being in this room is putting his and your life in danger. We have other monitors set up in our vehicles that will show you the same image of him. May we go there and talk?'

She didn't answer, just looked longingly up at the screen. Saul started to stand, raising Sarah as he did. 'Come on Sarah. DCI Strange will need to ask us some questions to help him get Jacob out of there. The quicker we answer them, the quicker they can get him out.'

Sarah didn't protest as Saul led her slowly out of the room. Her eyes stayed transfixed on Jacob's image until she was out of the door. The rhythmic beating of his heart monitor diminishing as they left the room and walked silently down the corridor, back into the dusk of early evening, the last strobing talons of a setting sun enlivening the flattened peaks of the Cheviot Hills behind Featherstone Hall.

'Is he here?' Saul asked pointedly as they walked across the gravel towards the MIU.

'Not yet John. We'll talk about that soon. We need to understand a little more about Rob Adams first.' Strange answered firmly.

As they approached the MIU, Jessica was standing at its far end, away from the entrance. Saul flashed her a pained smile, which she returned with an understanding nod. Sarah didn't notice her. She was still in shock as Saul led her up the steps to the MIU and then into the interview room. Strange followed them in.

'Could you get some coffees for us please?' Strange asked Buglass, as he softly shut the door to the room.

Saul led Sarah around the table and sat her down, pulling a chair out of the corner to sit next to her. Strange sat down opposite.

'I promise Sarah, I won't keep you long and you can go and sit in front of one of the monitors and see Jacob. There are just a few questions I need to ask you. Is that alright.'

Sarah looked towards Strange, her features heavy and drawn, eyes still confused and startled. 'I just want you to get him out Jerry. I don't care how, I just want you to get him out.'

'And we are doing everything we can to make that happen. Could you tell me the last time you were in contact with Rob Adams?'

'I talked to him this morning, I don't know what time exactly. About nine-ish. He sounded normal. He had been in hospital most of the night and was going into the office today.'

'You haven't had any texts or e-mails off him since then?'

'No, I haven't heard from him at all since then.'

'What time did he leave with Jacob last night?'

'It was about half five. He sent me a text when he dropped him off. Why would he do that?   Why would he take Jacob?   I don't understand.' Sarah said while chewing on the scraggy nail of an index finger, her voice raising in volume with the last question.

'That's what we are trying to find out Sarah.'   Strange answered, his tone gentle. 'Did you ever visit his offices?'

'No. He always came to the house or we would meet at the Children's Hospital.'

'Sir.' Saul interrupted. 'He seemed to be a genuine person. He was recommended to us by Jacob's paediatrician about six months ago. We had no reason to suspect that he had any plans to abduct Jacob. I think we need to understand if there is any link between him and Dr Ennis. I think we need to find that out pretty fast. We only have about five hours until midnight.' he finished firmly.

'Sarah. Could you please wait here a moment while I have a word with John.' Strange asked, rebuking Saul with a glare as he did. Sarah nodded. Strange motioned for Saul to follow him. They both left the room and Strange pulled the door closed behind him. Strange ushered Saul to the seats at the table where they both sat down.

'John, we need to find out as much as we can about this man. Sarah had a very close relationship with him and it's important that we explore that to see if there are any clues as to why he may have done this? I can't have you rushing the questioning John. Do I have to remind you that you are no longer on the case?'

'Do I have to remind you, Sir, that it is my son in that bloody crate?' Saul answered in a whispered snarl.

'No John, you don't, but your impatience is not going to help him.' Strange answered sharply, before his face softened and he continued. 'Look, I can't imagine how you are feeling and I am not going to even ask you to try and think professionally about this. We are doing everything we can. We have already found out that Rob Adams has not been seen at his offices for over a week. He definitely was not on locum duty last night. Checking back through his recent work history, we know that he and Dr Ennis's paths have crossed. So we know there is a link between them. We just need to discover what and why. Sarah may be able to help us with that. You were hardly ever there with him John. Sarah was, five days a week. There must be something he let slip during that time.'

'So they knew each other. Why isn't that bastard here yet Sir?' Saul said, his voice still resonating with a simmering fury as he stared at his superior.

'We are just trying to find him at the moment. Munro has been to the Institute. Ennis has left for the day. He is currently on his way to Ennis's house.'

'I doubt very much that he is going to be there, Sir. I think he has Rebecca Angus somewhere. That's where he'll be.'

'That's all well and good John, but we have no idea where that is and we have no evidence whatsoever to confirm that he even has her. So we will be going to his house as that is a location we know about.'

Saul banged a fist off the table, the sound reverberating around the contained space inside the MIU. 'We don't have time to wait on evidence for everything.' he shouted.

Strange grabbed Saul's fist, holding it fast on the table, stopping him banging it again. 'What would you suggest we do John?' Strange reprimanded. 'We have no idea where he is, but he may not be far away, he may be at home. We have no idea, even if he does have Rebecca, where he might be keeping her, but that might be at home too. So, apart from his home, where on earth would you like us to start?' Strange demanded.

Saul's features slowly morphed from livid to thoughtful as he absorbed Strange's rebuke. 'He may not be far away.' Saul repeated, deliberately, pondering upon each word. 'He may not be far away? Saul repeated again, this time faster, more a question. He pulled his hand free of Strange and stood up suddenly, his chair toppling over backwards.

'He's not far away at all, the bastards had her right under our noses all the time.' Saul scoffed, heading quickly for the door of the MIU.

'John, what do you mean?' Strange asked, following him as quickly as he could.

Saul was jogging now, over the open space between the MIU and his car, which he jumped into and slammed the door shut, revved the engine hard and spun away with a squeal of tyres and a plume of smoke in an instant.

'John!' Strange shouted ineffectually after him as he came to a halt in the billowing smoke. 'Shit.' he blasphemed, kicking his foot into the gravel. 'Where the hell is he going?'

7:05 pm

'What you need to understand about what happened next is that I had absolutely no idea it was Michael. You might think that is a cop out. After all, it was still somebody's son, even if I didn't think he was mine.' Rebecca said, looking at Dr Hanlon anxiously, circling the fingers of one hand around the bandages on the wrist of the other.

'I'm not here to judge you Rebecca. Regardless if it was Michael, or someone else, they were there that night because they wanted to be. It was a sex party. He was dressed in a Gimp suit with a bit in his mouth. Nothing screams, I want to be submissive, I want to be controlled any more than that get up.' Dr Hanlon answered reassuringly.

'It's just, this is going to be difficult. I know what I made him do. I know what I *forced* him to do.' Rebecca said, still concerned about what Dr Hanlon would think.

Dr Hanlon stood up, lifted his chair and limped toward her, placing his chair next to her and sitting down. He held her hands, stopping them from squeezing her wrists, and stroked the tops of them gently. 'Don't worry. If it gets difficult, we just slow down, or stop. We do something different. You get dressed, we grab a drink, whatever you want. This has to be in your own time. It has to be your story, your way. That is the important thing here, you trying to make some sense of what you call this nonsense.'

A nervous smile danced onto her face, then quickly pirouetted away as she took a deep breath and softly nodded. 'I got another text. It said, 'You are the Master. There are a couple by the Bar, Henry VIII and

Anne Boleyn. Introduce them to your slave and have them abuse him.' I quickly looked around the room, not for the couple, but to see where Madame Evangeline was. She had to be there. How would she know about the couple otherwise? I saw a glimpse of someone who looked like her, so headed in that direction, pulling my Gimps reins forcefully. I lost sight of whoever it was. I felt an anxious, exhilarating excitement at that point. I knew she was teasing me, playing with me and I just adored that, being the submissive myself. But I also knew what she was trying to do. She was trying to teach me to switch, to become the Dom. She had given me a Gimp to play with and she wanted to see what I would do.'

'What I did was take him over to the couple. I pulled the zip on the front of my cat suit down, all the way to my navel, exposing the swell of my breasts and my tight stomach. I strode up to them purposefully, my Gimps reigns over my shoulder. I tugged them hard as I approached. They smiled towards me as he let out a groan of pain. I was feeling a little euphoric with the power I felt, but my stomach was also churning with nervous, terrifying anticipation. 'Hello, I'm Madame Rebecca.' I started, my voice low and full of sultry timbre, my expression smouldering, or at least, I hoped it was smouldering. 'This is my Slave. I would love to watch you,' I directed to Anne, 'Tea bagging him, while you,' I looked at Henry, 'give him head.' I finished. They turned their heads to each other, a tacit glance exchanged before they both looked back at me, smiling. 'Certainly Madame, it would be our Royal pleasure.' And they did.'

'We walked over to one of the booths that was unoccupied and I watched as Anne lay down on her back and my Gimp sat astride her, dropping his bollocks into her mouth, which she then started to suck and chew voraciously. Henry thrust Anne's skirts up to her waist. She was naked underneath. He loosened his codpiece and threw it to one side, positioning himself between Anne's open thighs, his large erection entering her. As he started to rhythmically move in and out,

Henry lowered his head to where my Gimp's semi erect penis was and started sucking. I watched the three of them, one of my hands sneaking inside my open cat suit to caress a hard and throbbing nipple. I started to pull it harder and harder as the tempo of the threesome in front of me increased in rampant ferocity. My Gimp screamed as Anne started to convulse through the beginning of an orgasm, squeezing his balls tightly between her teeth. Henry was nearing that point too and his teeth were doing likewise around my Gimps shaft. The moaning got louder, the groaning got louder, the screams from my Gimp got louder as they all came within a few seconds of each other, both Henry and Anne biting down hard on my Gimp's privates.'

Rebecca fell silent and her body began to shake. She closed her eyes tightly and screwed up her face. Dr Hanlon squeezed her quivering hands. 'It's alright.' he said, comforting her. 'Whatever it is, just let it out. Just scream if you feel the need.'

She screamed, her eyes opening wide, her body almost convulsing. 'It was my son Doc, it was my bloody son and I enjoyed it. I watched two complete strangers have sex with him, inflicting excruciating pain on him, and I enjoyed it. That is not right, Doc. That is so many kinds of wrong.' she started to sob as her chest wracked, tears streaming down her newly applied makeup. Dr Hanlon leant over and wrapped his arms around her, pulling her tightly into his chest. 'You didn't know who he was. Just keep that thought in your head. Just keep reminding yourself of that. You didn't know who he was.' he said, consoling her.

She sobbed into his chest, the words muffled by his cardigan. 'But I do now, and I don't want to live with that knowledge in my head.' She cried for a while longer, Dr Hanlon comforting her with tender strokes up and down her back, letting the emotion flow, then slowly ebb from her.

When her sobs had all but subsided and only the most imperceptible of shaking could be felt, he slowly released his embrace and sat back slightly, allowing her to sit up and look at him. Makeup was now smeared over her face, exposing the scarring below the surface.

'Rebecca. There is something important that you need to appreciate. You can keep on blaming yourself. You can carry the guilt of knowing it was your son, to your grave if you must, but what you have to appreciate is that he was there, that night, because he wanted to be. You may not have known it was him, but you can be damn well sure he knew it was you. What you need to try and get into your head, to help you understand, is why.'

'Will that really make any difference? It will never change what happened. I will still have killed him, I will still have fucked him and I will still have allowed him to be a sexual plaything.'

'That's why we are here.' he smiled affectionately, raising a hand and rubbing some mascara away from her eye. 'To see if it does make a difference. I think it will. Once you know everything.' He paused, winking at her. 'Now, stop changing the subject and tell me what happened next?'

She let out a little stuttering anxious giggle and pushed a hand playfully into his chest. 'Point taken.' she said, taking a tissue from the top of the dresser and rubbing the tearstained makeup from her face. She turned back to the mirror and, grabbing some cotton wool balls, started to take all the makeup off.

'What happened next was much the same for the next few hours. Me putting my Gimp into more and more sexually provocative predicaments. For a while I enjoyed watching, enjoyed drinking, enjoyed the odd pill, but as time passed, I started to become anxious. Madame Evangeline always called me between ten and half past. She didn't that night. I had a text at ten fifteen telling me to enjoy the power and that she would call later. I kept looking around the room to see if I could see her. All I felt was disappointment when I didn't. I was starting to get a little disconsolate as the minutes passed. I thought I would be spending New Year's Eve with my lover. It was eleven thirty and I still hadn't heard from her. I hadn't had a text for over an hour.'

'I was thinking of leaving, letting my Gimp loose to his own devices when eventually my little white phone did ring. I answered it. 'What you need to learn, as a Master, is never to show any weakness.' she said to me, before I could speak. 'You might be a gibbering wreck inside, but never let it manifest itself in your actions. Never let your impatience bubble over. It's time to leave now.' she instructed. I told my gimp to put his trunks on and we headed for the exit. Out in the street I hailed a taxi, and we climbed in as Madame Evangeline gave me instructions of where to go next. 'Be patient lover. You will have me soon.' she finished. I laughed. My emotions had gone from disconsolate to jubilant in a moment, my smile beguiled and beaming, having heard from her, knowing she knew me so well. 'Hopefully very soon.' I answered as she hung up.'

'We took the taxi to Settle Avenue, not far from my flat, and got out on the main street as instructed. We were both a little tipsy at that point as we staggered down the street toward my flat. At the end of the row of shops, we turned left and there, as she said, was a black limousine. A tall, very handsome chauffeur got out and opened the door for us, doffing his cap politely as we entered. Once in, the driver headed off out of Leith, towards Portobello and the A1. I was watching out of the window, waiting to see her along the way, waiting anxiously to pick her up and enjoy her. There were a lot of cars on the road, it being New Year, and it seemed every traffic light was red, so it took a while to get out onto the main road. I spent midnight in the limousine, trying to call Michael to wish him a Happy New Year. It just went to voicemail. So I had a one way conversation with my Gimp instead. He just sat staunchly, in silence, hopefully listening to my ramblings.'

'As we departed the suburbs, the driver pulled into a layby just off the main road. Madame Evangeline jumped into the limousine and in a second we sped off again, the driver blackening the windows so we couldn't see out. She sat on the floor between my legs and kissed me with a fierce passion, biting my lip as she broke the kiss. 'Your patience will be rewarded. Perhaps not in heaven, but it will be rewarded.' she said, smiling lewdly at me then looking toward my gimp. 'Have you enjoyed him?' she asked, stroking an arm down his firm thigh, devouring the toned body beneath his skin tight outfit with her eyes. 'I have enjoyed watching him.' I answered. She laughed at that and turned her attention back toward me. 'Before the night is out, you will have enjoyed more than watching him. Seven sins.' she said. 'Seven for you, seven for me. He is ours and we will abuse him as we please. One rule only. On your sin, I do exactly what you want, on my sin, you do exactly what I please. No compromise. If you don't agree, we just leave it now.' she teased, tantalisingly, stroking a hand down my thigh as she stroked the thigh of my Gimp.'

''Oh, I agree.' I answered without hesitation, my heart beating with the thrill of the game, of the unknown. 'Then you begin. What is your desire, how can I appease your mortal sin?' she asked theatrically, throwing an arm into the air for effect. 'For the next thirty minutes, I just want you both to kiss me, everywhere. Every last centimetre of my body.' I ordered, unzipping my cat suit all the way and slinking onto the floor of the limousine to join her, my Gimp following as Madame Evangeline smiled and ran a sultry tongue over her cherry red lips, removing my cat suit as she started to kiss.'

'It was exquisite, it was delicate and it was delectable, every last part of my skin tingling under the tender caress of their kisses impressed upon my willing, eager flesh. I didn't open my eyes at all in that time, the anticipation of not knowing the destination of their next kiss, utter bliss. Waves of elation lapped over me as they explored my most intimate places, my body rising to their touch, yearning for fulfilment, never quite reaching that point of total ecstasy as they gently touched and teased. The kissing stopped and before I could open my eyes, I felt something being placed over them. 'Now it's my sin.' said Madame Evangeline, tightening and tying the blindfold behind my head. 'Stretch your arms out and reach for the door handles.' she ordered, which I did. She tied my hands to them. 'Now spread your legs.' I obliged and she then tied my feet to the bottom seat, wide apart. I couldn't see a thing and had no way of protecting myself. I was completely vulnerable.'

'I heard something click open and a rustling of *things*. Something started to buzz. A second later I felt a jolt of exquisite pain as something clamped onto my nipples simultaneously, biting into the flesh. There was a pronounced swish and I let out a small yelp as a whip ripped across my stomach. The buzzing got louder, its source getting closer to my head, suddenly a firm vibration resonated on my lips, forcing them apart, making me take the vibrator in my mouth. The whipping continued. Someone started tugging at the strap that tied the nipple clamps together, causing them to dig in deeper, to increase the pain. Then it all stopped. The clamps were removed, the vibrator taken away and the whipping abated. There was silence. Nothing moved. Then what felt like a feather circled over my red raw nipples and along the weals left by the whip, enticing the aggravated skin, before I screamed again as the sudden introduction of ice on my stomach tensed my whole body in an instant. Then that stopped, and the pain started again. That cycle went on for another half hour, pain, then titillation, then pain, the vibrator exploring every orifice in my body. The car came to a halt as the last vestige of ice melted and dripped from my simmering skin. I felt the bindings on my hands and feet loosen and stretched my body to get the circulation in my limbs moving again. I reached up to take the blindfold off but a hand stopped me. 'Not yet.' Madame Evangeline said as she led me from the car, still naked, into the chilly night air. The cold clung to my warm body, raising goose bumps, stimulating my already erect nipples. I was led into a building, down what felt like a corridor, the darkness perceptible, even behind my blindfold, then into a room where I could feel warmth, the subtle flickering of light and the unmistakable odour of vanilla. I heard a door shut behind me and then my blindfold was removed. We were in a room with a spectacularly gothic fire place, a roaring fire in the grate, candles dancing suggestively in each corner, the whole ambiance warm and inviting.'

Rebecca paused and sighed deeply, a haunted expression inveigling its way onto her face. She looked directly at Dr Hanlon. 'Looking back, I realise now what she was doing. She was dressed the same as me. Made up the same as me. We could have been twin sisters. We were even trading sins. Challenging. She was moulding me, shaping me, grooming me even, to be as domineering, as masterful as she was. I know it was sex, but in my mind I wanted sensuality. I wanted to make love to my lover. That's where my sins took us. Madame Evangeline, well, she had a different agenda. I can see that now. Every one of her sins, led me to be more and more intimate with my Gimp and less involved with her. She was leading me on a journey to lose my virginity.'

Dr Hanlon's brow furrowed and he said. 'Really?'

'Not necessarily in the anatomical sense. I'm sure my hymen was broken years ago, but I had never had a man inside me, until that night. We traded sins for the next few hours, making love or having sex all over the room, in every position, every location, with every unimaginable depravation sprinkled on top during her sins. Then we came to her last. Up to that point while I had carried out many sexual acts on my Gimp, he hadn't been inside me. 'Now, my darling, this is my ultimate fantasy.' Madame Evangeline said, leading me to the sheepskin rugs in front of the fire and lying me on my back. She was naked too, and sat astride me for a few moments, lettings her body, her dangling breasts course along the length of my skin, gently touching, tingling. She did that all the way to my toes, then stepped to one side and led my Gimp between my open thighs.'

Rebecca started to cry, softly as she spoke, silent tears biting a stream of decimation on her scar kissed cheeks. 'He was quivering, I could tell, and I was too, nervous and excited all in one breath. He entered me and gently leant over my body, resting hands on the floor either side of my chest, his suit sensually rubbing up against my stomach as he started to gently move in and out. Madame Evangeline straddled both of us and knelt down so that her head was visible to me by the side of his. She looked down on me, her eyes alive with desire, gorging upon the sexual platter she had created. 'Tell me how it feels, taking a man for the first time.' she asked with a simmering urgency. My gimps movements were getting faster and I could feel him swelling inside me, feel the girth of him starting to throb. It was euphoric, feeling my walls start to pulse in time, feeling the tip of his erection tickling my most sensitive spot inside, feeling the base of his penis caressing my exposed clitoris. 'Heavenly.' I said through short, surging pants, my own body starting to course with the tingling of orgasm. She grinned wickedly.'

Rebecca was sobbing uncontrollably, her body shaking ferociously, Dr Hanlon holding her tight around the waist, trying to stop her hands riving the bandage off her wrists. Pain contorted her features as she forced herself to speak, to relive the memories.

''Tell me how it feels,' she started, ripping the bit out of my gimps mouth and grabbing the edge of the mask on his neck, slowly starting to pull it back. He was pumping harder now and I could feel him start to tense, his erection throbbing deep inside me. I could feel my orgasm rising too, forcing me back into the floor, forcing my head back and forcing my eyes closed with the intensity.'

She started to kick and writhe under Dr Hanlon's firm grip, head bucking, trying to bang into his, her arms now flailing, her voice rising in anguished intensity as she started to spit the words out.

"To have this man,' she continued, slowly pulling the mask back off his face. I forced my eyes open as she said that, taking in the stubbled chin and contorted mouth and cheeks of my Gimp just as he came, just as his head shot back and he started to jerk inside me. I came a second later, the intensity thrusting me back even further into the soft rugs as I screamed in pleasure.'

She screamed, an ear splitting raucous roar of desolation, her whole body tensing and stiffening, quivering with the release of grief before the tension left her suddenly and she slumped limply back into Dr Hanlon's arms, crying as she continued.

'Fuck you!' she finished, pulling the last bit of the mask off his head and throwing it to one side. I looked up in an orgasmic daze, spent, firstly into Madame Evangeline's eyes. They were on fire, intense, the reflection of the fires flames a maelstrom in her pupils as she nuzzled her scarlet cheek into my Gimps hair. I looked down from her face into his. To his satisfied, sweating, euphoric smile beaming down at me. The smile of my son.'

Rebecca was sobbing, her tears uncontrollable, her body softly shaking in Dr Hanlon's embrace, her fingers scratching at the riven bandages on her wrists. 'He was smiling Doc, he was smiling. He knew it was me and he was smiling!' she whimpered, staring at him incredulously. 'It took a second or two for my mind to register who it was, but when it did, shock kicked in straight away and I screamed at him. 'Michael, what the hell are you doing?' I started to scramble back from him, trying to get as far away as I could. His expression turned confused instantly and he started to stand, looking to Madame Evangeline who was doing likewise. 'I don't understand.' he said to her. 'You said she wanted this too.' he questioned, imploringly. Madame Evangeline just smiled, casting her sultry satiated façade between the two of us. I stood up quickly, the sudden change of altitude just after an orgasm making me feel dizzy, the shock of seeing Michael making me nauseous. Adrenaline was still coursing through me and I was livid. I glared at him and, rushing forward, pushed him in the chest shouting 'That was wrong Michael, I am your mother, how could you!' He stumbled backwards, one of his feet catching on Madame Evangeline's leg, making him topple into the side of the fireplace, banging his head on it as he fell to the floor, his face contorted in the agony of his realisation.'

Rebecca cuddled in to Dr Hanlon's chest, sinking her head into the comforting cardigan, wrapping an arm around his waist, seeking sanctuary as she softly spoke.

'That was the second last thing I saw, his absolute grief, his utter despondency. The last, well, that was Madame Evangeline, smiling at me, whispering, 'Now, you truly are a Dominatrix!' just as I fainted.'

7:38 pm

'He's not at home Sir.' relayed DI Munro over the conference phone on the table in the MIU.

'Shit.' Strange exclaimed, rubbing a hand over his chin. 'Mick, can you say there for now please. Forensics have just informed us that Ennis's fingerprints were all over the snake warehouse. We need to get a warrant to search his place.'

Strange turned to the plasma screens. 'Sir,' he started, directed to the Chief Superintendent. 'Could you sort out a warrant quickly for a search of Dr Ennis's property please? Justification is forensic evidence linking him to a known crime.' Strange asked, pacing the short distance between the table and the whiteboards.

'I'll do that immediately Jerry. Should be with you in half an hour.'

'Thank you Sir. Mick, do you have any idea where else Dr Ennis may be in the meantime. Did the Institute give you any ideas? Is he a member of a Gym, of a Gentlemen's club, anything like that?' queried Strange, resting his palms on the table and leaning into the phone.

'No Sir, no indications of anything like that. We can do some door to door here while we are waiting and see if any of his neighbours may know his whereabouts.'

'Good idea Mick. Keep in touch with anything at all you find out and as soon as you get the warrant through, get in there straight away.'

'No problem Sir.' Munro answered, then hung up.

'Right, Steven, how are you coming along with those connections? Have you made any progress with changing the time of the heartbeat at all?' Strange asked.

Reynolds turned in his chair and faced Strange, a look of nervous excitement visible. 'We might just have done it Sir. It looks like the bot uses a parameter string for the time. We have simulated sending it a different time, just waiting to see if that changes on the connection back to here.' he said. His stutter was gone, supressed as he was embroiled in his passion. He turned back to his monitors and opened up an application on his computer. 'Yes!' he shouted, bum leaving his seat as his body shot up triumphantly.

'Yes what Steven?' Strange asked, coming up and sitting down beside him.

'We've changed the time on that connection. The heartbeat is now saying 16:00 hours. It means if we can decrypt all of the other heartbeat connections, we have a way of changing what time the bomb explodes. It doesn't mean we can stop it at the moment, but at least we can keep extending the time until we can figure out how to stop it.'

'Excellent work Steven. Now what help do you need to decrypt the remainder of the heartbeat connections and how long do you think it will take?'

'They are all using 256 bit triple DES encryption algorithms which take about thirty minutes to decrypt. Given there are more than three thousand of them and we only have around four hours.' he paused, the mental calculation evident on his features as his lips counted silently. 'I'm going to need about fifty computers running flat out in that four hours to decrypt them all.'

'Right, give Tech at HQ a call and get in anyone you need. We've got all the computers here too. Steven,' Strange reinforced, whatever you need, just ask. If you get any resistance just let me know.'

'I'm on it Sir.' he said with obvious relish, picking up the phone straight away.'

'Great news.' Strange said to the room, positively, before he turned to the whiteboard and checked his notes.

'Phyllis, are there any updates on the checks at Pison and with the Old Waverley Hotel?'

'Yes Sir. With regard to the Hotel, they have confirmed that both Mrs Seymour and DI Saul stayed there. They have CCTV of the Room Service Waiter attending the room at the time stated and also of them both entering the room earlier in the evening and leaving the room the following morning. No record of them leaving in between.'

'Okay.' Strange said, mulling the information over in his head as he went to the whiteboard and updated the notes. 'In one way that is good, in another, not so good. How about the limousine and the chauffeur?'

'That's who DI Saxon is talking to at the minute Sir. We should hear back from her soon.'

The door to the interview room opened and Sarah popped her head around, the main room suddenly falling silent.

'Is everything alright Sarah?' asked Strange, walking around the table towards her.

'Everything is fine Jerry. Thanks for setting up the monitor in there.' Sarah answered as he came up beside her. 'I would like to go and talk to Jessica Seymour, if you don't mind.'

Strange looked surprised, putting his hands into his pockets and shooting her a quizzical stare. 'Is that wise? She is the woman your husband is having an affair with, she is the woman who is implicated in Michael Angus's murder so therefore she is the woman who may be involved in the abduction of your son.' Strange asked bluntly.

'I know Jerry, and trust me, I don't want to fight with her. She may be all of those things, but she is also someone John loves, may not be involved with Michael's death at all and therefore may not be involved in Jacob's abduction. I know how alone I feel right now. I can imagine she is feeling the same. I just want to talk, that's all.' Sarah answered, gently stroking the top of Strange's arm.

He observed her features for a few moments, looking for any sign of anger, any sign of resentment in her countenance. He saw none. 'Alright, I am trusting you. Please don't let yourself down.' Strange said, returning her affectionate smile.

'I won't Jerry. Can I grab a coffee for us?'

'Yes, help yourself.' he answered, moving back to the whiteboard. 'Right, where are we.' he said, looking at the board.

Sarah filled two cups from the percolator and left the MIU, the conversations within fading as she started to walk around to the back where the Visitor Unit was located. The smaller unit came into view as she rounded the corner, Jessica sanding at the door looking out towards the house. Her relaxed stance tightened as she saw Sarah approach and she stepped out of the Unit towards her.

'I haven't come to fight.' Sarah said as she got closer. 'I've come with coffee.' she continued, proffering the cup to Jessica, a tired smile on her face. 'Can we talk?' she finished.

'Would you like to sit down?' asked Jessica, standing back and motioning in the direction of the seats within the unit.

'To be honest, I wouldn't mind a walk in the fresh air. I've been stuck in the interview room for the past hour crying my eyes out.' she answered.

Jessica smiled back at her and took a step to be by her side, both of them heading out over the grass at a slow pace.

'I'm sorry.' Sarah said.

Jessica looked at her, nearly stopping in her stride, taken aback. 'What have you got to be sorry about? It should be me who is sorry.' Jessica answered.

'You have nothing to be sorry for. John does. He should have told me about the two of you a long time ago. If he had, you would have been together much more in the past two years. No, I'm sorry for having the two of you followed. I shouldn't have done that, it was wrong.' Sarah said, running the little finger with the remaining false nail around the rim of her coffee cup. She was clutching the taggie entwined in her fingers tight in the palm of the hand holding her cup.

'I would say you had good cause. Your husband has been cheating on you. I have been totally complicit in that. You have every right to be angry with me.' Jessica answered, mimicking Sarah's actions on her coffee cup, walking in tandem with her steps.

Sarah smiled and looked sideways at her, taking in her profile. 'I can see why he likes you. You are very beautiful. I sat outside your office this morning in the café opposite, thinking about what I would say to you when I saw you. I was angry then. Very angry. But angry at John. My friend Allie reminded me of something. I had an affair when I was younger. She asked me, did John jump, or was he pushed. I pushed him.'

Jessica looked back towards her, a slightly awkward expression on her features as she sought the right words to say. 'I know you have more insight into John than I do, but I find he can keep things to himself and not open up.'

Sarah let out a little laugh. 'Jessica, I would really like to say I do have more insight into him after the time we have spent together, but I don't think I do. We shared experiences, we had wonderful times, we had horrendous times and I have memories, good and bad, that I will cherish forever, but I never really knew John. He never let me in and I never let him in. Not all the way. I hope the two of you are different, I really do because he is a good, good man. Has he told you anything about his childhood? Anything other than he doesn't want to talk about it.' Sarah asked.

Jessica didn't answer for a moment, deliberation painted onto her face. Eventually she simply said. 'Yes.'

Sarah stopped and caught her breath as a sudden sob rose in her throat, her eyes welling up. 'Good, that's good.' she mumbled, rubbing her face with her free hand, quickly wiping the tears away as she started to walk again.

They walked in silence for a while, turning around and heading back towards the units, sipping their coffee. Eventually Sarah spoke again.

'Are you Madame Evangeline?' she asked, simply.

'Do you know, you are the first person to ask me that directly. There have been lots of questions about where I was and what I was doing, but not that one. Everyone must be thinking it. No. I'm not.' she answered, pausing, and then continued. 'In certain ways I wish I was. I can see a lot of suffering happening, with you, with John, with Jacob. I've been watching that building since I arrived here this afternoon and that's what I have been thinking. I could end this. I could say, yes, I am Madame Evangeline. Take me into the room and I will admit to killing Michal Angus and all this will end.'

'So why don't you? No, sorry, that's not fair, that's me being selfish. It's my son in there and I will do anything to get him out but it is not fair to even ask you to consider that. God knows what's going to happen to the person who does go in there. Look what they have done to an innocent child.'

'Don't be sorry. This isn't just down to you and it's not selfish. You are a mother, and that's the way a mother should feel.' A distant emptiness crossed her features as she said the last words, her eyes lost in that space for a moment before she continued. 'Why don't I? They have enough evidence to suggest I was involved, so why don't I? I don't really know Jacob. But I know John. I love John and Jacob is his son. I might not be a mother, I might not be his mother, but I know how a mother feels.' Jessica finished the sentence with a firm resolve resounding through her voice, emboldening her demeanour.

'I think I have sat around feeling like a helpless victim for long enough today. If there is something I can do to help Jacob, then that's exactly what I am going to do. I am going into that room to tell whoever the hell is listening that I am Madame Evangeline and that I killed Michael Angus.'

8:05 pm

Saul kicked the boarded up door with venom, planks splintering and bursting inwards through the door frame, his foot following. He looked around the derelict, floodlit area at the base of the tower entrance to the old Lunatic Asylum, opposite the Fielding Institute, to see if anyone had heard the noise. Only the augmenting breeze, becoming a wind, ruffling the leafless gnarled branches of surrounding trees came to his ears. He ducked and entered the building, torch in hand.

The torchlight picked out broken windows, flaking paintwork, rubbish littering the floor as its narrow beam circled the entrance hallway. There was an overwhelming odour of dampness, decay and urine mingled together, almost palpable in its alkaline intensity. Corridors headed off to the left and to the right, with an entrance to what looked like a main hall in front of him. Saul darted the torch beam around the floor, looking for signs of footprints or a disturbance in the dust and dirt. Off to the left some of the rubbish looked to have been kicked to one side. He headed off in that direction.

Tiny slivers of light from the Security Lamps on the tower squeezed through slits in the boarded up windows, their beams alive with dancing dust as he walked down the corridor, his torch exposing glimpses of abandoned offices to his right. He let the beam investigate each room as he passed, searching out any sign of occupancy before moving onto the next. Tiles gave way to ripped up parquet flooring as he went further into the hospital, the torch beam picking out some scuffed dirt heading off to an opening on the right. In the opening was a door hanging off its hinges leading to a descending stairwell. It was in complete darkness. He shone the torch onto the steps just as a large rat scurried down them. He stepped through the broken door and headed down the circular stairs, the darkness engulfing him from behind as he moved further away from the rivulets of lights coming through the upstairs windows. The sound of the chattering trees also abated, leaving him surrounded by silent nothingness, only the iris of the torch shedding light into his world. The circular beam charted his course all the way down the stairs into another corridor which led away to his left. In the distance, a gentle light oozed from a door that was slightly ajar. He cautiously walked towards it, torch beam on the ground to ensure he didn't trip over anything and make a sound. He stared at the floor, noticing tram marks in the dust and the odd footprint. He let the beam scan from left to right, noticing closed iron cell doors on either side. Half way towards the light, he saw a normal door on his right, closed, with a lot of scuff marks and footprints on the floor outside. He placed an ear up against it and listened for a second. He could hear a faint thrum. He continued down the corridor, the atmosphere close, cold and cloying, the odour even more intense, now flowered with the unmistakable aroma of faeces.

Saul arrived at the slightly open Cell door and switched his torch off, his eyes scanning the gap, looking and listening for signs of life within. His movements were alert as he gently pushed the door, taking in a wider area, seeing the faded, filthy padded walls. The room was silent. He pushed further, an empty wooden chair coming into view. It was bolted to the floor and unfastened head, arm, leg and chest restraints hung loose over its frame. A single light shone from a recessed lamp high in the padded ceiling above it. He forced the door open suddenly, pushing it back against the wall in the room, positioning himself ready for an attack coming from behind it. There was no one there.

He walked up to the chair and noticed a red tinge to the edge of the restraints. He ran a finger along one of the wrist straps, looking at the residue imparted, then lifted the finger to his tongue and tasted it. It was blood. He took in the rest of the room, his attention caught by the small camera lens on the wall the chair was facing. His gaze moved from the camera, to the chair, to his blood stained finger, his countenance contemplative. He gave the cell one last scan, then walked quietly back down the corridor, to the door with the scuff marks outside. He tentatively held the circular door knob and twisted it slowly. It squeaked slightly and he grimaced at the sound, stopping and listening intently for any noise within the room. There was just the gentle thrum from inside. He turned the knob further until it clicked open, then carefully started to push. Within the darkness he could just make out tiny green flashes of light bouncing off the wall to the left of the door. He tensed once again, readying himself, as he forced the door completely open, stepping into the room quickly, prepared for an assault. None came. He put his flashlight on and highlighted the source of the green lights. They were LED's on the front of monitors on a desk to his right. He reached for the wall just inside the door to his left and, finding a light switch, flicked it on.

Apart from the desk, which was loaded with monitors, the only other thing in the drab, lifeless room was a chair in front of the desk. He sat down in it, eyes scanning the desk surface as he switched on the bank of monitors in front of him. There was a keyboard and mouse on the surface and next to them, an old white mobile phone. He took a handkerchief out of his inside pocket and gingerly picked the phone up, putting as little pressure as possible on the keypad as he opened the menu and went to the last call list. The last calls were dated 1st January 2013 at 12:03 am and 31st December 2011 at 11:35 pm. The number was withheld on both calls. He then switched to the text message screen and opened the last message. It simply said, 'Enjoy the power, I will see you soon. E x'. There was no phone number against the text. He wrapped in in the handkerchief and slid it into his inside jacket pocket, looking up to screens in front of him.

His attention was immediately drawn to a screen on his left which displayed an image of the drawing room in Featherstone Hall. He was drawn to it because there was someone in the room. It was Jessica. She was walking toward the crate and looking up at the plasma TV, at Jacob's serene face. Saul looked surprised and concerned, searching out a volume control. He found one and turned the volume up.

'What the hell are you doing Jess?' he said to himself as he leaned in closer, raising a hand to the screen and stroking a finger down the pixels of her body.

'Hello. Is anyone listening?' he heard Jessica ask, watching as she saw her own image on the Plasma TV and turn around to face the direction of the camera. She walked slowly towards the location of the camera, her body getting larger, until eventually, her whole head filled the screen in front of Saul.

'If you can hear me, me name is Jessica Seymour.' she started, her demeanour determined, her tone controlled with a commanding gravitas. 'I own Featherstone Hall. I also own the Limousine that brought Rebecca and Michael Angus to this location on the night of his murder. I was in Edinburgh on the 31st December 2011 and the 1st January 2012 at the same time they were at a Masquerade Ball. I came back here with them, and I killed Michael Angus.' she finished forcefully, glaring into the camera and holding her determined stare as she waited for a response.

'Jess, don't do this. You weren't there, you were with me.' Saul whispered under his breath, his features concerned as he stroked her cheek. He saw her turn to the left quickly, looking at someone then shaking her head before turning back to the screen.

'I am Madame Evangeline.' she stated, her countenance challenging anyone who was watching to disagree.

'Oh Jess, what a brave, selfless, bloody stupid thing to do.' Saul said, listening intently, as was Jessica, for any reply. Only the constant beep of the heart monitor invaded the silence of anticipation. He watched her face carefully, seeing the disappointment enter her eyes as no reply to her admission was forthcoming. She turned from the camera and he watched her figure shrink as she got further away and left the room. Only the beep, beep, beep remained.

He looked at the next screen. The image was of the cell he had just been in, the camera focused on the empty chair. There was a video control bar underneath the image. Saul moved the mouse and clicked the pointer on the Rewind Button. For a while the image stayed the same, just an empty chair with the time on a small digital clock in the top left hand corner of the screen continually decreasing. It went all the way back to 10:45 am before he saw any activity in the cell. It was in reverse, so what he saw was a wheelchair being pulled backward into the room and then someone lift a woman out of it and sit them in the wooden chair. He hit the pause button as the man doing the lifting turned back towards the wheelchair, his face captured by the camera.

Saul pushed himself back in the seat, clenching his fists in quiet victory as he took in the faces on the screen. The fake Dr Hanlon and the sleeping form of Rebecca Angus.

8:45 pm

Rebecca came back into the bedroom, her wig lopsided and her face ghost white and gaunt. She had washed all the makeup away, exposing her naked suffering once more. She smiled at Dr Hanlon as she sat back down, running an affectionate hand down his arm as she did.

'Why are there always carrots in your vomit?' she asked, passing Dr Hanlon a bemused, sheepish smile.

'They aren't carrots, they are sloughed off bits of epithelium, from your stomach lining. They usually get worn down by toxins or pathogens in your stomach. Probably due to all the medication you have been taking. Do you feel better, getting it all out?' he asked, leaning over and straightening her wig.

'Do you mean the vomit, or the memories?' she answered with a teasing smile before her face turned serious and reflective. 'I feel empty. I feel numb. I have buried that evening deep inside for so long. So deep that I had genuinely forgotten what happened. Or rather, had built a web of half-truths and suppositions, creating my own purgatory, inflicting my own guilt induced punishment. It's been cathartic. It doesn't change some of the facts. I still willingly had sex with my own son.'

'Willingly yes, knowingly no. You didn't know it was him. I can appreciate why you have felt so distraught about all of this. I can understand why you don't want to live in a world where these things have happened. Things that you think you have caused. But what I heard you say, quite clearly, was that Michael turned to Madame

Evangeline and stated 'You said she wanted this too.' What does that tell you Rebecca? What does that tell you about that night?'

'It makes me wonder why? Why did he think that? It still doesn't change the fact he is dead. It still doesn't change the fact that I ripped his heart out and ate it!' she answered, agitation entering her tone.

'One thing at a time Rebecca.' Dr Hanlon stated firmly, laying a hand over her wrists where she was starting to rub. 'It will never change the fact he is dead and any mother should feel grief because of that. You should not feel grief or remorse or guilt about killing him. That didn't happen. He fell when you pushed him away from you. He tripped over Madame Evangeline's leg and banged his head. That is what killed him. What happened in your flat, well, that's a different story and we will get to it, soon.' he finished as his trouser pocket started to vibrate. He took out a phone and quickly checked it, a slight look of concern crossing his countenance before his normally calm demeanour returned.

'I have to leave you for a while, but there is something I want you to watch, something that may help you understand why Michael thought the way he did. Let's go into the living room.' Dr Hanlon said.

He stood from the bed and offered his hand out for her to hold, then led her emaciated, slightly quivering frame into the living area, towards the sofa. The living space was open plan, a kitchen/diner to the right of the bedroom door they came out of. Next to this door was another, which was closed and padlocked. The living room itself was oak floored, with a large patterned rug underneath a beige fabric sofa, a coffee table in front of it. In one corner beyond this was a TV on a stand. Dr Hanlon sat Rebecca down on the sofa.

'On the table is a DVD.' he said, resting a hand on top of the DVD case. 'I want you to watch it in your own time. There is food and drink in the fridge. Please help yourself. There are clothes in the wardrobe in your bedroom. Think about getting dressed. Everything here is at your disposal. Treat it as your own. The only thing I ask is that you don't try and go into the second bedroom, which is locked. I will be locking the front door when I leave too and you will not be able to get out. Is that clear?' he asked.

'Do you trust me enough to leave me on my own?' she asked, seriously. 'I'm not sure I trust myself.'

Dr Hanlon smiled at her and said reassuringly, 'I trust you implicitly. I know you want to understand why this happened. The DVD will help and when I get back, and I will be coming back very soon, we will talk about what happened in your flat.'

'Alright, please don't be too long.' she answered timidly, reaching over and picking the DVD up from the table, turning it inquisitively in her hands. Dr Hanlon stood, leant over and kissed her on the brow and then limped towards the front door of the apartment.

'I won't be too long.' he said, smiling towards her before he turned, opened the door and left.

She heard the lock being set from the outside. She stood up, DVD in hand and walked to the front door, wiggled the handle and then tried to turn the Yale lock. It didn't budge. She then walked across the room and picked up the padlock on the second bedroom door and rattled that. It was thick and solid. She put her ear up against the door. There was no sound. She walked back towards the TV unit, opening the DVD case as she went, and slotted the silver disk into the DVD player. She switched the TV on and, grabbing the remote control, went back and sat down on the sofa and pressed the 'Play' button.

'Hi Mum!' the smiling animated face of Michael shouted from the screen, filling it as he came closer to the camera, adjusting the focus.

Rebecca yelped and jumped straight back off the sofa, throwing herself across the floor on her knees and stopping right in front of the screen. Her hands shot up and started to touch Michael's enlarged features as he adjusted the camera. Rebecca's eyes were wide open with wonderment, tears trickling from her eyes once more as, her lips quivering, she mumbled, 'Oh god, my baby boy, my baby boy!'

Michael backed away from the camera after repositioning it, a bed coming into view behind him as he did, the poster covered walls and clothes strewn floor of his student digs becoming visible as well.

'I've been wanting to tell you this for a while, but don't really know how to. I'm not sure how you are going to react, so I thought I would just do this little video, to get it out.' Michael said nervously, his animated arms enacting his words as he slowly backed away from the camera, closer to the bed. As he did, a pair of slender legs came into view, lying on the bed, shoeless, but with the bottom of a knee length skirt visible.

Rebecca's eyes were transfixed on his face, absorbed by the sight and sound of him more than the words he was saying, her fingers stroking his form as he moved.

'I would like to introduce you...' he started to say, a look of pained embarrassment crossing his face before he continued, 'God, that sounds so flipping formal. Oh Jesus, this is harder than I thought. Mum, look, please don't have a cow. I've got a girlfriend, okay, but she's older than me. When I say older, what I mean is, she's about your age.' he said, visibly cringing as he said the words, backing up further, the woman's torso coming into view, a slim elegant arm rising to wave at the camera.

'But I love her, and I really would like to introduce you to her.' he continued, a warm, affectionate grin spreading over his face as he jumped on the bed alongside her, and kissed her passionately on the lips before turning back to the camera. 'Mum, I would like you to meet Eve.' he finished proudly.

Rebecca's eyes slowly moved from her son's face to the waving, smiling features of the woman lying beside him. She froze, her hand becoming static in mid-air, millimetres away from the screen, her face locking in a similar surprised glare. As a distant whisper, Rebecca vaguely heard her say the words 'Hi Mrs Angus, pleased to meet you.' as she took in her all too familiar façade.

The face of Madame Evangeline.

9:15 pm

Strange looked up at the new image on the plasma screen in the centre of the bank of monitors. There were three figures on it. The first was the current time, 09:15:32, counting upwards by the second. The second was the number of heartbeat connections still to decrypt, 2896, and counting down at the rate of one every five seconds. The third showed another time, 01:18:00, the time, at the present decryption rate, that all the heartbeat connections would be decrypted.

'How many people are online now Steven? At this rate we will be blowing up before the decryption has completed.' Strange asked nervously.

'We've got thirty nine people online now Sir. We will have another ten online in the next fifteen minutes. That should bring us right on track.'

'Thank you Steven, excellent work.' Strange looked back from the screen to the table where DI Saxon was scribbling notes furiously onto a pad in front of her, shaking her head disconsolately as she did. He addressed her, concern in his tone. 'Is everything alright Leigh?'

DI Saxon looked up at him, frustration in her features. 'Dead ends Sir. Mrs Seymour's chauffeur has a cast iron alibi for the night in question. He was at a family New Year's Eve Party with fifty other people. We have CCTV footage of him returning the car to the office car park and leaving. We also have CCTV footage of the car coming back out but no images whatsoever of who was driving it. There is no relevant forensic evidence from the vehicle either. No prints or DNA relating to DI Saul. There was DNA for Rebecca and Michael Angus but we know they were in the car. There were fingerprints for Mrs Seymour which you would expect as it is her vehicle. Any other prints found in the car have been linked back to Axiom employees all of whom have valid alibis for the night in question. I can't see where else to go with this line of enquiry.' Saxon finished.

Strange came around the table and sat down next to her, angling her writing pad toward him. 'That's fine Leigh. If there is nothing there, there's nothing there. Try not to fret about that, otherwise you will lose your focus.' He looked down at her notes, at a line of questions, the majority with crosses next to them. He pointed to two without crosses. 'So the next thing is Dr Adams. You are still waiting on information back on his whereabouts and associates, that's the next most important thing for you to focus on, okay? You are doing a great job. I know it is difficult being under this type of time pressure, but you are coping well. Just stay focused.' he instructed with a sympathetic smile.

'I'll chase those things up right away. Thank you Sir.' she answered, taking a deep breath, some of her anxiety being released.

'Good girl.' Strange answered looking up from her as Corporal Garry entered the MIU and slumped down in a chair next to Saxon.

'No joy Sir. Mrs Seymour laid it on the line, admitted into the camera that she had killed Michael and that she was Madame Evangeline and not a fucking peep.' Garry relayed tersely.

'It was a long shot Gaz. Even if she is Madame Evangeline, we have no evidence to prove it. I think our 'Unknown Caller' wants us to present that evidence. More particularly, I think he wants John to present it.'

'I understand that Sir, but we are running out of time and there seems to be no evidence forthcoming and Saul is nowhere to be seen. That could literally leave us in a fucking huge hole come midnight. At some point we should think about trying to manually disarm that frigging thing.' he stated with obvious irritation.

'Gaz, I appreciate that you are a man of action and want to do something, but the risk of going anywhere near that thing is too great. You said that yourself. We do have Steven, your guys and the Tech team doing the decryption and we do have a good lead in Dr Ennis, who may be our 'Unknown Caller'. Be patient and focus on seeing if there is another way to disarm it without going anywhere near it.' Strange answered considerately but firmly.

The conference phone on the table in front of them rang, Strange punching the answer button immediately as he saw the number on the display.

'Mick, give me some good news.' Strange said in anticipation.

'We haven't found Ennis Sir, but he's involved in this, the sick bastard is definitely involved.'

'What have you found?' asked Strange, leaning into the phone, as did Saxon and Garry, listening intently.

'He's got a BSDM Dungeon in his basement. Chains, manacles, whips, bondage wheels, the lot. Puts him directly into the scene that Rebecca Angus was involved in.'

Strange shook his head, slightly agitated. 'Yes Mick, but that's not evidence, that's just coincidence.'

'No Sir, the evidence we found in his loft. There was a locked cabinet up there, which we have broken into. Inside are rows and rows of jars. In each jar, in formaldehyde, are either parts of or whole hearts. On the front of each jar are two punched dymo labels, one a name and one a date. There are twenty three jars in the cabinet Sir, twenty fucking three.'

'What are you saying Mick.' asked Strange, concerned.

'They are his trophies Sir. Twenty three victims, twenty three trophies and on the twentieth jar, the name 'Michael Angus', the date '01/01/2012'.

9:45 pm

'She called it 'Her Temptation'. I put a hand forward as she stood in front of me, tracing one of my fingers down from the fork of the tattooed tongue, all the way down to the skin covering her pulsing button. She laughed and took a step back. 'Patience, my darling.' she teased, turning to her left just as two men coming from the field passed on her right, one staring straight at me with a lewd, penetrating glare. It was Dr Ennis, his gaze staying on me as he and the other gentleman passed by. I didn't think anything of it at the time, but now I wonder if he also saw Evangeline?'

Saul rewound the video again, staring at the screen incredulously, letting the same clip replay again: over and over again, as he had for the last five minutes. He was absolutely absorbed in the image, taking in every detail of Rebecca's face as she relayed her story, oblivious to anything else.

He never heard the soft soled footfalls sneaking quietly down the corridor outside. He didn't sense the large, looming figure fill the frame of the open doorway. He only realised someone was there, dragging him back from captivation, when the person spoke.

'It's a pity you had to see that Saul. A pity for you. A pleasure for me.' Dr Ennis said, brooding in the doorway, standing tall, his thumbs forced tightly into his waistcoat pocket, a crooked, cold humoured grin on his face.

'You knew Rebecca Angus way before she was in your care. You knew she was with Madame Evangeline.' Saul stated, fully returned from his contemplation, turning in his chair to face Dr Ennis.

'Oh, I knew her. I knew what a tease she was. Always watching, never getting involved. She was so beautiful, so enigmatic. I watched her become a sultry, sensuous commanding Dom and I wanted her.'

'You knew she was with Madame Evangeline.' Saul repeated, tensing in the chair, holding onto the arms tightly.

'I knew she was with a woman. I never saw who that woman was. She didn't interest me. Rebecca did.' he said matter of fact, watching every movement Saul was making.

'But you used that. You used that to get her committed. You said that Madame Evangeline was part of her DID. She was real, she was always real! You must have known who she was!' Saul said, his voice raised, anger entering his tone, his knuckles white, his hands shaking as he gripped the chair.

'I couldn't give a fuck about Madame Evangeline. All she ever became was a distraction. I wanted Rebecca. I wanted her here, where I could watch her being abused, any time I pleased.' he leered, goading Saul.

'You sick fuck!' Saul shouted, launching himself from the chair, straight toward Dr Ennis. Dr Ennis was anticipating the lunge and sidestepped Saul, throwing an elbow into Saul's back as he passed him, knocking him to the floor of the corridor outside the room. Saul spun onto his side quickly as Dr Ennis loomed over him and shot a foot out viciously towards his groin. Dr Ennis moved to one side again and Saul's foot connected with thin air. Dr Ennis grabbed the leg and yanked Saul up, strength evident in the action, spinning him to his left and banging his torso into the corridor wall.

Saul's head cracked into the porcelain tiles, stunning him slightly for a second, long enough for Dr Ennis to grab his other leg and flip him over onto his stomach. He knelt over Saul, forcing a knee into his back and grabbing both arms quickly. Saul shook his head, trying to shift the daze of the knock and started to writhe under the grip. Dr Ennis had his arms in a lock, up Saul's back, and lowered an elbow onto his neck, bringing his head down close to Saul's ear.

'You have no idea. No idea at all just how much of a sick fuck I really am. You have no idea how much pleasure I get out of restraint, especially face down restraint.' he hissed in a vitriolic whisper as Saul bucked below him. He pushed his elbow down further, forcing Saul's head into the uncompromising floor, restricting his windpipe, making him gag for air.

'What pleasures me most, is being this close, being right next to your head, hearing the sound labour in your throat, hearing your lungs start to constrict, hearing your voice rattle with the whispered wraiths of your last, pitiful breath.' he continued as Saul's head started to shake and his body started to convulse.

'Seeing your eyes bulge, seeing your tongue fatten and shake in your mouth and seeing your lips turn thick and blue.' he added, applying more pressure the Saul's neck.

'Feeling your body go limp beneath me and feeling the life drain out of you.' he sneered as Saul's body stopped shaking and went still.

'Smelling the exquisite stench of your death.'

10:00 pm

'You get used to it.' said Sarah as she noticed Jessica looking anxiously at the screen on her mobile, just as she did the same on hers. They were sitting inside the Visitor Unit, just finishing off another cup of hot coffee. The evening chill was setting in and the coffee was an attempt to warm themselves up. Jessica had her coat on and Sarah was wearing Strange's jacket, but the chill was still invading their bones. Jessica gave her a questioning gaze. Sarah pointed down at the screen on her mobile.

'Not knowing where John is. Buggering off at the drop of a hat without thought or concern for who he is leaving. Waiting impatiently for him to drop a considerate text to let you know what the hell he is up to. Just the absolute single minded focus on the job.' Sarah added, sympathetically. 'He doesn't think that you worry about him. He doesn't think that you wonder what madmen might be out there, with a grudge, intent on stopping him make it home. It's hard. Do you think you are ready for it?' asked Sarah, placing a hand, the one holding the taggie, on top of Jessica's which were cupped in her knee, thumb of one circling the palm of the other.

Jessica bit her lip, nervousness seeping through her precise deportment, allying with the evening chill to make her body gently shake. She looked down at the taggie, then back up to Sarah.

'I guess, being the other woman, I have had a lot of experience waiting for him. I used to worry that he wouldn't come back to me mainly.' she replied candidly. 'I am starting to understand the hopelessness of not knowing what is going on, of not knowing what is happening to him. Am I ready? Are you ever ready? Do you ever get used to it?' Jessica pondered, then asked the last question to Sarah.

'No, you don't. It's just another thing you learn to block out. Another thing you learn to hide from each other. At least, that's what I did. I hope it is different for you. You seem to talk, which is a big start, especially with John. Have you always found it easy to talk to him?' Sarah asked, innocently.

Jessica frowned, looking uncomfortable at the question.

'Sorry.' Sarah said, quickly. 'I'm not digging and trust me, I am not asking to be catty or nasty. It's just, I don't know, what you did for Jacob earlier….' she said, leaving the sentence hanging in the air.

'Forgive me, I am just very conscious I am the other woman. I really don't want to rub our relationship in your face. The first time we met we were very open with each other. I think the bottle of wine helped to loosen tongues. I told him about a dark place in my life and he told me how he was feeling about Jacob.' Jessica replied, looking down at the taggie again as she ran one of her fingers over its fabric.

'I know John struggles with Jacob's condition. I know he couldn't talk to me about that so I am pleased he has found someone he can talk to.'

Jessica smiled, its curves wearing sadness. 'We spent that evening talking about babies.' she looked up at Sarah, squeezing the taggie as she did. 'We talked about your baby Jacob, and about my baby. We both shared our feelings of loss.'

'Sorry, I didn't mean to be pry.' Sarah said apologetically, noticing Rebecca's lips twitch slightly as she tried to contain her emotion.

'It's alright. Sometimes I catch his reflection.' she started, looking down at the taggie again. 'In something like this bit of cloth, in another child's eyes, staring back at me. Sometimes he smiles. Mostly he is sad. He haunts me from his lonely grave.' She looked up and stared into Sarah's eyes, guilt lining the sadness in her face. 'I had an abortion.'

Sarah's eyes widened in absolute surprise, her brow then furrowing in empathy, her own lips quivering, mirroring Jessica's. She looked down, partly to hide the tears glistening in her eyes, partly to look at the scraggy taggie they were both holding. She raised it up between them, Jessica's hand falling away from it.

'I didn't buy this for Jacob. I had an affair when I was thirteen. He was thirty. I fell pregnant and kept it from my parents for a long time. I bought this for her, for Ellie. I was nearly twenty seven weeks pregnant when they found out. They went to court and fought for me to have an abortion. They argued that my mental wellbeing was in jeopardy. They said I had been raped by a paedophile and bringing up his child would scar me for life. The courts agreed. So I had my baby. I went through labour and had my baby. They tried to take her away immediately but I didn't let them. I fought and I screamed and for a moment, for the briefest of moments, I held her hand, and stroked her perfectly formed, angelic little body with this taggie. I catch her reflection all the time, every time I look at Jacob. She haunts me too.' Sarah finished, a gentle trickle of tears meandering down her cheeks.

They looked knowingly into each other eyes: their hollow, sorrowful eyes. Sarah reached for Jessica's hand and, taking one of her fingers, she slotted it through one of the tags on the edge of the taggie.

'For our babies. For all of our babies. Thank you for trying to save my baby Jacob.' Sarah said as she held the taggie, and Jessica's hand, tight.

10:05 pm

A harsh, repetitive squeak emanated from a wheel on the rusty old trolley as Dr Ennis pushed it down the corridor towards the light coming from the open cell door in the distance. On the top of the trolley were a number of implements. A hammer, some nails, a long bladed kitchen knife and a pair of pliers. He was whistling to himself as he nonchalantly entered the padded cell and positioned the trolley next to the chair in the centre of the room.

Saul's lifeless body was strapped in the chair, totally naked. All of the restraints were in place, on his head, over his chest, down his arms and around his legs. There was a subtle movement of the strap around his chest. His hands were positioned palm up and tied tightly around the wrists.

Dr Ennis continued his jovial whistling and adjusted the black gloves he was wearing. He picked up the hammer and a nail from the top of the trolley. He positioning the nail into Saul's left palm, circling it delicately to find the right position, then with a ferocious swing of his arm, smashed it with the hammer, straight through skin and bone, whistling as he did.

Saul screamed, his whole body tensing as his eyes shot open instantly, bulging from his head, darting around frantically as they tried to comprehend what was happening. They angled down to see a pool of blood collecting around his open palm, dripping down onto the floor. They looked in front of him to the sneering, sadistic countenance of Dr Ennis glaring back at him, whistling still. Dr Ennis smirked as he picked up another nail and scraped it all the way down Saul's right arm, drawing blood as it broke the skin before settling in his right palm.

Panic shot into Saul's face as he screamed 'No!' a second before Dr Ennis slammed the hammer against the second nail, the word augmenting into a shrilling howl of agony.

'In my world Saul, this type of pain is a precursor to pleasure. It releases endorphins into your body that try to counteract the pain. They also arouse you, sexually.' Dr Ennis said, squatting down between Saul's open thighs and wrapping a hand around his semi erect penis. A gloved hand. A gloved hand whose palm was covered in sharp metal pins. Dr Ennis squeezed and started rubbing it up and down Saul's hardening shaft.

'Get off you fucking bastard, get off.' Saul screamed, spittle dribbling from his mouth as he tried to shake his head, forcing his body against the restraints, his face living the excruciating pain.

'It's you who will get off Saul and you can't do a thing about it. Your body won't let you. As much as you try to ignore what I am doing, your body wants it, your body is enjoying it and your body craves the pleasure. Your mind might not, but your body does.' he said, squeezing and tugging his penis faster. Saul closed his eyes excruciatingly, shaking his head frantically with what little movement he could make, his body jittering as he tried hard to distract his mind from what was happening to him, from the overwhelming agony.

Dr Ennis laughed, tugging harder, feeling Saul's shaft thicken and throb between his hands. 'It's no good Saul. No. Good. At. All.' Dr Ennis finished slowly, speeding up his tugging. Saul's body shuddered, his penis pulsing, his throat opening into another ear splitting scream as he ejaculated, his body jerking, then slumping in the seat as the last throb of ejaculation cease. Saul began to whimper, eyes closed, the darkness of despair painted across his sweat stained face.

'You mother fucker.' Saul groaned, disconsolately.

'I think you will find that it was Michael Angus who was the mother fucker. That was a thrill too, knowing that he had Rebecca. Knowing that she had lost her virginity to her son.' Dr Ennis sneered as he raised a finger covered in Saul's ejaculate, and rubbed it into his lips, licking it off with a lewd tongue.

'Did you kill Michael Angus? Did you kill him just so you could have Rebecca committed?' Saul asked, surprise evident in his laboured tone.

Dr Ennis burst out laughing, a harsh, maniacal noise as he reached for another nail from the trolley. 'You should know something about me Saul. It might help you appreciate what is going to happen to you. Every New Year's Day, since the age of twenty, I have killed someone. I have killed lots of people in between those times, but they were either accidental or, as in your case, opportune. I had set out on New Year's Eve 2011 with the specific intention of killing someone, as I always did. I attended a Masquerade Ball, and noticed Rebecca there, pimping her Gimp around. I had seen her many times before and as I said to you earlier, I wanted her.'

Dr Ennis knelt down on the floor in front of Saul's left foot, placed a nail on the top of it and thrust the hammer down hard onto it, puncturing through the skin and bone, Saul screeching in agony instantly. Dr Ennis smiled.

'I watched her all night, admiring the way she dominated her Gimp, fantasising about what I wanted to do with her luscious body before I killed her. When they left the club, I followed them. I thought they were going back to her flat. I knew where she lived, I had followed her before. I was surprised when they got out of the taxi on the high street, but I did likewise and followed behind them at a discreet distance. Then I lost them. They turned a corner and when I got to it, they were gone. At the time, I didn't realise they were in the limousine that drove by. I went to her flat, knowing that if she wasn't there already, she would be there soon. She wasn't there, so I picked the lock, went into her bedroom, opened the curtains so that the streetlight cast a glow into the darkness, and made myself comfortable under her bed, patiently waiting for her to come home.'

Dr Ennis picked up another nail from the trolley and knelt down next to Saul's right foot. His eye line was with Saul's crotch and he smirked as he saw his penis semi erect again. He placed the nail against the foot and, looking up to Saul's pleading face, malevolently drove the nail home, devouring the anguished cries of Saul with avarice.

'It was 4:30 am when I heard the front door. There were muffled voices, more than one person, and some shuffling and bumping outside the bedroom. My initial though was that the two of them were drunk and trying to navigate across the living room. The bedroom door opened and two sets of feet entered, one a man, one a woman. They seemed to be carrying something, which they placed on the bed, and then they both left the room, closing the door, after which I heard the front door shut. I waited for another half an hour in silence before quietly edging myself out from under the bed. I raised my head slowly, making out two shapes on the bed in the ruddy glow of the streetlights. One was Rebecca, naked. The other was Michael, still in his Gimp suit.'

Dr Ennis stood up in front of Saul and looked admiringly at his inflicted stigmata. He picked up another nail and twirled it in his fingers in front of Saul's eyes.

'Neither of them were moving. I checked their pulses. Michael was dead and Rebecca was heavily sedated. Sometimes,' Dr Ennis started, crouching down again, smiling at Saul, 'circumstances are opportune.' he continued as he placed the tip of the nail against Saul's scrotum and let the head of the hammer gently tap against it. 'I had the opportunity to take my New Year's Day heart, incriminate Rebecca for a murder and mess her mind up so bad, that she would be under my care, under my domination, for a very, very long time.' He lifted the hammer, eyes shining with delirium and pummelled the nail straight through Saul's scrotum.

Saul's face contorted as he tried to contain the excruciating pain, tension screaming through his pulsing veins, his eyes bulging, circling wildly, frantically deranged.

Dr Ennis stood between Saul's thighs and raised a hand to his chest, massaging the skin around his heart, letting his fingernail impress themselves into the pliant flesh.

'So I ripped the skin open on Michael's chest, rived the ribs apart and tore out his still warm heart. His blood started to seep onto the bed so I rolled Rebecca over into it, covering her body with the viscose life force. I forced a few morsels of heart into her mouth, closing it and covering her nose so she had to swallow. She gagged but didn't wake from her sedation. I washed her hands and forearms in the blood pooling in his open chest cavity and then caked her mouth with it. I took out my small Tupperware container, and secreted my prize, Michael's heart, inside it. A few weeks later I had my second prize, Rebecca Angus under my care, to do with as I pleased.'

Dr Ennis had two hands against Saul's chest now and was digging his fingers into the skin, breaking the surface with the pressure he was applying.

'Why did you let her go? If she meant that much to you, if you did so much to get her, why did you let her go?'

Dr Ennis forced a finger into a small slit that he had worked open on Saul's chest. 'I think I may have gone too far, with her mind. I think I pushed her into madness, and to be honest, because of that, she bored me. Ordinarily I would have just killed her, face down, but with the scrutiny I was under, the scrutiny *you* put me under, it seemed easier just to transfer her out.'

'So why me Ennis, why Jessica, why the fuck have you involved my son in this. If you want revenge against me then fill your fucking boots, rip my heart out and put it in your little plastic box, keep it as a puny trophy, but let my son go.'

Dr Ennis laughed again as he inveigled a second finger in the lesion he was making, savouring the discomfort Saul was experiencing. Saul smarted as he started to dig into the flesh below. 'You think I have your son. You think I have had Rebecca hidden away in here. And you call yourself a Detective. Someone knows what I have done Saul. Someone knows and they are trying to expose me. I am taking the opportunity to exact some sweet revenge before I have to disappear. I have no idea who our friend Dr Hanlon really is yet, but when I do find out, you can be assured, he will suffer a worse fate than you.'

'Is that right now, a worse fate than being nailed to a chair?' came a voice from the doorway to the cell, a voice with an Irish lilt.

Dr Ennis spun around quickly and grabbed the knife off the top of the trolley, dropping the hammer as he did. 'Dr Hanlon. I was hoping you would make an appearance.' he said as he faced the old Irishman in the beige cardigan, tan slacks and Jesus sandals.

'I hadn't expected you to figure out about this place Gordon, I didn't think you were that intelligent.' Dr Hanlon goaded, seeing the rouge rise in Dr Ennis neck above the collar.

'You arrogant bastard.' sneered Ennis as he thrust himself towards Hanlon, and slashed the knife in an upward arc toward his chest. Hanlon stepped back quickly, Ennis wrong footed by the swiftness with which the old man moved. Hanlon raised a knee and dropped an arm, trapping Ennis thrusting arm between them, then banged his other hand down on Ennis wrist, knocking the knife to the floor. Ennis swung his other arm around, the fist at the end of it smacking into Hanlon's jaw, jolting the old man, who lifted both hands as he staggered under the impact and grabbed Ennis jacket lapels. Ennis pushed forward into the hands, forcing Hanlon back against the cell wall, raising his own hands as he did, grabbing Hanlon by the neck. As Ennis began squeezing, the skin started to peel away from Hanlon's neck, his hands slipping with it, surprising him. Hanlon took advantage of the moment, clamping his hands either side of Ennis's head and twisting his arms viciously. There was a loud snap as Ennis's neck broke and he crumpled to the floor at Hanlon's feet.

Saul looked on, confused, as the old man, strips of skin dangling from his neck and chin, deftly stepped over the now prone figure of Ennis and strode towards him. He reached for the hammer on the floor and wrapped the claw end of it around the nail in Saul's right hand. 'This may hurt a tad.' he said as he tried to lever the nail out without digging the hammer into Saul's hand.

'It can't hurt any more than when they went in.' Saul said, grimacing as the nail moved against bone. Dr Hanlon removed the first one, then started on the next, concentration on his face.

'Who are you?' Saul asked between gritted teeth as the nail in his other hand was prised out, Dr Hanlon crouching down to take the ones out of his feet.

Dr Hanlon smiled up at Saul as he positioned the claw around the nail in his left foot and pulled it out. 'Who I am isn't important.' he started in a clipped British accent. 'Why you are here is important.' he continued in his soft Irish twang, removing the nail from his right foot. 'What you do next, is the most important thing of all.' he ended, in a tone Saul recognised.

'Rob?' Saul said, surprised, observing what he thought had been loose skin on Dr Hanlon's chin. It wasn't skin, it was latex. Dr Hanlon was wearing a mask.

'Rob Adams, Ben Hanlon, your 'Unknown Caller', none of them are important.' Dr Hanlon said, carefully positioning the claw of the hammer around the nail in his genitals, softly rocking it to loosen the end before he yanked it out. Saul yelped. He threw the nail and the hammer onto the floor and then grabbed Saul's shirt, which was in a pile with his other clothes in a corner of the room. He tore strips off the shirt and started to bandage Saul's wounds, kneeling on the floor in front of him.

'Whoever you are. You have your killer now. Ennis is dead. He admitted to ripping Michael's heart out. He admitted to setting Rebecca Angus up. Can you please let my son go?' Saul asked, imploringly.

Dr Hanlon looked at him, looked deep into his tormented eyes and shook his head sadly. 'Gordon Ennis did not kill Michael Angus. He butchered him, yes, but only after he was dead. There is only one person who was complicit in his death. Madame Evangeline. You know that John. You know who she is. You have all the evidence you need and I expect you in that room in Featherstone Hall before midnight.'

Dr Hanlon finished dressing Saul's wounds and then started to release his restraints, the head first. As soon as it was free, Saul shook it from side to side disconsolately. 'It can't be Jessica. It can't be. She was with me all night. It's impossible.'

'Then you have a predicament John. A choice. Jacob or Jessica. Only you know the truth, only you have the facts.' Dr Hanlon said, loosening the last of Saul's restraints and standing up.

Saul moved in his seat, his body squirming in agony as he tried to stand, tried to lunge towards Dr Hanlon. He sank back down, broken. 'It's not possible. She was with me all night. No one left the room. They have it on CCTV that no one left the room.' Saul repeated.

Dr Hanlon started to back out of the cell, stepping over the body of Dr Ennis as he did. He stood in the doorway for a moment, taking in Saul's defeated demeanour before he spoke. 'John, think on one thing: Even Fallen Angels have wings.'

10:30 pm

'We have another five teams of Detectives drafted in now Jerry. Three teams are assisting DI Munro with location searches to try and find Dr Ennis. Two teams are working on identifying the victims of Dr Ennis. We are still containing this with regards to the press, but I think we only have until morning at the latest before we will have to make a statement. It has gone way beyond one death and one kidnapping, this is now into serial killer territory. Do you need any further resource at the Hall?' asked the Chief Superintendent.

Strange was standing with an arm across his chest, the other arms resting upwards, the hand of it supporting his chin. He looked pensively towards his superior. 'I don't need anyone else at the Hall Sir. I am concerned that we are running out of obvious leads. As much as we are trying to extend the detonation of the bomb, all that does is give us more time. It doesn't help us get Jacob out or find Dr Ennis, if it is Dr Ennis behind this. If it isn't Dr Ennis, then we are feeding on the remnants of scraps in terms of evidence, none of which are leading us anywhere. The same is true with regard to Madame Evangeline. There is nothing concrete. At the moment Sir, time is still the biggest problem.'

'I appreciate that Jerry. I think you and the team are doing everything that you can on this. I can't see any other direction that you could have taken. You have two prime suspects, one there, one we are hunting down and you have a method of dealing with the bomb. I would say so far, that is a decent day's work.'

'It will be Sir, when we get Jacob out. Thank you for your support.' Strange finished, then glanced across to the countdown screen.

'1,267 connections left and a time of 12:06 Steven! What's happening with the time?' Strange stepped towards Reynolds, concerned.

'Some c...connections are taking a little longer that others to decrypt Sir.' Reynolds answered nervously. 'There will be five more people working on this in the next ten minutes. That will c...come back in, to around 11:45.'

'Steven, if anything, and I mean anything gets in your way on this, let me know immediately please.' Strange said, patting Reynolds on the shoulder as he moved past him and approached the coffee percolator.

He poured himself a coffee and stood there watching the incessant drip of coffee from the filter into the pot for a moment, listening to its rhythmic heartbeat, lost in his own thoughts. His contemplation was interrupted by the conference phone ringing. He turned to the table and answered it.

'Mick, have you got good news?'

'Sir, we know where Saul was and we know where Ennis is. We were just driving towards the Fielding Institute when Buglass saw Saul limping out of the old asylum buildings. He go in his car and drove off. We have just been into the building Sir. Ennis's body is in there Sir. He is dead. In the cell where we found Ennis, there is a chair covered in blood. It looks like someone has recently been strapped into it and tortured.'

'Do you think that's Ennis?'

'I don't think it was him being tortured. He may have been doing the torturing. SOCO and the Duty Medical Examiner are on their way. One other thing Sir. There is a room with a bank of screens in it. One of the screens is showing the feed from Featherstone Hall. One shows a feed of the cell where the body is. Unfortunately there are no recordings of what went on in there. But it looks like this is a location Dr Ennis was working from.'

'Good work Mick. Can you ensure someone from Tech Forensics gets there quickly? We need them to check out the setup there to see if there is anything that can help us with the bomb. Did you see where John went?'

'No Sir, he floored the car and was gone in an instant, straight past us. From the brief glimpse I saw of him, he looked in a bad way. Sir, there was no one else down there, in the cell. We have to consider the possibility it was Saul who killed Dr Ennis.'

10:57 pm

Rebecca watched intently as the lock on the front door started to slowly turn. She took a sip of wine, an amused smile crossing her features as the door was pushed slowly open and Dr Hanlon tentatively put his head around it.

'You are fine Doc. I'm not standing behind it with a meat cleaver. I am on the sofa, enjoying a pleasant Rioja.' she said as he looked toward her, his expression turning jovial.

'Oh, I wasn't worried about what you would do to me, I was worried about what bits of your body I would find strewn all over the living room.' he joked as he entered and pushed the door closed behind him, approaching the sofa.

'If your knives weren't as blunt as a Nun's chuff, it might have been a different story.' she teased, before continuing. 'Is it chilly outside?' Rebecca asked as he sat down beside her, looking at the scarf around his neck.

'For an old codger like me it is.' he answered, pulling it a little tighter, feigning a shiver as he did. He then took at her relaxed demeanour, running his eyes over her, nodding appreciatively as he did. 'You are looking remarkably good and sounding extremely lucid for a Category A Mental Patient. That's a lovely top you are wearing, it suits you.'

'Blowing your own trumpet Doc, it was you who bought it, not me, I just picked it out of the wardrobe.' she answered. As well as the purple long sleeved round necked top, she was also wearing a pair of jeans. She sat on the sofa with her legs curled up underneath her and had an arm resting on the back of the sofa, supporting her head with its hand, which was tousling the hair on an auburn shoulder length wig. She had a full face of makeup on again, concealing the inflictions of her incarceration well, only the subtle ridges and rivulets of scarring visible close up.

Rebecca reached over to the table, where there was a second glass of wine and, picking it up, offered it to Dr Hanlon, who accepted it. She held her glass towards his and said, 'Cheers Doc.' as they clinked glasses together.

'I take it you have watched the DVD?' Dr Hanlon asked as he relaxed back into the sofa, taking a sip of wine.

'I have. It was enlightening. For the first ten minutes I was a gibbering wreck. I wasn't watching the content, just watching Michael. Seeing him living, breathing, speaking and just being alive all over again. It was hard. It just reinforced what I know I have lost.' she answered, her words tinged with sadness.

'Did it help you make sense of why he did what he did?'

She was silent for a moment, looking down into the rippling surface of the wine in the glass, composing her thoughts before she answered.

'When you strip it all back, when you take away the 'things' that happened, the 'people' who have been influencing those 'things' and you get back to Michael and what he felt it becomes very simple. He loved his mum. Far more than a normal person would consider morally healthy, but that is how he felt.'

'We've had that conversation a few times today Rebecca, it's not always about the morality, it is about understanding.' Dr Hanlon said softly, seeing the emotion bubbling in her eyes.

'I know. I'm not judging him, I'm just understanding him. Probably for the first time. I can see how the way I have nurtured him over the years has contributed towards the way he felt about me. My love for him, my time for him was never compromised. I was there for him always. I can see now why that wasn't necessarily the best thing, for both of us. The only person I had an emotional involvement with after Hannah died was Michael. Any emotion I felt, love, anger, frustration, probably even sexual frustration was only ever shared with Michael. For a long time, well into his teenage years, his years of sexual awakening, it was the same for him. He would talk to me about everything that he felt, every emotion. Or at least I though he did. I can see how we relied on each other, I can see where the feelings he had for me came from. I can see that while he had those feelings towards me, he would probably never have acted upon them if he hadn't met Eve.'

'Ah, Eve, or Madame Evangeline. So how do you feel about her part in this?' asked Dr Hanlon.

Rebecca took another sip of wine, looking at Dr Hanlon thoughtfully. 'All she did was give us exactly what we wanted. Not necessarily what we needed, but exactly what we wanted. I know how I felt: sorry, I know how I still feel about her. She brought something into my life that I craved, that I desired. She did the same for Michael. He loved her and if you watch those DVD's you can see how happy he was. What I don't understand, yet, is why. Why did she give us what we wanted? Why did she lead us into temptation?' she was staring intently at Dr Hanlon as she asked the last question, watching every movement of his features. Before he had a chance to answer, she added, 'It resonates with another question I keep asking. Why are you doing this?'

'To lead you on the path to redemption.' he answered, seriously, holding Rebecca's challenging stare.

'So am I redeemed?' she asked, simply.

'That is not for me to say Rebecca, it is for you to feel. Do you still replay music in your mind to distract you from what happened?' he asked.

'I will always replay music in my mind. But at the moment, it's not to distract me, it's to remind me. I don't feel redeemed. I understand now why Michael was there that evening. I understand how he fell and banged his head. I still know that it was me who caused that and I still killed him. I don't understand what happened at the flat.'

'That's where I can help you. What happened at the flat was Michael saved your life. Dr Ennis was going to kill you that night. He was under your bed when you were taken back to your flat and his intention was to molest you, rape you and cut out your heart. His plan changed when he saw Michael dead on your bed. He took his heart instead and then set the scene up so it would look as though you had done that to Michael. He then committed you, to his Institute, under his control, to do whatever he wanted with you.'

Rebecca looked shocked, and took a gulp of wine before she spoke. 'Jesus, why would he want to do that, why would he want to kill me?'

'While you were watching other people in the clubs, he had been watching you. He saw you as a challenge. He is genuinely a psychopath, so don't try to rationalise why you in particular too much. My understanding is that you would have been one of many that he has killed.'

'Perhaps he should have, it would have saved me the many failed suicide attempts.' she said, a slight tinge of ironic humour in her tone.

'I can say, unequivocally, that I am pleased he did not kill you and that you didn't kill yourself. I have said this to you before, you are a remarkable woman who has been exposed to extraordinary circumstances. I genuinely do want to help you on the path to redemption. So now you know just about everything that happened that night. The how, most of the why's. Let me ask you this question now. Do you feel like killing yourself?'

'At the moment, just at the moment, no, I don't want to kill myself. There are questions I still want answers to and I don't think you can give them to me. I need to understand more about Madame Evangeline. I also need to understand what happens next. I am a committed psychopath, surely someone must be looking for me? As much as I now know what happened, I am still a convicted murderer.' she stated, rationally.

'What happens next Rebecca, is entirely down to you. Call the police, tell them you are here. Kill yourself. Go on the run. It's your choice. There is something I would like you to do for me though before we get to that decision.'

She laughed, 'You are really selling those choices Doc. What would you like me to do?'

He smiled back at her. 'Just keeping it real. Let me show you.' he said, rising from the sofa and approaching the locked bedroom door. He took a key out of his pocket and unlocked it, inviting her over. She approached the door tentatively, her expression quizzical as she stood next to him and looked into the room.

'Before you make your mind up, I would like you consider another option.'

11:32 pm

The car was swerving from side to side down the drive, its headlights illuminating the trees lining it before their glare was consumed by the Arc lights in front of Featherstone Hall. Saul was flopping from side to side as well, struggling to hold the wheel with his injured hands, struggling to concentrate on the road through the pain that was ingrained on his tortured face. He took his bandaged foot off the accelerator and placed it on the brake, agony breathed into the scream he emitted as he tried to exert pressure and slow the car down. It didn't slow down enough and smacked into the side of a police van parked on the drive, coming to a shuddering halt. The airbag inflated straight into Saul's face as his body was thrust forward and then jolted back on impact.

The noise of the impact had people running from every direction toward the black SLK. Corporal Garry arrived first and yanked the door of the car open, Saul's battered form falling straight onto the gravel drive, howling on impact. Saul had no socks or shoes on, only makeshift bandages, dirty and bloody, on his feet. He wore no shirt, trickles of dried blood visible around the open lesion in his chest. His tuxedo was ripped and filthy. Garry picked him up and sat him on the driveway as Strange, Sarah and Jessica arrived.

They all scrambled to the driveway around him, finding a gap to get close, all laying hands on him in an attempt to comfort, concerned shrieks calling his name. More officers rushed in behind them, anxious to see how they could help.

'Can you all just calm the fuck down and give me some space.' Saul shouted angrily, his face contorted with the pain of movement as he did. As one, they all sat back from him, silence descending upon the scene.

'Look, I know I look like shit, but we don't have time to fuck about with me.' He reached an arm over to his inside jacket pocket, wincing continually, and took out the white mobile phone, handing it to Strange.

'Sir, this is the phone Madame Evangeline gave Rebecca Angus. It has calls and texts from her. It proves she exists. You need to get the Tech guys to see if they can find anything that might help us identify who she is. She is the one who was involved in Michael's death.' he instructed, staring fleetingly at Jessica as he did.

'John, we need to talk about Dr Ennis.' Strange said, passing the phone onto Reynolds who was standing behind him.

'All you need to know about Ennis for now is that he is not our 'Unknown Caller', and while he ripped the heart out of Michael Angus, he didn't kill him. What you need to know about our 'Unknown Caller' is that he, Dr Hanlon and Rob Adams are one in the same person. What you need to focus on is anything that might lead you to him. What I need now are some painkillers and five minutes alone with Jessica. You aren't getting another fucking thing out of me, until I get those two things.'

'Shit.' exclaimed Strange. 'Five minutes John. That's all. Gaz, Jessica, please help Saul to the Unit around the back. Sarah, can you wait in the interview room until they are finished please. Come on everyone, back to work, let's see what we can find out about this phone and revisit leads on our 'Unknown Caller'. We only have twenty five minutes before that bomb explodes.'

11:38 pm

Garry closed the door of the Visitor Unit, leaving Saul and Jessica alone inside. Saul popped painkillers into his mouth and took a quick gulp of water from the cup Jessica had given him, wincing with pain as he swallowed. He was sitting beside Jessica, then awkwardly started to shuffle his seat around, intent on facing her.

'John, let me do that.' Jessica instructed, stopping him and pulling her seat around instead. She leaned over and tried to kiss him. He turned his head away, shaking it disconsolately.

'John, what is it?' she questioned, sitting back slightly, surprised by his reaction.

'Madame Evangeline Jess. Who the fuck is Madame Evangeline?' he asked, the question loaded with accusation. He placed his hands with an effort onto her knees, one on each leg.

'John, I don't have a clue who she is. Why would you think I do?' she answered, her demeanour stiffening in concern.

He glared at her, accusation turning to confusion. 'Neither do I Jess. I know I was with you every single moment of that evening.' he said, shaking his head and leaning forward into her a little, the fingers of his hands creeping inside the hem of her dress, stroking her outer thighs.

'Yet we know it was your property where Michael was murdered. It was your limousine that brought him here.' he added, shaking his head and lowering it towards her knee, his hands snaking further up her thighs.

Jessica looked down at his confused, frightened eyes and raised her hands, putting one on each cheek, holding his face tight, her own countenance reflecting his confusion. 'I can't explain those things John. I wish I could.'

'Then perhaps you could explain this.' he said, tensing suddenly and thrusting his hands all the way inside her dress, forcing it up towards her hips.

'What are you doing John?' she screamed, trying to wriggle from his grasp, kicking her legs. She forced her body back, intent on trying to distance herself from him, but it only allowed Saul to push her dress up over her hips, exposing her panties, exposing the bottom of her stomach, exposing the cherry red forked tongue of a tattoo, snaking out the top of them, toward her belly button.

'Could you tell me,' Saul spat, through pain and through the effort of pinning her down. 'why you and Madame Evangeline have the exact same forked tongue tattoo.'

Jessica stopped squirming, a look of sheer astonishment screaming from her eyes as she looked down at the tip of her tattoo, then to Saul's ferocious and imploring glare. She burst into tears, her body sagging back into the seat, her hands reaching for the hem of her dress, trying to lower it over her hips. 'I don't know John. I really don't. I am not Madame Evangeline. I thought you believed that, I really thought you believed that.' she cried, the tone hurt and violated as she turned her legs away from him and pulled her dress all the way down.

Saul still stared at her, the fury fading, an utter confused desolation replacing it as his head dropped and he began to weep. 'I don't know what to believe Jess. I know you were with me. I know that. But all these things. He wants me to go into that room Jess and make a choice. You or Jacob. You having that tattoo is the first bit of conclusive evidence we have. But I know you can't be Madame Evangeline.' He sunk his head into his hands, weeping disconsolately.

Jessica looked down at his beleaguered, broken body and reached her hands out, lifting his torso, pulling him into her, cuddling him into her chest. 'John, there is no choice. It doesn't matter what you believe. If you think the evidence is there, go into that room and tell him. What's important is Jacob. We have to get Jacob out.'

11:45 pm

The door of the Visitor Unit opened and Jessica supported Saul out into the chill night time air, both with tear stained faces. Strange, Sarah and Garry were waiting for them.

'Is everything alright?' asked Strange, concerned.

Both Saul and Jessica nodded together. Saul approached Sarah, putting his arms out, embracing her tightly. 'I'm sorry for all of this. It is all my fault.' he whispered into her ear, holding back tears.

'John, all I want is Jacob safe, I don't care whose fault it is.' Sarah answered, her voice crackling with tension.

Saul broke away and slowly started to walk around the side of the MIU, towards Featherstone Hall, Jessica supporting him. 'Sir,' he started, addressing Strange. 'Jessica and I are going into the Hall. It's what he wants. I don't believe that she is Madame Evangeline, but we have to go in there.'

'John, any minute now we will have extended the time the bomb will explode. You don't have to do this now, not until we find more evidence, not until we find out what is on the phone at least.' Strange answered.

'Sir, this is personal, he wants me in there, before midnight. All I can do is tell him the truth.' Saul said, holding tight onto Jessica's arm, casting her a pained smile.

Reynolds was running toward them as they came around the side of the MIU. 'Sir, all the c...connections are decrypted and we have just extended the trigger to activate at 23:00 tomorrow.'

Strange walked towards Reynolds and threw his arms around him, patting his back affectionately. 'Excellent work Steven. That is great news. I wish I could say take a break but I need you to continue looking at the mobile and I need you to get the guys set up to trace calls from the line in the Drawing Room now. Can you do that for me please?'

'No problem Sir.' Reynolds answered as he turned and ran back to the MIU.

There was a palpable drop in tension as the small group continued their walk to the Hall.

'Ennis is a killer Sir.' Saul said to Strange as they walked.

'We know John. Mick and a number of teams are looking into twenty three possible murders. Did you kill him John?' Strange asked straight out.

'No Sir. It was our 'Unknown Caller'. In self-defence. Ennis went for him with a knife and he protected himself. It was Ennis who ripped the heart out of Michael Angus. He was planning to kill Rebecca Angus.'

'What about Rebecca Angus, was there any sign of her?'

'She had been there Sir. Our 'Unknown Caller' has her somewhere. I talked to him.' Saul answered as they reached the door of the Hall.

'Go in there and talk to him again. Go in there and make him see the error of his ways. Go in there and do the right thing John, that's all you can do.'

11:50 pm

'This is DI Saul. I have Jessica Seymour with me. I have reason to believe she was involved in the murder of Michael Angus.' Saul announced. He and Jessica were standing with their backs to the fire, looking out over the Drawing Room toward the bookcases, toward the camera. They waited for a moment, the bleep of the heart beat the only sound above Saul's laboured breathing.

The Bakelite phone started to ring. Jessica aided Saul across the floor to it and he picked it up.

'I'm pleased you made it back John. It's good to see you have Jessica with you too. Do you have something you would like to tell me?'

'We have evidence to prove that Jessica Seymour owns Featherstone Hall, the place Michael Angus was killed. We have evidence to prove that she owns the Limousine that brought Rebecca Angus, Michael Angus and Madame Evangeline to Featherstone Hall in the early hours on the 1st January 2012. We have evidence to prove that Jessica Seymour was in Edinburgh at the same time as both Michael and Rebecca Angus on that date and the day before.' Saul relayed, then paused.

He had been looking at the opposite wall as he spoke, looking intently at the Cezanne picture, at the disjointed perspectives of the table, at the apples on its top. At all the apples. He looked from it to the crate. The wooden crate in the middle of the room. The wooden crate they were under strict instructions not to touch. He turned to Jessica, to his lover, to the woman with the forked tongue on her stomach. His face displayed an overwhelming sadness, a tear trickling down his cheek.

'I'm sorry Jessica, I truly am.' he whispered to her, reaching for her hand and holding it tight, his face grimacing under the physical pain, despairing under the mental torture.

'We have reason to believe that Jessica Seymour is Madame Evangeline and was involved in the murder of Michael Angus.'

Saul sniffled, trying to contain his tears, the heart monitor beeping, a lonely tone echoing a hollow life. The hollow life of Jacob, his countenance angelically serene as Saul looked up at the screen. The phone line crackled with static, but otherwise was silent. Jessica looked at Saul anxiously.

'Anything else John?' came the question, a few seconds later.

Jessica shook Saul's hand, attracting his attention, distracting him from staring at Jacob. 'Tell him John!' she whispered harshly, in astonishment. 'You have to tell him everything!'

Saul shook his head and mouthed the word 'Sorry' to her, his face desolate.

'No, there is nothing else.' Saul answered, his lips quivering with emotion as he did.

'Thank you John. I appreciate all the efforts yourself and your team have put into finding the real killer of Michael Angus. If nothing else, I hope you understand how grave a miscarriage of justice took place. If nothing else, the beast that was Gordon Ennis is now exposed. It is 11:56 pm. Unfortunately, you have not presented the evidence I wanted to see regarding Madame Evangeline. I would leave the building as quickly as you can. The crate will blow up in four minutes.'

11:56 pm

Jessica supported Saul out of the Drawing Room and into the corridor. 'John, why didn't you tell him about the tattoo?' she asked incredulously.

'It's wrong Jess. He is still playing games with me. I know you were with me that night. I know you cannot be Madame Evangeline. He wanted me to choose. I chose what I believe to be true. I believe in you.' Saul said as Jessica hurried them down the corridor.

'John, what about Jacob. You do know what could happen!' she said, her voice rising with panic.

'We have to find another way to help him, one that doesn't involve sacrificing you to the whim of a madman.' he answered, a spirited determination entering his tone. 'Let's go and find out if they have managed to trace that call.'

They walked out into the antiseptic glare of the arc lights, vapour wraiths dancing from their lips as the cold air surrounded them. Sarah was pacing nervously just outside the cordon tape. Strange was running out of the MIU toward the tape, Garry following closely behind. They all reached the tape at the same time.

'He didn't go for it Sir. We didn't have the evidence he wanted. As far as he is concerned, the crate will explode any minute now. Did you get a trace?' Saul asked.

'We did, the call came from a payphone on the Quayside in Newcastle. Officers are on their way now.' Strange answered.

'Look guys.' started Garry, 'I know we have altered the trigger, but I would still suggest we back away from the building just for the moment, at least until after twelve.'

'Why?' asked a nervous Sarah in surprise. 'You have changed the trigger, there isn't any risk, is there?'

Strange shot Garry a reproaching glare. 'It's alright Sarah.' he said, coming up beside her and wrapping a comforting arm around her shoulder. 'It's just a precaution.' he finished, gently directing her away from the building, back towards the MIU. Jessica led Saul in the same direction. Garry stayed at the tape, a look of concern on his face.

As they approached the MIU, Reynolds came running out of the door, his features animated, arms waving as he shouted towards Strange.

'Sir, Sir. The white mobile, it's ringing Sir!' he puffed as he arrived in front of Strange, passing over the device. Strange looked down at the words on the display of the phone.

The words said: Madame Evangeline.

Strange glanced between Saul, Jessica and Sarah in bemusement as he raised the phone to his ear and pressed the answer button.

'Hello, this is DCI Strange. Is this Madame Evangeline?' he asked.

There was a click on the line and a recorded voice kicked in. 'The time now is 23:59:48 seconds precisely.' It was the voice of the 'Unknown Caller', of Dr Hanlon, of Rob Adams. 'The crate will explode in ten seconds.'

Strange had just activated the bomb.

11:59:50 pm

'It's the trigger, it's another fucking trigger!' Strange screamed, panic on his face as he threw the phone to the ground, pushing Sarah, Saul, Jessica and Reynolds towards the MIU as he shouted to everyone else. 'Get out of the way, get out of the way. The crate is going to explode!' waving his arms frantically to the various officers stationed around the perimeter tape. They all started to run towards the MIU or towards the nearest vehicle.

11:59:52 pm

The words 'crate' and 'explode' hammered into Sarah's head in the confusion of Strange's panicked warnings. She moved in the direction that he was pushing her for a second, until the two words made themselves heard and she screamed 'Jacob!' with every last ounce of breath in her lungs. She turned instantly, ducking under Strange's arm and started to sprint towards the Hall, her face contorted with anguish.

11:59:53 pm

Saul reached out to grab Sarah's arm as he saw her turn, as his face reflected the enormity of what Strange had shouted. She slipped through his fingers, his hand clasping thin air. He tried to turn after her, but his feet gave way underneath him as he did and he crumpled to the floor, reaching out an arm toward her as he fell, screaming out after her. 'Sarah, don't!'

11:59:54 pm

Garry was running from behind Sarah and saw her dart between Strange and Saul and head back toward him, toward the Hall at pace. She was heading slightly to his right so he change direction to head her off. He kept his eyes firmly fixed on her. He could see in her darting, startled glare that she knew he was going to try and stop her. It was going to come down to a choice. Would she veer left? Would she veer right? He looked for the signs in her demeanour, looked for her pumping legs twitch in a particular way, looked for a drop in the shoulder, a tilt of the head. He saw all of them, which suggested that she was going left. She was upon him and he leapt left to grab her waist, catching nothing as he slammed into the ground, just as she pulled to the right and sprinted past him.

11:59:56 pm

Jessica knelt down on the gravel, scraping her knees against the harsh stone as she bent over and started to lift Saul from where he was spread-eagled on the ground. She pulled his torso up, managing to raise him into a sitting position.

'We have to stop her! We have to save Jacob!' he screamed at Jessica imploringly, 'Help Me!'

'No John, you don't have the strength, I've got to get you to safety.' she answered, kneeling up and thrusting her arms through Johns arms from behind, clasping them around his chest as she dragged him backward, towards the MIU.

11:59:57 pm

Strange stopped in mid stride, seeing Saul fall to the floor out of the corner of his eye. He turned and rushed the few steps back to where he had fallen, stepping in front of Jessica, who had just hauled him back into a sitting position. Strange grabbed his battered legs, Saul looking up at him in anguish.

'Jerry, we can't let her do this, we have to stop her! We have to get Jacob!'

'It's too late John, we have to think of you now.'

11:56:58 pm

Sarah bounded up the steps to the front entrance, and sprinted down the corridor, learning from her earlier mistake and slowing down slightly as she turned into the drawing room. She leapt for the crate, her hand scraping the side, the last little false finger nail flying off. She knelt down beside the crate, hugging the wood as tightly as she could, looking up to the plasma TV on the wall, staring at it, eyes dilated with the darkness of despair, but glistening with a mother's love as she took in Jacob's serene face.

'I'm here Jacob. Mummy is here. Mummy will always be here. I am so sorry my beautiful baby boy.' she cried, into his worn and tattered taggie.

11:56:59 pm

Garry was back on his feet again, shaking his head in frustration as he ran towards the lumbering trio in front of him, noticing Saul kicking furiously, trying to extricate himself from their grip, screaming, 'I need to stop Sarah! I need to save Jacob!' at the top of his voice.

He came up alongside Strange and grabbed one of Saul's legs off him, taking the load from the older man. 'Look mate, it's too late for her, do your mates, who are trying to save your life a favour and stop fucking struggling.' he shouted at Saul as the three of them picked up some speed, getting closer to the MIU.

12:00:00 am

Jessica's irises contracted, a sudden burst of brightness shining from her dilated pupils, sparkling into the emerald, reflecting the explosion happening in front of her. The sound battered her eardrums, forcing her to fall to the floor, dropping Saul and raising her hands quickly to cover her ears, to block out the deafening roar. Searing hot air smacked into her face, jittering the skin with its force, drying the moisture from her tear stained eyes, forcing her short hair backwards. Debris followed, whistling particles of rubble biting into her flesh where they landed on her face, gouging lesions as they ricochet.

She didn't close her eyes, staring down the explosion defiantly, her lips rippling back from her teeth, exposing a rictus grin. From below she heard mumbled words, releasing the hands from her ears to hear, looking downwards to Saul. To his ripped, torn and filthy tuxedo. To his beaten, stigmatised, bleeding, broken body. To his shaking arms reaching abjectly out in front of him. To his tormented, grief stained face.

'Jesus, what have I done, what have I done.' Saul cried, over and over again, his litany of guilt seeping into her mind, enlivening her smile, rising with the spreading satisfaction that was painting itself onto her face. She looked back up, smirking euphorically ahead. Her emerald irises glowed, flecked ruby, pupils reflecting flames which danced in the devastation of betrayal that her final words bestowed:

'Et tu, my darling, Et tu Brute.'

12:01 am

The emptiness of forever shrank, then grew, the pupil changing size under volition. The green iris surrounding it moved effortlessly in tandem, framing the imperceptible communication in a dazzling glow. The white of the eye remained static, as did the lashes and lids, as did the young face the eye lived in. The rest of his body was prone too, lying flat on a cot bed.

'His name is Jacob.' Dr Hanlon said, leaning over the cot and watching the young boy's eyes intently. 'He has a condition called Pinocchio Paralysis. At least, that is the non-clinical term his parents gave it. He can't move at all. Apart from his pupils. He has only just learned how to do that in the last few days.'

'Can you hear what I am saying Jacob?' Dr Hanlon asked, clearly and concisely. Rebecca leaned in closer too, focusing on his left eye. She saw the iris contract once, then slowly expand to normal dilation.

'That is amazing Doc, absolutely amazing.' Rebecca said, her own pupils wide with awe as she observed the silent interaction.

'It is remarkable. Jacob is a very special little boy.' Dr Hanlon said. 'Rest your eyes now Jacob, we will talk more later.'

He motioned for Rebecca to leave the room and followed her, picking up a holdall from the top of a chest of drawers. He pulled the door closed then walked back to the sofa with Rebecca, both of them sitting down.

'So Doc, as much as it was lovely to see little Jacob, I'm not quite sure how that relates to having another choice?' she asked, perplexed.

'Jacob needs someone to look after him. Someone who is good with children, someone who has spent a lot of time with them.' Dr Hanlon said.

'You just mentioned his parents Doc, why can't they look after him?' Rebecca queried.

'It's complicated. Let's just say his parents have let him down and he needs someone who can give him their undivided attention.'

'And you think that someone is me. Rebecca the Psycho. Rebecca the murderer. Rebecca the escaped mental patient. You think that puts me in a better position than his parents to look after him?' she asked, incredulously.

'Yes.' he answered simply, his expression unwaveringly sincere and serious.

Rebecca breathed out heavily, shaking her head, smiling at the ludicrousness of the suggestion. 'How is that ever going to work? The second I step out of that door, you know and I know it's only a matter of time before they catch up with me.'

'Not necessarily.' Dr Hanlon started, reaching into the holdall and pulling out a plastic wallet. He opened the wallet and took out two passports, some flight tickets and a credit card and handed them over to Rebecca.

She took them off him and inquisitively opened the first passport, her countenance expressing an even higher level of surprise. 'The picture is mine, but the name isn't?' she said, looking inside the second passport. 'The same with Jacob.' She opened the flight tickets, 'Italy?' she questioned.

'An opportunity for a new start. A new life for you, a new life for Jacob. That is the other choice Rebecca. It is entirely down to you if you take it, but think about, seriously. You have all the skills, all the understanding and all the empathy.' He paused, reaching over to hold her hand tightly. 'You have all the love that little boy needs. You will find his love unequivocal too.'

'It's ludicrous Doc, absolutely ludicrous.' she said, shaking her head.

'All I ask, is that you spend the rest of the night thinking about it.' He leant over to the holdall and took out a mobile phone, placing it on the table. 'If, after that, you still think it is ludicrous, then give yourself up. Or let the authorities know where Jacob is and kill yourself.' he finished, a wry grin in amongst his serious demeanour.

She started at him quizzically, trying hard to read something, anything in his eyes, in his steadfast expression. 'Why?' she asked, simply.

He didn't answer for a moment, just returned her gaze, weighing up what to say next. 'We let you down Rebecca. What Dr Ennis put you through, should never have happened.'

'There you go with the 'We' again Doc? Who the hell is 'We'?' she asked, an obvious annoyance entering her tone.

Dr Hanlon smiled at her, unabashed by her tone. 'Who we are is unimportant. Why you are here is important. Why Jacob is here is important. The choice in all of this is entirely yours.' he answered, standing up and looking down at her still petulant façade.

'And that is all I get, after everything you have done for me, that is all I get?' she questioned, leaning upwards on the sofa onto her knees, her body coming in line with Dr Hanlon's chest as she looked up towards him.

'You can have a hug if you like?' he answered playfully.

'That's not what I meant and you know it.' she said in frustration.

'From me, that is all you will get. However, it is entirely your prerogative, if you decide not to kill yourself, to find out more. I can't stop you doing that. Now though, I really have to leave and personally, I would like a hug before I go.'

Thirty Six Hours Later

A brilliantly bright midday sun hung blissfully alone in a cloudless, pale blue sky. The pale blue sky enlivened the serenely calm surface of Lake Garda, the sun's reflection glistening and swaying under the gentle swell of the water. A motorboat sped by, splicing through the serenity, both with its noise and with the wake it created. The noise dissipated as it headed off further down the lake. The wake rippled towards the shoreline, dispelling its surge gently onto a pebbled beach edging the lush verdant lawns of a large Villa standing proudly alone in its vast grounds, along a mile of the shoreline, looking out over the lake. The lawns gave way to ebulliently fruitful orchards.

A small wooden jetty stretched out from the shore, a stone path leading from it through the well cut grass, meandering up to the veranda at the front of the Villa. Under the veranda were a number of deck chairs angled to face the lake and drink in the blistering Italian sun. One of the chairs was occupied, a slim, attractive woman with a short blonde bob reclining in it, reading documents in a manila folder as she sipped a long cool daiquiri. The only things she wore were mirrored sunglasses and a tiny cherry red bikini.

The shadow of a tall, handsome dark haired man crept over her relaxing body as he stepped out of the open sliding doors in the Villa and stood behind her, drinking in the spectacular view of Lake Garda, with its craggy mountain ranges framing it on the distant opposite shoreline.

'It's good to be home.' he said as he looked down towards the woman on the deck chair, smiling. She reclined her head, looking up towards him and pouted her lips.

'Don't I get a kiss?' she tantalisingly asked, reaching up an arm and searching out his hand, letting hers wrap around it, squeezing it tight.

He leant over from behind and placed his willing lips onto her eager pout, kissing her long, kissing her deep, kissing her passionately. Their tongues stayed entwined as he circled the head of the deck chair to its side and slowly descended onto his knees, prolonging the kiss fervently, his free hand cupping her well defined cheekbone, fingers caressing her elfin earlobe. After many minutes, their lips parted, and he looked down upon her lovingly, removing the sunglasses to take in her mischievously sparking emerald eyes.

'And who was I kissing?' he asked, letting a finger tingle a trail from her cheek, down her neck, through the gentle swell of her cleavage, over her trembling stomach, to the cherry red tattooed tongue lustfully poking out the top of her cherry red bikini briefs.

'Well, it wasn't Jessica Seymour you were kissing. Unfortunately she was involved in a fatal car crash yesterday afternoon. Died on impact. The car exploded, leaving nothing but dust, not even bones. It was a terrible tragedy. Poor John, losing his son, his wife and his lover all in one day. How must he feel?' she playfully answered.

'You have created a monster there. I really did think he would choose Jacob over you. Your wiles are more persuasive than even I imagined.' he responded, smiling, before adding, 'Was it Madame Evangeline who I kissed?' circling a finger on the tip of the tattooed tongue, letting it slide to the fabric of the bikini.

'I know you would like it to be but no, it wasn't her. I think we still have a role for Madame Evangeline to fulfil, so you might yet have the opportunity for a kiss. Today my gorgeous husband, you were kissing me, Eve. Would you rather have been kissing Rebecca? Would you rather have been exploring her gnarled tongue, caressing her scarred and ravaged flesh?' she replied, her voice brazen and wilful.

He raised the finger that had been circling her tattoo to her lewdly grinning lips and rested it over them.

'You are wicked, so irresistibly wicked.' he said, watching her eyes brighten in acknowledgement before continuing, deliberately ignoring her question. 'Where is she? Has she left the flat yet?'

'About half an hour ago. With Jacob. The tracker has them approaching the airport. Your wiles are more persuasive than I ever imagined, Dr Hanlon. For an old fart, you certainly turned her head.' Eve teased.

He smiled down at her, taking in the folder lying on the deck chair that Eve had been reading. There was a name on the front.

'Fenny Bentley.' he said, looking from the folder to Eve, quizzically.

'You know me Adam,' she started, tantalisingly, 'I am always thinking about the next temptation. As I said, we still have a need for Madame Evangeline.'

Behind them, from the Villa, came the sound of a phone ringing. He stood up, kissing Eve playfully as he did, and entered through the open door, into a sumptuously decorated living area bathed in swathes of leather, mahogany and marble. An enormous tapestry of 'The Last Supper' hung from the wall directly opposite the door he came in through. He approach a marble table in the middle of the room, piles of neatly stacked manila folders on top of it, as well as the phone and a remote control. He picked both up together, pressing a button on the remote control as he started to speak into the phone.

The tapestry started to move, bunching up in concertina from the left, exposing a bank of TV's, ten deep by twenty across, two hundred in total, each one showing a different location, a different room, a different scene, a different person.

To the left of this was a wide corridor, running to the front of the house, rooms heading off each side of it. Cezanne's 'Skulls' hung on one wall, on the opposite wall, a self-portrait, entitled 'Reflections In Shadows', signed 'J. Saul'. At the end of the corridor a solid oak front door was framed either side by stained glass panels depicting biblical scenes.

Through the stained glass could be seen the main driveway leading up to the property. A small fountain sat in the middle of the driveway, a cherub version of Eros spurting water from his mouth in the middle of it. The driveway was flanked with borders of manicured lawns, leading off into acres of orchards, with enormous shining bright red apples burgeoning thousands of trees.

Half a mile from the house, past the orchards, large wrought iron gates flanked by marble pillars crossed the driveway, a high stone wall heading out in either direction marking the boundary of the land. Supported on the marble pillars was a marble arch. Engraved into the arch, in letters two feet tall, inlaid with pure gold, was a word.

And the word was: Eden.

The story continues...

'Her Moons Denouement'

The sequel to 'Angels Bleed'

Is now available in paperback and e-book at Amazon

See the cover image, read the book pitch

and the first chapter preview on the next few pages

MAX HARDY

HER MOONS DENOUEMENT

Even Fallen Angels Have Wings

'Even Fallen Angels Have Wings'

In the midst of a bustling Fringe Festival in Edinburgh, a strange sideshow pops up. Billboards proclaiming 'Even Fallen Angels Have Wings' stand either side of a ten foot tall crucifix, an unconscious, near naked man nailed hand and foot to it.

'Even Fallen Angels Have Wings'

Two hours later the sideshow is a Crime Scene. DI Fenny Bentley arrives to find a dead body on the ground at the foot of the crucifix, a single self-inflicted gunshot wound through the head, large feathered wings stretching out from the back with blood pooling around them.

'Even Fallen Angels Have Wings'

DI John Saul is on compassionate leave, supposedly recovering from the devastating personal loss he suffered during his last case. But he can't leave that case alone. It consumes his every waking moment. And he can't sleep.

'Even Fallen Angels Have Wings'

DI Saul switches on a TV and hears those words on the news about the crime in Edinburgh. The same words spoken to him by a killer on his last case. A case which involved DI Bentley.

'Even Fallen Angels Have Wings'

Words that lead DI Bentley on a journey where everything he believes in, is ripped apart. Where a woman he believes doesn't exist, hounds his every move.

Words that lead DI Saul on a journey of impossible realisation. Where a woman he believes dead, haunts his every move.

A woman that embroils them both in a trail of murder, debauchery, suicide and revelation. A woman who laughs at her own Moons Denouement. A woman called Madame Evangeline.

Chapter 1

The rusting, squeaky rubber wheels bounced erratically over the uneven shoe-shined cobbles on the narrow, steeply inclined side street leading up towards the Royal Mile in Edinburgh. The wheels supported a twelve foot high distressed mahogany cabinet which was agitatedly shaking and rocking as it was being pushed up the incline. It was being pushed from behind by a hunched back man, dressed in Jester's motley, dull and threadbare, all vivacity faded from the colours. Tarnished silver bells jingled on the end of the Fools Hat framing his ruddy, sweating face which was grimacing under the strain of his labour.

Up ahead, streams of people passed the entrance to the alleyway and the vociferous hubbub of the main street in the middle of a Fringe Festival began to pervade the alley, drowning out the jangling bells as with one last huge effort, the Jester rolled the cabinet off the cobbles and onto the flag stoned pavement of the Royal Mile.

The din was infectious, swirling through the open air under a cloudless midday sun streamed blue sky, intoxicating the milling throngs who were devouring the street entertainment. A slow meandering wave of people navigated their way around crowds surrounding the jugglers, magicians, living statues, fire-eaters and sword swallowers, bobbing heads trying to catch sight of the wares. Up and down the pavements, sandwich boards and posters proclaimed the evening gigs, touts standing next to them shouting out the same message and forcing flyers into the hands of every person that passed by.

The Jester slowly negotiated the cabinet along the pavement, patiently going with the flow, until he came to a small square by St Giles Cathedral, where there was a relatively open space in front of the imposing building. He manoeuvred the cabinet into place in front of steps to the entrance of the Cathedral, the front doors of it facing out onto the street. He opened a drawer in the bottom of the cabinet and proceeded to remove half a dozen buckets filled with stones from within and placed them in a semi-circle about five metres in front of it.

A few passers-by stopped to watch as the Jester skipped back to the cabinet and started to unfasten the doors. Swinging one of the doors open he turned to the small crowd, smiling broadly.

'Good morrow to you kind Lords and Ladies. Today, I have for you revelations of the like you will have never encountered. They will truly blow your mind. Please, please, avail yourselves of a stone or two from the buckets in front of you while I finish setting up the show.' he encouraged animatedly, his hunched body prancing to open the other door, revealing a large white sheet, fully ten foot tall by ten foot wide, covering something within the cabinet. At the top of the cabinet three metal rods with clasps on the end held the sheet in place. Emblazoned on the sheet in blood red letters, each a foot tall were the words 'Even Fallen Angels Have Wings'. The same words were written on the inside of the open doors.

The jester turned back towards the growing, inquisitive crowd with a broad, almost manic grin on his face and skipped towards the throng building behind the buckets. From the bottom of the cabinet he had picked up what looked like a metal tube with a bladder on the end, which he proceeded to tap off the heads of the crowd as he jauntily skipped the line.

'Fear and Faith. Faith and Fear. Fear and Faith.' he started to sing while bopping the bladder off people, who smiled in nervous expectancy. He suddenly stopped in front of a young, tall skinny man in the middle of the line and stared into his eyes intently.

'In whose faith is your fear founded?' the Jester started to sing, rattling the bladder and shaking the tarnished bells on his hat in rhythmic accompaniment. 'Which God's atonement do you seek?' he continued, turning to the young woman who was with the man and tapping the bladder off her forehead, chest and shoulders in the sign of a crucifix. 'Whose penance keeps your soul grounded, when spirits avarice is preached?' he finished, stooping down and grabbing a few stones from the bucket in front of him. He skipped back a few steps and took in his ever growing audience.

'Ladies and Lords. Would you help me uncover the truth? Would you help me tear down the veil of deception? I am not without sin, but I am prepared to cast the first stone.' the Jester preached, raising one of the stones above his head in his free hand. He smiled broadly as he watched the crowd look down to the stones they held, then turned and threw his towards the clasps holding the sheet in place, tapping from foot to foot as he took a second stone and threw that. He turned back to the crowd, grinning and skipping. 'Help me derail the veil, help me expose the truth.' he encouraged, throwing another stone which pinged off one of the clasps, slightly dislodging the sheet.

A stone shot out from the crowd and smacked into the sheet well below the clasps with a dull thud, causing the blood red words to billow and dance. More followed, from the hands of people whose faces were still perplexed, but also enlivened with the temptation of the revelation, joining in the crowd reflex. Stones pinged of the woodwork, splatted into the sheet, the odd few making contact with the clasps, shaking them and loosening the cover.

Her Moons Denouement   Max Hardy

Suddenly, the sheet came away from the clasp on the right side of the cabinet and fell down, partly revealing what lay behind. There were panicked gasps and screams from the crowd and as one, the group shuffled back, dropping whatever stones they still had in their hands to the ground. A few started to push their way out and away from the scene. Many more, the majority, stood transfixed in morbid curiosity, staring intently at an outstretched, blood-stained arm, the hand of which was nailed through the palm to a wooden plank.

The Jester stopped skipping and walked slowly over to the cabinet, his stride imperceptibly lengthening, his shoulders widening as his gait started to un-hunch, even though the lump was still on his back. He grabbed the flapping corner of the sheet and yanked it forcefully off the remaining two clasps to further screams and gasps of astonishment.

In the cabinet was a crucifix, ten foot tall. Nailed to it palm and foot was a scrawny silver haired man, naked apart from a dirt stained loin cloth. He was unconscious, head lolling to one side, blood meandering down his brow: from the barbed wire crown that was gouging into it. Behind the crucifix, on the back of the cabinet there were pictures. Smiling faces. Smiling faces of young, vibrant women, the carefree snapshots resonating with the beautiful bright day, but at odds with the macabre scene in front of them.

'Is your fear founded in his faith!' shouted the Jester, turning back to the remaining crowd and pointing his bladder towards the man on the crucifix. 'Do you want to know the truth of his faith! What he does in the name of his faith!' His voice was rising in volume, simmering with vitriol as he stood up fully from his feigned stoop and pointed the bladder towards one of the pictures.

'Demi Simpson, twenty three, a prostitute, went missing in 2008.' he pointed to the next picture. 'Josie Richards, nineteen, a lap dancer, went missing in 2010.' And the next. 'Shelley Crabtree, seventeen, seven-fuckin-teen,' he spat, 'still in sixth form, went missing three weeks ago.'

The crowd were in stunned silence, but through the Jesters rant could be heard the raised tones of someone pushing through them, the bobbing peaked cap of a policeman visible above their heads.

'Come one people, let me through, what's all the screaming about.' PC Simpson started just as he got to the front of the crowd and saw the vista in front of him. 'Bloody hell mate, what's going on here!' he said as he walked into the open area in front of the cabinet, his incredulous gaze moving between the crucifix and the Jester.

Instantly, the Jester pulled the bladder from the end of the tube he was holding and pointed it towards the PC. The tube was the barrel of a gun. 'Please stop there PC?' he asked calmly, holding the gun steadily at the policeman's chest.

Pandemonium broke out behind them as those in the front of the crowd saw that it was a gun the Jester was holding, panic pulsing in waves as people turned to flee, screaming, while some stood fast in their curiosity and still more on the periphery sought to see.

'Simpson. Bill Simpson. Now I don't know what your beef is Sir, but could I ask you to just keep calm and put the gun down please.' Simpson asked as he stopped suddenly, putting both hands out in front of him in placation.

'You have nothing to fear from me Bill. Quite the contrary. Today I am here to help you. Today I am here to expose the crimes of this man to the world.' the Jester answered, smiling radiantly, the gun not wavering.

'What do you think this man has done?' asked Simpson, his eyes darting from the crucifix, to the Jester, to the frantic crowd and the other peaked caps he saw pushing through it.

'It's not what we think Bill, it's what we can prove. In the bottom drawer of the cabinet are folders, each one of which contains conclusive evidence of that man's, no, that *monsters* involvement in those seven poor women's deaths.'

'Okay Sir, so perhaps you could put down the gun and we can talk about that. Talk about who this man is and what he has done.' Simpson suggested, seeing other policeman emerging from the pulsing crowd and gesturing for them to hold back.

'His name is Liam O'Driscoll. Archbishop Liam O'Driscoll.' he shouted, so that the curious still in the crowd behind the ever expanding line of policeman could hear. 'The highest authority of the Catholic Church in Scotland. You may have unburdened your sins to him in confessional. He may have asked you to do three Hail Mary's. That wasn't enough of a penance for these women. No. Their penance was to be bound face down on the alter in the Cathedral behind you as he sodomised them while strangling them to death. All in the name of his God.'

'Jesus.' stuttered Simpson, losing his composure for a moment at the revelation. 'Please don't think about shooting him. If you have evidence that can prove he has done those things...' he continued before the Jester interrupted, laughing.

'Bill, Bill, I'm not going to kill him. I am giving him to you so that justice can be exacted, so that the lies and deceit that are spread in the name of his God can be exposed. For far too long his seed have committed debauchery under the fear of his faith and we say NO MORE!' he finished the sentence shouting, flexing his shoulders, his eyes alive with fervour.

'We will no longer sit in the shadows of your Gods and let their impotence prevail. Even Fallen Angels Have Wings!' he sang, stretching his arms out as he did, still keeping the gun levelled at Simpson. There was a rip of Velcro from the hump on his back and out of the Jesters Motley, two giant feathered wings sprouted, fully the length of his arms, shimmering and fluttering in the brilliant sunlight. Simpson stepped back in surprise, an astonished shriek escaping his gaping mouth, in tandem with gasps from the rest of the crowd.

'We want justice. Justice for Demi, justice for Josie, justice for Shelley. We want justice for every Angel that has died. Justice for every Angel left to bleed in the fear founded by the disease of their seed. We want the world to see the truth.'

The Jester quickly turned the gun in his outstretched hand from pointing at Simpson and forced it into the temple of his own head.

'We are the Fallen Angels!' he shouted, smiling wildly at the crowd, and pulled the trigger.

Visit my website at

www.maxhardy.co.uk

or Facebook at

www.facebook.com/themaxhardy

or Twitter at

www.twitter.com/themaxhardy

e-mail to

max.hardy@live.co.uk

Printed in Great Britain
by Amazon.co.uk, Ltd.,
Marston Gate.